INFINITY
REAPER

ADAM SILVERA

SIMON & SCHUSTER

First published in Great Britain in 2021 by Simon & Schuster UK Ltd

First published in the USA in 2021 by Quill Tree Books, an imprint of
HarperCollins Publishers, 195 Broadway, New York, NY 10007.

1 3 5 7 9 10 8 6 4 2

Simon & Schuster UK Ltd
1st Floor, 222 Gray's Inn Road
London WC1X 8HB

www.simonandschuster.co.uk
www.simonandschuster.com.au
www.simonandschuster.co.in

Simon & Schuster Australia, Sydney
Simon & Schuster India, New Delhi

A CIP catalogue record for this book
is available from the British Library.

PB ISBN 978-1-4711-8782-7
eBook ISBN 978-1-4711-8783-4
eAudio ISBN 978-1-4711-9984-4

This book is a work of fiction. Names, characters, places
and incidents are either the product of the author's imagination or
are used fictitiously. Any resemblance to actual people living or
dead, events or locales is entirely coincidental.

Printed and bound by CPI Group (UK) Ltd, Croydon, CR0 4YY

INFINITY
REAPER

For those who don't want to keep fighting. Fight on.

Shout-outs to Becky Albertalli and Elliot Knight,
who were always with me even when they couldn't be.

THE WORLD OF GLEAMCRAFT

Gleamcrafters—practitioners with powers. Applicable to both celestials and specters.

Celestials—their true origins unknown, these people carry powers that have a connection to the stars and sky. Some powers are presented at birth, others surface later in life. The range of their abilities is wide. Celestials can be distinguished by the way their eyes glow like different corners of the universe as they use their gleam. Notable group: the Spell Walkers.

Specters—sixty years ago, alchemy was developed as a way to use the blood of creatures to give humans powers. People who receive their powers this way are known as specters, and the range of their abilities is limited to the blood of that creature's breed. Specters can be distinguished by the way their eyes burn like eclipses as they use their gleam. Notable Group: The Blood Casters.

DRAMATIS PERSONAE

SPELL WALKERS AND ALLIES

Emil Rey—a reincarnated specter with phoenix blood who can cast gray and gold fire, self-heal his mortal wounds, sense feelings from other phoenixes, fly, and resurrect. Known as Fire-Wing and Infinity Son.

Brighton Rey—the creator of the online series Celestials of New York. Drank Reaper's Blood for the powers of a phoenix, hydra, and ghost.

Maribelle Lucero—a celestial who can levitate and glide.

Iris Simone-Chambers—a celestial with powerhouse strength and skin impervious to most gleam attacks. New leader of the Spell Walkers.

Atlas Haas (Deceased)—a celestial who could conjure winds.

Wesley Young—a celestial who runs at swift-speed.

Eva Nafisi—a celestial who can heal others but gets harmed in the process.

Prudencia Mendez—a celestial with the power of telekinesis.

Carolina Rey—Emil and Brighton's mother. No powers of her own.

Ruth Rodriquez—a celestial who can create clones of herself.

Bautista de León (Deceased)—a reincarnated specter with phoenix blood who could cast gold fire, self-heal his mortal wounds, resurrect, and remember details from his past life. Founder of the Spell Walkers.

Sera Córdova (Deceased)—an alchemist and celestial who had psychic visions. Founding member.

BLOOD CASTERS AND ALLIES

Ness Arroyo—a specter with shifter blood who can change his appearance at will.

Luna Marnette—a supreme alchemist who created the Blood Casters. No powers of her own.

Dione Henri—a specter with hydra blood who can grow extra/regrow missing body parts and

Stanton—a specter with basilisk blood who has serpentine senses and venomous, acidic, petrifying, and paralytic abilities.

June—a specter with ghost blood who can phase through solid objects and possess people.

POLITICIANS

Senator Edward Iron—a presidential candidate who opposes gleamcraft. No powers of his own.

Barrett Bishop—a vice-presidential candidate and chief architect of the Bounds. No powers of his own.

Congresswoman Nicolette Sunstar—a celestial presidential candidate who can create burning hot dazzling lights.

Senator Shine Lu—a celestial vice-presidential candidate who can turn invisible.

HALO KNIGHTS AND PHOENIXES

Tala Castillo—a Halo Knight with no powers of her own.

Wyatt Warwick—a Halo Knight with no powers of his own.

Nox—an obsidian phoenix that excels at tracking.

Roxana—a light howler phoenix with stormlike powers.

OTHER NOTABLE CHARACTERS

Keon Máximo (Deceased)—an alchemist and specter with phoenix blood who could cast gray fire, self-heal his mortal wounds, and resurrect. He developed the alchemy to give normal people powers and became the first specter.

Kirk Bennett—the curator for the phoenix exhibit at the Museum of Natural Creatures.

Dr. Billie Bowes—a celestial who can cast illusions.

The Silver Star Slayer—a conservative YouTuber.

But true rulers are not born. We are made.

—MARIE LU,

THE ROSE SOCIETY

ONE

BRIGHT NIGHT

BRIGHTON

I drink every last drop of Reaper's Blood while looking up at the Crowned Dreamer.

The elixir smells like burning bodies and tastes like iron and charcoal. The blood from the century phoenix, the golden-strand hydra, and the dead ghosts is heavy on my tongue like mud. My throat is burning and I'm this close to spitting out the rest, but I force myself to swallow it all because this Reaper's Blood is game changing. I wasn't lucky enough to be born with powers—to be born a celestial. But now that I've absorbed these creatures' abilities, the world will get to welcome me as their new champion—a one-of-a-kind, unkillable specter.

I drop the empty bottle and it rolls toward my brother, who has been stabbed. Emil is eyeing me like a stranger as I lick my

1

lips clean and dry them with the back of my hand. I'm about to help him up when I stumble, falling onto my knees. My vision becomes fuzzy. It's as if everyone in the church's garden is spinning slowly, then faster, faster, faster. My entire body feels like countless fingertips are grazing my skin. I suck in the sharpest breath of my life, like someone has been strangling me and finally lets go, and before I can full-on panic about whatever is happening, light surrounds me.

I'm glowing. I'm nowhere near as bright as the Crowned Dreamer above me, but I still feel like my own constellation—the Bright Brighton, the Bright King, whatever you want to call it. I have no idea if all specters experience this warm white glow when getting their powers. The only specters in my life I could ask are special cases who wouldn't remember—Emil, who was reborn with his phoenix powers, and Maribelle Lucero, who just discovered hours ago that she isn't a regular celestial. Her biological father was a specter—the very founder of the Spell Walkers—marking her as the first-known celestial-specter hybrid. But I'm a special case too. I feel it; I feel this change in me, even when the glowing stops.

Emil is stunned, but his expression turns back to pained. "Hel-help me," he breathes. Blue blood from the dead phoenix, Gravesend, is wet and sticky on Emil's chest, but it's his own red blood spilling out his wound that needs attention. Luna Marnette, the supreme alchemist who created the Reaper's Blood I just drank, stabbed him with an infinity-ender blade. She must've gotten Emil so deep with that infinity-ender blade that he can't even tap into his phoenix powers to heal himself.

I cradle Emil's head. "I got you, bro."

I flinch as spellwork explodes across the Alpha Church of New Life's garden. The fighting hasn't stopped because my brother is dying. It's like the Blood Casters and their acolytes won't rest until every Spell Walker is dead. In the fray, I see my friends Prundenica Mendez; Wesley Young; and Iris Simone-Chambers, the leader of the Spell Walkers. Despite their innate powers, they're struggling to contain Stanton, a specter with the blood and the powers of a basilisk, and Dione, a specter with the speed of a hyrda and the extra arms to match.

Then I see Maribelle, our most powerful player, as she crouches beside Luna with absolute murder in her eyes. "You had my parents and boyfriend killed so you could live forever. Now I get to watch you bleed out."

Luna is fading in and out as she stares at the stars like they can still make her powerful. Not happening. Her silver hair is plastered to her sweaty forehead and she's pressing down on the hole I blasted through her stomach with my wand's spell. "You won't . . . you . . ." Luna tries to speak but keeps choking on her own words. It triggers a flashback of Dad gagging on his own blood. It's so vicious that I turn away, even though Luna deserves every ounce of pain.

Unlike Luna, I'll never have to fear death again thanks to the Reaper's Blood.

But my brother does.

"Maribelle! Maribelle, we have to get Emil to the hospital."

Then June appears out of nowhere—moon-white skin, dark silver hair, big empty eyes. She's a specter with ghost blood, the

3

only Blood Caster with those powers, we think. And she possessed Maribelle and made her kill Atlas Haas, the love of her life and one of my very favorite Spell Walkers. I keep calling Maribelle's name, but it's like her need for vengeance has me on mute. There's no stopping her as she scoops up the oblivion dagger, the one that's made of bone and can vanquish ghosts, and chases the young assassin around the garden.

Back home when I told Maribelle my plan to steal the Reaper's Blood away from Luna, she didn't question it. She wants Luna to die powerless, and I don't want to die at all; we're both coming out winners. Except it's all pointless for me if Emil doesn't live too. I have to get him out of here. I try lifting him, but it's a struggle; it's like he has rocks hidden in his power-proof vest. It's a shame that none of my new abilities is powerhouse strength, but I still manage to muscle up and get Emil on his feet, and he wraps his arm around my shoulders.

An acolyte runs at us with an ax, hopping over the hydra beheaded for the potion, his feet now slick with yellow blood. I'm counting on him slipping on the grass, but he stays upright. Emil can't protect us, but it's okay. I'm going to be his hero the way he's been mine the past month. I take a deep breath and extend my hand, visualizing phoenix fire blasting from my palm. The acolyte keeps pursuing us. I keep my hand ready, concentrating on how badly I want to take him out, and he's suddenly wrenched backward as if flicked away by some invisible hand.

How did I do that? Is this a ghost blood power?

I realize it wasn't me when Prudencia appears at our side with her eyes glowing like skipping stars. The eyes that look like doorways into different corners of the universe are how you can identify anyone as a celestial, but that's only if the celestial activates their powers around you. Prudencia has only ever shown us her beautiful brown eyes since we met her in high school, and now here she is saving our backs and fighting this war with us. Her forehead is split open, and her glistening celestial blood is running down the side of her face.

"What happened? Who hurt you?" I ask.

Prudencia waves the question away as she observes Emil's wound. "We have to get him medical attention."

It was only hours ago when Prudencia and I last saw each other at Nova, the elementary school for celestials that was being used as a haven. Iris was forbidding me from going on any more missions, and even though Prudencia told me to stop risking my life, to stay with my family, to stay with her, I followed Maribelle like a true hero.

From the ground, Luna groans.

"Whoa," Prudencia says. "So we stopped her?"

She must've missed everything while fighting for her life. My grand entrance, blasting Luna with the last spell in my wand, saving Emil, and drinking the Reaper's Blood. Even the glowing. Those moments were historic, and she missed them; I should've set up a camera to upload everything online later for everyone to see.

"I took her down," I say, pointing at the steel wand on the ground.

She doesn't call me a hero or tell me I did a great job.

Iris shouts as she barrels through acolytes like a quarterback, laying out six before she reaches us. There's blood setting into her dyed-green buzz cut and even more across her knuckles. She clearly bested every idiot who thought they could take on one of the city's strongest celestials. "Enforcers are storming in," she says, panting. "I counted a dozen, but more will be on the way. Time to retreat."

Enforcers file through the church's garden door, protected in their sea-green armor as they aim their wands at every single one of us—celestials, specters, the human acolytes who want to become more—and bombard us with spellwork of all colors. Now would be a spectacular time for my ghostly abilities to kick in so I can phase through the solid wall behind us, maybe even teleport us over, but when all I feel is some painful nausea and dizziness, I drop with Emil to the ground and spells fly over our heads. Iris leaps forward and shields us, her arms crossed over her chest; her dark brown skin is resistant to this spellwork. Prudencia uses her power to sweep other spells away, but she's careful not to fire them back at the enforcers.

This past January, a terrorist attack known as the Blackout was blamed on the last four original Spell Walkers, but we all know now that the Blood Casters were actually responsible. Except the enforcers have never gotten that memo—they've been tasked with eliminating the new wave of Spell Walkers, even though it's not their fault. Unlike the Spell Walkers, the Blood Casters don't save innocent lives. Something is off as to why the enforcers don't work harder to take them down and lock them up.

Wesley dashes to us, skidding to a halt. His height and curvy build remind me of one of my favorite childhood wrestlers, except that guy doesn't have Wesley's brown man bun. But the wrestler was definitely sporting bruises above his eye and cut lips like Wes does now. "Heads up, friends, we are very cornered right about now," he says.

"Didn't notice," Iris says as she smacks a lightning spell away.

There are puddles of blue, yellow, gray, and red blood all across the garden. I wasn't here when the massacre first started, but it's still disturbing to see the hydra head facing skyward with its tongue hanging out of its massive mouth, and the dead blue phoenix lying on its side.

Sharp movements catch my attention, and Dione lunges into the squad of enforcers. Using her six arms, she chops one in the throat, snaps the neck of another, punches one between his eyes, and snatches the wands of two and blasts them dead.

This garden is becoming a graveyard.

"Prudencia, cover me," Iris says as she runs to the gate, wrenches apart the spiked poles like they're made of clay, and begins punching away at the brick wall behind it. "Wes, get Maribelle!"

I turn to find Maribelle slashing at the air with the oblivion dagger, constantly missing June as she teleports all around. Wesley dashes over, and immediately has to take a step back before he can get stabbed. He's trying to drag Maribelle away, but she's not having it, so he grabs her by the legs, lifts her onto his shoulder, and runs back to us.

"Put me down!" Maribelle shouts, trying to break out of his grip like a phoenix locked in a cage.

"We're not leaving you behind," Wesley says.

Maribelle hammers Wesley in the back with the dagger's bone handle until he releases her. She scans around as June suddenly rises out of the ground and places her hands on Luna, protecting her leader. Maribelle hurls the dagger, and it flips through the air as quick as a blink, but June and Luna have faded faster into the night.

"She got away—they both got away!"

A spell narrowly misses her, and Maribelle turns to assess the danger. More enforcers trying to kill her. It's clear she's fed up when one eye glows like a sailing comet and the other burns like an eclipse. Dark yellow flames burst into life from her fists to her elbows, and she casts the fire toward the enforcers. She's quick with a fire-arrow to the cauldron when Stanton, the basilisk specter, makes a move for the remaining elixir; all the Reaper's Blood goes up in flames.

"Hurry!" Prudencia shouts at Iris. Her power isn't trained enough to keep fending off all this spellwork, and more enforcers are arriving on the scene with fully charged wands.

Iris breaks the wall open with a mighty punch, creating a hole big enough for everyone to go through.

"Gravesend," Emil says weakly.

"Gravesend is dead," I say.

"Don't leave her."

Of course Emil cares about the corpse of a phoenix, like it really matters right now if someone takes Gravesend and makes a scarf out of her feathers. But as more spells fire our way, I take the lead and get Emil out of there. Iris sees me struggling and she carries Emil with ease straight into the back of her Jeep.

"Where's Eva?" I ask. Eva is Iris's girlfriend, and a powerful celestial in her own right. Emil needs her healing powers fast.

"Eva is Philadelphia-bound with your mother and others," Iris says.

"I have a connection at the Lynx facility," Wesley says from outside the door. "We should be able to get discreet care."

Prudencia hops in the front passenger seat. "We need somewhere closer. He's losing blood fast."

Wesley racks his brain. "Aldebaran! There's good people at Aldebaran."

"Lead the way," Iris says.

Wesley dashes ahead on foot and Iris hits the gas, peeling off. I look out the rearview window and see Maribelle is gliding behind. I don't know when she's planning on coming back for Atlas's car, which we used to arrive here tonight, and I don't care. Emil's eyes are closing, and I slap him awake.

"Emil, come on. Bro, look at me."

I was so busy using up each charge in the wand that I didn't see Luna gut my brother with that infinity-ender. If I were my own wand, my own walking weapon, I would've had unlimited power to handle business. Blood rushes to my head seeing Emil in this state. He's not going to die. This is not how this ends.

"I should've gotten here sooner."

Prudencia turns from her front seat. "You should've never left Nova. We had no idea if you were even alive."

"I was with Maribelle. She was cast out too."

"No one kicked you out, Brighton."

I look down at Emil.

Prudencia shakes her head. "You're not actually blaming your brother while he's bleeding. Be better than that."

"But it's true! He rejected me from joining the next mission. You too, Iris."

Iris remains focused on the road, swerving around cars to keep up with Wesley. "Don't come for me when I'm doing my damn best to save your brother's life."

"You should've taken the time to train me!"

"Too busy saving the rest of the city," Iris says.

Life whizzes by out the window. People are on their porches and fire escapes staring up at the glorious Crowned Dreamer, even though authorities cautioned everyone to stay inside until it passed. Unlike basic constellations such as the Great Bear or the Hunter that only strengthen select powers, the Crowned Dreamer is a prime constellation that elevates all gleamcrafters, celestials, and specters alike. The media is making it sound like celestials are the problem tonight. It's alchemists like Luna who need prime constellations like this one to turn people into specters.

"I promise you're no longer superior to me," I say.

"And I promise I'm not trying to win some pissing contest with you," Iris says, steering left.

There's a question forming on Prudencia's lips as she begins inspecting mine in the flashes of streetlight. "You didn't . . . Brighton, you didn't . . ."

"Someone had to be brave," I say.

Prudencia looks like she might slap me. "Stop confusing reck-lessness with courage! That elixir can kill you!"

I'm not going to let anyone talk to me like I'm some idiot,

10

not even Pru. I know similar elixirs have been tested on people. As soon as the Crowned Dreamer rose on my eighteenth birthday, September 1, the Spell Walkers started tracking specters who were exhibiting powers from multiple creatures—a clear first. Emil's powers manifested when we were fighting one.

"It worked for the other specters," I say.

Prudencia's gaze is uncomfortable. "Do you mean other specters like Orton, who literally burned to death on his own fire? Brighton, your father died because his blood couldn't handle the hydra essence in him—"

"I know why my father died!"

"Then why are you playing with fire like this? This behavior is why Iris didn't want you out on the battlefield! You think you're so tough, but Emil is one of the strongest gleamcrafters on our side, and look at him!"

"Imagine what I'll be able to do once my powers kick in. Cast fire, walk through walls, regrow limbs, race through the streets. Fly! Maybe I'll be able to possess people too and—"

"The stars be damned, possessing people isn't helping you look good. These powers aren't yours to have. That elixir was created for Luna with her parents' blood. There might be negative side effects. You're so irresponsible—"

"I don't remember you giving Emil any of these talks!"

"Emil didn't choose to become a specter, and he is actively working to figure out how to bind these powers, whereas you've thrown yourself into a dangerous combination of gleam, one that might kill you."

I stay true to what I told Emil.

11

I would rather die powerless than watch him doing everything I can't.

We pull into a parking lot, and Iris brakes so hard I have to steady Emil's neck.

The Aldebaran Center for Gleam Care is bright red and shaped like a ring. Out the window I see Wesley is at the entrance, sweating and taking deep breaths as he speaks with three practitioners. The practitioners rush to us, their midnight-blue cloaks swaying, and they gently carry Emil out of the car and onto a stretcher. I swear a couple of them are admiring him, like he's some celebrity. The thing is, Emil *has* become a celebrity, especially to celestials, ever since he went viral multiple times. He's lucky we're not in a regular hospital, where the workers might handcuff him until enforcers could arrive to lock him up in the Bounds.

Footsteps drop behind me out of nowhere—it's Maribelle landing. She's caught the eye of the female practitioner, who glares at her, which isn't uncommon. Maribelle's mother, Aurora, was the one caught on camera bombing the Nightlocke Conservatory, and since then, celestials have had a harder time living in peace. Still, with the way the practitioner is looking at her, you'd think Maribelle blew up the conservatory herself. The practitioner looks away, assessing everyone. Iris, Wesley, and Prudencia are already pretty beat—bleeding, dirty, bruising. I got off good, no one touched me; it's like I've got phasing powers already. I was careful and more alert because being taken hostage by the Blood Casters one time was more than enough for me.

I catch up to the practitioners who are handling Emil right as the elevator doors are closing.

"Family only," one practitioner says.

"He's my brother."

Damn right he's quiet. If they know him, they should know me. Emil's only been featured on my YouTube channel multiple times.

They'll all know me soon enough.

The elevator rises to the top level, the fourteenth floor. The lights in the hallway are warm and bright, and it reminds me of being onstage delivering my salutatorian speech. I stumble, dizzy, but right myself. The practitioners wheel Emil into a private room with white walls, wide windows, and most notably, a ceiling that is shuttered open, which is standard in most Gleam Cares so the night sky can heal and strengthen celestials—and specters too, but to a lesser degree.

This practitioner is taking his sweet, sweet time cutting open Emil's power-proof vest. I shout at him to hurry the hell up, that Emil was stabbed with an infinity-ender blade. Emil is white in the face, and I stay close, holding his hand, even when someone asks me to give them space because my brother has to know that I'm here with him. Eva Nafisi could save Emil's life in moments, but the Spell Walkers never bring her out into battle because losing the healer would be a great loss for us and a great gain for our many enemies. I'm relieved when the female practitioner reveals a moderate healing ability of her own. Her power isn't as colorful as Eva's, which glows like a rainbow, but the muted red lights are helping replenish Emil's blood. Slowly, but surely. The only thing is she doesn't seem to be strong enough to fully seal the cut. They might have to give him old-fashioned stitches.

I wish Emil and I could heal each other, power to power.

All this blood is making me light-headed. I should sit, have some water, but this reminds me too much of Dad dying. Emil didn't want to fight, but I pushed him. The room spins when I think about Emil dying. He deserves to live; come on, this is someone who cares so much about making sure we don't abandon a dead phoenix. The lights fixed on the wall are growing dimmer. I don't feel the Crowned Dreamer working to make me more powerful, to keep me upright. My grip loosens around Emil's hand and I stumble backward.

I once asked Dad what it felt like living with his blood poisoning. He said it was all over the place: body shivers, flushing skin, dizziness, vicious heartbeats. Sometimes his breath would shorten, like mine now, getting cut in half, then those halves cut in half, and the closest I can compare anything to this suffocation is when I had anxiety attacks over exams, or even worse, the ones when Dad would return home from hospital appointments with shorter life sentences.

I collapse, looking up at the fading Crowned Dreamer from the floor, and as my eyes close, I have that blood-and-bones feeling that the Reaper's Blood isn't going to make me immortal—it's going to poison me to death.

TWO
PRISONER

NESS

Who am I going to be? The Senator's prisoner out in the world or one who's locked up in the Bounds?

We're below deck when the Senator invites me to get some air at the front of the ship to think over the big decision ahead of me. Between him punching me in the nose, getting shot with a stunning spell by enforcers hours ago, and the boat speeding toward the island, my balance is especially off as I go up the narrow stairway and step out onto the stern.

There are two men fully dressed in black outfits guarding the stairway, and neither pays me any attention, even though we know each other good and well. The Senator's head of security, Jax Jann, has always reminded me of an Olympian swimmer with his stretched torso and long arms and legs. He has thick eyebrows

15

and red hair that's pulled into a ponytail. He's the most impressive telekinetic I've ever seen; there's no way any assassin will ever land a shot on the Senator as long as he's around. The other, Zenon Ramsey, has dark blond hair that completely covers his eyes, which lulls people into thinking he's not paying attention when in reality he's watching more than most. He has the rare ability to see things through other people's perspectives—literally. I've heard it only works on people in a short distance, but that's all he needs to be a security guard for a two-mile radius.

The Senator has always employed celestials to protect our family, and having celestial bodyguards when he's actively campaigning against the community always felt like a special sort of magic trick until I learned how well they were being paid to keep him alive. That's more than I can say for being a Blood Caster who was working to make Luna immortal. What is shocking to me is how Jax and Zenon regarded me like I wasn't supposed to have been blown to smithereens at the Nightlocke Conservatory.

How many others know that the Senator tried to have his own son killed so he could paint the Spell Walkers as dangers to society?

Even if there was some way I could take down Jax and Zenon and get away on a life raft, a piercing screech high above in the sky tells me that I wouldn't get very far. A phoenix that is four times the size of an eagle swoops down toward the river, its crystal-blue belly skimming the surface as it searches for any intruders or escapees. This phoenix with drenched indigo feathers is a sky swimmer, which I can identify because the Senator once returned home from a hunting trip with the head of one; it might

16

still be mounted in his office at the manor.

"Quite a sight," the Senator says as he follows me to the bow of the ship.

At first I think he's talking about the sky swimmer, but he's staring straight ahead at our destination. The New York Bounds is a collection of small stone castles, huddled together like someone pushed all the rooks of a chessboard together. The towers are windowless, designed that way so inmates will be disconnected from the stars, dampening their abilities. Solitary confinement is the cruelest punishment, burying celestials so deep underground that it's as if all the stars have vanished from the universe.

I've seen this up front.

The Senator brought me here after my mother was killed.

We toured the Bounds so I could understand the creative measures that the prison's correctional architects had to put in place to seal away their powerful inmates. On one level, there were two men floating inside tanks of water, with only their heads above the surface so they could breathe and eat; their waste was their own problem. The fire caster couldn't summon his gleam at all, and if the lightning striker wanted to make a move, well, that was his life to take. On another level, electric traps were installed around the edges of a cell to prevent a woman who could melt herself into a puddle from escaping. Her neighbor was a man who could camouflage himself against any surface, so the engineers installed sprinklers that sprayed paint of different colors to always keep track of him.

The last person we visited that day was a convict in solitary confinement. He'd been imprisoned for using his heating powers

17

to boil the blood of his family. The screams echoing through the corridors had me so nervous that I had stayed hidden behind my then-bodyguard, Logan Hesse. But when the security guard opened the cell, I realized I had no reason to be scared. The inmate's hands and ankles and waist were bound by iron chains. He had no fight in him as we observed him like some animal in a zoo. The next day, the celestial was found dead in his cell, with red handprints burned onto his pale face. When the Senator told me the news, he mocked the dead man with an impression of his suicide. I laughed so hard before returning to schoolwork.

I hate who I was.

The boat docks at the pier.

The island is known for having its traps, like sand basilisks waiting to swallow people whole, but when the Senator steps onto the beach before me, I trust that he knows more than I do right now. I'm weighing in my head if I'm ready for this steep climb with jagged rocks up to the prison when an older man walks out from a cluster of trees. The flashlight guiding his path illuminates his features and I recognize him instantly.

He runs this island.

Barrett Bishop is very pale, as if he only ever comes out at night. I last saw him the morning of the Blackout, and there are now more wrinkles around his eyes, and graying hair that stops at his shoulders. He's dragging the maroon jacket for his three-piece suit because he doesn't care about appearances as much as the Senator. The contrast has worked for them this election cycle. The Senator is the put-together candidate who is best qualified to serve as president, but Bishop's everyman vibes paired with his experience as the chief architect of the Bounds have made him a dream choice for vice president. Their supporters cheer him on at every rally, even when he says the most dangerous things.

"Edward," Bishop says in a hoarse voice, regarding the Senator. Then his icy-blue eyes turn to me. "You brought your ghost."

"I did indeed," the Senator says.

Bishop directs the flashlight toward my eyes, toying around with me like I'm some bored cat, before turning it off. "What are we doing with the ghost? Burying him deep in the Bounds?"

"It's his choice," the Senator says.

The little light spots fade, and Bishop's grin suggests he wants to make me his personal prisoner. If I were locked up, leaving me in a cell to regret all my wrongs would be punishment enough. But the correctional architects who hate gleamcraft have to show their dominance. They have to prove to all of us, everywhere, that our powers can be beaten by ordinary means. They have dark imaginations and enough hate to go home at night without feeling absolutely inhuman.

I once had that hate too.

Following our visit to the Bounds, the Senator asked me how I would've punished the man who killed my mother if we'd ever tracked him down. The celestial had cast an illusion and tricked Mom into believing he was her friend before gutting her. I spent all day thinking over the question and during dinner I told the Senator that I would chain the celestial to a chair, bring in his family, and kill them all in front of him. No illusions. Only reality.

"We can't murder people," the Senator had said.

19

But that's clearly a lie. He organized my death and pinned it on innocent celestials. The truth is that he can't be caught with blood on his hands.

So what's my move?

I hated being used by the Senator to spread messages to other young people that all celestials are dangers, but what he's got planned for me now is even more extreme. Back on the boat he said he wants me to use my shifting abilities to impersonate Congresswoman Sunstar and her team to counter the support she's being shown in the presidential race. I don't know the exact details of the plan, but if there's any chance of me posing as her somewhere in public, then I might be able to flee.

Right now I stand no chance of escaping this labyrinth—four towers with multiple levels, armed guards, and traps galore.

I turn to the Senator to give him his answer, and the fading Crowned Dreamer is reflecting off his glasses. I have no idea what went down tonight with the immortality ritual. I hope Emil was able to find his brother and get away with the phoenix; I hope he didn't die for that bird. If I'm ever going to have a chance to see him again, I have to be as calculating and patient as Luna has been her entire life.

I have to become a pawn who takes down the king. To outsmart the man who fools the world without a single shifter's muscle.

"I'll work for you," I say.

"Smart choice, Eduardo," the Senator says with a quick that-settles-it clap.

"I was really looking forward to making a game out of your

imprisonment," Bishop says. "But we'll make do."

"Let's go home, then," the Senator says.

Home. That cold manor stopped being my home before the Blackout. It's a cage of a different kind. But if I can bide my time and wait for the Senator to leave a crack in the door, I can slip out and never look back.

Hopefully I can escape before helping the Senator become the President.

THREE
DEATH'S HOLD

MARIBELLE

Months ago—I can't remember, four months, maybe five—there was a celestial on a street corner advertising her ability to see into the past and future. I'm not normally this desperate, but I was willing to try anything to uncover the truth behind my parents' deaths. Atlas had warned me to not get my hopes up; I should've trusted his instincts more. Mama always said I had a tendency to get lost in my foggy mind and someone clear-headed like Atlas could be good for me. The celestial and her crystal ball were useless, but all this time later I finally have my answer: June, the specter with ghost blood, possessed my mother and framed her for the Blackout so the country would lose faith in the Spell Walkers.

Then June possessed me and made me kill Atlas.

I needed space from everyone, so I'm up on the sky deck of the Aldebaran Center, legs dangling over the edge, fourteen stories high, and the Crowned Dreamer's starlight prickles my skin one last time before completely fading into the night. It's done. Luna's last shot of becoming immortal. I wouldn't say no to crates of star-touched wine and boxes of blaze cake as a thank-you for the miracles Brighton and I worked tonight.

I did come away with one gift. The oblivion dagger twirling between my fingers is beautiful. Not because of its look, stars no. The rare dagger looks like rotted bone and carries the dark gray stains of all the ghosts that have been slain by it—most recently Luna's parents. The dagger is deceptively heavy too, heavy like the celestial's crystal ball, which I had hurled across her velvet-decked room once I realized her reading was a hoax, some side hustle to make money. The oblivion dagger is beautiful because it's the weapon I'll be able to use to end June forever.

I'm exhausted—beat down, bone tired, sore muscles. The last time I rested was when I collapsed onto Atlas's corpse hours ago in the museum, immediately after my new powers revealed themselves to me and everyone around me in a ring of fire. But I can't sleep without Atlas tonight. This feeling reminds me of those dark lonely nights after the Blackout, when I forced everyone away, even my then–best friend, Iris, who was grieving her own parents too. But then Atlas became a light. Some afternoons I needed him to help me out of bed. Other times I was strong enough to do it myself. Right now the idea of crawling into any bed without him terrifies me.

The cold wind blows back my dark hair. I wish Papa was

around to braid it for me like he did when I was growing up. But he's not.

Death has a hold on me, taking everyone I love.

Mama, Papa. Atlas. Simone, Konrad.

It didn't have to be this way. If I'd known that the founders of the Spell Walkers were actually my birth parents, I would've understood that my power to glide was only a hint of what I'm capable of after inheriting Bautista de León's phoenix abilities. I would've known that the strong instincts that kept me alive in combat were more of a sixth sense, an extension of Sera Córdova's danger-detecting visions. I could've strengthened my powers and kept Mama and Papa at home before they left to try and save the world. Before they set our movement back by years.

I could've used my power to keep Atlas alive.

While we're waiting to see what the deal is with Emil, and if Brighton is coming back with me after so we can track down the Blood Casters together, I should pick up Atlas's car, which I left a couple blocks away from the Alpha Church of New Life. I don't have a sheath yet for the oblivion dagger, and it's too thick to fit into my boot, so I conceal it back inside the padded pocket of my power-proof vest.

I reenter the building through a pyramid-shaped door, and a pair of practitioners watch me cautiously, as if I might blow up the facility the way they believe my mother blew up the conservatory. These practitioners are on the younger side, maybe a few years older than me, so maybe they weren't paying attention eight years ago when the Spell Walkers helped out a dozen Gleam Cares by raising millions for high-tech upgrades. People paid for

24

photo shoots with my parents and Iris's parents. And Iris and I felt like royalty when donors were requesting personal greetings and birthday wishes for the children in their lives. But the most money came from people who wanted to know what it felt like to fly—and not just fly, but fly with then-beloved Spell Walkers. Why go skydiving when the Luceros could take you flying around your neighborhood for a few minutes?

Things weren't perfect then, and they'll never be perfect, but I would kill for those times.

I will kill for those times.

I round the corner, and someone is sobbing. Prudencia is sitting on the floor, crying into her hands. Emil must be dead. I know he has a good heart, but it only seems fair. If Emil hadn't released June when we finally had a hold on her in the Apollo Arena, then Atlas would be alive right now.

"Did Emil die?" I ask.

Prudencia can barely get any words out, and she doesn't bother wiping any tears from her glossy brown eyes. "I don't know. The practitioners are working on him already, but Brighton . . . he's unconscious too, and they have a team trying to save him."

From what I understand, Brighton and Emil are the closest people in her life. Prudencia's parents were killed too, and now she's also on the edge of losing everyone she loves. She only got involved in this war because she wanted to see this through with her best friends. Will she stay with the Spell Walkers if they die, or go back to her celestial-hating aunt? I don't know.

"There's still hope," I say. It's true—I don't waste my breath on empty words. "Specters have been known to faint early in

25

their journeys—after consuming elixirs, when their powers first surface. Their bodies have to adjust. And the Reaper's Blood is a whole other level. I'm sure Brighton will pull through."

"Brighton isn't supposed to be a specter," Prudencia says.

Well, no one is supposed to be a specter. Myself included. But Emil's ambitions to create the power-binding potion Bautista and Sera were working on before they died feels like an impossible task. It may not be easy to get an experienced alchemist to turn someone into a specter, but that task isn't as daunting as reverting every specter back into an ordinary person. That star has long fallen out of sight, as the old proverb goes.

"Brighton made his choice," I say.

"And you chose to help him, which makes me want to send you flying through the wall . . . but I also know Brighton. Even if you didn't help him, he would've shown up. If anything, you kept him alive." Prudencia stares straight ahead at the opposite wall, which has a calming poster of celestials running on water. I can't imagine it's having any positive effect on her right now. "What was his reasoning for drinking the Reaper's Blood?" she asks.

When Brighton first presented his plan, I could see through what some people, even Prudencia, probably mistake as charm. "He said he had to be the one to drink it. He said it would be too risky for me since we don't know enough about the blood type of someone who inherited both celestial and specter properties."

"Oh yeah, like he didn't have his own risks. Like how his own father didn't survive having hydra essence in him, or how Luna prepared this elixir with blood from *her* parents' ghosts, or how it was all untested and he knew all of this, but he did it anyway!"

She's hyperventilating, and it reminds me of the many days following the deaths of my parents, when I would cry and scream so hard that Atlas and Iris and the others couldn't even understand what I was trying to say.

"He's going to die," Prudencia says.

"Maybe. Gleamcrafters are not promised the luxury of time. You should've understood that already from losing your parents."

She stands. "What are you talking about?"

"I never kept secrets from Atlas. You had your reasons for not telling Brighton you're a celestial, I get it. But how do you think he felt when you trusted Iris, an absolute stranger, with your big secret before you trusted him?"

"I never wanted to be exploited by him. Look at the way he was using Emil to boost his own status and fame. And Brighton and I are different than you and Atlas."

"I was open with the person I love and you weren't."

Prudencia rolls her eyes. "You don't know me."

"You went on missions involving dangerous people, knowing that you may even have to expose your telekinesis, to keep Brighton alive."

"And keep Emil alive!" She's shaking. This anger would be useful against the Blood Casters if she ever wanted to get serious.

"Can you honestly say that you would've gone on all these missions where you knew that Emil was being protected by Spell Walkers if Brighton wasn't there?"

Prudencia takes a deep breath. There are words on the tip of her tongue, but she keeps them to herself and walks away. Hiding from her truth seems to be her signature.

If Wesley hadn't pulled me away from June, I would invite him to go with me to pick up Atlas's car. But I'm pissed, so I head down the stairs to avoid him and Iris, and once I'm outside, I jump into the air and glide through the shadows of the night with the wind in my ears.

It doesn't take too long to arrive at the church. I'm careful because there is still one enforcer tank parked out front, with an ambulance truck and police cars nearby. The body bags with dead acolytes should be brought out soon enough. Police officers are taking statements and I wonder if the eyewitnesses are exaggerating details about what happened like so many have in the past.

I unlock Atlas's car, but before I make my way back to Aldebaran for updates on Brighton, I open the storage compartment and pull out the wine bottle that's holding Atlas's ashes. I cremated him myself with the power that manifested after his death; I'll die before I let a poet get their hands on that story.

I'm not an expert on ghosts. It's not an enemy force we've crossed swords with before, and I grew up knowing just the obvious details, like how ghosts can only appear under night skies and how they only wander the world if they were violently murdered. But I learned something valuable because of Luna's ritual. An alchemist proficient in necromancy can summon a wandering ghost; they just need something of the person from when they were alive and the presence of the person who killed them. It doesn't seem cosmically fair to the ghosts, but if there's one bright side to June possessing me when she shot Atlas in the heart with

28

a spell, it's that I should count as his killer too.

But first I'll kill June and avenge him.

I press Atlas's ashes against my heart, daydreaming of the night when I get to summon his ghost and peacefully send him off into the stars.

FOUR

NIGHTMARE

EMIL

My brother is a nightmare.

The streets are crowded with enforcers casting spells into the night as their tanks blaze in gold fire. Brighton has flown higher than every building around him, and he freezes in the air, admiring his chaos. He has three heads with eyes as dark as black holes, and streams of phoenix fire are flowing from the palms of his six hands. I fly into the air to tackle him, to get him to stop, but he's untouchable. I go through him like he's made of air. I float in front of his face, begging him to stop, and there's nothing but cruel laughter echoing from all three of his heads. The city is his to destroy. Finally, when I'm brave enough to stop my brother and conjure fire of my own, Brighton unleashes an inferno toward me and—

I snap awake, groaning and panting.

My brother was a nightmare. That's all. It was all a nightmare. Brighton wouldn't ever go dark like that. It's all in my head.

I remember pieces of conversation, of an argument between Brighton and Prudencia, but neither of them are with me now. I'm alone in a room with bright white walls and lights that hurt my eyes, so I shift to the see-through ceiling and stare out into the night sky. I don't know what time it is, or even what day it is, but I don't see the Crowned Dreamer or its glow stretched across the darkness. Not even a single star in sight. This constellation is rare and won't return to the sky until I'm an old man, assuming I get to live that long. Maybe my next life will see it, or the one after that, or however many lives I get to have before someone gets me good with an infinity-ender.

This bed I'm in is too firm, and I'm hot, so I remove the sheet and realize I'm shirtless. There's dried blood around my stomach from where Luna stabbed me. The wound is closed, but it looks odd, like discolored, stretched-out skin; someone's healed me. But I don't think it was Eva. Eva's power seals all open wounds in ways that you have to look twice to tell that work was even done in the first place. She also absorbs all the pain, and I still feel this dull pounding and sharp twinges. Don't get me wrong, I'm grateful that someone kept me alive. I'm just appreciating how good we have it with a powerful healer like Eva on our side.

Surrounding the gash are the scars from when Ness sliced me to trick Luna and the Blood Casters into believing he was still loyal to their gang. I don't think these will ever fully heal. But

31

Ness did this to save my life, and even when he finally had the chance to run away into anonymity, he returned to Nova when we were under attack to save me again. Then he got taken captive by enforcers, and I doubt he escaped. He's probably dead somewhere, even though I'm not worth dying for.

There's a gentle knock at the door. I look up to see a short practitioner with freckles dotting her face and curly red hair flowing over the shoulders of her midnight-blue cloak. Her electric-green eyes widen when she sees me staring back at her. "Emil Rey," she says with a hint of motherly pride. "I'm Dr. Bowes. It's an honor to have been part of the team that—that—that, uh, that worked on you." Her cheeks are flushed and she's shaking her head as if she wants to leave the room and come back in to restart this entire interaction.

"Hi, thanks . . ." These first words aren't much, but they're rough against my throat.

"Relax," Dr. Bowes says as she hands me a cup of water, and I drink from the metal straw.

She asks me a series of questions, and I answer everything in as few words as possible: I rate the pain seven out of ten; I'd like the lights dimmed; I'm starving and vegan; I'm exhausted. She dims the lights and puts in a request for someone to prepare a meal for me. I bring the blanket over my chest again. The last time my scrawny body was exposed was when Ness was washing the cuts he inflicted on me, and he did all of that with his eyes closed because he knows I'm struggling with how I look, even with everything else I got going on. I can tell Dr. Bowes senses my discomfort because she helps me into some patient-wear—mustard yellow with black stars—and that's one less thing on my mind.

"Emil, the authorities are going to need a report on what happened tonight," Dr. Bowes says as she pulls up a chair.

"The Blood Casters," I say.

She nods. "Iris mentioned this while we were treating her too. I understand she's been in touch with your mother and has advised her to keep her distance for the time being." Makes sense, but I know that can't be easy on Ma. "I have to thank you for your service to this country, Emil. It takes a brave soul to fight this fight. I don't think I'd have it in me, even with your powers. I grew up watching Bautista and his Spell Walkers charge into combat. That was back when they were welcomed heroes—celebrities too, of course." Dr. Bowes smiles wistfully before pressing her hand against her heart. "I cried for weeks after he died, and it was years before I took down his posters."

The way she's looking at me makes me question whether she knows that Bautista is my past life. But that's impossible. The public doesn't know that reincarnation is real, since even specters with phoenix blood like me aren't resurrected as the same person. The way she's going on about Bautista so admirably makes me think she'd be chill if I let her in on the secret, but it's my original life as Keon Máximo, the alchemist who turned himself into the first specter, that I want to keep close to the chest. The only person I told who isn't directly involved in this war between the Spell Walkers and the Blood Casters is my former boss at the museum, Kirk Bennett. Then he betrayed me for his own research and fame.

I play it cool about Bautista. "He was a hero."

"As are you. My son is so proud of me for helping a Spell Walker. You probably hear this a lot, but he's your biggest fan. We've been working on his costume for Halloween. He's going as you."

The blood that didn't spill out of me back in the garden rushes straight to my face. There were a couple years where Brighton and I dressed up as the Spell Walkers for Halloween. He had to be Bautista, of course, because of that alpha, big-brother bone in him, and I chose to be Lestor Lucero because I thought he was cute, I can't even lie. But look at us now. Brighton's fantasies got the best of him tonight and he drank Reaper's Blood so he could fit in with the Spell Walkers. I'm Bautista's real-life scion. These lives were never costumes, but Dr. Bowes's son is going to dress up as me, even though I might be dead before Halloween. And what then? Will her son mourn me the same way she grieved Bautista? He doesn't know me, and she didn't know him. This cycle of worship and grief needs to come to an end.

I offer a quick thanks—that's the best I got.

"Where's my brother?"

I might have to deck him if he's out in the hallway bragging into some camera about this Reaper's Blood business.

For a moment, Dr. Bowes looks as if someone has come around the corner and surprised her. She composes herself and says, "Don't be alarmed."

"Too late. What's wrong?"

"I understand Brighton drank a potion tonight," Dr. Bowes says. "Traffic increases in all our facilities during the appearance of every prime constellation as people pursue specter conversion.

34

Believe me, we're already bracing ourselves for the Cloaked Phantom next weekend. My alchemy courses while pursuing my PhD couldn't have prepared me for this new, dangerous trend of people experimenting with multiple essences. The results have been disastrous. There have been so many reports of people combusting, others eaten alive from within, limbs falling off."

I absolutely didn't need her to paint this picture of Brighton's legs and arms falling off, like rotted teeth out of a mouth, while he screams and dies in a fiery blaze, but there's no shaking that out of my head.

"It's very tricky," she says. "But I assure you my team and I are doing our best to stabilize him."

"You can't guarantee that." I'm shaking. It's like all the promises the doctors and alchemists fed us about saving Dad. "The elixir was created by Luna Marnette herself. It's next level. She's responsible for the Blood Casters and all these other hybrid specters. She was going to use this potion to live forever."

"Immortality is impossible," Dr. Bowes says.

"I bet you think stealing blood from ghosts is impossible too, but here we are."

Dr. Bowes is stone-faced as she absorbs all of this. "You're all fighting a battle beyond our comprehension, aren't you?"

I don't answer her. "Can I please see Brighton?"

She helps me out of bed, and I'm dizzy. I settle into the wheelchair she's insisting I use. Good call. She guides me to another room four doors down.

Inside, Brighton is in bed with his eyes closed, but this isn't some peaceful sleep. He's the palest I've ever seen him. There are IVs injected into his arms, delivering clear, light blue and dark red fluids into his veins. There's a ventilator helping him breathe, and it's nicer than the one we had at home for Dad. I know that I should feel relieved, but it's actually freaking me out that Brighton's condition must be so severe that he needs the best equipment available.

I get out of the wheelchair, holding his hand and fighting back tears.

"He's stable at the moment," Dr. Bowes says.

"Our dad died from blood poisoning."

"I'm aware," Dr. Bowes says.

How much do strangers know about me? I feel uncomfortable, like cameras are following me everywhere I go.

"The hydra essence turned on him," I say. "Won't it kill Brighton too?"

"We're working to purify the blood before an infection can spread, but considering there are three foreign essences working against his system, the chances of Brighton's body failing are higher than most. But you all came to the right place; I've treated many specter aspirants before. You won't believe how many people try to get powers without hiring an alchemist. It's like when my husband tattooed himself as a teenager to save a buck. It didn't turn out well." Dr. Bowes looks sheepish as she realizes that she's gone and made this about herself. "I promise I will do everything I can to make sure your brother goes home with you."

She's too confident. If Ma were here right now, she would go off on Dr. Bowes for not giving it to us straight.

I hope Brighton lives, even if it means reliving all the heartache we went through watching Dad in pain.

"How much time do you think he has?"

"It's too early to tell, but I would prepare for a few months if we can't successfully purify his blood."

Months—and that's if we're extremely lucky. "What if we could cancel out the essences? Do you think that will stop his sickness?"

"It's a popular theory, but no one has ever been able to eradicate a specter's powers. Once creature blood is fused into a person, those abilities become as permanent as a celestial's. Enforcers have means to temporarily dampen powers, of course, but even that takes considerable resources. I'm afraid that there is no known cure for specters presently."

Brighton always says that something being unlikely doesn't make it impossible. I hope I get to hear him say it again.

I squeeze his hand. There are no stars in the sky right now to pray to, but the moment they're back I'm counting on each and every one of them to guide him back to health.

"Dr. Bowes, can you make sure your son won't say anything about us being here? I want Brighton to get as much assistance from you and your team as possible. I'm happy to, I don't know, autograph something for your son if we can count on some privacy."

Dr. Bowes shakes her head. "That's not necessary . . . but if you don't mind, I'm sure it'll make his day. He dreams of becoming a Spell Walker when he grows up."

There should be concern in her voice, not pride. I don't know what powers Dr. Bowes or her son have, but I hope he grows out of his Spell Walker hype before he finds himself in a battle that can kill him. Everything can change so quickly. Check out Brighton. One moment he was saving my life, and in the next, he was doing the unthinkable because staying on the sidelines wasn't enough.

Nightmares may be terrifying, but dreams are dangerous.

FIVE

IRON MANOR

NESS

It's been a while since I've been in a town car.

Luna wasn't comfortable with the Blood Casters traveling in packs unless we were protecting her or there was a very urgent reason. That way, if one of us got caught, the others could complete the mission. Stanton travels through sewers. Dione leaps from rooftop to rooftop. June teleports short distances, usually only appearing long enough for someone to wonder if they're seeing things. And I always blended in on public transportation, an experience I was denied growing up because my fame was growing in political circles. But the Senator keeps his team together. Jax is driving, and Zenon is vision-hopping through the eyes of other drivers to determine the safest path, as well as to make sure we're not being followed. The partition is down as the Senator and Bishop discuss the news that's just come in about a brawl between the Spell Walkers and Blood Casters at a church.

"Which church?" the Senator asks Bishop, who's reading the update off his tablet.

"The Alpha Church of New Life," I say with a smirk, even though I know this isn't good news.

Bishop confirms with a nod.

"What do you know?" the Senator asks.

"That while you were busy with me, Luna was becoming the most powerful person on this planet," I say.

The Senator taps the panel between us, a sign that he's nervous, even though his expression won't betray him. These are the details I pay attention to when I have to impersonate someone. I'm already plotting on when I can pose as him to stage my escape.

"Any casualties?" he asks.

"A dead hydra and a few idiot acolytes," Bishop says.

No mention of the phoenix or Emil. Maybe they did get away. Luna has always sworn that the key to success was merging the three essences, but maybe she's taking her chances on just the blood from the ghosts and hydra. It would still be tricky, but she'll definitely be killable if we ever cross paths again.

"Very well," the Senator says to Bishop. "You'll make a statement in the morning while I meet with some donors."

Business as usual. As if the son who is supposed to be dead because of a plan he engineered isn't going to be alive and well in his home. I wonder if he'll lock me up in the manor's panic room.

We're driving through my old neighborhood, Whitestone,

which sits at the top of Queens, and it's even more painfully residential than I remember. I've seen so much life and color since working the field as a Blood Caster that the sight of these houses makes me feel like my life is reversing. I've gotten used to seeing kids out so late that they're either ignoring their curfew or their parents don't care. I've passed teens in parks where they're huddled together, sharing a joint, as if the smell won't stick to their clothes. By the time I was old enough to test any sort of freedom like that, my mother had already been killed and the Senator's career was rising, so he insisted on my protection. Maybe this entire time he was always keeping me alive so he could one day martyrize me.

I feel sick as I see the familiar laurel hedges that hide the estate. The gate opens and we drive around the small fountain of my grandfather Burgundy Iron, who turned his fear of celestials into fortunes when he invented the first power-proof vests and manufactured them for the government. The manor is three stories high and grayer than Grandpa's fountain. I truly hate it here.

"Where am I staying?" I ask as I push open the front door.

"Your room, of course," the Senator says.

Not much has changed as I enter my old home. Same rug over the cork-colored hardwood floor. Same living room reserved for friends of the Senator but never my own. Same sunroom where Mom used to eat pitahaya while reading some nonfiction book. Same dining area that started feeling more like a boardroom given how often the Senator was having his campaign staff over. Same creak on the seventh step of the stairs. Same portraits of outspoken political figures lining the hallway as I pass the Senator's office and open the door to my bedroom.

Most of the room has stayed the same. All the walls are white except for one that I had wallpapered with black diamonds. The green curtains are open, and I can see that the Crowned Dreamer has vanished from the sky. My colorful candles line the built-in bookcase that's stacked with biographies of politicians who rewrote history to fool me and millions of others into thinking all celestials are dangerous. I stop in front of my desk and stare at the pictures that don't belong.

Back in mid-February, one month after the world thought I died, I came across this article about grieving parents who had lost children of their own. This one mother spiraled because she was already pregnant with another child and she no longer trusted herself to keep them alive. These young parents raised funds so fewer children would have to die from the type of cancer that claimed theirs. The one that gripped me the most was the father who refused to remove a single sock or toy or juice cup from his daughter's room to preserve her memory. I'd wondered if the Senator would leave my room untouched. But he didn't.

Sometime in April, the Senator did a walkthrough of my bedroom for Wolf News. He had planted all these framed pictures of us together: the night he was elected senator; our fancy sailing trip through the Caribbean Sea while visiting the Dominican Republic, a trip that was planned for Mom to spend time with her distant relatives; and day one of eighth grade, which I should've realized was a publicity stunt since it was the first time Mom wasn't around to take me to school. The Senator lingered the longest around the picture of us waving together in our tailored suits on the steps of a courthouse in the Bronx, moments after he announced that he was running for president.

"Eduardo is the reason I believe I can lead our great nation," the Senator had said to the reporter. "Especially after losing Esmeralda."

Then he took this ridiculous long silence that editors deemed worthy of keeping in the final cut.

I slide the picture off my desk and directly into my empty trash can, hating how I probably got my actor bones from the Senator. Thinking about acting reminds me of the picture I actually *have* been missing since I've been gone. I scan around for it since it's no longer on my bedside table, but it's not in here. The picture was of me and Mom on opening night of my first school play. I was dressed as the grandson of this dragon tamer and Mom was kissing the top of my head. The Senator wasn't around because of some last-minute fundraiser. I was upset back then because he didn't show up, but I'm pissed now because he completely removed a great physical memory of that night.

I head for the door right as the Senator and Jax come down the hallway. Jax shoves me back into the room, and I almost fall.

"Control your lackey," I say.

"Jax doesn't need control. He cooperates," the Senator says. "You need to follow his lead."

"You need to give me back my picture of me and Mom."

The Senator stops to consider this and then chuckles. "The one of you from some play? I wasn't in it, so we had it trashed."

"You had no right."

"Dead men have no possessions, and you were supposed to be

43

one. If you wanted that picture so badly, you could've come back to life for that occasion." The Senator claps. "Well then, I have private matters to discuss with Bishop and must alert select others about your return. If you need anything from the kitchens, Jax will have it sent up for you, and he'll escort you to the bathroom as needed."

"For my protection?" I ask mockingly.

"For my campaign's protection," the Senator says. "Welcome home, Eduardo. Have a good night."

Jax telekinetically closes the door in my face.

In all my nightmares of the Senator discovering I'm alive, I never thought I would return here. Dead within the day always seemed more likely. There's still time for that if I don't cooperate.

I sit on my bed, exhausted. I'd forgotten how comfortable it was. I've come a long way from sleeping on stiff mattresses, couches, subway benches, and even the floor of that supplies closet when I manipulated Emil and the Spell Walkers into taking me hostage. This would all feel a little easier if Emil were here with me. If we could talk about our own lives instead of how to save everyone else's.

But my life here won't be easy. He's going to keep me disconnected. There's never been a TV in my room, and the Senator certainly won't give me one now so he can continue controlling the narrative. Still, there's one narrative he can't control: he'll never fool me again into thinking this luxurious house isn't a prison. Except with traditional jails, the prisoners are expected to keep their heads low and behave while they serve their time. Here at home, the Senator is going to corrupt me further.

SIX

LIKE FATHER,
LIKE SON

BRIGHTON

I wake up with a tube down my throat and wires in my arms, and I freak out.

Emil calls for help and nurses rush in, instructing me to relax and let their machines help me breathe a little longer. But Emil crying makes me want to panic even more, so I stare out the window instead. The blackness of the sky has been replaced with bright oranges and pinks and blues. The sun is rising. Has it been a few hours since I fainted? I'm guessing so since Ma would be by my side too if it'd been any longer than that.

When I'm calming down, I can't help but think about this one time when Dad woke up in his hospital room alone. He was so scared, which felt backward. Children aren't the ones who are supposed to tuck their parents back into bed after they've had a nightmare, or check their closets to make sure basilisks aren't nesting in there. Dad explained that his fear was about dying alone, and that struck all of us. Since that moment, we always made sure someone was there when Dad woke up, even if that meant we missed class, work, birthdays, Emil's tutoring sessions, and my extracurricular clubs.

I lucked out having Emil here to keep me company. Even luckier that he's alive. But I'm definitely logging away that Prudencia isn't here.

An hour later, a nurse returns to stop the intubation. My throat feels dry and swollen when he removes the tube, but I'm able to breathe okay. A practitioner, Dr. Bowes, checks my temperature, tests my senses, and assesses my energy levels. I'm burning up, and Emil presses a cold towel against my forehead. I used to be on the outside looking in whenever I watched Dad try and stay strong as nurses poked and prodded him. But the grass isn't greener on the other side with Emil watching me suffer. I'm getting hotter and hotter. This happened to Emil when his powers first appeared. That could be a good thing, except for the fact that it was also what happened to Dad on and off before he died. Emil helps me remove my shirt, but it's not making enough of a difference.

The question I'm building up the nerve to ask is making me nauseous and so nervous that I'm shaking. "I'm dying, right?"

Dr. Bowes's solemn expression says it all. "It appears your body is rejecting the elixir you consumed. We believe you may have a few more months ahead of you."

I don't get it—I glowed after drinking the Reaper's Blood. That has to mean something. "But the elixir was mixed and consumed when the Crowned Dreamer was at its zenith."

"Blood alchemy for specters has been around for decades, but there are no surefire methods," she says.

Even with all of Luna's calculations, the elixir could've turned on her too. If I spared her from everything I'm going through, I hope she suffered from my spell before dying. There are worse legacies I could have.

"We're preparing some more tests to run and afterward we can explore some alternative practices to cleanse your blood," Dr. Bowes says. "Do you need anything else for the time being, Brighton?"

"I need a minute."

Dr. Bowes says something before leaving, but I don't hear her because I'm too busy sorting through my own thoughts about how the elixir backfired.

Emil and I are quiet when we're alone. He gets me ice chips to chew on, and he's making me feel guilty with how sad he looks, so I focus on the sky some more. I wonder how many more skies I'll get to see before I die. If I'll get to see Ma. Talk things out with Prudencia. If Emil and I—

"Did you mean what you said back at the church?" Emil asks, ending the silence.

I said a lot of things back there, but I realize he's asking me about what I said before I drank the Reaper's Blood. How I would rather die like Dad than live powerless. "Just get your I-told-you-so out of the way," I say.

"Not happening. Everyone ignores their big brother," Emil says.

"I'm older. I was born first . . . thought I was born first. We don't actually know."

"I've got two extra lifetimes on you. I win."

Even though he's forcing this humor, this is the smoothest conversation we've had in weeks. Everything else has been this battle about how best to approach our positions in this war. Strangely enough, the last time it felt this easy talking to Emil was after we found out he was adopted. We had talked about how we were always going to be brothers, no matter what.

"Remember my bully in seventh grade?" I ask. "The one who hated my early YouTube videos?"

"First time I ever hit someone who wasn't you," Emil says.

We got into a number of fights with each other growing up, and it was always over something stupid. One time he was practicing his drawing, so he traced a superhero over one of my comic books and left pen marks all over the page. Another time I kept hogging the TV to play an RPG where you get to build your own celestial. But those fights were different from the ones we got into with other people at school or on our block. Watching Emil deck that other kid was something I wish I'd gotten on camera so I could play it on repeat.

"It was incredible," I say.

"Until he hit me back and punched you too."

"Hey, we got jumped together. Even back then."

"Simpler times," Emil says.

Truly. It's not that I would trade this gang war for schoolyard smackdowns. I just wish this all turned out differently. That Emil and I could've been the powerful Reys of Light like we dreamed

48

about when we were younger.

"I wish I wasn't your brother," Emil says.

Somehow, that hits harder than finding out I'm dying.

"No, that came off wrong," Emil says, red in the face. "Sorry. I wish you were an only child. I love being your brother, Bright, but our brotherhood is what got you involved in this war in the first place. If Dad hadn't found me on that street corner, you would be safe at home and covering all this action for your Celestials of New York. You wouldn't be—"

"What, dying? No, but I wouldn't be happy either."

"I know, but you never got caught up in any of this until you were living in my shadow. You wouldn't have felt so competitive or incomplete. I'm just saying, I wish another family found me."

"No, what you're saying is you wish I wasn't involved. Guess what, Infinity Son, I'm the one who stopped Luna, not you. If I hadn't been there you would be dead and Luna would be immortal. How is that good for anyone? For the world?"

Emil hops out of his seat and kicks it over. "I don't care about the world! I care about you!"

"This is why I'm the one who should have powers! I could prove that not all specters are bad, that we can trust ordinary people with powers. That we can all be more like Bautista. Be more like you."

It pains me to use Emil as a shining example, but it's true. Power didn't corrupt him, and corruption seems to be the popular narrative about any specter. This country is doing itself a gigantic disservice by assuming everyone will abuse their abilities. Right now, enforcers are the only authorized special-ops

49

unit tasked with taking down gleamcrafters. Some celestials have been hired as enforcers, sure, but the majority are humans who are fighting back with wands, gem-grenades, and other weapons boosted by gleamcraft. But what if we trusted more people with powers? What if we could use creature blood to strengthen soldiers in the military, police officers, bodyguards, and protectors of all kinds? We can't assume that everything will go wrong just because a select few might abuse that privilege.

"For the hundredth time," Emil says, shaking. "I don't want these powers. They are not the solution to my problems."

"Maybe you would feel differently if you saw Dad die!"

That shuts him up.

We're both breathing heavily. My cheeks are wet with tears and sweat. My fist is shaking so hard, I could probably punch a wall and not feel a thing. "I always hoped Dad would pass peacefully in his sleep with all of us surrounding him. I wasn't ready to be alone with him when it all happened so violently. One minute he was telling me why he no longer loved his favorite book and the next he was gripping it so hard that he tore the cover. I kneeled before him and he grabbed my hand and his eyes went wide and—"

"Brighton, stop, just stop—"

"—he spat blood all over me and he was crying and it smelled and I begged him to hold it together and then his hand went limp. His head bumped into mine so hard, and my reflexes shoved him back and his eyes stared back at me and never blinked again. I screamed for him to wake up even though I knew he was gone."

I'm panting.

This is the first time I've gotten this off my chest. It's the kind of relief that reminds me of taking off my backpack, which was always loaded with textbooks. There are still so many more details when I play Dad's death back in my head, but Emil doesn't need any more. He's already crying hard, like it's Dad's funeral all over again.

"I don't want to die with you thinking this only happened because I'm power-hungry," I say as he stares me down like I've committed the most unforgivable act. "I drank the Reaper's Blood because I thought those powers would protect me in this terrifying world where one day you're healthy and the next day you're dying." My throat is strained, and my voice lowers to a whisper. "Whenever I die, I hope you're not around. You'll be scarred so badly you'll remember it in every lifetime."

SEVEN
THE JOURNAL

EMIL

Believe me, I invited Brighton multiple times in the past to open up about Dad's death, and I get that he was trying to protect me, but I never in a million lifetimes would've thought that he would weaponize those graphic details against me.

I'm down the hall and back in my own room, face-planted into my pillow, while Prudencia massages my shoulder to comfort me. I'm crying really damn hard, eyes stinging, and I wouldn't have thrown down money on having any more tears left, but I've got plenty flowing because I can't get this picture out of my head of Dad crying and crashing into Brighton. I don't know how Brighton wasn't in therapy every week. Even I was in counseling, and I didn't experience everything he went through.

"That wasn't fair of him," Prudencia says.

I didn't put her through everything Brighton told me. She loved my dad too and doesn't need these visuals. "Brighton's been carrying this on his shoulders alone for months," I say as I roll over to my side, and my latest wound aches. "I get why he couldn't keep it together."

"He was wrong to share it in an outburst, when you were least expecting it."

I'm not denying that.

I keep trying to focus on the good memories of Dad, like when he rented a car and drove us all to the Poconos for a surprise family vacation, or when we marathoned these nature specials about phoenixes in the wild, just the two of us. But all I can think about is what must've been going through his head during his final moments. Did he want to apologize to Brighton for spitting blood on his face? Was he happy, even a tiny bit, that if he had to go, he was at least with his only biological son?

I'm facing the facts. My parents were only expecting to bring one son home when Brighton was born, but when Dad stepped out of the hospital to get balloons for Ma and discovered me out on a street corner, he brought me back, thinking I was abandoned. He had no idea that I wasn't a newborn, but instead someone who was reborn in a blaze of fire. None of us knew until a few weeks ago when we pieced it together with the Spell Walkers. I know Dad loved me. But if someone put a wand to his head and asked which son he would've wanted with him when he died, it makes sense now more than ever that he would've chosen Brighton.

"Hey," Iris says as she walks in with a phone in one of her bandaged hands. "How are you healing?"

"Getting there," I say. Movement is one thing, but the infinity-ender blade is built to kill phoenixes and prevent them from resurrecting. The first time I was wounded, my powers were still there, but weaker. I'll have to see what's good with them when the time inevitably comes for me to use them again. "How are you doing?"

"Punching through bricks put a strain on my fists, but the salve they put on me should have me demolishing more walls in no time," Iris says.

"Thanks for getting us out of there," Prudencia says. "It was getting close."

Iris nods. "What's the deal with Brighton?"

I'm not sure how to answer that in the grand scheme of things. "I don't know."

"Well, you need to talk to your mother. Carolina keeps threatening to hop on a bus from Philadelphia to get back here if one of you don't call her."

"I'm not telling her about the Reaper's Blood," I say.

"Your family, your business," Iris says. "We haven't told your mother we're camped out in Gleam Care, but our plan is to have Eva and Carolina arrive tomorrow afternoon. Wesley will hopefully have figured out our next haven by then."

"More hiding," I say.

"Feel free to take your chances back at your apartment. Let me know if the Blood Casters come knocking on your door again."

I first joined the Spell Walkers after Ness, posing as Atlas, surprised me at home to lure me back to Luna. But thankfully the real Atlas showed up and saved me and Brighton. There's no world where we can ever live there again without freaking out every minute, worrying that the Blood Casters, or anyone else who wants me dead, will kill us all in our sleep. More havens it is.

Iris dials a number. "Eva, babe. Is Carolina around? I'll put Emil on the line. . . . Great . . . I love you too."

It's beautiful that Iris and Eva, and all the Spell Walkers, have been able to pull off love while existing in the heart of this war we're fighting. But I don't know how to factor in romance while trying to survive. Atlas's death doesn't make me any more eager to figure it out, but I'm regretting not exploring that energy with Ness when I had the chance. Maybe it would've been better to have loved, lost, and all that.

I take the phone from Iris and talk into it. "Ma?"

"My Emilio, what's going on? Why haven't you reached out sooner?"

I step out into the hallway and walk toward Brighton's room. "Sorry, Ma, there's been so much going on. But Brighton and I are together again."

"That's the only reason I haven't completely lost it. Eva says you all won. You stopped Luna. So it's all over now."

"We won," I say. The greater truth behind that victory is going to break her heart. "But I don't think it's over yet. We still have some loose ends to tie up."

"What do you mean?"

"Don't worry. I'm going to take care of everything."

"Where's Brighton? I want to talk to him."

Through the triangular window of Brighton's door, I see he's staring at the sky. "He's resting right now. Have you been able to sleep?"

"No, but Wesley's wonderful girlfriend, Ruth, has already prepared a bed for me. I can try to sleep now that I've heard your voice."

It helps so much to know that she's got something good going for her in Philadelphia. "Please rest, Ma. Call us in the morning when you're on the way."

"I will. I love you boys so much."

"Love you too."

We hang up.

I'm going to get Ma the closest-to-normal life that I can, a life that Brighton better get on board with because I'm over all of this chaos and what it's done to our family. If I can't save him with the power-binding potion, then Ma is going to know that I did everything in my power to keep her only biological son alive. It's the least I can do for all the trouble I brought into her life.

I return to my room. Prudencia is resting on my bed, and Iris is picking at one of her bandages.

"Thanks," I say, giving Iris her phone back.

"Carolina calming down?" Iris asks.

"Yeah, but once she finds out about the Reaper's Blood, it's going to set her off. I have to focus on the power-binding potion."

"Which you were already doing," she says.

"No, my focus was split because of the Crowned Dreamer. But now that I held up my end of the deal and stopped Luna, I'm giving my full attention to this potion to save Brighton."

Iris doesn't argue. "The world thanks you. Well, the whole

56

world isn't thanking any of us. But you get it."

"What's the plan?" Prudencia asks.

"We haven't been able to figure out what those ingredients in Bautista's journal mean. I bet he and Sera were close; we just got to finish the job. It's time we straight-up ask an alchemist to decode everything for us, and fast, so we can save Brighton too."

Iris scoffs. "Sorry, but you do realize that the majority of senior alchemists in New York swore allegiance to Luna, right? Even some of the younger alchemists who didn't agree with her still respected her work. It's unlikely that Luna survived that attack, and once word gets out that you had a hand in killing her, they're all going to try and make a name for themselves."

"And what better way to do that than getting us," Prudencia says.

I can stop fighting all I want, but that won't stop others from hunting me.

"Then we don't ask an alchemist," I say. "Dr. Bowes studied alchemy. She might recognize the ingredients."

Prudencia considers this for a moment. "After everything with Kirk, we have to be careful. Do we trust her?"

"She hasn't sold us out," Iris says. "Yet."

"Dr. Bowes wouldn't. She has loved the Spell Walkers her entire life."

"It's a start," Prudencia says, headed for the door. "The journal is in the car."

I follow her downstairs, and when we get to Iris's car, she unlocks the trunk with her power. The journal is inside her back-pack, and I'm so damn grateful she didn't leave it behind in Nova when I was busy trying to protect Gravesend. Prudencia hands me the journal, and hope sparks in me, looking at it again. It's cased in dark blue leather, and there's an illustrated fire-orb on the cover, gold like the flames Bautista could create. In the elevator back up, I flip through and find the pages with the ingredients we couldn't translate.

We find Dr. Bowes's office, and her door is open. She looks up from her computer. "Emil, Prudencia. Come in, please." We sit on the little yellow sofa she has in her office, and I breathe in the smell of the pink roses beside me. "Fifteenth anniversary last week," she says when she sees me eyeing them. There's a picture of Dr. Bowes with her family in Egypt and another of her in a ball pit with her son. She should be home with her son and husband, not working overtime to keep us all alive. "What can I do for you?"

"I hate to ask, but we need your help," I say.

"And discretion," Prudencia adds.

Dr. Bowes straightens up. "I'll do my best."

"I know we can't fully eliminate the essence of creatures once they're introduced into a human's body, but we're hoping that if we can lock away all the powers that come with being a specter, they'll stop eating away at Brighton." I tap the cover of the journal. "This belonged to Bautista and Sera Córdova."

Dr. Bowes eyes the journal like it's unearthed treasure. "I remember all the murmurings about what an impressive alchemist Sera was. There were even rumors that she and Bautista were romantically involved."

I'm not going into Bautista's family tree, especially not where Maribelle and I sit on it. "I don't know anything about that, but their notes are confusing."

"There are all these ingredients we can't translate," Prudencia says. "We've looked through textbooks, online searches. Nothing comes up."

"Which ingredients?" Dr. Bowes asks.

I read them out: "Ghost husk, cumulus powder, feather-rock, dry-tear, burnt-berry, crimson root, grim-ash, and water from the Shade Sea. Do any of these sound familiar?"

Dr. Bowes shakes her head. "Not a single one."

"Could they be archaic names?" Prudencia asks.

"Possibly, but I think it's more likely that these names were invented. Over the years, alchemists have worked to define their legacies with groundbreaking works. Even the great devastation Keon Máximo caused by creating specters is historic," Dr. Bowes says. I keep a straight face, not owning up to my first life. "Rival alchemists since then have wanted to leave their mark on the world, and some began stealing the formulas of others and framing them as their own. By using code names that only the original alchemist will understand, their work is protected."

It sucks that we can't summon Sera's ghost and ask her to let us in on the secret, but we know good and well that ghosts only speak in howls that make you hopeless and miserable. Not that I need any help in that department.

I close the journal. "So we're screwed."

"There's got to be another way," Prudencia says.

"What, we just throw a bunch of ingredients in a cauldron and luck into the right combo?"

"Planets aren't formed in a day," Dr. Bowes says.

I know she's using the expression, but unlike planets, this potion isn't going to create itself. "Smarter minds with legit resources have tried figuring out how to bind someone's power and come up with nothing. We could spend the rest of our lives experimenting with this formula only to discover Sera was totally off base. This is . . ." I try taking deep breaths, but I'm losing to my anxiety. "This is why I didn't want to get involved in the first place. This is so much bigger than me, and I can't deliver the win." I get up, handing the journal to Prudencia. "I'm done. I was never going to be the next Bautista. Sorry."

Maybe Brighton was right. Maybe the wrong brother got powers.

EIGHT
HIGH AND
MIGHTY

BRIGHTON

There's too many people in this room, for star's sake. Emil is reviewing test results with Dr. Bowes, and judging by his face it's not looking promising. Wesley is leaning by the window and texting his contacts to figure out the next haven. Iris thankfully takes her phone call with Eva out into the hallway. There've been tons of practitioners too, but with everyone coming in and out, I haven't seen Prudencia or Maribelle since we arrived a couple nights ago. One person is grieving her boyfriend. The other isn't. I won't be around when Prudencia regrets shunning me like this; that'll be her future therapist's problem.

Another practitioner, Dr. Oshiro, comes in, but I'm okay with them. Their methods of helping are simpler than the others. When I was a kid I assumed that all Gleam Care practitioners had healing powers, but Dad explained that if the world had that many willing healers, there would be fewer patients in hospitals. Unfortunately, that's not the case, but Dr. Oshiro's cooling abilities are very helpful at lowering my high temperature. They ask me to take deep breaths and I brace myself for their freezing touch as they place their tattooed hand on my forehead. It feels like those first moments when I step out into a snowstorm, cursing myself for not wearing some ski mask to protect my face from the cold, but then their touch cools my entire body down in seconds, and it feels like I've been relaxing in a pool all day to escape the summer heat. It's not the kind of power I would've risked my life for, but it's got its uses.

I couldn't sleep last night. The side effects from the blood poisoning can be agonizing, but I'm more haunted by how much I hurt Emil yesterday. Apologizing seems pointless. This wasn't like other past situations where all my own rage came before his feelings, like once when he wouldn't turn off this podcast when I was trying to study so I told him that I was actually trying to succeed in life and not get rejected everywhere like he was with his pathetic grades. I knew Emil tried really hard with his schoolwork, but I didn't care in that moment. It took weeks before things felt right between us. This time I would need true immortality to live long enough to make it up to him.

Dr. Oshiro and Dr. Bowes leave together, and Iris returns before the door can close.

"Your mom's on," Iris says, handing me the phone.

I don't think I am ready to tell Ma everything. This reminds me of when I was studying for finals and, even with days and days of prepping, I still didn't feel prepared. But it didn't matter whether or not I was ready once the exam was in front of me—I just had to go for it.

A lot of people in my situation might ask for privacy, but I've lived so much of my life online that I don't care. Especially not when everyone here knows my condition.

I take a deep breath and try to sound as strong as possible. "Hello?"

"My shining star," Ma says with a crack in her voice. "I'm so happy you came back, but you can't run away again. I told your brother the same thing, remember? We are each other's responsibility."

Tears are trying to break through as every moment feels like I'm inching toward my end. I feel guilty enough that she got hurt because I was pissed at Emil and the Spell Walkers when they told me I couldn't go on any more missions, but now putting her through this? I would rather speak about anything else. Ask her about her favorite memory with Abuelita. The first meal she taught herself to cook. If watching me and Emil grow up together makes her wish she had her own sibling. What she misses the most about Dad.

I can't die without being honest.

"I'm sorry. I won't run away again. I promise."

"Good. I'm excited to see you and your brother in a couple hours. Are you well?"

"I've been better. Ma, I came back because I wanted to help beat the Blood Casters. I survived and I held my own, but you should know I'm getting medical attention right now."

The parallels between me and Emil both being treated in Gleam Care when we had to break big specter-related news to Ma isn't lost on me. Except this is all my fault.

"What happened?" Ma asks. "Were you burnt? Is anything broken?"

"No one hurt me out there. It's just . . . it's been hard living in Emil's shadow, and I decided to take action. My dreams got the best of me."

She's quiet for so long that I have to check that the call hasn't dropped. "Got the best of you how?"

"I drank the Reaper's Blood, and now I'm really sick. I wanted those ultimate powers and—"

"Brighton Miguel Rey! How . . . ? You . . . You're smarter than this! The hydra blood ruined your father. What made you think you were the exception to the rule?"

"So many reasons, Ma! For one, your mother was a celestial, so I hoped it would better brace me to welcome other powers into my system." Everyone's eyes are on me, and Emil is approaching. He reaches for the phone, and I smack his hand away. "I could've saved lives if this had worked. I could've been safe from death forever."

Ma is sobbing, and it immediately transports me back to when I called her to give her the news about Dad. I never thought words could hurt someone so much.

"I can't lose you too," she says. "I can't believe I'm losing you because you were so selfish—"

"Selfish?!"

"Yes, selfish! You are always putting yourself before others, Brighton, and your father and I didn't raise you to be so high and mighty! You—"

I'm burning hot, like I swallowed a star and I'm milliseconds away from exploding. "This is why Dad was always the better parent! If I told him I was dying, he wouldn't have been shouting about how little he thinks of me!"

I throw the phone across the room, and the screen shatters against the wall.

Emil is staring at me like I'm a hydra that chewed up a phoenix and spit out its bones. Wesley's jaw has dropped and frozen in place. Iris is staring at her broken phone and probably dreaming up which arm of mine she's going to rip out first so I can't ever destroy her property again.

"Don't look at me like you know how she was talking to me," I spit out.

Emil stares me dead in the eyes. "Bright, if you need to swing at someone, I'll be your punching bag, but don't go off on our mother like she spoon-fed you the Reaper's Blood and expect me to take your side. You crossed the line, big-time."

He storms out of the room.

Iris picks up the phone and examines it before dropping it in the bin. "That was my last phone. Wesley, do you mind getting some new ones?"

"We're low on funds," Wesley says.

"Then cash in on favors. Someone somewhere has to have a connection to a bulk buyer," Iris says on her way out too.

"You got it."

Wesley comes to the foot of my bed like he's about to say something, but he gives me this look of pity before taking off. He's got it so good being born with power. When he was living on the streets, he used his swift-speed for his own selfish means, but no one is ever calling him out on it. But when it comes to me, I'm the bane of my family because no one believes I could be just as good and powerful, if not better and more, than any Spell Walker in this building.

I'm left alone. I squeeze my eyes shut and try to force myself to rest so I don't have to think about how little my own mother and brother think of me.

NINE

OBLIVION'S EDGE

MARIBELLE

I slowly wake up, wondering why I don't feel his chin between my shoulders or his breath on my cheek or his hands locked in mine. I'm not actually in bed with Atlas. I'm alone in his car. I begin shaking as I realize it was only a dream. I scream and punch at the wheel, the horn honking a dozen times. I don't know how long I was asleep. Minutes, I'm guessing. When I parked the car outside of the Aldebaran Center, reclined the seat, and used my power-proof vest as a pillow, I doubted I would get any rest. But it seems my body will only take my revenge into account for so long before it shuts down.

I wipe my eyes dry and go inside the hospital. Immediately I see Prudencia, Wesley, and Iris being escorted into a faculty cafeteria. Great. I won't have to deal with any of them when I get upstairs to check on Brighton. I ride the elevator and go to the room everyone crowded last night before I sought air on the sky deck, and I let myself in.

Brighton is watching TV on this cart that someone must have brought in for him. "Good timing. We made the news," he says.

I stand by him and watch.

Senator Iron's pick for vice president, General Bishop, is on site at the Alpha Church of New Life. His tie is loose, and his sleeves are rolled up, revealing the dark green arrow tattoos on his pale skin. He keeps trying to remind the public that he is one of them, that he's gotten his hands dirty. People overlook that General Bishop was never working-class. His family lived luxuriously from all the riches his grandfather made by creating the Bounds.

"Am I surprised we're here again?" General Bishop says to all the reporters. "Of course not. These gleam gangs only care about winning their war, not the well-being of your neighbors, your homes. These young acolytes, all aspiring to become specters, were slaughtered in this church last night. Let that sentence sit with you. . . . Is no life, is no place, sacred to these Spell Walkers?" His expression is furious, leaning into the tough-guy persona their supporters are cheering on. "It may not have been your child killed last night, but what's to stop them from being seduced by power and ending up dead?"

Brighton looks down.

I turn off the TV.

"If there's a bright side to all of this," Brighton says, "I probably won't be alive to see Iron and Bishop win this election."

He's right. Senator Iron and General Bishop will most likely take the White House. If they're going to do everything in their power to take away ours, I'm going to make sure I don't go down alone.

I'm dragging June into the grave with me.

I dig my thumb into my palm for the first time in months. It's a technique Atlas passed on to me, one he taught himself after his parents were convicted for using their powers to rob a bank and sent to the San Diego Bounds. If I press my thumb into my palm, I'll feel how real I am. It worked even when I was in the haze of grief from losing my parents.

"You would've been a great partner," I say, taking a seat. "The Casters weren't ready for the storm we were about to unleash on them."

"Nice to know someone believed in me," he says.

"That didn't work out in your favor."

"You gave me a chance. Emil, Prudencia, Ma, and the others didn't."

"Maybe not, but love gets in the way."

"I'm not sure how much they love me," Brighton says. "I said some really horrible things to Emil and Ma, and Prudencia hasn't visited me once."

"Prudencia cares. I see right through her act," I say. It's not my business. But Prudencia protecting her heart so Brighton can't be used against her the way Atlas was killed because of me seems pointless. Brighton is already dying.

He tries to sit up. "What do you mean? I—"

Spellwork thunders outside, and I rush to the window to see

what's going on. There are a couple vans and four motorcycles blocking the entrance. I identify acolytes by their gray jumpsuits. They're battling the hospital's security guards, both sides firing spells out of their wands. It's hard to make out any faces from the fourteenth floor, but there's no mistaking the six-armed girl holding her own wands—Dione. If one Blood Caster is here, the others can't be far off.

"What's going on?" Brighton asks.

"Blood Casters," I say. "Go find cover."

I hit the gray button that opens the shuttered panel in the domed ceiling, designed to allow celestials to accelerate their healing by sleeping under the night sky. I need to get outside faster, so once the clearing is open wide enough, I levitate to the edge, slide down the side of the dome, and dive off the building. Wind roars in my ears as I keep my hands to my sides, and I must look like a missile. When I'm near the ground, I activate my power, thrust backward a few feet, and glide down in a circle. I drop into the parking lot, and when my psychic sense signals that there's danger, I dive behind a car, catching myself in the air so I don't slam on the concrete. More spells are being shot into the car, and I move away before it can explode and take me with it.

The front doors open and Iris and Wesley run out alongside three more security guards. Even though it's clear that the acolytes are directly across from them, they keep looking around. Iris points—Eva and Ruth are here, and they're helping Carolina out of a green van. None of them have the offensive powers needed to take on the acolytes. Iris yells at them to stay inside the car, but they don't seem to hear her. She runs across the path as spells crash into her, simply slowing her down, until Dione charges across the lot and tackles her.

Acolytes fire spells at the green van as it begins to drive my way. Ruth is in the driver's seat, but another Ruth is also still helping Eva and Carolina. It's unclear which one is the clone until the one on foot vanishes in a purple glow. Four acolytes hop on their motorcycles and chase after the van. I knock down one acolyte with a fire-arrow before he gets too far, but everyone else vanishes from sight as they go out of the exit. Wind blasts past me; it's Wesley chasing after them to protect his girlfriend, maybe even their daughter if Ruth brought Esther along.

I run for Atlas's car, knowing my skin can't resist the spells like Iris's can. I grab my power-proof vest from the front seat and put it on, quickly like my parents trained me, and I grab the oblivion dagger.

I jump and glide into the battle, hurling fire-arrows at the acolytes. I land behind Dione, and before she can hammer Iris with her six fists, I slice her back with the dagger. Dione screams, whirls around, and punches me four times. Spit flies out of my mouth, and she snatches the dagger from me. Dione hooks one arm around my head, flips me over her shoulder, and slams me on my back. She hovers over me, pinning down my arms with two of hers and twirling the oblivion dagger with another. I try kicking at her head, but a fourth arm catches my foot. She drives the dagger down toward my throat, but Iris's hand slides underneath, and the bone blade goes through her palm, her glistening blood spilling onto me. Iris punches Dione in the face with her other hand, and I can hear bones cracking as Dione flies backward.

Iris bites down on her lip as she slowly pulls the oblivion dagger out of her hand, the bone clattering as she drops it to the ground. We take cover behind a pillar. Iris examining the blood gushing out of the hole in her hand reminds me of when we were children in the park and she jumped on my back so she could experience what it was like to levitate. We ran toward the edge of the staircase and I carried us into the air, but I couldn't hold her for very long. We fell, and she landed on a pile of broken glass that pierced her skin. At least Iris isn't crying this time.

"Fly after Eva—she's with Carolina, Ruth, and Esther."

"Ruth drove off," I say.

We peek around the pillar to see Eva and Carolina being pursued by acolytes.

"We have to get them," Iris says, taking off at a sprint.

But that's when I see June standing by the driveway's entrance sign—and she's staring at me.

I grab the dagger and go straight for June, ignoring Iris shouting for me to help her because she's not in charge of me. I don't owe her just because a dagger was driven through her hand for me. If she hadn't kept my true lineage a secret from me, I would've understood my powers better and saved our parents and Atlas. Iris will rescue Eva and have her hand healed. I have to kill June while she's stupid enough to show her face.

I glide after June as she takes off running through the bushes and heads downhill. June darts into the street and has to phase through an oncoming car, though it's too late for the driver, who swerves to miss her and crashes into another car. June stands

72

in the center of her chaos as the other cars honking masks the sounds of spellwork back at the hospital. I drop down onto the street, swinging the dagger. June fades out and kicks me from behind, and I crash into the hood of a car. Then my psychic sense goes into overload as she keeps reappearing around and attacking me. Punch to my back, elbow to my neck, kick to my ribs. She punches my shoulder from behind so hard that I think she's dislocated it, and I don't have Atlas around to pop it back in. My eyes flutter from dizziness as she slams my face against the hood.

She tries to wrestle the dagger away from me, and my arm is too busted to keep a tight grip. Dark yellow flames burst from my fist and burn her hands. Is this why she and the Blood Casters came back—for the dagger? Or did they hunt us down to get revenge for their creator? I don't know if June even has enough humanity in her to care for Luna like a mother, but I hope she was forced to watch Luna choke to death on her own blood.

I cast a stream of fire at June, obscuring her vision as I levitate about ten feet high, and when she walks through my flames, expecting to find me still on the ground, I hurl the dagger down at her with my good arm. June sees me just in time, and the dagger phases through her, clattering against the ground. She's untouchable. . . .

June slowly turns to her shoulder, eyeing it curiously. Gray-and-red blood drips down her solid body.

The oblivion dagger can harm her when she's incorporeal.

We both learn this at the same time.

I drop down, grab and throw the dagger again, but June

vanishes through the ground this time. I wait for her to pop back up, but she doesn't. The gray-and-red blood on the bone dagger is the most promising sight I've seen in days.

There's a crack in June's armor, and I'm going to break her apart.

TEN
POISON

BRIGHTON

There haven't been a lot of times that I've missed being that ordinary Brighton who was college-bound about a month ago, but I would give a lot right now to be healthy in some dorm room watching a TV show with some roommate I low-key hate. Instead I'm staring out the window in a hospital as a battle unfolds, and I think someone may be coming to kill me before I can die of unnatural causes.

An alarm blares, and against every practitioner's instructions, I run. I've just made it to the door when I crash so hard into Emil that we collapse on top of each other. He groans and I rub my forehead.

"We got to go," Emil says as we help each other up.

"You think?"

I've got nothing on but the hospital garb. There's no time to even put on the socks Emil took off me when I got too hot, or grab my sneakers in case we make it outside. My body is aching, but Emil drags me down the hall. Overhead lights are flashing yellow and orange, which I know is an emergency signal from this zombie horror movie that took place in an abandoned Gleam Care facility.

"Where's Prudencia?" I ask.

"I don't know," Emil says.

We've just reached the end of the hall when Dr. Bowes calls our names from behind. She abandons her high heels and catches up to us. "Let's get you somewhere safe until security can handle the threat."

"They're Blood Casters. Your guards are going to get ripped apart!" I say.

The bang of a spell shocks us all, and Dr. Bowes pulls us out of harm's way. The poster behind us is set on fire. I turn to find three acolytes armed with wands. I hate every celestial who has donated their blood to power all of these so-called defensive weapons, as if it's not easy for dangerous people to get their hands on them too. These acolytes don't care about using the power of others, if that's what it takes to become specters and have their own powers one day. But if Luna is dead, why are they bothering? Are they serving a new leader?

Dr. Bowes opens the stairway door, and Emil and I go down as quickly as we can, fighting past our pain.

"Eleventh floor," Dr. Bowes says, following us.

Spells rain down on us as the acolytes catch up. Emil swings open the door, and Dr. Bowes pauses before closing it behind her. Her eyes glow with twinned crescent moons as she holds out her hands, swinging them in dips and curves like a pendulum. Suddenly, there are projections of the three of us soundlessly continuing down the stairs.

"The illusions will only make it down a floor or two before they vanish, but that should be long enough to protect two heroes," Dr. Bowes says with beaming pride. It sounds like Dr. Bowes isn't strong enough to cast the grand illusions that masked us from the public eye in Nova, but this stage trick saved our lives.

She leads us to a laboratory and swipes us in with her key card. She turns off the lights so we can hide. It's pitch black until Emil creates a little bulb of fire, wincing in pain as he guides us behind a counter that's littered with vials and magnifying glasses and documents. He presses his palm against the wound on his side. The infinity-ender affected his powers when Ness sliced him the first time, but it's going to hurt even more after being stabbed by Luna. Once we're all situated, Emil closes his hand and the fire goes out. The lab is nothing but heavy breathing in darkness.

"Maybe I should help," Emil whispers. "They're here for us."

"They're here for me. I'm the one who killed Luna."

I should be brave and turn myself in so the other patients don't get hurt. Even though I already know I'm dying, I don't have it in me. My time is running out, and I want as much of it as possible. The stars didn't give me the powers I wanted to protect the people, so everyone can be their own hero.

There's a bang outside the door. Two bangs, three bangs, four bangs. Have the acolytes found us? Something smashes outside. The door opens and hallway lights spill into the entrance for a moment before closing again. There are light footsteps roaming the room.

"Tsk, tsk," a man says with a slight hiss.

I pointlessly mouth Stanton's name to Emil, but he should recognize the voice of the specter with basilisk blood too. Terror reawakens within me from being held captive by Stanton. He's so strong and vicious. He only kept me alive so he could use me to send a signal to Emil, who'd flown away with the urn containing the ghosts of Luna's parents. But that doesn't mean he went easy on me. He strangled me and beat me unconscious. I didn't hesitate to give him my password so he could upload that video for Emil on my own YouTube channel. I didn't want to risk extra torture. Now he's found me again, and I don't think he'll be keeping me alive this time.

If I had a wand, I would blast him in the heart.

If I had powers, I would set him ablaze.

I concentrate and stare at my palm. I'm hoping fear will trigger my powers the way it did Emil's. But I'm still cloaked in darkness without a flicker of flame appearing.

"Maybe, just maybe, they're behind that counter," Stanton teases.

Emil pins me against the counter.

"He obviously knows we're here," I whisper. "Why am I even whispering?" I ask out loud and stand. "You found us." I can't make him out in the shadows. "You can go ahead and turn on the lights."

"What's wrong? Can't see in the dark or sense your prey's heartbeat? Their scent? I bet you're wishing Luna needed basilisk blood for the powers you stole from her," Stanton says from the far right corner of the room.

"I didn't get any powers. It was all a bust."

"Luna will be happy to hear that," Stanton's voice says from the other corner.

"She's alive?!"

"Hanging on there after some scum hit her with a cheap shot."

"She told me I shouldn't've missed in the graveyard. I was honoring her wishes."

I'm trying to sound braver than I am, but I'm so nervous. Dr. Bowes shaking against the counter isn't helping. Our greatest defense is Emil, and he's not at full power. But Stanton is moving soundlessly, and we can't try to beat someone we can't even see.

"Some light," I tell Emil.

Emil casts fire—and illuminates Stanton's face right in front of us.

"Hello," Stanton says. He grabs Emil by the throat and swings him into a glass cabinet that shatters so loudly it's like someone shot a spell through it.

It's pitch black again without Emil's firelight. I don't even hear him groaning. I got to fight my way to him. I scramble for something heavy to try and defend myself. I can hear Dr. Bowes running off toward Emil. She screams, and I realize she's probably stepped in glass. Then Stanton's nails dig into my shoulders and I'm hurled into the shadows; I can't even try to brace myself since I have no idea when I might collide with something. I bang against a wall and crash onto a cart with loaded vials. The breath is knocked out of me, and I'm wheezing hard. Shards of glass dig into my arms, and thick liquids spill onto my hair like the stickiest shampoo. Sharp pain runs through my back and elbows. I'm dizzy in this darkness, and I roll onto my stomach.

Stanton presses his boot down on my neck. "There are so many ways to kill you before I bring Luna your head. Petrification. Poison. I've always been curious about reaching into someone's chest while they're petrified and ripping out their heart to see how much pain they feel. . . ."

He's a basilisk that plays with his food. His only motivation is blood.

"I can petrify you and make you watch as I torture your brother. . . ." He presses down harder on my neck. "Or I can end you right now."

The door opens, revealing a silhouette with glowing eyes. The lights come on as Stanton's foot rises, and before he can slam it down on me, Prudencia telekinetically catches it. She's struggling to suspend him. Her power isn't as strong without the Crowned Dreamer. I roll a few inches, enough for Prudencia to release her hold. Stanton's foot slams against the floor like a heavy step.

Stanton laughs. "You're not strong enough to stop me."

Prudencia telekinetically throws various instruments and shards of glass at him. His skin is getting cut up, and still he's smiling with his terrible teeth.

Dr. Bowes rises, and eight illusions pop up—two Brightons, two Emils, two Prudencias, two Dr. Boweses. They're running around Stanton and he swipes at them, going through them like air. Then Stanton closes his eyes for a moment, spins, and lunges straight at the real Dr. Bowes, snapping her neck. The illusions vanish before her body can hit the floor.

Her death isn't that shocking. She's the first of four in this room.

Before I'm added to the count, I gather all my strength and grab a shard of glass, then jump onto Stanton's shoulders and stab him in the chest. He's trying to shake me off, but I keep digging and digging even though the glass is cutting into me. He wants to grab me, but Prudencia is binding his hands. Stanton bites my hand and his teeth sharpen, extending into fangs like a real basilisk that puncture straight through my palm. It's the greatest pain I've felt since the Reaper's Blood warped against me. Fire feels like it's shooting through my veins, so hot that it wants to melt my bones. I fall off him.

My hand is bleeding.

Prudencia keeps Stanton fixed in place before he can charge at her.

Gold and gray flames light up the corner; Emil, sprawled out on the floor, is carrying a glowing orb, although it appears he's too weak to throw it. Prudencia releases her hold on Stanton, and he is so close to reaching her when she telekinetically pulls Emil's fire-orb as if she's tugging a rope, and it strikes Stanton in the back. She dives out of the way and Stanton slams headfirst into the wall and collapses, still.

"You okay?" Prudencia asks me as she gets up.

I can't even speak. My bloody hand is shaking uncontrollably,

81

and the fire within is pulsing. No better time to be in a hospital, but seeing Dr. Bowes's head angled so unnaturally reminds me of how mortal we all are. How mortal I wouldn't have been with the reaper powers.

Prudencia assists Emil as he tries getting up by himself. He's groaning as his power automatically heals the glass cuts across his face and arms.

"Whoa." Maribelle appears, stepping over Stanton, while pressing her fist against her shoulder. "You've been busy." So has she, judging by the blood on her face and the fresh coat of gray-and-red blood on her oblivion dagger. June must be dead.

"Stanton killed Dr. Bowes," Prudencia says, unable to look at her corpse.

I groan in pain, and Maribelle crouches beside me, her eyes immediately going to the bite mark on my hand. Everything is getting blurry, and I'm suddenly cold.

"That's basilisk venom. We need an antidote," Maribelle says.

"What's going to happen to me?" I ask.

"It can kill you within days," she says.

My life sentence keeps shrinking. "Find an antidote!"

Prudencia frantically checks the cabinets, and Emil tries to help but he's too slow and weak. We're in a hospital that specializes in gleam injuries; finding an antidote really shouldn't be that hard.

Iris barges in, at first surprised to see Stanton on the floor, but then she steps on him as she makes her way over to Maribelle, holding her bloodied hand to her chest. "Where did you go?!"

"I had to get June," Maribelle says, still searching for an antidote.

"I hope to the highest stars you killed her, because Dione bested me!"

"You lost a fight; get over it," Maribelle says.

"I lost more than a fight! The acolytes captured Eva and Carolina and got away."

Emil and I turn to each other at the same time, like a person and their reflection, wondering what this means for our mother especially.

Then my hand fully tenses, so rigid that I can't even twitch my finger. It's like thick clay is drying all over me. My veins are shifting to a dark green, the venom slithering up my arm, and going straight for my heart.

ELEVEN
REUNION

NESS

Everything is hazy in the moments after I wake up, especially as I try to figure out why there are fresh scars across my ribs and another above my ankle. Everything clicks as soon as I get a closer look, because my complexion isn't on this paler side. I'm fresh out of a nightmare where I was torturing Emil with the infinity-ender dagger. The whole thing was more monstrous than how it happened in real life, but maybe it represented how Emil felt in that moment, and that's why I shifted into him while I was sleeping.

Judging by the sun, it looks like I've slept the entire day away. I can't believe the Senator hasn't put me to work yet.

I remain in Emil's form and stare at the scars that his phoenix powers couldn't heal. We had a moment in some art supplies room at Nova where I helped clean his wounds while keeping my eyes shut because he didn't want me to see his body; even the form I'm looking at right now is mostly imagined since Emil always hides himself in baggy shirts. There's a lot I would give up right now just to touch him again. To explore our feelings. Maybe even discover each other without any clothes on.

"That Spell Walker your boyfriend?" Jax asks from the door, his presence completely surprising me.

My blood rushes to Emil's cheeks, and I glow gray as I revert back into myself. "No," I say as I throw on one of my old shirts. I have no idea how long Jax has been watching me. I can't have the Senator thinking that Emil is someone I'm interested in. "He's just another good guy that got hurt because of me. Many more to come thanks to you all."

Jax doesn't take the bait. "Tell me. How many times have you turned into other people to see what they look like naked?"

I sit up in bed. "That's not how this works."

"That's a shame."

I wasn't best friends with my bodyguard Logan, but there was always decency between us. "Any chance of Logan relieving you from your shift?"

"He took leave after your 'death.' Took it personally," Jax says. "But don't worry. I'm not going anywhere."

Let him think that he's the one that's got me cornered, even though every time he smirks and crosses his arms or taps his left foot, he's giving me what I need if I get the opportunity to shift into him and escape.

I got good at picking up details on people years ago. Samples came back from this family photo shoot where my smile was so convincing, even though I'd been pissed at my parents that morning. I was only eleven then and thought it was bizarre how smiles could be faked. I kept studying other people from there, trying to figure out their tells. Which smiles from Mom were lies? Was Dad's smile real when he saw me onstage for school plays? Or the one when I drew him in third grade for Hero Day?

This all came in handy at the beginning of February when I stood under the Cloaked Phantom—the twice-a-year constellation that elevates shifting abilities—and drank Luna's potion to get my powers. She appreciated how well I paid attention to others, and even though our sessions were brutal before I could really get a handle on shifting, it's all played a part in why I'm so good at what I do.

I have to use this to my advantage, but plotting against the Senator and his team is tricky. There's no telling when Zenon is looking out of my eyes to see what I'm up to. I can't take notes about any plans. I can't mess with the window, which has been welded shut. I can't set aside anything I might use as a weapon. I have to operate like there's a camera on me at all times; I don't know that there isn't. I've been spending a lot of time in bed, eyes closed to black him out. It's a good thing he can't see into my head, I guess.

The lights in my room switch off. I turn, thinking it's Jax still messing with me, but the hallway is dark too, and he's looking around suspiciously.

"Status on power," Jax requests into his wrist communicator.

"Scouting perimeter now," Zenon's voice responds. Then,

seconds later: "Intruders. We're surrounded."

"Have you identified them?" Jax asks.

"I can't make eyes on them," Zenon says.

That means that whoever is surrounding the manor must be spread out or not looking at each other. When a person is alone, Zenon can only identify them if he recognizes their body or clothes, or if they're staring into a mirrored surface like a puddle or glass.

"I'm taking Eduardo to the panic room," Jax says.

The panic room has existed in the manor since the Senator was a child, but he's had it updated over the years as he's made more enemies. It has everything we could need—independent high-speed internet connection, fridges with enough food to last two weeks, top-of-the-line wands, bathroom with function- ing shower, foldout beds, and, most importantly, the strongest power-deflecting gleam-shield that money can buy. I don't want to go down there. I can't risk tripling the number of locks keep- ing me in the manor.

It's a long shot, but what if Emil is here to rescue me? If he suspected that the enforcers got their hands on me, then maybe he would've thought the family home would be a good place to check out. Then again, it's damning to break into the house of the presidential candidate who is running on a platform of how dangerous celestials are. If the Spell Walkers are risking their necks for me, it's only because Emil made the case that I came back for them during the invasion at Nova.

Then I'm hit with a terrible thought that would track against me: What if Emil just thinks I ran away again and never comes looking for me?

Jax tells me to follow him, and I cooperate to buy time to figure out my next move. I'm tense as we go down the hall. Glass shatters from the downstairs foyer, and we pause at the top of the stairs. The backup security alarm goes off for mere seconds before being disconnected. Even I couldn't have disabled the alarm that quickly; maybe Wesley dashed in and handled it.

While Jax is distracted, I run toward the Senator's office so I can open the window and climb down the terrace. I don't make it far before I'm telekinetically yanked back so hard that it feels like my spine might snap. I'm suspended in the air, all my joints stiff as Jax rotates me toward him.

"You're not going anywhere," Jax says with glowing eyes.

Zenon's voice booms from Jax's communicator: "Above you!"

We both look up. My heart sinks when it's not a Spell Walker falling from the ceiling, but a Blood Caster. Dione drops fast like this one time she fearlessly jumped out of a building to escape enforcers. She tackles Jax in front of the office with her six arms, pinning him down before he can defend himself, and she unleashes a flurry of punches on his face and chest.

The telekinetic hold on me breaks.

I have to run. If I'm not fast enough, being locked up won't be my biggest problem. The Casters will torture me for betraying them, bone by bone. I don't want to be around to see if Luna succeeded in her ritual. I can't go through the office without risking Dione grabbing me with one of her arms. I run downstairs, rounding the corner and sprinting through the dining room and into the kitchen. The Senator and Zenon are standing in the doorway, and I skid to a halt. But Zenon knew to expect me, and he slams me against the wall before I can reverse course.

"Why are the Blood Casters attacking?" the Senator asks.

"You tell me," I say.

"I bring you home and the gang arrives not even twenty-four hours later! If you sent them a message—"

"I ran away from them, remember? You're the one who spoke with Luna last. Maybe she's trying to clean her hands of you for good."

He looks like he wants to throttle me.

"Acolytes approaching," Zenon says as his glowing eyes flash like twinkling stars. "They're all armed." He releases me and aims his own wand at the doorway.

Unless he's a sharpshooter, I'm our best shot. I take a deep breath, and the familiar gray light washes over me as I transform into Dione. This is the first time the Senator has seen me use my power. I hate that in saving myself I'm also saving him. I step out into the dining room with my shoulders hunched, doing my best to impersonate Dione's mask of determination when she's hunting. The acolytes freeze when they see me.

"What are you doing down here?" I bark in Dione's voice. She's never patient with the acolytes. "Go upstairs and spread out."

They follow my orders. This will buy us a minute at most— just until they find Dione laying into Jax. I have to escape before Stanton shows up. If he's focused on hunting me, my morph won't mean anything. He'll be tracking my scent.

"Get to the panic room," the Senator says as they all come out of the kitchen.

If I'm locked in that room with the Senator, only one of us will come out alive.

"Someone's coming in," Zenon says, pointing at a wall without a door.

We're all confused until my nightmare comes true—Luna and June emerge from the wall holding hands. Luna's silver hair is dirty, and there's blood all over the same ceremonial cape she wore the night I got my powers. More bloodstains decorate the stomach of her silky white blouse. If she's been wounded and is still managing to hold herself upright like this, this must mean she's won.

She's unkillable.

Zenon fires multiple spells from his wand but they sail through Luna and June as if they aren't really there.

Luna's green eyes study me. "Dione, dear, why haven't you snapped this fool's neck?" She's right. Dione's allegiance is always to the woman who gave her power when she felt defenseless in the world. "Drop the charade, darling Ness."

I cross my arms as I revert back to myself.

"Family reunions are so beautiful," Luna says. "Especially when someone returns from the dead." She appears distracted for a beat, then pulls herself out of her reverie. "I must say, Senator, this welcome doesn't feel very welcoming. First we're greeted with spells, and now no one is even offering us a seat. Get your house in order."

"Maybe if you'd given us some notice," the Senator says. "If you're here for the specter of yours who's been detained in the Bounds, I cannot advise Bishop to release him under any circumstances. It won't do well with our supporters."

Luna waves him away. "I hold no present concerns for Stanton. He's a soldier who understands the great sacrifices we must make."

Stanton's locked up? I don't even have to know why right now. This is great news.

"Then why are you here?" the Senator asks.

"To discuss our futures. Is the living room this way?" Luna asks as she and dead-eyed June walk past us. "Beautiful dining room, by the way," she calls over her shoulder, walking through the manor as if she owns it.

Footsteps on the stairs catch my attention. Dione glares at me, four of her arms retreating back into her sides; I clock her bloody fists before they vanish. Jax might be dead.

"Don't you dare put on my face again," Dione says to me as she catches up to Luna.

Great. I've pissed her off too.

We all gather in the living room, but Dione sends the acolytes to the kitchen. I lean against the fireplace's mantel, wishing I could shift into a bird and fly out through the chimney. Luna takes a seat in the Senator's armchair, forcing him to sit on the couch. Zenon seems shifty as he keeps watch on Dione and June.

"I held up my end of the deal, Luna," the Senator says. "Do you want to explain to me why Eduardo is still alive?"

"If you wanted your son dead, you could've gotten your own hands bloody. You still can. By all means." Luna relaxes into the chair with her hands folded over her knee. "I suspect he's alive because you recognize the influence his power can have in securing you this election."

I wave to them. "I'm standing right here. Maybe you can take this discussion about whether or not I should be alive or dead to another room."

"You'll be dismissed shortly," Luna says. "I saved your life when your father sought to make you a martyr. I gave you power and security. Most importantly, I gave you my trust. You betrayed me by divulging my grandest design to the Spell Walkers, and ruined decades of work." She stops and coughs blood, using the sleeve of her blouse to wipe it from her lips. It's a beautiful sight; she isn't unkillable. "I don't intend to die alone, Ness. For your punishment, you'll play a role in making sure all of the Spell Walkers go down with me." She turns to the Senator. "I believe this goal will be of great interest to you as we approach Election Day."

"I'm winning in the polls," the Senator says. "What makes you think I need your help?"

"I've always admired your commitment to a plan, Senator, but do not forget who ultimately engineered everything," Luna says. He blushes. "The knowledge I hold on how your son's powers work will take us both very far in our shared agenda."

I'm about to shout in her face when Dione dashes in front of me and holds me back with her muscular, tattooed arm. "I'm done working for you, Luna! Both of you!"

"Then innocent lives will be taken," Luna says. She nods at June, who vanishes.

We're all kept in suspense as Luna smiles on.

Zenon leans toward the Senator. "The girl is returning with

92

two more people, sir. Both blindfolded."

I'm expecting one of them to be Emil, but when June finishes reappearing, she's holding on to the wrists of an older woman I immediately recognize as his mother and a young woman with brown skin and dark hair. June removes the latter's blindfold. It's Eva Nafisi, the Spell Walkers' healer. She has a black eye and bruising across her wrists. She must've been forced to heal Luna from whatever wound someone inflicted on her; man, I hope it was Emil who attacked her. June removes Carolina's blindfold. Carolina is absolutely petrified, as expected of any hostage until a disturbing shock takes over: she's actually seeing Luna and the Senator—the damn presidential candidate—sitting across from one another like a casual evening between neighbors.

Luna locks eyes with me and points at Carolina. "You'll cooperate, or we'll cast a spell straight through her head. Eva is a very talented girl, but even this will be beyond her means."

Carolina is shaking so hard. I won't be the reason she's killed.

The Senator smiles—one of those terrible, honest smiles. "What's the plan?"

"Lock these two away somewhere," Luna says, gesturing at Carolina and Eva. "Send Ness away. He clearly can't be trusted to know the work that's ahead of him."

"Zenon, escort our guests to the panic room. Reverse the controls from protection to entrapment," the Senator says. Then another smile, this one playful. "Go to your room, Eduardo."

If this is some game, I can't win. I'm not even being given the rules. But I can't give up yet. There's got to be a chance where I can cheat my way to victory.

93

Carolina and Eva struggle as Zenon and June force them downstairs. Dione takes it upon herself to watch after me since she took down Jax.

I look over my shoulder one last time as we leave Luna and the Senator alone. Is this what it was like when they sat down to plot the Blackout—to plot my death? Are they plotting it again?

I wish I'd died the first time.

TWELVE
THE LUMINARY UNION

MARIBELLE

It doesn't seem likely that Brighton will survive the night.

A practitioner at Aldebaran was able to inject an antidote, but all that did was slow down the venom. It was too risky to hang around, so we rushed Brighton to the Clayton Center for Recovery out on Long Island, a high-end private practice also run by celestials. If Aldebaran is a single star, this facility is a constellation in terms of how they can assist him. The bill won't be pretty, but between Brighton's infected arm and the blood poisoning, he's going to need around-the-clock attention unless a miracle happens. What he doesn't need is me here.

I have to go hunt.

I roam the halls. The walls are sterile-white, as if the facility opened this morning, and fixed onto them are bronze sconces shaped like hands to represent their healers. It's creepy, and I can't wait until I don't have to look at them anymore. I finally track down a supplies room, empty some employee's duffel bag, and load up. My newfound phoenix powers haven't healed any of my bruising or the cut on my forehead from my fight with June, so I pack a few first-aid kits. I throw in water bottles, a blanket, and I hide the oblivion dagger between folds of gauze before leaving the room.

There's an indoor garden, where the alchemists grow their own herbs. It's really serene and inviting, but there's no time for peace. Not when June and Luna are still alive. Not when they've taken Eva and Carolina.

It's possible Luna has already had them executed. Brighton ruined her life's work.

I don't wish a single broken bone on Carolina, but Eva especially doesn't deserve to be caught in this cross fire.

A couple years ago, Iris's parents were using a clubhouse for celestial senior citizens as a haven. Mama and Papa had flown to Colombia for humanitarian work, and I'd hung back with the Simone-Chambers family so I wouldn't fall behind on home-schooling. On the third day of my stay, Eva came into our care after a foster family doubted their abilities to protect her from traffickers. Eva and Iris were magnetized to each other immediately, but wires kept getting crossed. Eva thought Iris was only complimenting her neck scarf because she wanted one for herself, and Iris thought that there was no way that a pacifist like Eva could ever fall for a fighter with powerhouse strength. On the same night I finally convinced Iris to be direct and make a move,

Eva surprised her with a swimming lesson in the clubhouse pool. Iris confessed her feelings, and they shared their first kiss while drying up poolside. One of my favorite moments is when we were all scrolling through Pinterest and Iris loved this model's green hair so much that we locked ourselves in the bathroom to dye her hair the same shade, laughing so hard when we couldn't scrub away the stains on the floor.

Eva was—no, is—a great friend. She's loyal to Iris, naturally, but even after Iris and I drifted after the Blackout, Eva regularly checked in on my mental health. I'll always appreciate how she didn't take Iris's side when we all found out that she kept my true lineage a secret from me.

It's twisted that Eva has been taken by her former best friend, but if Dione harms her, Iris will be sure to rip off her arms, one by one, until they don't grow back.

I swing the duffel bag onto my shoulder and pass the waiting area that's closest to Brighton's room, where he's still unconscious. Iris is asleep on a bench, and Emil is resting his head on Prudencia's shoulder. I'm not losing sleep over this, but Emil looking so broken does manage to stop me in my tracks. My parents and Atlas were killed. But Emil has to watch his brother waste away, so soon after going through the same thing with his father, and stars know what the Casters have done with his mother. Grieving before someone is dead is its own beast.

I make my way for the exit, planning on driving back into the city to hunt down any Brew dealers. Threatening to burn them alive, much like celestials have been punished for generations, should get them talking about where they get their supplies.

The doors open before I can reach them, but no one comes in. I stop, and even though my psychic sense isn't alerting me to any danger, I don't have a good feeling about this. Then I hear quiet footsteps—whoever is near me certainly has a light step, but Papa personally trained me to have a good ear. I pretend like I'm unaware, and as they pass me, I strike. My fist connects with someone's forearm. The last time I fought someone invisible was with Atlas, and he had exposed them by creating a windstorm that swept all sorts of trash through the air, and a newspaper pressed against the celestial's face. I'm all I have.

"Stop!" the invisible intruder—an older woman, I believe— says.

We've been found out again, because apparently we can't trust anyone, not even a facility that is staffed by celestials who have been outspoken against Senator Iron. This invisible celestial has probably been hired to assassinate Brighton. I feel all the more validated about quitting the Spell Walkers; I'm tired of working so hard to save people who have no problem turning on us for money, favors, revenge.

"Prudencia, help!" I shout down the hall.

I back myself against the wall so the intruder can't sneak behind me and I jump into a scissor kick but I don't hit her. She tells me to stop again, even using my name, but I follow her voice and hit her with a jab in what feels like her shoulder. Prudencia, Emil, and a groggy Iris come running out of the waiting area, but none of them can make sense of the threat. I go for the crescent kick, aiming for where I've calculated her head would be judging by the height of the shoulder, but she catches my foot and shoves

98

me to the floor. I stretch out my hands, dark yellow flames surrounding them.

"WAIT!"

A pale woman in her midthirties appears as quick as a blink—shoulder-length jet-black hair with a signature gold streak, a wrinkle-free white shirt underneath a blue plaid blazer, silver bracelets dangling from one wrist and an emerald watch clasped on the other, and light brown eyes that are frightened by my fire. It's Congresswoman Sunstar's running mate, Senator Shine Lu.

"What are you doing here?" I ask.

"We want to help," Shine says.

"Who's we?" Iris asks.

Shine releases my foot and speaks into her wristwatch. "I've made contact. Come in."

The door opens and two women with power-proof vests underneath their black jackets enter. One keeps moving past all of us while the other guards the door after Nicolette Sunstar appears. Sunstar is in a white pantsuit that pops against her dark skin and hair. The click-clack of her yellow high heels infuriates me. Here we all are, beat and bloodied, and Sunstar and Lu are styled like they're going to a fashion show. We all have targets on our backs, but it's very clear which of us have to hide out in defunct schools and senior citizen clubhouses and who gets to go home to gorgeous lofts with their own security.

"Hello, Spell Walkers," Sunstar says.

"How did you find us?" Iris asks.

"You're not exactly hidden. We'll arrange for a crew of illusionists to conceal you during your stay here."

"Fantastic," I say dryly. "What are you doing here?"

Sunstar looks past us, and her bodyguard signals something with her fist. "How about we have some privacy?"

This better be good. I was finally freeing myself fully from the Spell Walkers, and suddenly I'm following everyone into an empty employee lounge. The bodyguard closes the door on her way out. Sunstar and Lu sit at a round table, and Emil and Prudencia are clearly sheepish about joining them. I don't care if they're running for president and vice president, they're still two women who haven't been there for us. They don't get my respect. They shouldn't get Iris's either, but she sits down.

"Care to join us, Maribelle?" Sunstar asks.

The last open seat is beside Iris. I cross my arms and lean against the wall. "I'm good standing. What are you and Lu doing here?"

"You can call me Shine," Lu says. "We're pleased to meet you all."

Her name is a very traditional one among celestials, the most popular being Star. I was almost stuck with Skye before Mama came to her senses; a celestial named Skye who can fly is already an annoying nursery rhyme. But I understand the very important branding that Shine is pushing here. Their campaign slogan—*Shine Like a Star*—is catchy and cute and I don't care.

Prudencia taps Emil's hand. "We're newly eighteen. You've got our vote. We attended the Friday Dreamers Festival last month and loved everything you had to say."

Emil nods. "Yeah, I'm really rooting for you."

"Thank you both," Sunstar says. "We never pretend to be

perfect, but we know this victory is of great importance for celestials everywhere. And even for well-intentioned specters such as yourself, Emil. I don't know if you're one of those specters we've seen over the years who are trying to do the right thing like Bautista de León, but our administration wants to ban that practice."

Emil is red in the face. "I want that too, I promise. I didn't do this to myself."

"Were you drugged?" Shine asks.

He shakes his head. "It's complicated."

"And none of your business," I say to Sunstar and Shine. "You don't get to sneak your way in here and call for a meeting as if we're in this together. Just because you haven't condemned us doesn't mean you support us. Now, my patience is running very thin, so make good use of this next minute and explain why you're gracing us with your presence. Otherwise I'm leaving to hunt down every last Blood Caster myself."

Sunstar folds her hands. "That ties beautifully with why we're here. We're very sorry for not publicly supporting you, but if we aren't careful with this campaign, then everything will become worse for every celestial—and every innocent specter." She eyes Emil, who blushes. "We don't understand the cause of the Blackout, but we know something happened behind the curtains. I promise we support you and will make right on that soon by saying so publicly. I don't want to mislead the American people. If we can secure the White House, we'll be able to set a precedent for how gleamcrafters deserve to be treated globally."

I'm tired of having to defend my humanity. My life shouldn't be a debating point.

"How do you intend on doing that?" Iris asks.

"We want to abolish the Enforcer Program," Sunstar says. "Every time an innocent celestial is brutalized and killed because of corrupt enforcers, the narrative increases that we're all dangerous. That we must be stopped by the wands containing power sourced from our own blood. We need honest protectors who would devote themselves to detaining the Blood Casters and other rogues."

"And who would that be?" I ask.

"You all," Sunstar says.

"And the other vigilante factions born out of great intentions," Shine adds.

Sunstar is beaming. "We're calling it the Luminary Union, named so because this division will be a global guiding light in heroism, illuminating security practices that should've always been in place. Every Luminary will be vetted by a council of celestials who don't operate with hate in their hearts. Every faction trying to do the right thing won't have to be classified as vigilantes. Your work will be authorized and supported by the government."

"Every faction that folds into the Luminary Union will be paid, of course," Shine says. "We've discreetly donated to your campaigns for funds this past year. Our discretion will become unnecessary if we can build this division."

This was always part of the dream for my parents—Iris's too. They wanted their work more than trusted, but a welcomed service to make the world a better place. This world didn't deserve them.

"First off, go easy on the light metaphors. We get it," I say. "Secondly, why would we submit ourselves to the government? So you can control the way we save the world?"

Iris turns to me. "I seem to remember you quitting the group. You don't get to be part of this decision."

I can't take her in hand-to-hand combat, but I want to throttle her anyway.

"You mean the group that my biological parents founded? I'm the true heir to the Spell Walkers. I'm the one who should be leading."

"Then maybe you should act like it," Iris says. Sunstar is trying to ask questions about my family, but Iris speaks over her. "We are protectors who need protecting too. My parents? Dead. Your parents? Dead. Atlas? Dead. Eva? Probably dead. And these are only the major deaths between the two of us. Our way clearly isn't working, and I'm crumbling from all of these losses! I'm open to a change. You should be too."

If that were true, she would patrol these streets with me and do everything it takes to end the source of our pain. "Eva's fate is unclear, Iris. But Atlas's isn't. You get to be open to all the changes you want because there's still a glimmer of hope that you'll get to reap the benefits. I have no one, and I'm going to end every last person responsible for that."

Sunstar rises and approaches me. I straighten up and her eyes clock my fists. "Maribelle, please. Whether or not you're an active Spell Walker is irrelevant to the public. If the country is going to believe our vision, we need everyone's cooperation."

"*Your* vision. I'm not lying low so you can win your election.

Why don't you keep this big idea in your pocket for another few weeks?"

"Backdoor plans aren't formulas for building trust. The Luminary Union will need years to build, and to accomplish this, I'll need to be voted in for a second term as well. But this entire agenda is futile if you go rogue. Honor your parents by helping shape the country for the better."

I could burn Sunstar right here, right now. She hasn't offered a single condolence and yet she's trying to use the memory of my parents against me. I shoulder-bump her out of my way, and Shine pops out of her seat as if she's ready for another fight.

"Try me," I warn her. "I've never seen an invisible woman on fire."

Prudencia rushes between us with glowing eyes and her hand outstretched. The door swings open. "We are not each other's enemies. But I know we can't stop you, Maribelle. Take care."

I cast one last look at the two women who are trying to claim the White House, the boy who isn't cut out for this war, his best friend who has my respect, and the girl who used to be a sister to me. Then I leave, the one-woman army who won't die fighting. I'll live by doing what surely won't be accepted in any Luminary Union guidelines—killing.

THIRTEEN
THE HEROIC CRIME

EMIL

Everyone would've been better off if I'd never been reborn.

Dad would've never found me on the street and brought me into the family. Brighton wouldn't have been so deep in this war that he thought getting poisoned by the Reaper's Blood was the only way to win. Ma would be home, maybe missing Brighton if he'd still gone off to Los Angeles for school. Ness could've tricked the Spell Walkers into taking him hostage, and moved to another country, shifting so frequently that no one can track him. Eva would be safe with Iris, able to do good work with her powers, not forced to heal a terrifying alchemist. Dr. Bowes would be home with her son and husband.

But those aren't the lives anyone gets to live. They're all either dying like Brighton or already dead like Dad.

I'm not right in the head over this. Prudencia keeps reminding me that I didn't have a choice in being reborn, but what about the choices I have made since becoming a so-called chosen one? I stupidly thought I could get in and out of this war, like I would have some astounding light-bulb moment about the power-binding potion. Come on, I was never going to be able to piss off someone like Luna and enjoy an early retirement. Of course she's sending out her Blood Casters to abduct and assassinate us. I'll never forgive myself for involving Brighton, Ma, and Prudencia.

I've been thinking about how Maribelle and Iris were able to keep going after the Blackout. They had Atlas and Eva to comfort them, to distract them, to love them. I don't know how they're going to keep it together now, but there's another choice I'm especially regretting myself. I should've run away with Ness and taken Gravesend with me, escaped to the other side of the world, where we could've raised her in peace. Ness and I would've had time to figure out our whole deal. Maybe we would've been great friends, maybe we could've been something more, but now I'll never know.

I'm done being alive, but I can't say that out loud because no one ever wants to hear that you're over your life when others have lost theirs. Especially when it's your fault.

Ever since Sunstar and Shine's visit yesterday, I've felt safer with the illusionists hiding us, but even with all the vetting Sunstar's people did before employing those celestials to use their powers of illusion to protect her, and now us, I still can't shake this feeling that someone in that crew might sell us out, since it's popular to blame the Spell Walkers for everything bad that's happened to gleamcrafters since the Blackout. Maybe Senator Iron and General Bishop's extreme methods will lose steam if all the Spell Walkers are dead before the election, and some votes can swing back to Sunstar.

I stand outside Brighton's room, wondering when his new practitioners can give me a solid update on his condition. It's really been a team effort. Dr. Swensen uses her power of hypnosis to keep Brighton asleep so he doesn't have to suffer through the pain. Dr. Salinas has been treating the basilisk venom with antidotes she's been brewing fresh, all custom because of the Reaper's Blood poisoning.

When Dr. Swensen finally comes out and tells me that Brighton needs more rest and that I look like I should get some too, I thank her for everything she's doing and head for the cafeteria instead. I need to throw back a big salad or something. I've had nothing substantial in my stomach since yesterday morning when Prudencia brought me this grilled tofu soup and stayed with me until I finished it.

I stop in place when I see an illusionist guard speaking into her headset by the side entrance, her eyes glowing. My heart is pounding instantly, and I'm ready to try and push past the pain and hurl a fire-arrow her way, but when she's done maneuvering her hands around, carving a door-shaped hole beyond the actual open door, I see that she's letting Wesley, Ruth, and their baby daughter inside the facility.

I forgot they were coming today.

Wesley looks concerned as he pushes the stroller toward me. "Emil, buddy, you okay?"

I don't get how people who full-on know what's what with someone's situation can ask them if they're okay. I'm clearly not. I haven't slept for more than two hours at a time for days. I've barely eaten. My mother is dead or being tortured by the most dangerous gang in the city. My brother is in critical condition. There's not a lot going on for me to make me feel anything close to okay.

"I'm fine," I say, because I don't have it in me to go off on someone well-meaning.

I turn my attention to Ruth, who has this cautious smile, like she wants to be pleasant for our official meeting but can also see that I'm suffering. She's wearing one of her Mighty Wear shirts, a clothing line she started because she recognized there isn't enough attire for fat celestials such as herself and Wesley. Brighton used to show me pictures from her account, especially when they featured Wesley, and her hair was black in all of her previous posts, but now it's dyed light brown. Her brown skin seems well moisturized too, and Brighton always pointed to her as an influencer who seemed to really believe in the products she was promoting.

"You seem like you need a hug. May I?" Ruth asks without stepping any closer. "You're not hurting my feelings if not. I know everyone isn't a hugger."

"You can hug me," I say under my breath.

Ruth wraps her arms around me, and I relax my forehead on her shoulder. I already get a sense of what Brighton means by Ruth's influencer abilities. She's instantly sold me on this hug, and unlike an ab roller this fit guy on Instagram once convinced me to buy, I actually needed this. Her hair smells like vanilla, and it reminds me of when Ness asked for vanilla candles during his interrogation. I hug Ruth harder, wishing I could transport myself back to those simpler times where I could visit Ness in that supplies room at Nova and have honest conversations.

Wesley and Ruth introduce me to their squirming four-month-old daughter, Esther, who shares Ruth's complexion and brown eyes, but her button nose and slightly pointed ears, like an elf in a fantasy novel, are all Wesley's.

I lead them to their room, right beside the one I'm sharing with Prudencia, who is still asleep when I peek in.

"Is Iris around?" Ruth asks as she takes Esther out of the stroller.

"Her room is down the hall, but I haven't seen her today."

"Has she been going out to search for Eva?" Wesley asks.

I nod. I offered to go with her, but she made it clear that she didn't want to have to protect me since my powers are barely working. I'm sure there's more to it.

"At least it's a safer place to stay, even if someone follows her back," Wesley says. "The illusions made the center look busy. Bit of a dead zone in here." He blushes while spinning his hands around, as if he can rewind time and take back the words. "I don't mean dead zone like Brighton is going to die, or that everyone here is going to die, obviously, because we're choosing to be here too, and we wouldn't bring Esther if we thought it were high-risk, you know."

Ruth places a hand on Wesley's shoulder. "Calm down."

I don't know where they've been the past couple of days and I don't ask.

"I found out how we got discovered," Wesley says. "Dr. Bowes has a son, Darren. He texted some friends that his mother was taking care of us, and word got out online."

I asked for discretion, but Darren is fourteen, and his excitement got the best of him. I can't blame him. I probably would've been able to keep it together if Ma had told us she was treating a Spell Walker at the hospital, but Brighton would've bragged away.

"He's a fan of mine," I say, which feels gross. "Dr. Bowes told me. I was supposed to sign something for him."

"It's not your fault," Wesley says. "I told Darren the same thing."

"You saw him?"

Wesley nods. "I reached out to the father and got them to a safe house. They'll be relocating to a haven later tonight."

I might not be able to bring back anyone from the dead, but I can own up and ask for forgiveness face-to-face. "I want to see him."

Ruth is tearing up as she sways Esther back and forth. "You're a sweetheart for wanting to speak with Darren."

"I'm not trying to be sweet; I owe him an apology. He's growing up without a mother because of me." I wonder how much time I have without Ma before I'm dead too. "Can you take me to see him, or let me know where he is?"

"I can drive you," Ruth says.

"You drove here," Wesley says.

"Well, you stayed up all night with Esther."

"Which you did all the nights before that."

"You were preventing a ritual," Ruth says, beaming like she's won.

"You were caring for our daughter," Wesley counters, smiling because he knows he topped her by declaring that their daughter trumps the world. "Not to mention the dozens of celestials at the shelter. Also, babe, you're forgetting something huge about this trip. Rush. Hour. Traffic."

Ruth lets out a deep sigh and turns to me. "I'm so sorry, Emil, I absolutely break down in traffic. I once had to cast a clone to take over the wheel and it almost led to an accident when the clone vanished and . . ." She's shaking her head and offers me the most apologetic expression.

"It's okay," I say. "Seriously."

"Well, I'll be your chauffeur," Wesley says. "I'll check in with my contact at the safe house and arrange the visit."

While I wait, I go to the cafeteria. I drown my toasted tofu salad in ginger dressing and I lose my appetite halfway through my sweet potato fries. This is normally when Brighton would grab my plate and finish them off. But I'm sitting here all alone and I keep catching staff members stealing glances at me. I wonder how many of them have known me since I first went viral as Fire-Wing. They all definitely know me now as one of the Spell Walkers who has to be so fiercely protected that Sunstar and Shine got involved. I want to say hey and thank everyone for their work, but I don't have it in me.

I pull out my phone and tap into Instagram. I ignore the flood of comments and direct messages and type in Dr. Bowes's full name, Billie Bowes, in the search bar. The most recent picture was taken at the Friday Dreamers Festival in Central Park, the day I got my powers. It's wild how Dr. Bowes was there with her husband and son to support Sunstar at the same time I was there with Brighton and Prudencia. The world can feel so small sometimes. Darren is tagged in the picture, and I check out his profile. He hasn't posted anything since Dr. Bowes was killed. There's one post of him laying out a white T-shirt and fitted jeans on his bed, saying that this is the beginning of his Fire-Wing costume and that his mother is going to help him make a convincing power-proof vest with the Spell Walkers emblem so he can win this Halloween contest. I completely crack and cry so hard, burying my face into my arms, desperate for this life to be my last.

I jump when Wesley taps my shoulder. "Are you okay?"

I wipe my tears. "We good to bounce?"

"Yeah, we can go."

We leave the Clayton Center, and when I turn around, the guard who let us out is no longer there. It's like Wesley said, the illusion creates this impression that there's regular life happening here, one person crying into their phone, a doctor walking inside. You can't tell from the outside that we have illusionists stationed by every door in the facility's east wing. I don't know what the plan is unless someone has an actual emergency, but I'm trusting that Sunstar's team will be ready.

I didn't realize how much I missed fresh air until stepping outside, and once we're driving away, I keep the window down. I'll have to put the window back up once we're passing other drivers, but until then, I'm enjoying the breeze.

I tell Wesley I really like Ruth, and how my mother appreciated

112

the kindness Ruth showed her too back at the shelter. Before I spiral again about Ma's fate, Wesley distracts me with different stories of what a generous soul Ruth is. Whether she's donating clothes to other celestials and allies that she used to get from sponsors, or cloning herself to help out other parents with their own children, Ruth is constantly giving herself to others.

"She won't tell you this herself, but she's strong enough to create six clones at a time," Wesley says while keeping his eyes on the road. "For Valentine's Day, I wrote something in her card that was really bad. Cheesy-bad. It was something like 'Your love is so huge that I'm sure you have seven hearts in your chest,' and in response she cloned herself so that all the clones could roll their eyes at the same time."

I get a quick laugh out of it, which feels nice, like the fresh air. "Wow. You tried."

"Always do," Wesley says. "Even if I look like a clown, then we have another funny memory."

We start pulling into the city and I close the window, throwing on a beanie that will flatten my curls in case anyone recognizes me from their cars.

"You're lucky you have each other," I say.

"I'm lucky to have her. It feels like yesterday when I was using my powers to steal and survive, but Ruth has changed me. She turned her back on her rich, respected family and all the spoils strangers would give her if she did a single Instagram post, and all she does now is give and give and give. Her time, her energy, the shoes off her feet."

"Any chance we can send her on some Kindness Tour? We

need more Ruths in the world."

"Ooh, 'more Ruths in the world.' Going to use that in my next card," Wesley says with a chuckle. "There's something I've been hiding from everyone. Months ago, Atlas came with me when I bought this cottage for my family. We had a lot of fun that day. . . ." He trails off. He didn't know Atlas that long, but they were still tight like brothers. "I bought the place off this celestial we saved, and it's this safe space where Ruth and I can raise Esther in peace. It's where Ruth and I have been staying, and she wants to invite you all over when we leave the center."

I shake my head. "No way. We're not bringing danger to your home."

I'm already struggling with living with myself. How many more people have to get hurt before I fly away and live alone on some mountain on the other side of the world?

"Believe me, I'm not excited either, but you're all family. We'll take care of you."

"We suck at taking care of each other. Look at how many lives we've lost this week alone," I say.

Atlas, Gravesend, Dr. Bowes. Maybe Brighton, Ma, and Eva.

"It's the Heroic Crime," Wesley says as he pulls into a garage and parks the car.

"The what?"

"Something I coined. It's what happens when innocent people get caught in the cross fire of war. No matter how careful we're trying to be when saving the world, there will be casualties. The losses are brutal and real, and a lot of us would time-travel back and undo whatever acts cost us loved ones like Atlas and innocents like Dr. Bowes."

Maybe Luna was onto something all along with the Reaper's Blood. There wouldn't be so much grief in the world if we could all live forever. Dr. Bowes could be home making costumes with her son.

"Darren is going to hate me, right?"

Wesley squeezes my shoulder, which doesn't hold a candle to Ruth's hug, but I get it. "I know the feeling. I've been able to sit down with some kids and apologize for not being able to save their guardians. Some of them need a minute, but then they share stories and it doesn't bring them back, obviously, but we all feel better in that moment. Darren looks up to you, and he was clearly proud of his mother. Just go in there, remind him that it's not his fault, and that his mother was a hero who was creating a better world for him."

Unlike Dr. Bowes, I can't confirm if my own mother went down fighting or not. Or if it was quick and painless, or if they made her suffer for so long that she begged for death.

I keep my teary eyes to the ground, which works since we're trying not to be recognized as we walk down the street.

Wesley throws on his hood, telling me how earlier today when getting Darren and his father to this safe house that he wished he could've been wearing sunglasses, but people have been especially suspicious of sunglasses since the Blackout, swearing that they're for celestials hiding their glowing eyes so they can use their powers undetected. Not our problem this evening, but I think about how easy Ness could blend into a crowd. He didn't have to tense up like me as I'm passing people on the street, acting like I'm suddenly interested in the awning of a flower shop and the bagel shop on the corner.

We stop outside the tattoo shop, Orb Ink, and the sign on the door has been flipped to *Closed* and the blinds have been drawn. I realize that we're standing on a message in graffiti and I step back to get a closer look: *YOUR LIGHTS ARE OUT NEXT.* I've seen this hate speech targeted at celestials ever since the Blackout, and Senator Iron never condemns those behind it.

"Is this shop celestial-owned?" I ask.

"Yup." Wesley knocks on the door in a rhythm that must be code.

A woman approaches and she has dozens of small silver tattoos, like clocks and bricks and flowers, that seem to sparkle on her brown skin. Her dark eyes take me in before she unlocks the door.

"Hey again, Xyla. This is—"

"Pleasure," Xyla interrupts as she shifts her gaze back on Wesley. She definitely won't be dressing up as me for Halloween. "You have ten minutes before Flex arrives to escort the boy and his father. I'll be in the back finishing some paperwork. In and out, you got it?"

"Copy that," Wesley says as she lets us in and walks away. "Don't mind her, E. She might not be on the front lines but her job is risky too. I'm going to go grab Darren and Daniel."

I look around while Wesley heads into a room that I'm guessing gets used for private tattoo sessions. The shop's name is illustrated on the ceiling like a constellation. There are pictures of past clients with their tattoos: a star on a woman's forehead, a stallion galloping along someone's waistband, two hands shaping the universe on a man's forearm, a polygonal hydra with seven heads on someone's back that glows in the dark, and, my favorite, a crowned elder—the beautiful phoenix that is born old—with its storm-gray feathers and amber eyes perfectly drawn onto a woman's shoulder.

If I ever get a tattoo, I think I'd go for one of Gravesend. Then I could remember her when she was a beautiful newborn phoenix instead of bloodied and dead.

Wesley comes out the back with Darren and Mr. Bowes. Mr. Bowes is bald with a thick beard and Darren has shaggy black hair with his first specks of a mustache coming in. Darren is wearing a plain white T-shirt like me with camo pants and big headphones around his neck. He walks straight to a stool and flips through a binder with template tattoos. Mr. Bowes comes out to me and shakes my hand.

"I'm so sorry for your loss," I say. I shake my head because I hate how that sounds. That condolence barely did it for me after my dad died. "No, that's not enough. My brother and I are alive because of your wife. She deserved better."

"Billie really cared for her patients," Mr. Bowes says.

It doesn't feel right for me to say that she cared more about her family. They know that already. "She shouldn't have died because of us. I'm sorry that we brought danger her way."

Mr. Bowes nods. He's not contesting.

I cautiously walk over to Darren and sit opposite him. "Hey, Darren." He keeps flipping through the binder. Wesley told me that it can be harder to crack the shells of children who have lost their parents, but I'm only four years older than Darren. I don't get to act like some know-it-all. I connect with him the only way I know how. "I lost my dad a few months ago. I don't go sharing this secret online, but I have no problem telling you that I'm actually adopted. I just found out a few weeks ago. It was a total surprise because my dad always treated me like a Rey, and I know how lucky I am for that. A day hasn't gone by where I haven't missed him asking me about my day or telling me some story that sometimes ran long."

Darren closes the binder. He almost turns toward me, but stops.

"I cried a lot with my mother after my dad died. My brother, Brighton—you might know him from his Celestials of New York series—he kept a lot of his grief to himself. I'm not trying to tell you how to grieve, just that there's no one right way."

Darren looks me in the eye. "Why aren't you dead too?"

My breath is caught in my throat.

"Darren," Mr. Bowes says with a warning tone.

"No, he's fine," I say.

"I'm not fine!" Darren shouts, flinging the binder onto the floor. "I don't care about your dad, he didn't die because of me!" The commotion causes Xyla to come out from the back room and she looks as surprised as Wesley. "Why aren't you dead too? Are you better than my mom?"

"No, of course not—"

"Why didn't your neck get snapped?"

I didn't think he knew the details of how his mother was

118

killed. His father is telling Darren that enough is enough, but he's not letting up.

"I thought you were supposed to be one of the good guys!"

"I tried, I'm trying—"

"Tell that to my mother!"

I turn back to Wesley, ready to ask him if we should go, but no, I deserve this. When I turn back around, Darren is gone and Dr. Bowes is sitting across from me with a broken neck.

"My son has to grow up without a mother because of you," Dr. Bowes says in a raspy, otherworldly voice, blood spitting out of her mouth. "You should be dead!"

"I'm sorry, I'm sorry!"

I know this can't be real, I know the dead can't come back to life, I know we can't understand ghosts, but I know Dr. Bowes is right. I'm the one who should be dead.

"Remember this face!" Dr. Bowes screams as her eyes close and her flesh begins unraveling. She keeps repeating herself, burning this horror into my mind alongside the very real memory of Stanton snapping her neck, and through another repeat her voice becomes Darren's and the illusion ends. "Remember this face, remember this face," Darren cries with his eyes still closed like the short-lived illusion he cast over himself like a costume.

Mr. Bowes drags Darren by his arm, apologizes for his son's behavior, which is nonsense because I deserve to be trapped in a horror house, haunted by illusions of everyone who has died because of me.

I watch them as they leave the shop, and Darren turns one last

119

time before getting in the car, a threat in his eyes.

It's safe to say that I'll remember his face. It's the face of some-one who sees me as a villain in his story, and when he's older and stronger, and if I'm somehow still alive, he will hunt me down, take everything I love, and kill me.

FOURTEEN
THE ODDS

BRIGHTON

These past few days have been a fevered nightmare that have taken so much from me—my blood; my steady consciousness; my time, which was already running out. The two practitioners, Dr. Swensen and Dr. Salinas, tell me all about how I've lost four days. Somehow even with the most sleep I've ever had, I'm groggy, like I might pass out again any minute, but they keep talking at me about how difficult it is to cleanse my blood.

My arm feels even stiffer than before. They must've failed to save me. I inspect myself, discovering that my arm is tightly wrapped in a soothing silk bandage. Dr. Salinas tells me that it's made from basilisk cocoons. She goes over the list of antivenom serums she's given me, as if I'm going to be familiar with any of these things. What I do know is that this medical bill is going to be unimaginably expensive. Though the chances of anyone in my family living long enough to have to worry about paying a single dollar is slim, hopefully the bill doesn't follow Emil into his next life.

"Am I dying anytime soon?" I ask because I'm tired of them beating around the bush.

"The venom is still spreading, but we've managed to slow it down," Dr. Salinas says.

"But the blood poisoning from before is another matter," Dr. Swensen says.

Two hospitals, one verdict. I'm as good as dead.

"Where's Emil?"

"You can see him soon," Dr. Salinas says. "I want to give you a fresh wrap on your arm to avoid infection."

"I want to see my brother now!"

They back off and leave to get Emil.

This brings me back to Dad's funeral. Emil and Ma really went for it with their eulogies, but it felt impossible to remember the good after watching Dad die. Then one minute I was in the front row while Dad's boss at the Lucille Barker Theater shared a few words and the next I was standing at the podium with Emil at my side. I couldn't stop talking about what I miss already: Dad singing along to songs in Spanish that only Ma understood; asking him to quiz me on prep work so I could see him smile as I answered everything correctly; inviting me and Emil on grocery runs; how he never settled for one-word responses when asking about our day.

I was keeping it together while others delivered their eulogies, but I lost my mind when Dad's doctor was behind the podium and expressing his regrets. During all that time in the hospital, Dr. Queen was always so appreciative of Emil's kind nature and patience, but I was a nightmare to anyone, especially Dr. Queen, who stood in my way when I wanted to see Dad. At the funeral, I let him have it one last time, even though Emil and Prudencia begged me to calm down for Ma's sake if no one else. But I didn't stop until I chased Dr. Queen out of the funeral home, blaming him for putting Dad through that clinical trial that killed him sooner.

I decide what I do with my remaining time. No one else.

It's not long before there's a knock on the door and Emil comes in. He doesn't say anything; he just hugs me, which is a surprise given how I treated him. But when he starts crying I spit out the question I've been terrified to ask since being awake.

"Ma's dead, isn't she?"

Emil backs away, wiping his tears as he sits beside me on the bed. "No. I mean I don't know."

"Why don't you know? What has everyone been doing while I've been asleep?"

Apparently a lot has been going on, including a visit from Congresswoman Sunstar and Senator Lu, but what I don't hear is action. "So what, the Blood Casters haven't put out any message like when they wanted the urn back?"

"They traded last time because I took the urn, and Luna needed to kill the ghosts for her Crowned Dreamer deadline. But this time . . ."

"This time what? I took what Luna wanted? Fine, I'll post a video and offer myself up."

"No!" Emil is staring, but he can't stop me. "We don't even know if Ma is alive!"

"But if she is, this may be the only way to get her back. I'm dead anyway, Emil."

He shakes his head. "You already drank the Reaper's Blood, Bright. It's a done deal, like when Luna was trying to trade me off to Kirk for Gravesend because I didn't have any more value to her. You don't serve any purpose to her alive. She made that clear when she sent Stanton to assassinate you."

"Then maybe she'll get a kick out of seeing me die before her."

Emil looks so beat, like he's been awake enough for the both of us. His curls are growing, dirt is building up under his fingernails, and he smells like unwashed armpits. I'm about to ask him how he hasn't managed to take a shower during all this sitting around he's been doing when he looks at my wrapped-up arm. "How are you feeling?"

"Fantastic."

"Bright, you don't have to lie to me. I really wish we could see some therapists because I've been struggling too and—"

"We all are," I interrupt. "We're losing the war."

"Right, I know. I wasn't trying to make it about myself. I think we all could benefit from some professional help. More than Eva's services, which really wasn't fair to her."

"I got a list of things that's unfair too."

He looks at me like he's expecting me to go on.

Emil gets up. "I'm going to grab Dr. Salinas so she can replace your bandage. Do me a solid and treat her a little better than you have me and Ma."

I let him go. I'm not trying to fight everyone, but everything is getting worse and worse and I don't know how to bury my frustration and my fury. There are a lot of powers I wish I had, but reading thoughts could be really helpful so I can know for sure whether or not Emil has dark, ugly thoughts like I do. I can't be the only one.

He returns with Dr. Salinas, who asks me to relax as she unwraps the bandage. It stings, like a Band-Aid ripping off multiple scabs. I'm speechless when I see how different and monstrous my arm looks. Dark yellow scales are scattered everywhere from my fingers to my forearm and all the exposed skin is a deep green. It's like I'm turning into a basilisk.

"Will it heal?" Emil asks.

"There's a salve that can assist with the shedding," Dr. Salinas says. "But it takes a few months to return to its former state."

"But—" Emil stops himself. We all know I don't have a few months.

"Maybe it's time we start placing bets on how I'm going to die," I say. "We've got some solid options. Venom reaching my heart. Blood poisoning. I'm personally putting my money on the Blood Casters coming back to finish the job."

"Not funny," Emil says. "We're going to get you through this."

Thinking about my future distorts reality. This is all too much for one person, it's like one shot fired after the other. The poisonings, the death sentences. I feel like I'm blowing through the stages of grief. I've been living in denial and anger since the last night of the Crowned Dreamer. Depression is definitely creeping in because I don't have powers, especially now, when I would love to use them most to track down Ma—and punish everyone who even looked at her wrong. But there's no bargaining because there's nothing else I can do to become a specter, and any other trial will only kill me sooner. Sitting around this hospital room and thinking about how I don't want what little time is left to be spent here, I've reached acceptance.

"I don't want to die here," I say. "I want to go home or somewhere."

Dad was never trying to die in the hospital either. He wanted to die peacefully with us at his side. One out of two isn't the worst, but it's not how I'm going to go out.

"Bright, we have prime security here," Emil says.

"Fine, they're going to protect me so I can die in peace here? The odds are stacked against me."

"They might save your life! Come on, you always swear that just because something is unlikely doesn't make it imposs—"

"SHUT UP!"

I tense up, thinking about all the different dreams I've had over the years. Graduating college as valedictorian. Becoming a talk show host. Breaking records with the number of followers I have. Getting the timing right with Prudencia. Saving the world with Emil as the Reys of Light.

Unlikely, but not impossible are the best odds for any dreamer. But I'm done dreaming.

FIFTEEN

FIRE AND FLIGHT

MARIBELLE

No leads yet.

It's been one day since that ridiculous meeting with Sunstar. I lost too many hours oversleeping in Atlas's car, but I'm making up for it now. I've been patrolling Greenpoint for hours. It's a hot spot for every hipster wanting to down Brew, the illusionary potion that gives its drinker a taste of what it's like to have powers. One of Luna's greatest mistakes was confessing to Brighton that she's the creator of Brew. If I can track down a dealer, I can force them to give me information that will lead me to Luna and June.

Perched on top of a seven-story apartment building, I wait for a couple to round the corner before I jump off the ledge. Several feet above the ground I catch myself with a smooth glide like I'm walking down invisible steps. I tighten Atlas's old baseball cap I found in the trunk and try to not be recognized so I can move discreetly.

I pass a celestial-run gym where I can see a woman through the window using her stretched-out, elastic-like arms as a jump rope. It reminds me of when Iris's father, Konrad, would act like our coach and make exercising our powers fun. Mama and Papa always hoped I'd be able to fly on my own—and they always knew there was a chance my power of levitation would grow into flight. But they never told me that it might manifest in wings of fire. Not that it's happened yet.

The Night Elk Bar on the corner has some life to it for a Thursday night. There's a bouncer checking IDs underneath the tacky sign of an elk with crescent moons for eyes. I peek in and there's a celestial dancing with his clone to impress a group of women. The music is fast with solid beats that Atlas wouldn't have known what to do with.

Shortly after Atlas and Wesley began working with us, we hosted a welcome party at our haven. Iris DJ'd, playing all the hits that had us sharing headphones and dancing together. She played one of our favorites, this song in Spanish that begins slow before bursting with this beat that has you sweating by the end if you manage to keep up. I brought Atlas onto the dance floor and he didn't stand a chance against this song and had to conjure his winds to cool down. That was the first time I was properly charmed by him.

Atlas can't dance poorly anymore.

"Hey, you're Maribelle Lucero," the bouncer says.

I don't pay him any mind. I cover my face some more with the cap's brim and I walk away. I don't stop moving like an emotional zombie until over an hour later when the Brooklyn Bridge comes into view. This is where I met Atlas. I want to feel closer to him, more than just being in his car or hugging his ashes, both of which I left behind in a school parking lot.

The very top of this bridge is where I first told him I was in love with him.

It was in April, three months after the Blackout. Atlas had taken care of me, and that day, it was my turn to take care of him. He'd just found out his parents' prison sentence for robbing a bank was expanding for another five years.

"I was *this* close to having them back," Atlas had said, snapping his fingers. He was pacing from one edge of the bridge's crown to the other. He loved coming up here to relax with the wind in his ears. His blond hair was blowing in every direction and then he completely lost it. "I bet they didn't even do anything wrong! They're punishing them because I'm out here trying to do something right!"

He couldn't even visit them. Not without walking straight into the Bounds, where all the enforcers wanted him.

Atlas tried drying his eyes and catching his breath. "I'm sorry, Mari, I know my parents are still alive, I'll talk about this with Wes—"

"You're allowed to miss your parents too," I had told him.

It's just as true then as it is now—I preferred a quick death for my parents than a long life of mistreatment in the Bounds.

I locked my fingers in his. "You can talk to me about

anything. We make each other stronger the more vulnerable we are together." I had to honor my own words no matter how much they scared me. I stared into his teary gray eyes. "I love you, Atlas. You always have me."

The pain in his expression flickered away as he fully took me in. "I love you too, Mari."

We kissed with the winds pushing us closer together.

I eye that spot in the bridge now, scared to go there knowing he won't be able to hold me or tell me he loves me, but I hope it'll make me feel closer.

I levitate several feet and dark yellow flames crawl from my fists to my elbows. It took Emil weeks before he realized he could fly, and that was born out of panic like when he first discovered he was a specter. I'm more capable than he is—I'm the daughter of powerful Spell Walkers, I'm a celestial-specter hybrid, I have been strengthening the gleam in my veins my entire life.

When I was a girl, I only tapped into my power for the first time when I was pushed by my loved ones. I'm all I have now. I'll push myself.

I glide away from safety and toward the bridge. My yellow flames glow across the dark East River and I inch higher and higher, pushing past the height limits that have always separated me from everyone else graced with flight. My arms are shaking and my body is trembling and I'm sinking through the air. Atlas feels out of range more than ever, in this moment where I can't even reach his memory, and the flames roar and roar until they stretch past my hands and become burning wings that carry me up into the night. I push and push against the winds and imagine

Atlas and my parents beside me up until I land on top of the Brooklyn Bridge. I gaze at my wings, staying strong against the elements until I decide it's time for them to vanish.

I've caught the attention of people below who were posing for pictures with the cityscape. I doubt many of them know that this bridge continues to exist because of me and Atlas and Wesley and Iris fighting off terrorists.

I sit in the center, imagining meeting Atlas under different circumstances. He could've been below playing around with Wesley while Iris and I were out on a stroll. Atlas and I could've noticed each other and just like when I coached Iris on how to talk to Eva she could've pushed me to say hi to Atlas. But reimagining history like this hurts because the reality is that we were brought together by battle and forever separated by it too.

It's freezing up here, and I cast a fire-orb to keep me warm. I stare at the night sky, wishing I could find Atlas's face glowing in the stars. There are all these nonsense prime constellations that I'm supposed to care about as a celestial, but unless one can bring my loved ones back to life, I really don't. I break into tears and scream so loud and I'm so close to making it rain fire on everyone below me when the roaring wind gets so strong and loud that I can barely hear myself. I pretend that Atlas is around, casting the winds himself.

Then it begins pouring rain out of nowhere, dousing my fire-orb. I didn't know it would rain tonight, but weather always catches me by surprise. Atlas was the one who paid the most attention to forecasts so he wouldn't fly out into storms.

Lightning flashes across the dark cloudy sky and illuminates a massive phoenix that casts its shadow over me as it flies toward the city. The phoenix's feathers are yellow and brown and its belly and crown are black. It's the largest phoenix I've ever seen up close, the size of a racehorse, and as it moves away from me I see the silhouette of a rider—a young woman. My psychic sense thrums, warning me of some great danger. The rain stops pouring down on me and the river but continues to follow the phoenix like this bird is a storm cloud. I'm not familiar with this breed, I've never had any reason to study phoenixes since I've never been up against one, but as I stand there wet and shivering against the cold winds, I'm sure this might change.

The phoenix rider is a clear threat. Who is she hunting?

SIXTEEN
RESETTING

BRIGHTON

The Spell Walkers are honoring my wishes and packing up.

Iris dismissed the illusionists, which works out anyway since Sunstar is making her big announcement today and can use that extra protection. The doctors seem nervous without them, as if the Blood Casters have somehow tracked us here and have been waiting for the illusions to vanish so they can pounce. Dr. Swensen and Dr. Salinas have given me many reasons why I should stay, like how most times when I'm awake I can't even keep my head up, and how my temperature shoots up and drops right back down without warning, and how I've been throwing up all my food. But I refuse, so they train Emil and Prudencia on how to mix a cooling gel and give them the ingredients for an herbal potion that may settle my stomach.

I meet Ruth and the baby briefly when we're all gathered outside and she very generously offers to cook me whatever meal I want when we get to her place. She then takes Esther and rides in one car with Iris while Wesley drives the other with me, Emil, and Prudencia. Emil is the only one in the back with me, and I can keep to myself.

I've been having a lot of resets lately. There are some things I would've normally used my right hand for but now use my left, like brushing my teeth and scrolling through my phone. But then there are the major resets, like no longer planning different features for my online channels or expecting Ma to be around. No longer expecting myself to be around.

Until then, I wonder how long it's going to take before I get used to using my left hand. I have to redo the fingerprint scanner on my phone since it doesn't recognize my scaly index finger. I tap into Instagram and I have so many DMs, some from mutuals like genderqueer icon Lore asking me if I'm okay, but mostly from strangers who want to know if I was involved in the Alpha Church battle. Just like how I didn't tell anyone I drank a potion to try and kill Luna, not realizing it was Brew, I'm not trying to get into the story of the Reaper's Blood since it has an unhappy ending. I'm not one of those desperate souls on social media who needs attention so badly that they mistake basic sympathetic messages as true affection from their followers who are commenting while on the toilet. Part of me wants to put up a goodbye post so I can have the last word, but who cares?

I scroll through my feed. My favorite artist, Himalia Lim, has painted gold and gray wings across different buildings in the Bronx to celebrate Emil, and she's sharing some pictures of fans posing in front of them; I don't show Emil the posts. This celestial Reed Tyler cross-posts his clone dance challenge from TikTok using his actual clones, and it's these little moments that build up within ordinary people that make them want to become specters. Lore is starting a book club, apparently, and their first choice is a fantasy novel about a nonbinary celestial who opens a portal that sends them into an alternate New York where powers aren't real. If I lived in a gleam-free world, I would've been okay not having powers of my own. But that's a fantasy world, and my reality has proven lethal.

No one talks during the ride. Prudencia turns on the radio and she quietly sings along with her favorite Mexican band. There are thick trees down this mostly empty road, and after getting deeper into the suburbs of New Suffolk, we pull into the cobbled drive-way of a one-story cottage with dark green bricks and a maroon front door. The mailbox is marked with the house number, 149. Waves are crashing in the Great Peconic Bay, which is a quick walk away. If you were hanging up your power-proof vest, this is definitely a nice place to retire.

Wesley parks, and Emil races out of the car to help me out.

"I can open my own door," I snap.

"I'm just trying to help," Emil says quietly.

Prudencia looks like she might say something, but instead she locks her arm with Emil's and they walk into the house.

I don't care if they think I have a bad attitude. I get to be upset, for star's sake.

I carry my own bag inside. There are pictures everywhere of

Wesley, Ruth, and Esther from the walls to the table with the key bowl. Even the clock's face is a photo of Esther as a newborn. There's a piano by the sliding glass doors and a TV mounted above the fireplace. Emil, Prudencia, and Iris are awkwardly gathered around the cozy living room, unsure where to go.

"What's the setup?" Iris asks.

"We have three bedrooms," Wesley says in a hushed voice with Esther asleep in his arms. "I'm moving all of Esther's stuff into our room. So Iris and Prudencia in one room and Emil and Brighton in the other? We have some air mattresses we can blow up."

"I'll take the couch," Emil says.

"I'll take the other," Prudencia says and turns to Iris. "I want to give you some space if that's okay."

Iris gives the slightest nod. She checks her watch. "Sunstar's announcement is in thirty minutes. Let's meet out here then."

The guest room is simple. Twin-sized bed, private bathroom, and a desk with a view of the bay. Emil would've been in a sleeping bag on the floor if he weren't so frustrated with me. I charge my laptop, wanting to do some research on golden-strand hydras, but I spend the next twenty minutes propped up against the toilet, vomiting so much of this disgusting bile that my throat burns. Even though I'm tempted to stay in and rest, I wash up because I want to be with everyone else as they watch Sunstar's announcement. I missed enough when I was asleep for days. I'm not part of the team anymore, but I'm still going to have a say as long as I'm here. Everyone is already situated, and Prudencia creates some space for me on the couch, but I drag a chair from the wooden dining table and sit next to Ruth.

We watch Sunstar take the stage in a town hall meeting with hundreds in the audience. She addresses that this country is indeed having an issue with gleamcrafters abusing their powers, especially with the rise of specters, but she has issues with how the enforcers have been operating. Enforcers have been trusted to defend citizens from gleam abusers, and instead, they have been abusing their authoritative power against innocent gleamcrafters. Thankfully she has a proposition—the Luminary Union, an official government task force comprised of some of the greatest protectors in every city. The True Lighters in Chicago. The First Sparrows in Omaha. The Arrowed Souls in Dallas. The Sunbeams in Phoenix. The Zoom Force in Lexington. The Shadow Belles in New Orleans. There's a pause before she announces the Spell Walkers in New York and there's an immediate mix of cheers and boos. She closes her statement by saying that in order to create a bright future, they need to rebuild the programs in place to protect this country, and that by uniting all of these groups under the watchful eye of the government, she believes we can all beat back the darkness.

"Do you think this is going to work?" Ruth asks as she turns off the TV.

"It's a dream some may have been open to before the Blackout," Wesley says. "Luna ruined all chances of people treating us with sympathy."

"If we can't make that dream come true, good luck enjoying this home you're building for yourself," Iris says as she gets up, pacing. "We wouldn't be in this situation if we had a government that actually cared about us. I could have some help looking for Eva and Carolina. I wouldn't have to ask for tips online or try to recruit trackers or hit the streets myself. But no, they are cut off from us because of a crime that we're not even responsible for!" She slams her fist down on the dining table, snapping it in half. She's the shortest person in the room and with one punch she proves herself the strongest. Esther begins crying from the other room. "Sorry," Iris says as she goes out into the backyard.

"She apologizing for breaking our table or waking up Esther?" Wesley asks.

"Baby or friend?" Ruth asks, ignoring his joke.

"I'll take Esther for a run," he says. Off Ruth's look, he adds, "A light jog."

I'm left sitting there with Emil and Prudencia. Emil manually turns on the fireplace and watches the fire lick away at the logs. Prudencia stretches across the couch she's claimed as her own. I go back into my room, even though I don't really want to be alone right now. I bring my laptop into bed and try to distract myself with some YouTube videos, but all I really want to do is form some kind of plan that will get the Blood Casters to at least put us out of misery as to whether or not Ma is even alive.

I don't exactly have that blood-and-bones feeling like usual, but I suspect I have another major reset in my life—both of my parents are dead.

SEVENTEEN
PROPAGANDA

NESS

For the past couple days, I've been reading scripts, but not for anything I'm excited to star in. The campaign manager, Roslyn Fox, thought it would be a great strategy to counter Brighton's Spell Walkers of New York series with videos of our own. The Senator and Bishop have signed off on the scripts that will paint celestials as walking weapons that need to be controlled—all thanks to the shifting power that was supposed to help me reboot my life.

I've been propped in front of the camera for over twelve hours filming anti-celestial videos. I'm locked away in the attic that's been converted into a studio with only Roslyn for company. She looks murderous as she reviews our most recent take.

She has the same tight black bun she's been wearing since she was brought onto the Senator's staff one year after Mom was killed. Black eyeliner she probably put on for the Senator is smudging around her icy-blue eyes. She curses under her breath.

I don't have to be good at reading people to know she hates me.

We worked closely together back when I was more compliant because she wrote some of the speeches I delivered at the youth conferences she would book for me. One night I thanked her for giving me all these stages to release my anger and grief. Then she overstepped by inviting me to always talk to her about my feelings like I would've with Mom. I had the Senator shut that down immediately because no one was ever going to replace my mother. It was all business from there on out with Roslyn.

I'm sure she was thrilled when she thought I actually died in the Blackout. My resurrection has probably been really hard on her. I wish I'd been around when the Senator broke the news.

The difference between working with Roslyn now from before is that this time I know all the lines she's feeding me are lies. I won't be surprised if she keeps me going past midnight. I've been fed twice, but during those breaks I had to watch footage of Congresswoman Sunstar's staff to study their behavior and appearances so I can pose as them. But mostly I've been shifting into people who don't even exist. I'm given faces of randoms around the country and build a look. Someone's yellow teeth with someone else's lips with someone else's button nose with someone else's brown eyes with someone else's red buzz cut.

Then I lie about how celestials have ruined my life.

I've appeared as a teenager whose invisible high school coach spied on me in the locker room. The assistant to a boss who threatened to burn me from the inside out if I kept refusing dates with him. A victim who gave away my car keys because of "some young punk's mind control," which isn't even a known power in our world; it's something that's ripped out of science-fiction movies. A child who bullied a boy at school, so his mother blinded me with her blazing light—a power not-so-strikingly similar to Sunstar.

No one will use the word, but it's all propaganda.

"Again," Roslyn says from behind the camera. "Sell it to me."

"The young celestial threatened me if I didn't give him all the money," I say as an older bank teller with welling tears brought on by how tired I am. I don't want to say this last part, but I do. "He told me that the money was going to be donated to the Spell Walkers so they can build better defenses against the enforcers. His eyes were glowing as bright as the lightning in his hands. . . ."

The thing is, if anyone does the bare minimum to fact-check these stories, they won't be able to come up with anything to support it. But the problem is no one tries anymore. Headlines are read, articles are skimmed, and the reader passes that on to someone else, and they accept it as truth. Then that person tells someone else and it spreads like poison. By the time someone senses something is off and does their own research, it's too late. The damage has been done.

This is only one of the twenty-four stories I've filmed so far to further paint the Spell Walkers as villains. To make sure Sunstar never catches up in the polls. To limit the rights of celestials and increase demands for more enforcers.

The world is worse off because of me and my infinite faces.

EIGHTEEN
THE UNCHOSEN ONE

BRIGHTON

My body feels like it's on fire.

Since the middle of the night, I've been reapplying the cooling gel across my forehead, chest, arms, and even my feet. Then the morning brought insult to injury when I struggled with opening the childproof cap of my painkillers with my left hand. Also, pharmacies really shouldn't be allowed to call these pills painkillers if they're not going to kill the pain. I'm covered in sweat and biting back my cries when someone knocks on the door. I'm about to shout at Emil to go away when Ruth calls my name from the hallway.

"Yeah?" I ask, strained.

Ruth enters and her hand goes to her heart. She looks around the room, which is already a mess, and then her eyes glow like multiplying stars. A purple light flashes and her clone appears, matching every lock of hair behind her ear and every wrinkle in her shirt. The clone collects the plates from my half-eaten lunch and my empty glass and leaves. Ruth is gentle as she helps me out of bed so she can replace my drenched sheets. She parts the window's curtains to let more air in and it's dark out now. I've slept most of this day away.

"Do you want some company?" Ruth asks. "I could use some."

"Isn't that what clones are for?"

"It's hard talking with someone who knows everything about you because they are you. Believe me, I would run my own book club if my clones had their own opinions," Ruth says with a smile. "You should take your medicine with some food in your stomach."

"I'll eat in here."

"If you really want to, but it would mean a lot to me if you joined me in the living room. Pretty much everyone is out right now, so it's relaxed," she says.

I should try and eat some more, especially after everything I've been throwing up.

Ruth's clone returns with ice-cold water. Ruth and her clone exchange tired smiles before the clone fades in a pale purple light. If this had been weeks ago, it would've been cool seeing Ruth's power in action after hearing Wesley talk about it in our Spell Walkers of New York interview, the one that got Ruth a lot of slack from the conservative blogger Silver Star Slayer. But now it makes me extra envious.

We go out toward the living room, where someone is playing piano. It's a little choppy, but otherwise it's beautiful and calming. I'm expecting it to be Wesley or another clone, but it's Prudencia seated on the bench, her hands hovering over the keys, pressing down on them with her power. She loses concentration when I enter, and Esther begins squirming in the bassinet beside her feet. Prudencia's eyes glow and when she resumes playing Esther settles down.

"Where is everyone?" I ask as I sit on the couch in front of a foldout table since Iris destroyed the real dining table.

"Iris finally fell asleep, and Wesley and Emil are installing surveillance cameras along the road just to be safe," Ruth says with fear in her voice. She's risking her home for us.

She prepares a plate for me with mashed potatoes, gravy, steamed broccoli, roasted carrots, corn, and a salad with sunray dressing. Nothing that I can't eat easily with one hand.

"Thank you."

"My pleasure," Ruth says as she sits beside me on the couch. "I should've asked before, but are you okay with my clones being around? It's second nature to me, but I want to be more sensitive."

"No, you keep doing you. I'm actually curious about your powers. . . ." I stop, realizing that this is one of Prudencia's biggest issues with me. "Forget it. You don't have to talk about that."

"I'm happy to. It's been a journey," she says, beginning her story.

Ruth comes from a long line of celestials with cloning abilities. Their matriarch, Ruth the First, was born under the Twinned

Queen constellation, which only surfaces for two nights every century. She was so powerful that she could clone objects too. Fame turned Ruth the First into a purist and all the other children in her line followed suit. When the Twinned Queen returned eighteen years ago, Ruth's parents timed their pregnancy so they could have her under the constellation.

"They were so happy when they found out they were having a girl so they could name me after Ruth the First. But my mother's water broke three days before the constellation. Labor was painful and she did her best to keep me in, hiring healers to absorb her pain and drinking all these potions to numb herself, but it was all too much and she gave birth to me early."

Fast-forward several years and Ruth showed no sign of powers. Ruth couldn't clone herself or objects like her mother or project her spirit in her sleep like her father. Her parents had her tested by savants and were so ashamed to admit that their daughter was Ruth the First's descendant and showed no sign of gleam.

"I grew up embarrassed that I wasn't special," Ruth says.

"I know the feeling. My grandmother was psychic. Her power wasn't that strong, just these immediate future visions, like if someone was about to trip, but I still had hope for myself. And no . . ." I gesture at my entire body. "Here I am. The unchosen one."

"You might be better for it. My powers didn't manifest because of anything good. That savant recommended a forced isolation on me, and scenarios where I would need to escape somewhere to try and spark my power. My parents busied me with friends and playdates for weeks and then, one day, they took it all away.

I couldn't go outside and I was so lonely and crying all the time. Ten days later my clone appeared for the first time because I wanted someone to play with me."

I've lost my appetite.

Ruth looks back at her daughter, and I already know she would never torture Esther this way. "My mother called me her Twinned Princess . . . She tested me to clone objects like her, but the only thing that happened was another clone emerged so she could deal with my mother while I played with my first clone."

"That's horrifying. Why haven't you ever spoken about this?"

"It doesn't help our cause to paint celestials in such a terrible light. We have people on our side making grave mistakes like this, but if we can't show everyone that most of us are model citizens, especially after the Blackout, then we're never going to be granted the equality generations and generations of celestialkind have been fighting for."

I never thought that celestials could be as monstrous as the worst specters. That the Blood Casters aren't the only villains.

"Do you talk to your parents?"

Ruth shakes her head. "Not really. The older I got, the less I appreciated their attitude toward other celestials. They're wealthy and self-important and enrolled me in an elite private school for celestials to strengthen my powers so investors would care about my future. I always fought with them to make a difference with their money, but they only invested in our bloodline, so I took all the money I gained from social media partnerships, donated my fancy clothes, and gave up everything that felt like royalty. Then I started working at a hostel for celestials and I got good—okay,

I'm being humble, I got amazing—at tailoring clothes for celestials in need."

The music stops playing. Prudencia gently rocks the bassinet with her telekinesis, and she looks so beautiful using her power for such a simple reason.

"Do your parents know about Esther?" I ask.

"They do. They were impressed that Wesley is a Spell Walker, but they said his power would ruin our bloodline as if I care about that. Esther could have no powers and I'm happy if she doesn't. Though Wesley wants her to have a combination of our powers so she and her clones can dash around my parents' homes and rob them clean." She rolls her eyes and smiles.

Her story is so epic it would've done really well on Celestials of New York, but really it needs to be an eight-part docuseries.

"You don't want to make things right with them?" I ask, thinking about how I'm not going to get that chance with Ma.

"They gave birth to me, and they'll technically always be family, but they're not mine. I have Wesley and Esther. The other Spell Walkers. My friends at the havens. Emil isn't your blood, but you know he's your brother."

"Of course." He always will be.

"Family isn't about blood." Ruth nods very obviously at Prudencia. "Don't let the good ones get away."

NINETEEN

THE CLOAKED PHANTOM

NESS

The Senator has spent the afternoon watching final cuts of my propaganda videos.

We're up in the attic with Roslyn, and she's explained her updated rollout plan. The majority of videos will be fed out online through sock puppet accounts. The ones capable of doing the most damage to celestial reputations—also known as the Senator's favorites—will be offered to pro-Iron networks such as Wolf News for more prominent airing.

Roslyn pulls out a script from her folder. "I wrote this one last night. I created a victim who claims that Iris Simone-Chambers broke her arm and threatened to punch a hole in her stomach if she didn't turn over surveillance footage that would've identified her as guilty of a robbery."

The Senator slides the script back across the desk. "We can't involve detailed personal accounts like that. Not for the Spell Walkers or Sunstar or any of my opponents. If they sense something is off, it could open an investigation that would stanch the wound we're trying to widen. Only videos that can't be traced back to us." He turns to me, where I'm sitting in the corner by the window. "We can't have Eduardo's wonderful work go to waste. Isn't that right, son?"

I don't react. That's what he wants and I've given him enough.

Filming for the past two days has been absolutely draining. The closest I've come to actively using my power for long stretches of time like this is when I once went undercover as one of Luna's rival alchemists to get him some intel for blackmail. For how physically exhausting this has all been, it's got nothing on how it's affected me mentally. I'm the person behind all these masks of lies. Once these videos are out there, everyone who suffers—rights taken away, jailed, killed—will be because of my performances. The whole thing makes me want to morph into a little boy and cry into my mother's chest.

The Senator stands. "Great work, Roslyn. I have to finish getting ready, but we can discuss your phase two proposals on the way to Florida. Be downstairs in three." On the way out, he looks over his shoulder and says, "Behave while I'm away, Eduardo. Don't stay up too late." His laughter follows him out of the attic.

Roslyn lets out a happy sigh.

"How do you sleep at night, fraud?" I ask.

"A lot better since I started sharing a bed with your father," she says with a smile.

So they are together now—or at least, hooking up. It seems like there are only a handful of people on the Senator's team who know about me being alive. I haven't seen any other bodyguards except Jax and Zenon, and Jax truly should've been fired for the way he failed at his job during the break-in this week. But if it's really just those two, Bishop, and Roslyn, I have to manipulate them. Get into their heads.

"You're never going to be his First Lady," I tell her. "I know what it looks like when he talks to a woman he loves. That's not what's happening here."

"My love for him and his work is enough for the both of us," Roslyn says as she finishes packing up her laptop and files. "That'll keep me warm in the White House's master bedroom."

She leaves the attic.

I want to call her a monster, but that won't faze her. Roslyn needs time to become unsettled and I have to trust that I've planted a seed. I didn't even have to lie. My mom wasn't perfect. Her views weren't always in line with where mine are now, and she didn't always challenge her husband like she encouraged me with others, but she would've never supported all this cheating, let alone help engineer it. She didn't have to perform her loyalty to the Senator to get him to love her. I saw his private grief when she was killed.

I hope every corrupt person on this team ends up in prison like the criminals they are. Right on cue, Jax arrives—his face fully healed because of Eva—to lock me back in my cage after this torturous session in the attic. I would've been happier alone and peeling paint off my walls than having the Senator and Roslyn for company. But Jax doesn't take me to my bedroom. We go downstairs, where the Senator, Roslyn, and Zenon are waiting by the front door with luggage.

"We said bye already," I say to the Senator.

"But not to Jax and Zenon. They'll be joining me on this trip. Fear not, you won't be left alone," he says.

Dione steps out of the living room and leans against the grandfather clock. "Enough talk. You can go now," she says to the Senator.

He doesn't challenge her disrespect. He must understand already that she won't ever favor him. It's one of the reasons I trusted her after joining the gang.

I see the Senator and Roslyn in this new light knowing they're together and I'm thrilled when they leave with Jax and Zenon following them out. That leaves me with Dione. We're not friends, though I thought we could've been. She was always the most human in rooms with bloodthirsty Stanton and ghostly June. But she's quick to anger, doesn't show remorse around killing those who try to overpower her, and she's very loyal to Luna. I have to be smart around her if I'm going to make the most of this time away from the Senator and his team.

"Should we throw a party?" I ask.

"Anything that helps trash this place," Dione says, eyeing the grandfather clock as if she's considering tipping it over. "But I have to catch up with Luna."

"Where is she?"

Dione chuckles. "The Cloaked Phantom is hitting the sky tonight. Where do you think?"

"That's tonight?!"

The twice-a-year constellation that made me a shifter. How has it already been eight months since I've had these powers? I would've never thought I'd be back here in the manor, forced to be a weapon once again for the person I happily played dead to never see again.

"For someone who's credited as being very alert, this important detail flew right over your head."

"I wasn't exactly given a calendar with every upcoming prime constellation when forced back here. Take that up with the host you're working for."

Dione's eyes are daggers. "I don't work for your father. If Luna is successful, you won't have to work for him either."

This must be what Luna and the Senator discussed the evening she arrived—my replacement. Maybe she has someone in mind who will be more eager to help them fulfill their vision. "So who's the young bastard Luna is preying on this time?"

Dione grabs me by the arm and drags me down the steps to the basement. "It's not your business."

I struggle, but she's far stronger than me. "Dione, this is what she does! This is what she did with you too! Luna is an opportunistic predator who buys our loyalty with power, I know you know this!"

We reach the landing and Dione shoves me to the floor. "If you were loyal, you wouldn't be in this mess."

The panic room is a gigantic black box with one-way windows so those inside can keep track of the intruder's movements. It's protected by the gleam-shield, a dome of yellow energy. In a demonstration video provided by the supplier there was a celestial who cast fire at the gleam-shield and it rebounded back at them so quickly they didn't even have a chance to move. The Senator has mused about improving upon his grandfather's legacy and upgrading the power-proof vest with similar protections so enforcers will be extra armored against gleam attacks. Dione reads the twenty-digit security code posted on the wall and types it into the keypad; I once had those numbers, or similar ones assuming they've been changed, memorized in the event I had to lock myself in the panic room. The shield drops and Dione opens the door.

"Go in or be thrown in," she says.

"You're making a big mistake," I say as I pick myself up from the floor. "If you fail her she won't even bother with you. Look at Stanton! She's not even breaking him out! She will replace you like she's trying to replace me!"

Dione doesn't wait for me to go in peacefully. She grabs me by the wrist and throws me through the door and I roll into a couch. Someone gasps. She peeks in, stares at Eva, then slams the door behind her. In moments the gleam-shield is up and running again.

I massage the shoulder I landed on as I look up at my new roommates who are sitting together on one of the two beds. Emil's mother, Carolina, looks exhausted and it's possible—well, likely—that she's been crying too. For the most part, she's fine. Unlike Eva. Her brown skin seems paler, her hair is thinning on one side, she has a black eye the size of my fist, and there are bandages all over her arms. It's like she's been strung up like a punching bag, which is something we did once with a former chief enforcer who didn't get the memo that no one messes with Luna's Casters; here's hoping we can get Eva out of here before she finds a wand to her head like the chief did.

"Are you okay?" I ask.

Eva sits up. "Do we look okay?"

I don't say anything. No need for my stupid answer after my stupid question.

"Why are you locked away with us?" Eva asks.

"Everyone else is busy, so I needed a babysitter. Was Dione this terrible back when you were both friends?"

Eva shakes her head. "She used to be my favorite person."

Carolina comes and kneels beside me, taking my hands in hers. "Please tell me that my boys are okay."

"I was hoping you could tell me. I've been cut off from all live news since the invasion at Nova."

"Everyone made it out," Carolina says.

I get a recap on everything major that happened while I was busy reuniting with the Senator. The Spell Walkers took on the Blood Casters. Luna stabbed Emil with an infinity-ender dagger, and then Brighton showed up and shot her in the stomach with a spell before drinking the Reaper's Blood. But apparently the elixir didn't make him immortal, and he's likely going to die. Emil is still alive too, as far as they know. Take the wins when you get them, and that's a big win in my book.

"We don't know anything else," Carolina says.

"If there had been any mention of Emil or Brighton or any Spell Walker dying, I'm sure the Senator would've thrown a party."

155

Framing the deaths of her sons as cause of celebration doesn't help her mood. She releases my hands and sits on the couch. I join her. How relaxed Carolina is around me releases a lot of tension.

"I regret my last words to Brighton," Carolina says. "I called him 'high and mighty' for choosing those powers, and now I may never get to tell him how much I love him."

"He wasn't kind to you either," Eva says. "He's got to be regretting his words too."

"What did he say?" I ask.

Carolina doesn't meet my eyes. "That his father was the better parent. I often think that's true, but I've been trying my best."

"I'm sure your best has been great," I say.

Brighton doesn't know how great he's got it. I would kill to have my mom back instead of being left with a man who is using me to ruin the country.

This is the first time in days I don't feel watched. Not by Jax from outside my room or from Zenon wherever he is within the manor. My life for the past few years has been putting on all these metaphorical masks and some literal ones the past few months. The last time I've really let down my guard was when I was around Emil, and he caught me in a vulnerable moment where I had morphed into one of my victims. I think about him as I inhale a deep breath with my eyes closed and embrace this peace.

Eva snaps her fingers. Peace killed. "What were you talking about with Dione? You're being replaced?"

"Apparently," I say. "The Cloaked Phantom hits the sky tonight."

"Which constellation is that one again?" Carolina asks.

"Not as epic as the Crowned Dreamer," Eva says. "But it was one my mother admired because this constellation invites change. Sort of like the beginning of a new year. It's also really important to any celestials who can shift . . . and now apparently anyone looking to become a specter who can shift too."

She can judge me all she wants; she doesn't know me. "I would undo everything if I knew I was going to end up here again. All the propaganda I've been filming to build Iron's case against gleamcrafters will be some other specter's problem soon."

"Will they keep you down here with us?" Carolina asks.

I shrug. "Probably not. It's a lot smarter to throw me out of a helicopter and into some basilisk-infested waters. Good way to get rid of someone who's supposed to be dead."

Carolina rubs my shoulder. "I'm sure that won't be the case. You're his son."

I see where Emil gets his sweetness from. I don't need to tell her that the Blackout existed so I could be killed.

"I'm sorry we never got to properly meet before this," I say.

"Me too. You must mean something to Emil given how much he wanted to defend you."

"I think Emil would've done that for anyone. You raised him right. I swear I'll do everything I can to get you back to him in one piece. No one's harmed you, right?"

Her voice shakes before she can fully form her first words. "Senator Iron demanded that Eva heal his bruised-up bodyguard and when I defended her Dione struck me. Eva healed him and took care of me too after they all left."

I don't know how I'm going to do it but I'll make sure Dione

157

and Jax feel double the pain they put Eva and Carolina through.

Eva massages one of her bandages. "Healing is becoming harder. I haven't been under the stars in however many nights we've been trapped here and Luna keeps draining my blood, even though she's okay."

Her own sickness. Luna is probably mixing some potion to try and buy herself more time.

"I haven't been apart this long from Iris since we met," Eva says. "I'm not making it back to her."

She states it like a fact. I understand her in my own way.

"How'd you meet?" I ask.

Eva hesitates, but gives in. "Alchemists were hunting me for obvious reasons," she says, gesturing at her whole body. "My foster family couldn't protect me. I've always avoided violence, but I needed the Spell Walkers. Iris's mother, Finola, answered our call for help. She brought me into their haven and introduced me to Iris."

"Love at first sight?" I ask.

"No, not at all. It was better. Iris brought me a change of clothes and we talked until the sun came up, even though I was exhausted after weeks of never being able to get a full night's sleep." Eva is crying and I'm about to grab her some tissues when she continues. "Iris told me this story about how her parents took her to see the Moon Belle constellation when she was ten. Finola bought her a shirt off the street, but Iris didn't get to try it on beforehand. It was a perfect fit, and I couldn't help but feel like Iris was talking about us too. We fit, and I feel naked without her right now."

Carolina gets up and drapes a shivering Eva with a blanket around her shoulders and the kind of hug that makes me miss Mom even more. Then she turns to me. "Do you feel this way about my son?"

I'm so thrown off by the question; then I realize this is coming from a woman who understands she may never get to see her children grow into full adults who choose to have partners and start families. I don't know anything about Emil's dating history though I bet he had tons of guys attracted to him.

"I wouldn't say I feel naked without him," I admit. "But I feel cold without him. If that makes sense. It's like someone finally let me out into the sun and I was so into how warm it made me feel. But then I was forced back inside and I regret how much I sat around instead of actually embracing the day."

I would do things differently with Emil. I didn't kiss him when I left Nova or when I came back to save him. Kissing when a literal war is breaking out never comes to mind. If the stars cross for us again, I'll give it my all.

"He's the best person I know, and I haven't even known him that long," I say.

"That's my son," Carolina says proudly. "Ever since he was young Emil always wanted to make someone feel better. I didn't know until his teacher told me, but in sixth grade Emil wouldn't play with Brighton and their friends during recess because he was comforting a girl who had lost her sister. The boys were always close, but it only made them closer because Emil was so scared of losing Brighton too." Now she's crying. We have no idea if Emil and Brighton are dead or if one is alive and missing the other. Both thoughts are devastating. "When we lost Leo, Emil managed to hold on to his warmth. He fought so much to keep it together for us. My hero. Whenever he would give into his grief, the warmth would come back."

I chuckle, thinking about how Emil is true to his firefly nature. "Funny, I have a nickname for him and——"

The buzzing of the gleam-shield goes quiet and the door opens. Dione enters with Zenon behind her. But he's supposed to be gone.

"Storytime is over," Dione says. She turns to Zenon. "Do we have enough?"

"Should do the trick," Zenon says.

I stand. "You're not even supposed to be here!"

Dione stands behind Eva and Carolina. Her expression is mostly menacing, which always feels for show, but there's a hint of a conscience like when she hit pause on our mission to give some cash to a celestial whose eyes had been gouged out by some gleamphobic hunter. "We needed you to get up close and personal, Ness. How else are you going to play the roles if you don't understand your subjects?"

Play the roles? Then it hits me. "No, I will do everything else, I will keep making up fake people, but you can't make me impersonate them——"

"Shut up!" Dione shouts as her eyes glow and two extra sets of arms grow out of her sides. She chokes Eva and Carolina and pins down their hands. "You will become them or you will watch me rip them apart."

I hold up my hands in truce. "Let them go."

160

Dione releases them, and even though she has six hands she only uses one to drag me out by my wrist. I don't even get a chance to apologize to Eva and Carolina.

I got played tonight—the manipulator manipulated. If the Senator's team is still using me to morph into other people, then what's the plan for the new specter with shifter blood? Just a new Blood Caster? That can't be right. Any plan that Luna helps design runs deeper than new recruits.

For now, I've got to get ready to cause more damage while wearing the faces of two women who trusted me with their hearts.

TWENTY
DARK HEARTS

EMIL

It's midnight when I sneak out of the cottage to see the stars. The Cloaked Phantom is high in the dark sky, its light reflecting across the sea. The prime constellation is shaped like an old-school theater mask with the sly eyes twinkling the brightest. I'm out here tonight for Ness, knowing this alignment of stars is the reason he has his powers in the first place. Powers that couldn't keep him safe.

I head down to the beach, already wishing I brought a jacket with me. I keep my sneakers on since the sand is too cold, which would've been welcomed the couple times I've been out here with Prudencia during the day, but it's too chilly right now. I flex my fingers, trying to tap into my gleam to keep warm, but just like when I was barely able to create a fire-orb to attack Stanton back at Aldebaran, all my wounds—the ones inflicted by Ness and Luna—burn so badly that I'm almost brought to tears.

It seems impossible to be a soldier in this war. I mean, check me out, I haven't exactly been the most effective weapon in every battle.

Prudencia and I have had that exhausting conversation while out on the beach. I hate that I dragged her into this war, but I'm grateful she's here, especially with Brighton mostly keeping to himself. Prudencia isn't a soldier fully known to the public, but the Blood Casters must have pieced together her identity by now. She hasn't said it out loud, and I doubt she ever would, but I think she's worried her aunt, Maia, might meet the same fate as Ma. There's a lot of love lost from how gleamphobic Maia is, but Prudencia still cares.

Footsteps are shuffling in the sand behind me, and I spin around, nervous that an enforcer or Blood Caster has tracked us down. I'm ready to try and cast fire as if my life depends on it, but it's only Brighton. I'm not ruling out that he might be coming to swing at me too. He sits beside me and looks up at the Cloaked Phantom. Days ago he was glowing under the Crowned Dreamer, primed to become an unstoppable specter.

"Screw these constellations," Brighton breathes out.

He's pissed at something that was never for him. These prime constellations exist for celestials. For every branch of power out there, a lot of savants can trace its origins back to constellations. I'm definitely not an expert on them, but when I was younger the Feathered Figure constellation took to the sky and elevated all flying powers.

"They can actually be positive forces for celestials," I say, remembering how jaw-dropping it was to see so many celestials flying through the air that evening.

"But not specters like us," Brighton says, rubbing his left hand against his leg to warm up while his poisoned arm is wrapped up again in the cocoon cast. "Specters like you." I think he'll die before he understands how lucky he is that he's not a specter. "I wouldn't have gone for the Reaper's Blood if that gleam gene had just been activated in me. I don't know why Abuelita's psychic powers weren't passed down through Ma, but I would've made good use of them."

This imagined world does have its possibilities.

"You could've been some detective who gets visions about crimes and stops them from coming true," I say.

"Sounds more like a TV show," Brighton says. "You would probably be the hero who complains about being the hero for the entire series. But then at the end you're grateful for the fight because it changed your life for the better. You win the war and you get the guy."

I'm drawn to the Cloaked Phantom again as the gentle waves creep up on the sand. The splashing would usually soothe me, but it's not cutting it for me tonight.

"Except I can't get the guy when he's dead," I say. It's clear I'm no longer talking about this TV show Brighton is dreaming up. Our lives aren't someone's entertainment, or aren't supposed to be, at least.

"It's not like you loved him," Brighton says.

I'm shivering from the cold. "I don't have to love him to grieve him. Ness was important to me and we trusted each other. When we were under attack at Nova I was running around trying to find you because we had no idea you'd run off with Maribelle already. Ness risked his life posing as me to buy me more time. That's when he got captured and . . ."

I stop because I don't know what went down next. I don't know much about what even came before, like his relationship with his mother before she was killed or his father before he became so consumed with power that he used Ness to spread hate. I wonder if he's ever been involved with anyone romantically before or always single like me. I even want to know more about his transformation into a specter.

"There's so much I'm never going to know about Ness," I say. His story is going to remain some big mystery to me. And I'll always wonder about what would've happened between us if we got away together.

"I feel the same way about Prudencia," Brighton says.

"We've known her for four years," I say.

"But not really. If she hid being a celestial, what else don't we know about her? There's got to be more to the story. What really happened that led to her parents being killed by enforcers? Her life at home with Maia. And did she date what's-his-face, Dominic, because he was also a celestial? Did *he* know about her?"

The day Prudencia revealed her powers, she told me how her father was the only celestial between her parents, but I don't have the answers to any of Brighton's other questions. "Just ask her," I say.

"What's the point?" Brighton asks. "I'm dying and it's not

like I'm going to come back."

"Maybe it's not about you. Prudencia might open up to you if you're doing it for yourself, not Celestials of New York."

"Did she say that?"

I shake my head. I never press Prudencia about her feelings for Brighton. She kept to herself while she was dating Dominic too, and I always swore that was because she didn't want to mess with Brighton's head, but after everything this past month I guess she's more private than we realized. "Bright, talk to her. Unlike Ness, Prudencia is alive. If you only have a few months left to live, do you really want to spend that time not being honest?"

"You're right," Brighton says. I don't hear those words from him that often. He looks up at the sky, taking in the stars. "If this constellation is supposed to represent change, then I should consider making some."

He holds out his left fist, and at first I think he wants me to help him up, but I realize he's waiting for a fist bump. It's been a minute since we've done one. I guess having a real conversation that doesn't end with him yelling at me warrants one. Our knuckles meet and we whistle.

"What are you doing?" I ask as he gets up.

"I'm going to make sure I don't die with any regrets," Brighton says and he walks back to the cottage.

Brighton leaves me alone with the Cloaked Phantom, and I stay out here, wishing I had the same chance to make things right with Ness.

TWENTY-ONE
ULTIMATELY

BRIGHTON

It's really sinking in how short life is.

I walk back to the cottage, thinking about how I'll never own a house I can show off to my family. How everything I always wanted for myself—fame, power, success, family—won't ever happen. I made some stupid, arrogant choices and I'm paying the price for it now. But the conversations I've had lately with Ruth and Emil are inspiring me to make some better decisions before my time runs out.

Prudencia was in the shower when I left to go kill some tension with Emil but she's nowhere to be seen inside now. I go back outside and I find her in the grass clearing by the toolshed, sitting cross-legged in the air. Her eyes are closed and she's wobbling but mostly keeping her balance. There's always been something attractive about Prudencia concentrating that distracted me so much that I would sneak peeks, like whenever we did homework together or made signs for protests or the couple times she helped me edit my videos. But she's stunning in this moment, fully in her own element—wet dark hair pulled back by a rubber band, one of Ruth's *Every Body Is Super* shirts tucked into sweatpants, and elevated by the power she's kept secret for too many years.

I feel weird standing here and watching her, so I whisper her name to get her attention, louder and louder, until I accidentally scare her and she drops to the ground. I run over and help her up with my left hand. "I'm sorry, I didn't mean to freak you out."

Prudencia sucks in a breath while she massages her elbow. "It's okay."

"Do you need ice?" I turn to go back inside.

"No, it's fine. Between all the battles lately I can handle a little fall." She wipes the dirt from her hands onto her sweatpants. "What are you doing out here?"

"I was looking for you." The seconds of silence that follow are too much, so I quickly add, "How about you?"

Prudencia points at the Cloaked Phantom. "We didn't get a chance to appreciate the Crowned Dreamer at its zenith, so I figured I'd come out tonight and feel these stars on my skin."

I start backing away. "Okay, I'll leave you to that."

I need to be better about respecting her background.

Prudencia sits on the grass and stares ahead at the bay. "I could use a break," she says and I stop retreating. "Balancing myself in the air is pretty taxing. So, you were looking for me?"

"I just wanted to talk."

"About . . . ?"

"Everything. Nothing. Whatever feels right."

She pats the grass beside her. "Come sit."

The last time we got to sit like this in nature was on my birthday. I hosted that underwhelming meet-up for not even a dozen Brightsiders and went home with too much merch. I have way more clout now, I'm sure I could get hundreds of people. But this focus on strangers has always been my problem. I've always had a real friend right here by my side. Someone who could've been more if I put her before others.

"I'm really sorry," I say. It crushes me when I realize I have so much to apologize for. "My ego won every battle against you and Emil but it especially wasn't fair to you. Emil and I have been able to turn to our parents whenever we got on each other's nerves, but you've been alone with Maia, who hasn't been a good aunt to you. She didn't even let you be yourself. And I failed by not being someone you can trust."

Prudencia folds her arms over her knees and nods. "I really appreciate that, Brighton. I never wanted to take my powers to the grave, but I didn't want to embrace them anymore. It's been really lonely, though."

I don't want to ask because I'm scared of how it will make me feel, but this is the work I got to do to make up for all the times I put myself before her. "But you had Dominic, right? Celestial boyfriend who understood you?"

"It could've," she says. "If I'd told him."

"Why didn't you?"

"It didn't feel written in the stars," Prudencia says. "His family

169

is very proud of their gleamcraft. Practically purists. I liked Dominic a lot, but I wasn't going to lay out all my cards so my high school boyfriend's parents would like me."

"You were always too good for him anyway," I say.

"Is this still because he wouldn't do a CONY interview?" Prudencia asks with a grin.

I laugh. "All I'm saying is that if he was so proud to be a celestial he would've let me profile him."

"He would've if he didn't feel so competitive. You always had higher marks and more followers. I explained to him over and over that growing your platform was important for your dreams of hosting your own TV show and that it didn't matter for his ambitions as a pilot. But he still kept tabs on you."

It's strange to think that someone who could travel through shadows was jealous of me. "Well, he was lucky enough to date you. That's a big win."

The starlight on Prudencia's blushing cheeks tightens my chest. The constellation is about change and I hope she's as open to honoring that as I am. Her eyes glow like skipping stars and she looks like a maestro as she makes small rocks and branches dance around us. The movements are mostly delicate; even when a couple branches snap, she catches them before they can hit the ground and adds them into her telekinetic current.

"Mamí wasn't a celestial, but Papí was. The first in our family in seven generations. That's why our telekinesis isn't as naturally powerful. He didn't have anyone to teach him how to use his power, but I was lucky to have him. The most important lesson was focus." Prudencia's fingers move more forcefully, like she's giving the air a deep-tissue massage. "To suspend something in elevation, you have to maintain focus. You can't forget about a single rock or stick. You have to decide on the movements for each. It gets trickier when you're also carrying yourself . . ." She ascends, not as high as when I found her out here tonight, and then I suddenly feel like I'm being slowly sucked up to the sky. ". . . and when you're carrying others."

We're sitting across from each other in the air with nature swirling around us. She's beginning to sweat as she gracefully lowers us to the ground.

"Better landing this time," she jokes.

"Thanks for telling me all of that. It's like I get to know you all over again."

"I'm happy to tell you everything as long as it doesn't end up on Celestials of New York," Prudencia says with a smile, even though I know she's serious. She lies down on the grass and stares at the stars.

I'm running out of time to see her smile and float together. I'm so stupid, the kind of stupid that could've only been salutatorian if he cheated. I put hours and hours into Celestials of New York so that I could be the go-to platform for news about a community I don't belong to—one I had hoped to belong to if Abuelita's psychic powers manifested in me. I always dreamed of profiling myself: Brighton of New York. But that's never happening.

I inch closer and lie down beside her. The Cloaked Phantom is this sparkling, gigantic reminder to be the change you want to see.

"You know I've always wanted more in life than likes and views, right?" I ask with my heart in my throat as I rest my hand on top of Prudencia's and squeeze. "I've always had feelings for you, Pru. I even broke up with Nina because I saw you as more than a friend, but then you were dating Dominic, and I waited and it hurt and now we're single but all of this is happening. It's always felt like we've had this unspoken thing between us and our timing has never been great, but seeing as I could drop dead any moment there's literally no time like the present. I'm sorry for pushing you away at Nova when you asked me to choose you. I should've stayed and told you I love you."

Prudencia doesn't move. She doesn't rip her hand out from under mine but she doesn't embrace it either. My stupid streak continues thinking that if she ever had feelings for me that they would still exist after every awful thing I've done.

I pull my hand away. "I'm sorry. You've always been too extraordinary for someone like me. I'm not even talking about the powers." I get up. "I'll leave you alone. Enjoy the constellation."

Every step I take away from her I expect her to call my name but she never does. I sneak one last look over my shoulder and Prudencia is still stretched across the grass with her eyes on the Cloaked Phantom. She clearly doesn't want anything to change between us and that's that.

I go inside. Wesley is in the kitchen giving Esther her bottle. His hipster bun is down and his brown hair rests behind his neck and he looks exhausted. He mentions something about the constellation being beautiful tonight but I go straight to my room, switch off the light, and lock the door. It's like I told Emil earlier: Screw these constellations.

Screw the Cloaked Phantom for inspiring me to make a fool of myself.

Screw the Crowned Dreamer for killing me instead of making me immortal.

In bed, I feel fevered and itchy and nauseous as I think about how much stronger I'd be if I hadn't failed so many times in my short life: I wouldn't feel like such a runner-up if I'd gotten vale-dictorian instead of salutatorian; I would've felt more valued if my so-called fans bothered to come to my meet-up; I would've felt more powerful if I could've somehow stopped Dad from dying or had the means to avenge Ma or the Reaper's Blood to protect myself eternally; I could've built something with Prudencia if I didn't obsess over Celestials of New York; I could've been living my own life if I hadn't followed Emil to save his.

Ultimately, I'm always the sidekick and never the hero.

I won't have to be tired of that for much longer.

I grab my phone, its light harsh on my eyes until I lower the brightness. My Instagram feed is mostly pictures of people post-ing the Cloaked Phantom with captions about changes they want to make moving forward as if they ever honored their New Year's resolutions. These pictures are pissing me off all over again.

Someone knocks on the door and I shout, "What?!"

I'm not in the mood for some check-in from Emil or Wesley.

"Can I come in?" Prudencia asks from the other side of the door.

"Yeah," I say reluctantly. Here comes the I'm-sorry-you-

173

took-so-long-to-get-this-right talk.

She tries to let herself in, but the door is still locked. A second later, she telekinetically unlocks it from the outside. Prudencia walks straight through the darkness, the constellation's light filtering through the window, and she crawls on top of me in bed and kisses me. I've wanted this for years, wanted it like having powers of my own, and her lips feel better on mine than every cheek kiss she's given me as a friend. This isn't some quick kiss either, it has life to it. Her hands touch me all over and I give in and explore her too.

Everything about this kiss feels like she's telling me that she'll be sad to see me go.

When she starts taking off my shirt and telekinetically closes the door, it tells me something else.

TWENTY-TWO
HALO KNIGHT

MARIBELLE

Hunting is finally paying off thanks to the Cloaked Phantom.

Working alchemy circuits such as pharmacies and hospitals hasn't given me any intel except that some alchemists would rather burn by my phoenix fire than betray Luna's honor. But thankfully there's nothing like a ceremonial constellation that gets ordinary people itching for abilities of their own, because stars forbid celestials to have something that only belongs to us. Tonight is divided into two groups: those who will partner with alchemists to become specters and those who don't want to open themselves up to persecution for having real powers, so they seek out imaginary ones.

I tracked down a youngish Brew dealer tonight in Alphabet City and I slam her against a black van in a parking lot. She seems to understand fear as my fire-orb illuminates her face. The same for her would-be client as he drives away. I couldn't be happier about ruining his night and her payday.

The dealer releases her hold on the Brew. The vial shatters against the ground and gold liquid flows under my boot. "Please don't hurt me," she says.

The dark yellow fire-orb spins around my palm like a burning planet.

"Where is Luna?"

"Who?"

"My sources have already told me that Luna Marnette is heading up this operation," I say. The dealer is sweating as I inch the fire closer to her face. "Tell me where to find her unless you want to spend the night as a pile of ashes."

She's crying as she looks away from me. "I'm not lying! I don't even know who this Luna person is, okay? I got laid off and needed a job and my cousin knows someone who knows someone. I've only been doing this for a week, I swear!"

"Then who's your boss?"

"I don't know. I get a call from an unknown number telling me what time to pick up my vials at the Light Sky Tower. That's it!"

The Light Sky Tower. For all the work Luna was doing with studying the stars to plot her next move, residing in the tallest building in the city makes a lot of sense.

My parents dreamed of working with architects to build apartments and schools for celestials that were higher than most, but the reception wasn't well received because the powerless feared that would only result in more celestials who could be strengthened under the stars and become so strong that we could never be overpowered. This is how deep gleamphobia runs in some of these people—we can't even live high up without being viewed as threats.

I close my fist and the fire-orb extinguishes.

The dealer is shaking as I release her.

"Get out of here," I say.

This is the most compassion I can offer her in Atlas's honor. Back when we didn't know Ness was posing as an acolyte named Hope to try and trick us into taking him back to Nova with us, Atlas was the one who tried comforting Hope after we were fed some sob story. I was ready to walk away. Sometimes I question why he wanted someone like me. Especially since he started dating me when my heart was the most vengeful it had ever been up until now.

I run full speed and my dark yellow wings of fire burst to life and carry me out the parking lot and across Alphabet City, where celestials and others have taken to the streets to party under the constellation. The Light Sky Tower is in downtown Manhattan too, and I can already make out the shiny prism of a building emerging from the cluster of others. It's risky going at this alone, but it would be riskier to give Luna and June and the others a chance to relocate if they haven't already. If there's a chance to avenge Atlas and save Eva and Carolina, I have to strike now.

I reach the Tower and am aiming straight for the penthouse. If they're not up there, I will work my way down, even if it takes all night to get through what I remember to be over one hundred floors. I fly around so the security guards patrolling the terrace on the south side of the building don't see me. They may not be able to mark me immediately as the daughter of terrorists they believe me to be, but it doesn't take binoculars to spot someone with dark yellow wings making her way to the roof. I'm still new at flying, so this is taking a lot out of me, but I push through for Mama and Papa and Atlas. The flames around my arms are diminishing until I give it one last push that drags a scream out of me. The wings burn brighter and fuller and I sail over the roof's balcony, crashing onto the floor and rolling besides a huge telescope.

I survey my surroundings as I catch my breath. The lights are off beyond the glass doors. There's no sign of life out here. No one seems to be guarding the penthouse—no security, no acolytes, no Casters. I pull the oblivion dagger out from the new sheath I fashioned into my power-proof vest and burn off the door's handle and let myself in. Lights immediately come on. Of course this place has sensors. No one pops out with a wand to take me down.

My psychic sense isn't signaling any danger. But I remain cautious because I still don't fully understand this power. If I knew everything there was to know about Sera's visions, I could better figure out how to tune mine.

I still haven't had time to fully process everything about what it means to be Sera and Bautista's daughter. I only know that the world would find more grounds to hate me because not only do they blame Mama and Papa for the Blackout, but my biological parents founded the Spell Walkers they've deemed villains. I think back to my sentiment about how I'm done saving the world that doesn't want to remember my parents as heroes, and I feel it doubly now. I'm including myself too.

Those who wouldn't save me don't deserve my saving.

Those who would've deserve my avenging.

I proceed through the penthouse. Starlight filters through some of the bay windows. There's a dining table that can seat a dozen but no sign of recent life. Black ceramic pots rest in the white built-in bookshelves. Above the fireplace is a painting of a woman climbing out of the central mouth of a nine-headed hydra. The chandelier is the icing on this very expensive cake.

The bedrooms are down the hallway. One reeks of sweat and sewage and there's dried skin on the pillowcase. All signs point to Stanton. I eagerly go to the next room, wanting more to confirm that the Blood Casters have indeed been here. I find newspaper clippings about Senator Iron on a bureau. This could've been Ness keeping tabs on his father. There's nothing out of the ordinary in the next bedroom but there are drops of blood on the bathroom floor. It's red, not gray like June's, so maybe this was Dione's room.

I keep my dagger ready as I enter the suite. It's eight times the size of the biggest bedroom I've had throughout my history of haven homes, which was the archive room of the Amy Silverstreak Library in Queens. The walk-in closet is empty. The bed is made, but sticking out from underneath is a handkerchief stained with blood. This had to have been Luna's quarters—living large and dying slowly as she tried to master immortality. I shudder thinking about Luna forcing Eva to heal her of her wounds and even going so far to try and get her sickness improved, even though Eva can't even heal a common cold. But if anyone is going to figure out how to use the blood of a healer to save herself, it's the alchemist who engineered potions combining multiple creature essences.

I exit the suite and continue down the hall when I see lightning flash outside the window. I was sure to check the weather this morning, and yesterday morning, since seeing that phoenix two nights ago, and there was no forecast for storms. There have been no sightings since then but those of us on the bridge that night weren't the only ones to see them flying into the city. Multiple clips surfaced online, but no one knows where the rider settled. I was able to identify the phoenix and do a little research. The phoenix is a light howler and in a fight can be as fast as its personal lightning strikes.

Thunder roars and the second lightning flash reveals the phoenix and its rider.

Danger buzzes through my body the closer they get.

The rider is wearing a mask with a metallic golden beak and confirms my suspicion—she's a Halo Knight, protector of phoenixes. The light howler hovers over the balcony as the rider hugs a crossbow to her chest, somersaults on top of the telescope, and fires an arrow at me. I spin out of harm's way with a one-handed cartwheel. The arrow shatters the door and glass rains behind me.

Two can play this game.

I'm quick with a fire-arrow and blast the crossbow out of her grip. She flips off the telescope and lands in a defensive stance. She's wearing the customary leather jacket with yellow feathered sleeves and finger-cut gloves. "You have no right possessing that sacred fire," the Halo Knight says with fury and heartbreak in her voice as if I killed a phoenix right in front of her.

"I inherited my powers—"

Danger.

A dagger drops out of the Halo Knight's feathered sleeve and she hurls it at me. I shift in time for the dagger to sail past my head. The Halo tackles me back inside the penthouse and pins my shoulders with her knees. She fidgets with a small pocket in her black leather belt and I horizontally levitate into the air, grab on to her, and spin rapidly until she must be dizzy before slamming her down on the floor.

I punch the golden beak, knocking the mask fully off her face.

The Halo Knight has dark eye shadow over her intense glare, a long nose that rounds out like a button, sun-kissed cheeks that are flushed from the fight, full lips that are cracked like she's been biting them, and dark hair that's been braided into a crown that's coming undone.

Then her foot connects into my back and I roll off of her. We pick ourselves up and charge, locked in a dance of physical combat. She shoulder rolls across the dining table and hurls a chair my way. I dodge and she closes in on me quickly. I go for a crescent kick but she sneaks under my leg with an uppercut that I block. I use my power to flip over her, but she beautifully times her sweep kick to my landing and knocks me onto my back.

Halo Knights are self-appointed guardians trained by those who came before them to protect phoenixes against all human dangers—traffickers, hunters, alchemists. Seeing as all my enemies have been people, I've never had to fight a Halo Knight before.

I wonder if all their skills are as otherworldly as this one.

"What do you want from me?" I ask from the floor.

"Your blood, Spell Walker," she says.

"That line runs around the block," I say. My dark yellow wings carry me off the floor and I charge a fire-orb while hovering over the Halo Knight.

She runs away from me and whistles at her phoenix. "STRIKE!"

The light howler sways on its black talons as a ray of lightning spits out of its throat. I glide out of the way before the lightning strike can blow a hole through my body, but as it blasts apart the fireplace, the aftershock throws me across the room and I slam against the painting of the woman and the hydra. Colors dance across my vision as the Halo Knight crouches over me and stabs my arm with a needle.

"No more fire out of you," the Halo Knight says as she waves a tiny dart in my face. "No-Fly Tranquilizer. The same used to sedate phoenixes. You have roughly three minutes before you're unconscious."

I'll be impressed if I can make it three minutes. I want to punch her but I can't get my mind to connect with my fist.

"My parents were slaughtered at the Museum of Natural Creatures protecting a newborn century phoenix," the Halo Knight says.

The night Atlas was killed. "That wasn't me. The Halo Knights were dead by the time I arrived with the other Spell Walkers. We saved the century phoenix."

"Where is she?"

"Dead now. You have the Blood Casters to blame for that."

The elevator dings. The silver plate indicates that someone is coming from the sixtieth floor.

The Halo stands. "Is that them?" she asks.

"I don't know, I'm not psychic—well, long story." I'm beginning to feel delirious. "It could be Blood Casters or security since your pet blew apart a wall."

"Roxana isn't my pet."

I'm slipping into sleep, I can't get into the politics of her phoenix right now. "Get me out of here. When I wake up I will tell you everything about my powers and connect you with Emil Rey, who would've been there when your parents were murdered."

"Why would I trust you?"

"I want the Blood Casters dead too . . ."

The Halo Knight looks back and forth between the elevator and Roxana before she drags me by my legs to the balcony. The phoenix sinks onto its belly as the Halo rests me onto Roxana's feathered head that smells like rainwater. Spellwork rings through the penthouse, quickly drowned out by the heavy flapping of wings and thunder and rain as we fly away from danger. Then nothing as I fall asleep above the city.

TWENTY-THREE
SILVER AND SAPPHIRE

BRIGHTON

I'm so hot that I'm pulled out of a dream where Prudencia telekinetically carries me into the sky and kisses me with the moon behind her.

Prudencia's head is nestled against my left shoulder as my scaly arm is burning up like it's trapped inside a fireplace. The heat spreads across my body, and as much as I don't want to let her go, I slide out from under Prudencia. I step over the used condom and put on my boxers so I can get some ice-cold water to go with the medicine I need badly to cool down my temperature. I fall to my knees and I don't realize I'm screaming until Prudencia snaps out of bed in nothing but the bra and underwear she put back on after we had sex.

"Brighton, what's wrong?" Prudencia asks and her touch burns me even more.

I flinch. "It's hot, I'm so hot—AHHH!"

There must be some inferno around my heart. The poison is eating me alive.

Emil runs into the room with groggy eyes.

I hold my shaking arm and it hurts to breathe so much that I almost don't want to. "Emil, this is it, bro; I'm dying." I scream again as I punch down on the floor with my left fist to try and fight through the pain. It's a losing battle. I grind my teeth so hard they might crack and go down my throat and choke me to death before this poison can finish its dirty work.

"You're going to be okay," Prudencia lies with tears flowing down her cheeks.

Wesley, Ruth, and Iris are gathered outside the doorway as Esther cries down the hall.

Emil hugs me. "I love you, Bright."

The heat spikes to a whole new level and I shove Emil because I sense something explosive within me. My scaly arm glows like burning coal and I wish someone would press a wand to my head and put me out of misery. My vision becomes foggy like heavy clouds of smoke and clears moments later and I find something impossible.

My arm is blazing in silver and sapphire flames.

For a tenth of a second I trick myself into thinking the Reaper's Blood is working, until the fire incinerates my flesh and bones. Blood pools around my knees. I must look like someone

185

in a grotesque horror film. The flames erupt all around me until I'm completely consumed. I'll be nothing but ashes in moments. My shoulder tenses as a fist punches its way out, stretching until the rest of my arm follows.

The silver and sapphire flames disperse from everywhere except my good-as-new arm.

"It worked! The Reaper's Blood worked!"

I break out into a laugh, sweat and tears still on my face, and as the fire from the century phoenix vanishes within my reformed hand, I don't see anyone else laughing or celebrating. They're all stunned, but it's the horror in Prudencia's eyes and the dread in Emil's that really sets me back.

"What?" I ask.

I investigate my body to see if I'm missing something bad. But I only see something amazing.

"How do you feel?" Emil asks.

My temperature is cooling down. My arm is sore and stiff but nothing that flexing my fingers and some stretching can't fix. "Happy," I say with a smile that feels as big as the one I had when Prudencia and I stopped to catch our breath during sex—a smile that has felt buried in my face for years and was finally freed. I have wanted powers since I was a kid; I never gave up on that dream like Emil did. The Reaper's Blood seemed like it was going to take my life when instead it improved it infinitely. "I'm starting over with powers. It's everything I've wanted—almost everything. Only two out of the three essences have manifested so far, but I don't want to be greedy. This is a great start!"

I'm so excited I actually jump up and down, pumping my

new fist that's nearly identical to the one I've always had minus the nicks I've gained the past month from all the fights against specters and acolytes. I notice a thin white scar from where the fire ate away at my arm and trace it. Hydra essence killed Dad but it saved me.

I'm strong enough to save the world with these new powers.

"I want to start training," I say, moving for the door.

"You should probably put more clothes on first," Wesley says.

I'm still in my boxers. I don't care. They all just witnessed a miracle.

"Settle down," Prudencia says. "It's three in the morning and you were literally just on fire."

"But it stopped hurting. Emil, was it that bad for you?"

Emil shakes his head. "No. My fire never hurt me like that. Pru is right; let's take this slow. Century phoenixes are different than gray suns. I heard how war-hungry Gravesend's cries were; we don't know how that's going to play out for you."

Great, now they're going to blame all my instincts on some breed temperaments. I'm eager because if there's a chance my mother is still alive we're going to have to move fast to save her.

I sway on the spot and this dizziness feels different than all the other times since the Reaper's Blood has impacted my system. Then I remember what happened to Emil and Maribelle shortly after using their phoenix fire for the first time. "I'm going to faint," I say. I think about quickly reaching the bed so I can have a safe landing and I suddenly lunge forward so fast that I roll across the mattress and crash into the desk by the window. Prudencia massages the back of my head as she helps me onto the bed. "Did

187

I just swift-run? I wasn't even trying to do that!"

The powers are all manifesting. It's happening; it's all really happening. I rest my head on the pillow because I'm fading, but I'm already so excited to wake up knowing what's waiting for me when I do. That enthusiasm clearly isn't shared by anyone else in the room.

It's almost as if everyone would rather see me dead than alive with power.

TWENTY-FOUR
INFINITY SAVIOR

BRIGHTON

It wasn't a dream.

I sit up in bed and the thin white scar above my bicep proves every nightmarish thing I went through in the middle of the night to get my powers. I don't know what was the final push to access them—the Cloaked Phantom? Near death? Sex with someone I wanted to live for? Time?—but I'm not questioning this victory. I take a selfie on my phone to document this historic morning. I don't upload it yet. Timing is really important when it comes to social media, and my mind is already spinning with possibilities on the Brighton of New York feature that will show the world my humble beginnings on my journey to becoming the strongest specter ever.

Prudencia must've woken up already, so I get dressed to find her.

The glorious smell of breakfast doesn't make me nauseous today, and Wesley is in the kitchen spreading peanut butter and jelly on some bagels beside a steaming plate of hash browns, a pitcher of freshly squeezed orange juice, and bowls of sliced cantaloupe and kiwis.

"Morning, Super Specter," Wesley says before turning his attention to the empty baby bottle that's boiling in the pot. "Good sleep?"

"Does it count as sleep if I passed out because my body overheated from phoenix fire?"

"Whatever it was, you did more of it than the rest of us," Wesley says. "Esther wouldn't stop crying. I had to take her for a run."

"Perfect segue. Judging by Dione's powers I know swift-speed works differently for specters and celestials, but you mind giving me some pointers later? I need to get all my abilities in shape."

Wesley finishes making a plate of food and grabs one of the sterilized bottles. "I'm only saying yes so you can take Esther on a nighttime run the next time you wake her up. Emil's down at the beach if you want to bring him some breakfast. You should definitely eat everything you can. You'll need the energy for all the running around."

He goes back toward his room and someone shifts on the couch. Prudencia is asleep in her *Every Body Is Super* shirt with her hair hanging off the cushion. Why didn't she stay in bed with me? Did she stay up talking about me with Emil? I won't bother her now, but it's one of many questions I got to ask her. She never explained what brought her to my room last night. I thought we might talk about it after having sex, but she put some clothes back on, wrapped my arm around her, and went to sleep.

I prepare breakfast plates and carry them down to the beach on a tray. Any other day I would've complained about how hot the sun is but this is nothing compared to being encased in phoenix fire hours ago. Emil is standing in the water, the waves crashing against his already-tight jeans, which are going to be impossible to take off when drenched. I call his name three times before he finally hears me over the wind.

He's dripping as he walks over. "How are you feeling?"

I set down the tray and hand him his plate with the bagel and extra fruit.

"I feel ready to put this new lease on life to good use. The sooner I can figure out these powers, the sooner we can make a move against the Blood Casters." I believe in the stars now more than ever and I pray to every last one that Ma hasn't been killed because of me. Especially not after how horrible I was to her on our last phone call. "Maybe we can save our mother."

Emil stops reaching for his breakfast as if he's lost his appetite thinking about Ma's fate. Not having an answer is unsettling, and I keep assuming the worst but I can't operate that way until we know for sure. I'm not giving in to the grief because it'll make me weak and powerless like when Dad died. Not when I stand to be stronger and more powerful than ever—than anyone.

"I want to save her too, but we can't rush into this. My powers aren't working and you're new to yours. If something has happened to Ma, then—"

"Then we make sure they don't get away with it," I interrupt.

Emil lets out a deep sigh. "By locking them up in the Bounds, right? You need my help with the phoenix powers, but I'm not doing that if you're trying to become some assassin."

There's so much wrong with that, but I bite my tongue. Emil seems to be forgetting that learning new skills and absorbing information has always been easier for me. I was also working the camera during all his training lessons with Atlas on how to pull the fire out of him. I can do this myself if I have to, but I don't want to.

"The dream has always been to save the world with you— the Reys of Light! The Blood Casters won't stand a chance against us. We'll be . . . What was it I called you when I was trying to figure out your hero name? Uh . . . Unkillable Kings! Though we should rework that to Infinity Kings for branding. You're the Infinity Son and I'll be . . ." Given the nature of the potion and my deathly powers there's one name that feels right— Infinity Reaper. But between not having the ghost powers and Emil not wanting me to kill, I abandon the name. "I'm the Infinity Savior."

We fist-bump and whistle, but it's so halfhearted on his end that it's getting harder to keep a lid on my frustration.

"I know my extra shot at life isn't as flashy as you being reborn in phoenix fire, but I'm alive and I thought my brother would be excited about that."

"Chill out, Bright, you know I am, but that doesn't mean I'm hyped about the direction you're moving in. I'm not getting caught up in our branding when it's more important to figure

192

out the binding potions." He's studying my face like he's taking me in for the first time ever. "If we can miraculously brew the potion, I'm scared you won't drink one with me. I'm scared of who you'll become."

He's not technically my twin anymore, but we grew up close like we were. I can talk to him about anything and sometimes it feels like I have but nothing hits harder than words we've never exchanged: I scare him.

"I'm not going to lie, bro, there's no part of me that's eager to get rid of these powers. I've been waiting for this moment forever, but that doesn't mean I'll actually understand the downsides of gleamcrafting until I'm deep in it. This isn't going to work, though, if you treat me like some power addict from the jump."

"You literally risked your life for the most dangerous combination of powers," Emil counters.

"To not die and help fight back against the real dangers in this city. I know it's not a choice you would've made, but I promise I'll do everything I can to earn your trust. We're a team. Can we hug this out already?"

I stand and help him up. This hug reminds me of this past June, when Emil was missing Dad during Pride month. Last year our parents offered to accompany us to the parade, but Emil wanted to have fewer eyes on him as he entered that space for the first time, so only Prudencia and I went with him. He'd told Dad and Ma they could join next time and Emil regretted that so hard this past Pride when Dad wasn't around. I gave him the hug that Dad would've given him, which always felt like its own superpower.

I hope Emil feels easier around me. I've been messy with

him, even before we got involved with the Spell Walkers, and it's going to take more than a chat on the beach to fix a brotherhood that I was ready to move across the country to get away from, but I'm sure we'll be stronger than ever before. Literally.

I pat him on the back. "We good?"

"We will be," Emil says. He nods toward the cottage, to where Prudencia is making her way down to us. "Are you two good?"

"I hope so. Did she mention anything to you last night?"

"I mean, I put one and one together, but we didn't talk about any of that."

It wouldn't bother me personally if Prudencia did get into that with Emil. What matters is knowing where we stand.

"Morning," Prudencia says as she joins us.

I want to lean in for a kiss, but that doesn't feel right.

I'm getting worked up over the confusing energy in this triangle of ours. Everything has changed and everything is changing. I'm a specter. Prudencia and I kissed and had sex after years of nothing. Emil might be feeling like a third wheel in the same way Prudencia has understandably felt the same and that I have too. Then there's figuring out what we are to each other now that I'm alive to answer that unspoken question.

"How'd you sleep?" I ask.

"On and off," Prudencia says. She glances at Emil, who takes the hint.

"I'm going to start some research on your powers," Emil says.

"Let's kick off training this afternoon," I say.

We fist-bump and whistle and our connection isn't quite there but it's better than before. I'll take that progress.

"You two must've had a great chat," Prudencia says. "I don't know if I'm more surprised by the hug or Emil helping you train."

"We're working through our trust and I want to do the same with you, Pru. I got to cut right to it. Do you actually care about me romantically? Or did last night only happen because I was dying?"

The wind blows back her hair as she looks down at the sand. "I wanted to be with you because I wanted to be with you. I let down my guard because you showed me a side of you that finally made me feel safe but I don't know if I'm going to matter as much anymore now that you're a specter."

"Pru, I'm not choosing my powers over you. We can fight to have it all like Iris and Eva, Maribelle and Atlas, Wesley and Ruth."

"I don't want to be some power couple, Brighton," Prudencia says with an edge in her voice. "I want to be a person in the world who isn't hated for who I am."

"I want to help create that world for you!" I go back to what Emil said and I can see the same concerns building on her face. "Don't fear me. Trust me."

I hold her hand and I'm so relieved when she squeezes mine. I get my lips ready when she leans in, but she kisses me on the cheek.

"You're on probation, Brighton Miguel Rey. I will telekinetically throw you across the world if you break your promises."

"No need, Prudencia Yolanda Mendez." I stare into her brown eyes and she starts walking back to the cottage with a big enough grin. "Hey, Pru! Want to help me become the most powerful specter in the entire universe and the most followed person on Instagram?"

Prudencia's hand drops to her side and her fingers wiggle and a bucket's worth of sand sweeps into me. She's already running away and laughing and I chase after her, eager to learn how to run at swift-speed so we can have more ordinary moments made extraordinary because of who we are.

I'm finally on the path to having everything I've ever wanted.

TWENTY-FIVE
TRAINING: BRIGHTON EDITION

BRIGHTON

If our lives were a fictional TV show, season one would've focused on Emil and season two is all about me. Viewers would remember how I cheered for Emil during his training and had his back during the other fights, but they would be more hyped for me knowing I've wanted powers more than he ever has. Our show—*The Infinity Kings* or *The Infinity Cycle*—would have a slow start because Emil isn't necessarily the most exciting hero if we're being honest. But then, right as viewers fear they might have to say goodbye to me as I'm swallowed in silver and sapphire flames, I emerge stronger than ever. I'm the absolute fan favorite who will carry the series forward.

I'm embracing this spotlight.

I hold up my phone until I find the right angle for a selfie. I don't want to reveal anything in the house that could identify where we are but the sunlight spilling through the window is too harsh on my face. Just when I think I've got it, my phone is being wrestled out of my grip, and I'm nervous my regenerated hand is somehow acting on its own, but the phone flies behind me and straight to Prudencia.

Her eyes stop glowing and she places the phone on the floor where she's sitting with a notebook open. "Next time it goes straight into the fireplace."

"It's not too late," Emil adds while typing something into Ruth's laptop.

I drop down onto the couch. "I'm excited! This is huge for me; I want to capture these moments."

I've taken pictures on big days over the years: Emil and me on our sixteenth birthday, which we spent playing new video games while our parents catered to us all day; before my first date with Nina and then another with her kissing my cheek when we left the pizzeria; when I hit ten thousand subscribers on YouTube; right before I stepped onto the stage at graduation to deliver my salutatorian speech. The one that haunts me the most is from the morning of Dad's funeral when I didn't want to get out of bed. But it's also the most important. Before becoming a specter, the biggest change in my life was coming home after the burial and becoming the man of the house.

"Bright, we got to get the research done so we can understand your complex powers."

"Trial and error is all the more reason to document our sessions."

"So this isn't for your series?"

The way he asks that is as if I've been trying to hide my intention. I'm not sneaky. "Some of it will be, yeah. Just like we featured you on my accounts we're going to do the same for me. The world needs to know they've got another hero on their side." I can see it in his eyes that he thinks I'm only doing this for me. "We should do a live chat. Let everyone know what the Reys of Light can do." He looks like he might counter, so I add, "Trust is a two-way street, bro."

Emil nods. "You're right. But we should know what we're actually working with here before you plan some big reveal."

"I second that," Prudencia says.

"And I third it," I say. "We're all on the same page."

We divide and conquer. Emil is in charge of phoenix research, Prudencia is looking into ghosts, and I'm on hydra duty. I'm tempted to get my phone back so I can get a selfie out there and tease my big news. But I focus for an hour straight. This reminds me of my study groups before finals, except this time the world will be grading us on how well we manage to save everyone while not causing more harm.

Once Emil finishes his tofu salad, he shares his findings on century phoenixes, beginning with the basics about how they're rare because they only spawn every hundred years; we already knew that. He couldn't find any record of any other specter with that breed's power, which will make me stand out. But ultimately the problem with all phoenix specters is no one has ever come back as themselves. There's always new identities, and in Emil's case, he doesn't even have the memories of his past life.

Luna claimed the Reaper's Blood would heighten those powers to operate properly, between the purity of the creatures and the Crowned Dreamer elevating the gleam, but this has remained unproven.

"I found this on the Halo Knights' website: 'Century phoenixes are restless, war-hungry fighters with survival instincts so fierce they will kill anyone who threatens their lives because they don't want to be away from the world for another hundred years.' That's just . . ." Emil runs his hand through his hair, and his eyes glaze. "I felt Gravesend's cries when she hatched and I could tell she was ready for a fight, but I can't imagine her becoming a killer."

"The wilds are different," I say.

Prudencia is writing in Bautista's journal. "What I'm more concerned about is if your instincts will be affected by the powers. We'll monitor your behaviors, but you have to tell us if you feel—"

"Murdery?" I mime cutting someone's throat. Emil shakes his head and Prudencia looks away. "I'm kidding."

But they don't say anything. They're already treating me like I've wiped out an entire city. I keep reminding myself that I'm going to prove everyone wrong. I'm the right hero for this war.

Prudencia almost throws her phone because she's frustrated with the lack of information on specters with ghost blood, even coming up empty in some more taboo corners of the internet. We didn't know those specters existed until last month and the rest of the world hasn't caught on yet either. The only information Prudencia finds are people's accounts of being haunted, which doesn't do anything for us. It's a shame that I can't call up Orton, who died in his own phoenix flames, or invite June to an exclusive Ghost Specter of New York feature for my series.

The Global Hydrus Society has a wealth of information on hydras; I should've turned to them sooner instead of random articles. There's a video of a golden-strand hydra running across a beach, occasionally bursting into swift-speed, which Wesley will help me master later, but when the hydra runs through the palm trees she blends in—damn near perfectly. The Hydrus employee explains what's happening and I almost lose my head.

"So golden-strands live on tropical beaches," I say, so excited that I cut off Emil as he tries telling us about the diet of century phoenixes. "And they can apparently camouflage themselves against the sand, trees, and ocean. That's an extra power I wasn't expecting!"

"So it's geared toward nature?" Prudencia asks.

"I don't know, but powers work differently between creatures and humans anyway. I'm not seeing anything about golden-strands being able to regrow their limbs, only their heads, and I got my arm back obviously," I say, admiring my handiwork. "Since I can't walk through walls without the ghost power maybe I can still sneak up on the Blood Casters with this new power."

"Yeah, maybe," Emil says.

He's not the only hero anymore and he's going to have to get used to it.

Knowing what I know now about the camouflaging, it's especially heroic how I prevented Luna from drinking the Reaper's Blood. She would've been more than unkillable; she would've been lethal. I can picture Luna fading into the homes of her enemies, cloaking herself to gather intel, and incinerating them before leaving. That's only one dangerous combination she could've used with all of those powers.

Once I'm caught up on everything about golden-strands, I click around the site and find links about known hydra specters. Dione is listed with a picture of her captured from a surveillance camera. Her blood comes from a hillkiller and that breed is apparently known for living in forests and multiplying their heads in minutes. I switch over to the profile of a man, Lucas Samford, who has the blood of a rockborn hydra. Rockborns are the toughest to decapitate with their boulder-like exteriors, but once successful, they need weeks before they can grow another head. It took enforcers hours before they decapitated Lucas and burned his body in phoenix fire.

I go through several of these pages before landing on the history of a specter who called himself the Blood Beast. He was among the first wave of Blood Casters, back in the glory days when Bautista was an idolized hero for fighting against them. The Blood Beast had the essence from the death-throated hydra, notoriously the most vicious breed, and in his three months of having powers he had a high body count. An anonymous acolyte got his hands on Luna's journals, tempted to infuse himself with the death-throated powers to become as dangerous, but the trials the Blood Beast had gone through proved so demanding, like eating rotten raw meat for every meal, that the acolyte ultimately gave up on the dream of becoming a specter and published the findings online to inspire others to do the same.

The Blood Beast didn't live long. There's a video of his death with a warning for sensitive material. I put on my earphones and press play. It's gory. The Blood Beast is dashing around with six legs, six arms, and three heads. He annihilates enforcers who were relatively new at the time and smaller in numbers. But eventually, just like when Orton burned out, the Blood Beast must've pushed himself too hard and all his body parts fall off him until he's nothing but a chest surrounded by heads and arms and legs. He looks like a life-sized doll waiting for someone to assemble him.

If I push myself this far, would I die?

There's a blur and wind and I jump when Wesley taps my shoulder. "What are you watching?"

I slam down the laptop. "Uh . . ."

"You watching porn while your brother and girlfriend work?" Wesley asks.

"Not his girlfriend," Prudencia singsongs as she smiles my way.

"And not porn," I add. "It's just a screwed-up video of a specter who pushed his limits." They don't seem convinced but I know Emil and Prudencia well enough that they would hate watching that. "Wesley, we good to train?"

Wesley smirks and dashes out of the house and down toward the beach.

"I'll take that as a yes. Break time!"

"It's not a break. You're about to work some more," Emil says.

"What's work for you is fun for me."

I grab my phone and chase after Wesley. He's already lying in the sand of course and acting like he's asleep, as if it's taken me forever to reach him. It won't be long until I have control over my swift-speed.

Wesley introduces me to some stretches that are not kind on me. I've always knocked Emil's posture, but all the time I've spent editing videos on my laptop hasn't done me any favors either. Emil records us on my phone while Prudencia exercises her power by lifting herself in a pull-up position.

"The most important rule when running with swift-speed is to always be several steps ahead of yourself," Wesley says. "If you take off aimlessly, you'll fly over your bed, or worse, almost straight into a moving truck. Not that I know of any thirteen-year-old who was so eager for a new video game that he almost got flattened on the highway."

After Wesley is done lying about his past, he explains how much more aware of my surroundings I have to be than anyone running at standard speed because even though I can get away from dangers faster, I can also find myself facing them first too. My power is tricky since hydras can't keep up momentum for longer distances like Wesley and other swift-speeded celestials can. I could lose steam right in the middle of a battle and not be able to escape.

"Let's try it out," I say.

I take a sprinter's stance and focus on reaching the coastline. I expect the same jolt forward as all the roller coasters I rode on with Dad—always front row because he loved that adrenaline rush—but my running is as ordinary as ever. Wesley asks me to take deep breaths, which I do. To not think about it, but also concentrate, which I think I do. My burst of speed happened so effortlessly last night when I thought I was going to faint and I accidentally overshot my new power and ended up on the floor. But even that's not happening right now.

I call "Time-out!" to Wesley and "Cut!" to Emil.

The sun is beating me down. I thought this was going to be easier. Instead I feel like a joke in front of Prudencia, who is telekinetically juggling pears and apples with one hand and building a mound of sand with her other. She's going to be so powerful, and I'm going to be a one-hit wonder of a specter whose powers never surface again.

"Slow start," Wesley says.

I wipe the sweat off my head as I realize he's joking. "Not funny."

"Quick pause," Wesley says. Before I can tell him to shut up with the jokes he dashes away and returns with bottles of water for us. "Peace offering." He sits beside me on the sand. "It's a fun power, but it's not always an easy one, Brighton. I grew up with mine, which you know I abused too."

"After your parents kicked you out," I say, remembering our Spell Walkers of New York interview.

"Before too. I wasn't robbing anyone for my own survival yet but my parents were always so frustrated with me. They didn't plan on having me and gave it a shot. Big regrets since they couldn't ever keep up with me or get me to slow down. Instead of going home after school I kept exploring the city and one day my father told me that if I didn't honor curfew he was going to change the locks. I didn't think they'd kick me out; I was twelve. But they meant it."

Between Ruth's parents conceiving her to groom her into an all-powerful celestial and Wesley's parents locking him out for asserting some independence with his powers, it's a wonder Ruth and Wesley are so loving to their daughter. Really makes me appreciate how lucky I was to have Dad and Ma—to have Ma still. . . .

"My point is that swift-speed is a survival power. You can use it to rescue others and to save yourself." He pats me on the shoulder. "I don't look back that often. I pay attention to where I'm going next. And where I'm going next is inside that beautiful sea because I'm melting in this heat."

He dashes straight toward the water and runs on top of it, which I didn't realize he could do. I've followed a lot of his media hits over the years and I'm already daydreaming about running up walls like he has. But this is some advanced skill. Strong currents of water trail him like he's a Jet Ski until all of a sudden he drops beneath the surface.

I bust out laughing and turn to Emil. "Did you record that?"

"You told me to cut," Emil says.

"You had one job, bro." My laugh winds down when Wesley doesn't come back up. "Where is he?"

Prudencia runs toward the sea and is trying to part it but it's going to take a lot more than juggling fruit before she's strong enough to do that.

"There!" Emil points.

Wesley is not too far off, but he's struggling to stay above the surface. I run for him and my body is thrust forward so quickly that I might have whiplash. Sand kicks up around me as I pass

206

Prudencia. Water splashes around my ankles in a matter of seconds. I'm dashing! Dashing on water! I'm a heartbeat away from Wesley but I don't know how to hit the brakes on my power safely, so I just stop and fall beneath the surface. I tumble around for moments that feel longer than it took for me to run here. Wesley helps me out and he's laughing as I blow out all the water that shot up my nose.

"I can't believe it worked!" Wesley says as he paddles perfectly to stay afloat. "The victim-in-distress is the oldest trick in the book! Even I didn't fall for that as a kid!"

I almost snap at him, but I laugh instead because this is huge. I ran with purpose and direction and the adrenaline rush of needing to save him gave me the charge I was missing. Not only that, my first successful dash was on water. This is what I'm talking about—I'm next level.

We're swimming back to shore and Emil is standing there shocked. Of course he didn't manage to get this on camera either, but I'll let it slide this time since we really thought Wesley was in danger. Not that there's anything powerless Emil could've done about it.

Wesley pats me on the back. "You just needed some motivation. Let's try again now that you're more familiar."

I make sure Emil is recording before Wesley coaches me further. Thank the stars because I've really got the hang of this. It's like riding a bike. I dash all the way down to a distant neighbor's bonfire and reverse, making it back in under four minutes. I never realized it would feel so draining, but it's like when Emil described carrying his fire as heavy. Wielding gleam isn't easy.

Those of us who can endure are the real champions of this world.

After a few more successful runs, Wesley challenges me to a game of tag to test my abilities to keep sight of a moving target in the event I ever need to chase down other swift-speeders like he has in the past. Time moves differently when you can run at an above-average rate. It feels like I've been running for an hour, and when I stop to catch my breath, Prudencia tells me it's only been ten minutes. I call it quits before I can catch him.

Wesley skids by me, sand kicking up. "That was a better start, Brighton. You'll catch me one day."

"I'll outrun you one day," I say with a grin.

And that's a promise.

Over a massive lunch where I finish devouring the last of my steamed potatoes, brown rice, and black bean burger, Emil discovers that the city has a special guest. A Halo Knight and her phoenix have been spotted around New York, and they're causing rainstorms everywhere they fly. They were last seen at the Light Sky Tower last night, which she'd broken into, but there aren't any details to support why. That's her business and has nothing to do with us.

Emil is fascinated by the clips circulating online, but I return my attention to my own phone so I can rewatch the videos of me dashing. I realize now that when I was running toward that bonfire that Wesley should've followed me with the camera because the current footage is basically just me taking off and returning a few minutes later. It's easy enough to edit out the dead space, but maybe I can layer it with some voice-overs with what was going through my head; I haven't seen anyone else do that. The other videos of me chasing after Wesley are a good demonstration of my speed and these will be safe to share online.

The second I'm free from helping Emil and Prudencia clean up our plates, I bring my laptop to the backyard and review all the old footage of Atlas teaching Emil how to reach within and call for his power. There are so many reasons to miss Atlas, but right now I wish one of my favorite heroes were around to coach me the way he did Emil. This would be epic to share for an in memoriam piece.

I'm trying to center myself mentally when Emil and Prudencia join me outside.

"Studied up?" Prudencia asks.

"Ready to ace this," I say. I feel confident like this is an exam.

I prop my phone against the fence, hit record, and confirm that I'm visible before trying to cast fire. In the video, Atlas tells Emil to visualize his power to cast it, but that's easier said than done. I'm imagining the silver and sapphire flames in my possession, even the heat when it felt like I was burning alive, but that doesn't instantly conjure them. Atlas had it easier. He got to grow up with his powers at the same time he was learning how to talk and string together sentences. It's a lot harder for those of us learning later in life.

I can't even get a flicker.

"Come on," I say under my breath.

"What are you feeling?" Prudencia asks.

"Frustrated. I'm concentrating and visualizing everything like Atlas instructed."

Prudencia takes my hand and settles me. "It's more than that. Papí always said powers have to be powered. Frustration is holding you back. When I use my telekinesis, I'm giving myself control in a world where I don't always feel like I have some. What do you feel, Emil?"

"It always starts as fear," Emil says. "Like when Orton was trying to kill you, Bright. When I wanted to protect you more than anything, the fire came to life."

Prudencia releases me. "Dig deeper, Brighton."

"Don't just try to drag fire out of you," Emil adds.

I close my eyes.

I have my own fears. Emil's powers activated because he wanted to protect me, but I went for the Reaper's Blood because it meant that I wouldn't ever have to fear death again. I don't want to go through what Dad went through, I want the fullest life possible, and the phoenix fire gave me the second chance I desperately needed. Heat flushes over me and I don't dare peek to see anything that's happening; I keep stoking the flames. Emil and Prudencia are right; this is about more than me being able to cast fire and maybe one day fly. I might never be untouchable as a ghost, but with my hydra and phoenix powers I won't have to fear an easy death and will be able to save so many lives. I'm hotter and hotter thinking about how this world will celebrate me—magazine covers, documentaries on my life, book signings for my sure-to-be ghostwritten memoir, statues erected in my honor, teams of celestials and specters uniting under my watch.

I will have infinite glory.

From somewhere deep within I hear a pained screech like a phoenix being killed, like Gravesend being stabbed. I open my eyes and silver and sapphire flames are spiraling around my fists like snakes on fire.

Emil and Prudencia are staring at me, caution in their eyes, as if they're worried I'm going to be in tremendous pain again, but I'm fine. The weight of the flames isn't even as heavy as Emil made it out to be—or maybe I'm simply stronger than him.

"What do I do with these now?" I ask about the flames with a laugh.

"You can pull them back in," Emil says. "Think about grounding yourself and—"

Grounding myself is the last thing I want to do.

I thrust my fists toward the sky and bolts of silver and sapphire fire shoot into the air with a thunderous phoenix screech and explode above us like fireworks.

This power thrumming through me is the beginning.

The world will worship the Infinity Savior.

TWENTY-SIX
BRIGHTON OF NEW YORK

BRIGHTON

A couple hours after casting fire, I finish editing the video of my dreams. I project the final cut from my laptop onto the TV and I gather everyone in the living room—Emil, Prudencia, Iris, Wesley, and Ruth with Esther, who's asleep in her mother's arms.

"I promise you're not actually ready for this, but are you ready?" I ask.

I get an enthusiastic fist pump from Wesley and encouraging words from Ruth, but Emil, Prudencia, and Iris are a tougher audience. I respect that. As a creator, I always want people to like my work because they actually do and not just because they feel forced to pretend because it's me.

I hit play.

The video opens with darkness. Then, my voice: "The time

212

has come. . . ." I'm shown on the sand with a quick cut to me in the backyard. It must look pretty basic, but that's the point. These were my last ordinary moments before I consciously cast my new extraordinary powers. Then the screen splits. On the left I'm running, on the right I'm flicking my hand, but nothing happens. "For another Spell Walker to rise . . ." The focus is back on me on the beach, minutes after I ran across the sea to save Wesley, and I dash away from the camera, edited slightly to show me returning sooner than I did in real time because I scrapped the voice-over idea. Then it moves onto the most glorious moment in the backyard. I get chills watching myself, eyes closed in concentration, as wisps of smoke snaking around my wrists grow into the silver and sapphire flames. My eyes open, and while I grew up dreaming of the day that they would glow like some godlike corner of the universe, I still find these burning eclipses absolutely beautiful. We linger on my smile before shifting to quick cuts of me demonstrating my speed as I chase after one of the country's fastest celestials and me casting firebolts into the sky, the latter a talent that took us all by surprise. The video ends with me carrying fire in my hands before I dash out of sight; it took us a few tries to get that shot right, but we pulled it off.

"Incredible, right?" I ask.

"That's the trailer to a movie I'd watch," Wesley says.

"Very inspiring. You put all of that together so quickly too!" Ruth says.

"It's a shame you don't have footage of me sweeping sand in your face, but this works too," Prudencia says.

"It's pretty epic, Bright," Emil says.

Happiness surges through me, like watching my follower count increase in the past. "This is only meant to be a teaser of what's to come. My prologue, if you will."

Iris scoffs. "Then maybe you shouldn't open your story with a lie. I never cleared you to become a Spell Walker."

In the past twenty-four hours, I have been intimate with Prudencia for the first time, had a second shot at life, tapped into my new powers, and put together this video so I can finally have the big moment I've been dreaming about for years. Of course Iris has to ruin that.

"But you're down three team members," I say.

"Believe it or not, that hasn't affected my ability to count on my own."

"I've been in this fight when all I had was my camera. Now I have Emil's and Wesley's core powers—all in one host! We're trying to save Ma and Eva and you haven't been successful tracking them down alone. You need me."

Iris is staring at me but she seems to be looking through me. If I could read minds I'm sure all of her thoughts would be about Eva. "I might need you, but you won't be making that decision for me. There's nothing to suggest that our people haven't been killed already. So if all I have left is the legacy of the Spell Walkers, I'm going to make sure we don't do any more damage that will endanger celestials, and keep our numbers from decreasing any further so I don't have to suffer through another math lesson. The truth is, Brighton, I don't trust you."

She gets up and walks toward her room and I'm very tempted

214

to dash in front of her, but I control myself because I know that's out of line.

Working with the Spell Walkers has had many lows but it's also been a dream come true. As incredible as it would be to join the ranks like my brother and become even more famous than Bautista, I'm not going to let Iris put me in a corner like this. It's tough enough feeling like I'm on probation with Emil and Prudencia, but I'm not letting Iris have that power over me too.

"Her loss," I say.

"She's not saying you'll never be a Spell Walker," Prudencia says. "Just not right now."

I'm not going to sweat this because I have a lot to be proud of, even though I may never be an official Spell Walker and despite not getting all three sets of powers the Reaper's Blood promised. It'd be so easy to let Iris's slight get the best of me like when I didn't get to be valedictorian, but everything about me now is undisputedly unique. Someone can get better grades than me— while my focus was down because I was grieving, don't forget that—but it's not as if there's another specter running around who is going to stand a chance against me once I master my abilities.

I'm in a league of my own.

I grab my laptop and make a quick edit to the video, swapping out *Spell Walker* for *hero*. Before I do anything else I take a selfie, memorializing the Brighton whose extraordinary powers aren't known to the public. I type out my caption—*Brighton Rey just got a little Brighter. #BrightonOfNewYork*—and upload first on the Celestials of New York Instagram. Then I get the video up on YouTube and Twitter and I even finally cave in and make a

TikTok so I can dominate the primary online spaces. Every video has the event details for the livestream Emil and I are hosting in a couple hours on Instagram. I sit against the wall where I can charge my phone while hopping between all the apps and soaking up the comments. My views and following are skyrocketing, quickly catching up to Mr. Infinity Son himself.

There are so many questions about how I became a specter and I reply to some in my comments section, letting them know that all will be answered during the livestream. Followers around the world tell me all about their plans to watch—stay up late, be sneaky at school, take an early break at work.

I get a DM from Lore and they're happy that I'm doing better and they would love to do a Q&A in the near future. Even though I have more followers than them, Lore still has an impressive social reach to other important influencers whose radar I need to be on. My growth will be huge as the Infinity Savior, but I expect that's going to cap somewhere, so tapping into the audiences of the other influencers will be a great refresh. I promise Lore an interview when time allows; I have some missions to tend to first, after all.

"Someone wants to help make merchandise," I tell Prudencia while checking out the user's feed. It'd be helpful to have someone handle the administrative responsibilities and I can be the face of it all. "They seem legit."

"Why don't you follow up with them after getting ready? Your chat is in thirty minutes, superstar."

"Please make that my new nickname," I say.

"Dream on, dreamer," Prudencia says with a smile.

I'm having a hard time picking what to wear, especially without my full closet in front of me, until I remember every influencer who puts time into looking casual even though they controlled every single-sleeve roll and wrinkle. I don't need a tuxedo or some trying-too-hard-to-be-cool leather jacket. Ruth gives me her blessing to choose something from her closet, and even though she's not actively selling anything from her *Every Body Is Super* line, I make a mental note to credit her in the caption. I choose a blue shirt with white lettering since it's the closest one that matches my flames.

I go outside with Emil and Prudencia and the evening air is chilly. We go deep into the trees, finding a nondescript area with a couple rocks for us to sit on and enough moonlight so we can be seen. I review the talking points with Emil, making him repeat them back to me because I want this conversation to appear casual and we can't have that if he's sitting there with a notepad. Prudencia offers to hold the phone for us so we can stream at a wider angle, but I think it's going to be cozier if I'm shoulder to shoulder with Emil. This way I also get to see how many viewers are tuned in and read some of the comments.

"We're still not mentioning my past lives, right?" Emil asks.

We had this conversation back when we were doing the Spell Walkers of New York feature. "That's not my call. You and Pru were the ones who didn't want to bring it up."

"Because people might hate Emil for being Keon once upon a time ago," Prudencia says.

"Or they'll love him for being Bautista," I counter.

"Either way, they'll take it out on phoenixes once they realize specters can resurrect with their essence," Emil says. "I'd hate for the Blood Casters to get the jump on us and reveal this to turn the public against me, but they haven't done it yet. Hopefully they have their own reasons for keeping it quiet."

"Good point. The secret stays in the vault," I say.

I still think there can be something so powerful about the world knowing that Emil wasn't only adopted, but that he was reborn in fire from the two most popular specters in history, but the story isn't more important than the consequences.

"We shouldn't mention the ghost specters either," Prudencia says. "We don't need alchemists and necromancers pretending to be gods any more than they do."

The more and more politics are getting involved in my business, the less enthusiasm I have for this livestream. But I hype myself right back up because it's not like I have to hide any ghostly powers from the public anyway. I still get to show off.

Once it's nine on the dot, we go live.

"Hey, Brightsiders, it's your boy Brighton coming at you from somewhere in the world—I can't say where exactly because I've got some ruthless Blood Casters after me—and I'm here with my amazing brother, Emil, for the chat of a lifetime." I wrap my arm around his shoulders. "Say what's up, man."

Emil offers a shy wave. "Hey."

I'll never understand how he isn't fueled by all this attention. I'm so fired up right now, especially as the comments are rolling in. My favorite is from a fan who says they've been following me since my first YouTube video and how they're loving my journey. I shout out their handle and thank them. They immediately react with more love because I noticed them. The power in a simple hello is incredible.

The chat opened with nearly ten thousand viewers and in two minutes we're already passing one hundred thousand. "There are already so many of you, but we're going to wait a little longer to start to give everyone a chance to settle in," I say. "But I got a treat for you early birds." I watch my eyes burn like eclipses in the livestream and silver and sapphire flames slither around my fingers. The chat section explodes with fire emojis. We're nearing five hundred thousand viewers when I announce that we're good to start, which is amazing since it's relatively short notice, but I hope we cross a million viewers.

"So you've shown us what's new," Emil says. "I obviously know what's what, but do you want to walk all your epic Brightsiders on what went down?"

I'm glad he remembered to call them epic. Lore calls their fans "beauteous" so much that it's almost like they have ownership over the word. I want my brand to be epic heroism and this association will better connect me with my followers.

"My origin story has been a trip," I say. "Everything changed for us the day that specter tried to kill me. You saved my life, bro. You've saved it a lot of times since then too. But there was only so much I could do from behind the camera, especially when the brawl was breaking out."

"That night was wild," Emil says.

"You were almost killed. Luna Marnette stabbed you with an infinity-ender blade—a weapon designed to kill phoenixes for good! Show them your scar." I reach for his shirt but he grabs my

219

hand and pushes it back toward me. "Come on, show everyone what we've been through!"

"I'm not lifting my shirt," Emil says and then I remember all his body business.

"All good. It's not for those with weak stomachs anyway." Great recovery. This is why I've always thought I'd be a great TV host. "But yeah, one week ago tonight when the Crowned Dreamer was at its zenith, we were battling it out with the Blood Casters. We were down a man after Atlas was killed—may he rest well in the stars—and Luna was about to turn herself into a specter with this new concoction. I was able to take her down before she could drink the elixir and then something came over me and I went for it. I drank it all."

"And it poisoned your blood," Emil says. "You almost died like Dad."

I have a YouTube video I filmed a month after Dad died to explain why I hadn't been posting as regularly but I share all the details again for everyone new. "Between being scared for my life in Gleam Care and Stanton coming to assassinate me, I really thought I was a goner. But it turns out I'm strong enough so I could become a soldier like you."

There are so many comments from people hoping to become specters too.

"And Bautista de León," Emil says. "You've loved him since we were kids."

"I have! There's no denying that the majority of specters are abusing their powers. But then you have some shining stars like you and Bautista who have done a lot of good."

"With powers that aren't ours," Emil says. "I'm really hoping I can figure out that potion to disempower any specter. No more Blood Casters. No more us."

I nod along even though that was not a talking point for this discussion. "Until that time comes, we have a lot of work to do making this country safer from the true terrorists—the Blood Casters. Emil and I have both been captured and abused by them. We're lucky we're alive. But we don't know if that's true for our mother who they kidnapped."

"They took Eva Nafisi too. Some of you might remember her as the healer from Brighton's Spell Walkers interviews," Emil says like I forgot about her.

"Eva made me good as new. She's an incredible healer and an even more remarkable human. Eva and our mother are strong women, but they don't stand a chance against the Blood Casters. We need all of you to be our eyes around the city so we can bring them home safely," I say.

As Emil describes everything about the fight at the Aldebaran Center, I read through the questions that are coming in so fast that I can hardly keep up. People want advice on how to become specters. Others are sharing their own personal struggles that require heroic hands. There are some good ones too I want to address.

"I think it's time to answer some questions," I say. It's a safer move since Emil isn't exactly sticking to the script anyway. "I see a lot of you asking if I'm planning a rebrand on the series since Emil and I aren't celestials. Maybe I'll change it to 'Gleamcrafters of New York' so it's more inclusive. But honestly, I created

Celestials of New York because it was my way of feeling close to the lives of those with powers. Keeping up this format of interviewing strangers feels tricky with everything going on that I might make it my own until things settle down. If they ever do."

There's immediate support and even a suggestion that I follow Atlas's lead and how all his posts were dedicated to lives saved and lost. That could be a cool way to honor him.

"Let's see. . . ." There's one question that's been popping up the most and it's time to get it out of the way. "Okay, okay, okay! Am I a Spell Walker? The answer is . . . NOPE." I'm tempted to reveal how badly the group's ranks are fracturing, but I'm bigger than that. "I'm part of a more important unit—the Infinity Kings. Back when you all thought of Emil as Fire-Wing, I joked that he was the Infinity Son since he's got these amazing powers from a firebird of infinity."

Once again, my little twist saves the day. I don't have to reveal why I really gave him that name.

"I'm cool with you all using my name too," Emil says.

"And I'll always be Brighton, especially for all of you epic Brightsiders. But once I got my powers I thought it'd be cool to add an edge to my identity too. I came up with the Infinity Savior. What do you all think?"

Engagement is key when growing your following. I might be the influencer but it's important to let my followers think they have influence over me too. The Brightsiders are really taking to the name. One commenter suggests Infinity Brother and I wish I could block this person who would reduce me as if I'm still shadowing Emil on his missions and not my own individual person.

Thankfully their comment gets buried by all the love and that's when I notice we've crossed 1.3 million viewers.

"I'm so happy the name is a hit," I say with a hand to my heart. "I'll admit, being a specter with a bull's-eye on my back is really terrifying. But I've got a great support system." I glance over at Prudencia, wishing I could mention her. "I've always been able to turn to Emil and I'm lucky enough to have all of you out there cheering me on too." I really want to stay and chat all night, but if I answer all these questions now, then my followers, old and new, won't have any reason to keep hanging around. "Emil and I need to get some rest after an eventful day. I promise to do another chat soon."

I elbow Emil's side, waiting for him to initiate our send-off.

"Oh—uh. Before we were the Infinity Kings, we were the Reys of Light," Emil says.

"And now we're shining brighter than ever," I say and salute.

I end the livestream before I've lost my cool. To think last night I was dying and now I'm living my best life. I apologize to Emil over the shirt thing and get a fist bump and whistle out of him. My high only gets higher when Prudencia tells us that we did a great job and kisses me softly on the lips. I'm the luckiest human alive.

I spend the rest of the night in bed, scrolling through social media with Prudencia asleep on my chest. There's already amazing fan art of me fighting every known Blood Caster with my flames and those criminal specters are so screwed when this becomes a reality. I got some haters too who don't think I'm being real about everything. I go on their profiles and decide I'm not going to take abuse from jealous people with five hundred followers who want what I have, who wish they were me.

It's a hard pill to swallow that even superhumans need sleep, but I don't go willingly. I spend every last waking moment soaking up all the Infinity Savior love.

This is only the beginning.

TWENTY-SEVEN
BRIGHT STAR

MARIBELLE

The smell of fresh rosemary wakes me up, and the Halo Knight is standing over me. I instinctively want to punch her, but my grogginess works in her favor—we don't have to fight because we share the same enemy.

Without her mask it's easy to see in her eyes that she isn't eager to take me on either. Her leather jacket with the feathered sleeves is hanging off the back of an armchair, leaving her in a black tank top, which also means she can't surprise me with any more daggers. She removed my power-proof vest and it's nowhere in sight. She has a home field advantage wherever this is, and my psychic sense isn't ringing around her.

The Halo Knight takes a seat in the armchair and rests the rosemary on a side table. "Did you enjoy your sleep?"

I'm regaining control of my muscles as I sit up from the plush couch. We're in some minimalistic loft with high concrete ceilings and light bulbs strung around the round windows. The Cloaked Phantom isn't outside. "How long was I unconscious?"

"Thirty-one hours."

"What?!"

"The tranquilizer is intended for phoenixes the size of Roxana. You're lucky you're alive," she says as she crosses her legs.

"Then you owe me an apology for almost killing me."

Her amber eyes narrow. "Shouldn't be a concern of yours given your stolen phoenix powers."

She knows nothing about me.

"I was born with the powers, but they're new to me."

The Halo Knight scoffs. "Interesting. I didn't realize you were a phoenix doing one hell of an impression of a specter." She begins clapping and it's infuriatingly sarcastic. "Brava."

"I don't know whether or not I can resurrect. But it's possible since my biological father could. Bautista de León."

There are a million questions resting on her lips. The one she asks catches me off guard: "Who are you?"

The truth is, I don't know anymore.

I'm the daughter to four powerful parents, all dead. I'm a terrorist to some and a hero to others, even though I'm no longer a Spell Walker. I'm not Atlas's girlfriend anymore because Atlas isn't alive. I don't have any idea who I'll be if I even survive this fight.

"I'm someone born into chaos," I answer.

"So, Maribelle de León, you're a princess as far as specter royalty goes."

"Lucero," I correct. I feel strongly enough about that name. "Same question. Who are you?"

She hesitates, well aware that she has control over me as long as I'm on her turf, but she shares anyway. "Tala Castillo. All my life I've been taught that there is nothing more horrific than someone who kills a phoenix for their power. My parents told me all the stories about how your father was paraded as a champion, but we know that he was simply a thief dressed up as one."

In some ways, Tala might have a better understanding of Bautista than I do. Whenever Mama and Papa spoke about Bautista, they always framed him as the kind of person who didn't have the same greed for powers in his heart as other specters. But no matter what, the hero is always someone else's villain, and for the Halo Knights, that would've been Bautista among every other specter with phoenix blood.

"I'm not defending Bautista. I don't know him. The past few weeks have only brought so many revelations, including that I'm Bautista and Sera Córdova's daughter and the true power of phoenix specters. I'm sure Emil Rey is on your radar."

"Fire-Wing," Tala says.

That nickname from the media didn't exactly stick. "Well, Emil is Bautista reincarnated, and Bautista is the direct scion to Keon Máximo."

There's a world-shaking wonder in Tala's eyes. "But . . ."

Halo Knights put their faith in the concept of resurrection, and Emil is now walking proof.

I walk Tala through everything I've discovered since Emil came into my life one month ago: the family secrets my own parents kept from me but that Iris's parents shared with her; the ghost specters, in particular June; and the true intentions behind the Blood Casters pursuing Gravesend instead of an ordinary century phoenix.

Tala bites her lip. "So Luna is running around immortal."

"She isn't. No one is. Emil's brother Brighton drank the Reaper's Blood and he's dying because of it."

"Those powers were never his to have," Tala says.

"He could've done good with them."

Tala gets up and puts on her jacket. "If I only had a dollar for every time I heard that hollow-hearted sales pitch about a specter, I could afford a place like this instead of renting it from a true phoenix activist. Follow me upstairs."

Upstairs?

I'm wobbly but find my footing as we walk across the loft with its walls covered in mirrors and black-and-white photos of a woman interacting with different phoenixes in the wild. She must be the activist. Around the corner there is a spiral staircase that takes us to this rooftop garden with stone benches and a bubbling hot tub big enough for Roxana to curl inside. The light howler is underwater and somehow hears us approaching, or maybe even senses our presence, and her drenched head comes out from under the steaming water and shakes it off. I get splashed and the water is as hot as it looks. Not a problem for a phoenix, I suppose.

Tala kisses Roxana between her lightning-blue eyes, which

are as large as fists. "Phoenixes have existed before humans and yet the majority of us don't respect their glory. It's rare, but there are still some phoenixes alive today who have cycled through thousands of lives. If you want to talk about doing good by them, find other ways to honor them that don't involve sacrificing them for human benefit." She strokes the yellow feathers on her jacket's sleeve. "These feathers come from Roxana. Some are from shedding, most of from when she's died over the years."

"Died how?"

"The standard cycle of a light howler is one year before they pass and begin again a month later," Tala says. She grabs two green apples off a small tree, and the phoenix grabs one with her beak and chomps away. "From growing up in Cebu and spending some time in Cairo, I have protected Roxana from ever being killed by alchemists and hunters." She scratches the phoenix's neck but Roxana only cares about that apple. "I have vowed to put my life before all of hers."

"Did your parents do the same for their phoenixes?"

"All Halo Knights do. This is our oath," Tala says. "In return for our services we'll be reincarnated as phoenixes." She looks to the stars. "I'll be reunited with my parents one day. If not in this life, then the next."

I'd forgotten that this was built into their beliefs. Even as someone who is part specter and may have that ability, I still don't believe this to be true. "If a pair of phoenixes landed beside us right now, how would you know if they were your parents or not?"

"I'll feel it in my heart," Tala states simply. "The same way my ex-girlfriend Zahra knew the butterfly that landed on her shoulder during graduation was her grandmother reincarnated."

I cross my arms. "Faith isn't proof. I would love to believe any time that the wind blows is because my dead boyfriend is casting it in my direction, but I'm not going to pretend I'm not grieving."

Tala stands and Roxana perks up too. The slightest hint of danger pricks me. "Death is part of the cycle and the only death to fear is one that breaks the cycle."

"Then why are you hunting down your parents' killers, if this is natural?"

"Murder isn't natural."

Tala turns her back on me and hops onto the ledge of the roof. For a second I think she's going to jump. Roxana would have to be as fast as my research claims light howlers are to catch Tala because she would hit that ground in under a minute. I would know, having jumped off countless buildings. Tala teeters on her heels and toes, really trusting in herself to not fall over. I stand beside her.

"My parents were everything to me. My first loving hands, my compass. I am who I am because of them and I expected them to live longer to nurture the best parts of me and wring out the worst," Tala says.

Even though she's one harsh wind away from falling off the edge, Tala's composure is the most relaxed I've seen her. Not saying much, since our meeting involved physical combat and a flying arrow and dagger, but I find my own fists unclenching around her. I won't dismiss her as nothing but a weapon the same way the world does to me.

"My name means 'bright star,'" Tala says as she stares into the night sky. "My parents tried and tried to have children but my mother continued miscarrying. They prayed to their phoenix companions, a crowned elder and a sun swallower, one last time to help usher a child into this life, and nine months later I was born. I was their bright star in a life they personally considered dark without me. Now their love is gone."

"The love isn't gone," I say.

She jumps down from the ledge. "That's why this all hurts so much! I'm carrying their teachings, I exist because their prayers were answered by their companions, but their remembrance ceremony brought me no comfort. I yelled at our new commander during the hour of silence so we would have a strategy in place to avenge them. That night every other Halo Knight stood tall in a field as all our fallen were set ablaze by their phoenixes until they were nothing but ashes. Meanwhile I was on the ground and crying in the shadows."

This moment she had reminds me how furious I still am that the Blackout didn't allow me the chance to have a public ceremony for my parents.

"I cremated Atlas with my phoenix fire," I say. "I keep his ashes in a bottle he gave me." I reach for her shoulder to comfort her, but pull back. "I understand how lost you feel without your parents. Don't even get me started on losing a loved one. Pray to your holiest of phoenixes you never have to feel that burning fire of grief because it's real and it's unstoppable." Somewhere out in this city are the people responsible. "I've been feeling touched by death after all of my losses this year. It's time I start making others feel the same.

231

If you came here to avenge your parents, let that be your compass."

"I kept you alive so you could point me in the right direction. Introduce me to Emil Rey and then you're free to go."

"What if we partnered together? I don't have the Spell Walkers, and you don't have the Halo Knights, but we both want the Blood Casters dead."

Tala considers me and holds out her hand as if she's about to challenge me to an arm-wrestling match. "Do you vow to take lives for those that are lost?"

I take her hand in mine. "Absolutely."

Tala squeezes three times and I do the same unsure if that's important or not.

"May their deaths be forevermore," Tala says as she releases me. "So where is Emil?"

"He might still be in a hospital with his brother, but it's possible they've moved on by now."

"You told me you knew. I should've gotten Wyatt to come with me, his companion Nox is a brilliant tracker and—"

"I have other ways to find out," I say. "I just need my phone."

We return downstairs and Tala retrieves my power-proof vest, car keys, and phone from a box in the closet. Maybe she thought this would've slowed me down from escaping if I woke up when she wasn't around. She's very wrong. I unlock my phone, and when I search Brighton's profile on Instagram to send him a message, I see a new post. He's alive and well—too well.

Brighton's eyes are burning like an eclipse and he's carrying sapphire fire sourced from the phoenix that Tala's parents died defending.

TWENTY-EIGHT
ANOTHER
KNIGHT

EMIL

I really hope I'm living this life right.

I got to trust Brighton and let him prove himself, but I'm not an idiot; I know his ego can bring out the worst in him. Arrogance alone is one thing. Arrogance paired with superpowers is another. I'm responsible for Brighton now more than ever.

He's all over the news this morning. Clips from last night's live event are on every station and only a couple outlets are reporting it fairly. The others are excluding how we prevented the Blood Casters from achieving something that would've been catastrophic. All they see now is another target to fear at a time when there have been an increasing number of allegations against celestials. This isn't helping Sunstar and Shine as the election approaches or the community as a whole.

The reports are heartbreaking: there's an invisible high school coach spying on students in the locker rooms; the boss who threatened to burn his assistant from the inside out if she kept refusing dates with him; the mother who blinded the children who bullied her son at school; and so many more stories that paint gleam as weapons. Hope continues shrinking. I don't think I'll ever see this country as strong as I trick myself into thinking it can be.

I turn off the TV as Prudencia comes out of the shower fully dressed with a towel around her head. It was a lot harder to get sleep alone last night since Prudencia stayed in the room with Brighton, but I get it. They're finally giving themselves a shot and there's no better time than now. Life is short, especially when locked into a war, and having extra lives hasn't exactly done me any favors.

"How's Bright handling his fame?" I ask.

Prudencia lets out a deep sigh as she sits on the couch that used to be her bed. "I woke up to him literally drooling on his phone."

"Eighteen years of sharing a room with him and that's a first," I say.

"It would've been a little more charming if it didn't have me wondering how late he was up reading comments about himself." Prudencia's eyes glow as she telekinetically opens the window and lets some fresh air in. "I promise I don't intend on using my power for everyday things."

"You're making up for lost time."

"For a war I never wanted to fight in," Prudencia says. "But with Atlas dead, Maribelle gone, and your powers down, we're going to need extra help."

I'm about to tell her how I don't want her picking up my slack when a blurry wind sweeps toward us, and Brighton appears with his phone. "Whoa," he says as he balances himself. "I don't recommend doing that right when you wake up." He sits beside Prudencia. "Maribelle DM'd me last night. It must've been right after I fell asleep."

"What does she want?" Prudencia asks.

Brighton reads out the message: "The stars took care of you after all, Brighton. Your second shot at life couldn't have come at a better time. I'm working with a Halo Knight to take down the Blood Casters. But Tala wants answers on the deaths of her parents. Bring Emil to the eighteenth floor of the First Nebula Lofthouse. We can all work together and maybe even save Eva and your mother. No Spell Walkers."

"Wait, why does the Halo Knight want to meet with me?" I ask. "Does she think I killed her parents?"

Anxiety strangles me.

"I doubt it, bro. Maribelle is the first person to make a case on how you won't kill anyone. Tala probably wants to know what happened to her parents."

"Then she'll probably kill us for having phoenix blood."

Brighton pops up. "Maribelle does too, so unless her ghost slid into my DMs we should be fine."

"Quick history lesson, Bright: the Halo Knights killed Keon. What do you think is going to go down if she knows about my past lives?"

"We're going to keep you safe. Look, Iris has been searching for leads every day and returning back with nothing. This Halo

235

Knight may have her own connections that can lead us to saving Ma. You'll never be able to live with yourself if something happens to her that we could've prevented. I'm getting ready."

He dashes down the hallway.

He's so eager to get out of here that he isn't considering the obvious differences between us and Maribelle. Maribelle was born with her powers and I was reborn with mine. I'm not innocent because of everything my past lives have done, but Brighton is a traditional specter who stole his powers in this life. I'm not sure how that's going to end well for him.

"Don't let him pressure you into this," Prudencia says. "I'm going to let him know how unfair he's being."

"No, he's right. If there's a chance to save Ma, I have to take it."

Prudencia nods. "Maribelle said no Spell Walkers, but she didn't say anything about me. I'm going with you."

We get ready fast. It's so screwed up to sneak away after all the hospitality Ruth and Wesley have shown us, but I've pissed off Maribelle enough for one lifetime and I tell myself that we'll be back by day's end if not sooner. It's extra wrong when Prudencia takes Wesley's keys and we drive away with his car.

"Maribelle knows we're on the way," Brighton says, putting down his phone.

"Did you tell her I'm with you?" Prudencia asks.

"You said you didn't want to put a label on it yet."

"Not romantically. That I'm physically coming with you."

"Oh." Brighton retrieves his phone again. "One sec."

I spend the ride nervous that this is some kind of trap and

Brighton keeps shooting me down and telling me to be more trusting. My anxiety has only grown stronger since getting my powers and the last time I trusted someone new he was killed because of me. I keep arguing with myself that Ma being alive isn't some delusion, that Luna could be holding her hostage to use her as a tool later, but it's damn near impossible to hold out hope for Ness. His very existence could upend his father's entire campaign.

It takes us a couple of hours to reach Carroll Gardens in Brooklyn and we park a few blocks away from the First Nebula Lofthouse. Prudencia comes up with signals letting us know when it's safe for us to follow her down the streets. She's associated with us, but she fortunately isn't famous like us, the Infinity Kings. Two men come out a building pushing a stroller and force us to hit a one-eighty when we see a group of women in athleisure dribbling a basketball our way. Brighton and I become suddenly interested in counting the blackened gum marks on the sidewalk like when we were kids until they pass. I miss the days where I didn't have to wonder if strangers were going to celebrate or hate me.

Brighton and I get to the front of the building right as Prudencia comes out.

"Doorman talking to a nanny," Prudencia says. We follow her around the corner and there's a door by a dumpster. She telekinetically pulls it open. "Up we go."

"Why did Tala have to be in the penthouse?" I ask.

"It's only eighteen floors. I'll see you up there," Brighton says as his eyes glow like an eclipse. He blurs for a moment before

237

freezing in place.

Prudencia has him bound with her power. "We're all walking up together. If it is a trap, I don't want you finding out alone."

"You're the boss," Brighton says with a smile. This is some kind of game to him.

Once she lets him go, we all go up, mercifully not bumping into anyone along the way.

Brighton holds the door open at the top level. "This is going to be a lot more fun when we can all fly straight to the roof next time."

If I can ever fly again.

Prudencia knocks on the only door and Maribelle answers in moments.

It's been exactly a week since Maribelle last saw us at the meeting with Sunstar and Shine but the only person she regards now is Brighton with marvel in her eyes. "How are you feeling?"

"Stronger," Brighton answers. It's awkward watching him soak up this moment knowing that Prudencia is more than familiar that he had a poster of Maribelle in our bedroom. "Ready to work."

"Let's go."

Maribelle leads us inside the loft, but we barely get to explore it before we go up one final flight of steps to the roof. There's a young woman standing in the garden and petting the biggest phoenix I've ever seen up close. The phoenix could be safely mounted for flight and maybe even crush someone with one tackle. Judging by its yellow feathers I'm thinking it might be a breath spawn or a light howler. The former can explode on the spot to kill us all and the latter could strike us dead with lightning. I normally wouldn't spiral over the different ways a phoenix might kill me, but I'm not counting on my specter presence to be welcomed by this Halo Knight. One glare from Tala confirms this. The phoenix cocks its head like it's studying me. I wonder if it can sense the power that's not supposed to be in me or Brighton.

"Tala, this is—"

"Who killed my parents?" Tala asks, cutting off Maribelle.

"The Blood Casters," I say immediately.

"Which ones?"

I stand frozen on the spot. All the Halo Knights were wearing my masks and their complexions ranged. I share everything that I remember about that swift fight. There were five Halo Knights total wielding axes and swords and crossbows. One man was immediately killed by Dione before having her head cut off by a short woman. "Then June, this specter with ghost blood—I don't know if Maribelle explained all of that—possessed some man. Nimuel, I think." Tala's eyes water at the mention of his name. "June forced him to kill two Haloes. I warned the woman that he was possessed and she said she was his wife. When June didn't leave his body, the Halo told Nimuel she would see him in another life and stabbed him. But June escaped in time and then Stanton killed the woman."

Tala is vibrating with anger.

"I'm sorry for your loss. They fought bravely," I say.

She doesn't seem to welcome my condolences. "We will always put our lives on the line for the birds of many lives."

239

"Gravesend was supposed to be safe behind a vaulted shield, but my former boss traded her life for mine so he could get famous."

I don't tell Tala how I considered killing Gravesend myself, hoping it would make a difference during the ritual. I tense up reliving the moment Luna stabbed Gravesend and then me with the infinity-ender blade. I should've died at that church too.

"My parents died for that century phoenix, to make sure she could live and never be used," Tala says, and turns to Brighton. "Then you stole her essence for your own gain."

He really should dash downstairs and get far away. "Better me than Luna. I'll avenge Gravesend with her powers."

"Gravesend was supposed to have her own lives, her own futures!"

Tala crouches behind a bush of lilies and when she rises she's aiming a crossbow at us. Maribelle shouts at her to stop, but it's too late. An arrow flies toward Brighton, and he dashes out of the way and almost tumbles over the roof's ledge. Prudencia teleki-netically snatches the crossbow away from Tala and holds it close to her chest.

"Roxana, strike!"

The phoenix stands on its black talons and fires a lightning bolt toward Prudencia. I don't think she's going to be strong enough to deflect the light howler and thankfully Brighton dash-tackles her out of the way. The lightning bolt strikes the ground and the aftershock blasts me across the roof and I roll toward a small pool. My hearing is buzzy, but I think I can make out Maribelle shout-ing for Tala to stop. But maybe Tala can't hear either because she leaps straight at Brighton. He runs circles around her and Tala holds out one leg and immediately trips him.

Even if I could use my powers, I wouldn't dare use them against Tala, a Halo Knight who does honorable work for phoenixes, but that doesn't mean I'm going to let her try to beat my brother to death. I fight past all dizziness as I charge straight toward her, but Tala grabs me by the arm and flips me over her shoulder. She goes back and forth between punching me and Brighton, but her glare becomes deadlier.

"You started this," Tala says. "You're the first specter. The Blood Casters exist because of you!"

I'm trying to get my words out, but Tala's blows don't stop. My body is trying to heal itself, but new wounds keep coming, more blood keeps spilling. It's possible Tala might kill me before my healing power can save me.

I wonder who I'll be in my next life.

Before her next hit can collide, Maribelle wraps her arms around Tala and carries her into the air, demanding that she put an end to this.

I try catching my breath to ask Brighton if he's okay, but my power keeps involuntarily trying to heal me and I can't stop it. I have to endure the pain. Prudencia grabs my hand and I squeeze, squeeze, squeeze. For the first time in my life I feel like my grip might be strong enough to break someone's bones. Once the burn subsides, Prudencia fully turns her attention to Brighton, who isn't self-healing. There is pink and red bruising around his right eye that's closed shut. I wonder how he feels about being more trusting to strangers now that he's groaning in pain.

Commotion above catches my attention and Tala wrestles out of Maribelle's grip and drops down onto the rooftop. She shoulder rolls toward her crossbow and aims it at my chest. I don't have it in me to move. I close my eyes and wait.

"Tala, don't!" a guy shouts in an English accent.

I'm covered in shadows of massive wings and for a delirious moment I wonder if there's a British phoenix that speaks with the ease of humans like my favorite childhood cartoon. But of course that's nonsense. I look up to see who saved my life and there's a pale guy with brown hair riding what has to be an obsidian phoenix judging by its glittering black feathers. The guy is wearing a leather jacket with feathered sleeves as black as the phoenix—another Halo Knight.

The obsidian lands smoothly on the rooftop and if I wasn't already intimidated by the sheer size of this phoenix, a whole foot taller than the light howler, I fully tense up as those dark eyes that look hollowed out of its face stare at me. The Halo Knight dismounts and there's a dirty white satchel hanging from his broad shoulder. From what I can make out underneath his open jacket, his white shirt is pressed tight against his pecs. He extends his cautious hand toward Tala as he approaches me.

"Why are you following me, Wyatt?" Tala asks.

"You're my friend—and because Crest said he'd increase my book budget if Nox and I tracked you down." Wyatt offers Tala a dimpled smile that doesn't win her over. "You know Nox; he loves a hunt."

"I don't need your help."

"Clearly." Wyatt gestures at me and Brighton. He helps me up with his sweaty hands and we seem to be the exact same height judging by how I'm able to stare straight into his eyes, which are as blue as Brighton's flames. Between the patchy stubble arching along his jawline and the smell of cedarwood, it's as if Wyatt has been hiking in the wilderness for days. There are three thin scars down the side of his neck, possibly from a phoenix, but too small to come from Nox. He wraps my arm around his muscular shoulders and guides me to the stone bench to rest.

"Do you have any idea who they are?" Tala asks.

"Emil and Brighton Rey—the self-proclaimed Infinity Kings." Wyatt knows who we are. Time will tell if that's good or not. "Pardon me, darling, but I'm not familiar with you," he says to Prudencia.

"A friend," Prudencia says.

"Well, hello, friend." Wyatt turns to Maribelle with a hand on his heart. "You're Maribelle Lucero. My condolences. May Atlas's winds blow again in another life."

Tala allows his sympathy to sink in for a moment before pointing her finger at me. "Wyatt, that isn't just Emil Rey—he was also Bautista de León and Keon Máximo. Everything we have feared about phoenix specters is true. They can be reborn and he's the mastermind behind it all!"

I brace myself for Wyatt's kindness to shift to violence but he's still as a statue.

"I was reborn into this, but I don't have any of Bautista's or Keon's memories. I swear I'm my own person and I don't want to be a specter. I have a journal that belonged to Maribelle's parents, Bautista and Sera, and I'm trying to complete their work on a

243

power-binding potion. I want this cycle to end with me."

"Wait one second." Wyatt looks between me and Maribelle. "Maribelle, I thought your parents were two of the Spell Walkers that died during the Blackout. And Emil, you look nothing like Bautista or Keon but you're somehow Maribelle's father?"

"Bautista and Sera are my biological parents, but Aurora and Lestor Lucero raised me. Emil isn't my father," Maribelle says.

"But he technically is, yeah?" Wyatt replies. "His past life gave you yours. But what does that make you? I thought you were a celestial."

Maribelle's left eye burns like an eclipse and the right glows like sailing comets. Dark yellow flames encircle her fists. "I'm a hybrid."

"Didn't have to demonstrate; I would've believed you," Wyatt says as he digs inside his satchel and withdraws a logbook. "That said, this is all a lot." He mutters as he takes notes. "Emil is Maribelle's father, but not really. . . . Specters with phoenix blood can come back to life but apparently as new people. . . . Celestials and specters can procreate. . . . Oof . . ."

I keep my eyes on Tala the entire time in case she's feeling trigger-happy while Wyatt is writing away as if this has been a chill environment before his arrival.

"Did I miss anything?" Wyatt asks.

"The power-binding potion," I say.

"Aha! You'll make a fine assistant back at the Sanctuary," Wyatt says.

Tala looks like she might fire an arrow straight between Wyatt's blue eyes. "You're clearly still lacking oxygen from your

244

flight over if you think we're bringing specters onto any of our sacred bases."

Wyatt puts away his logbook. "Tala, please. We have more to gain as Haloes by learning from them than by avenging our fallen companions. Think of all the people who won't bother harming phoenixes if the authorities have a potion that can prevent them from using their powers. It's especially critical if word gets out that specters can resurrect if they possess phoenix blood. Crest will want word on this."

I don't know who Crest is, but Tala doesn't argue any further.

"It's best if we go sooner rather than later since you and Roxana have caught the city's attention," Wyatt says with a raised eyebrow. Something tells me this isn't the first time Tala has done her own thing. "The New Ember Sanctuary is located in Storm King State Park. Beautiful scenery all around, prepare your hearts." Wyatt hops onto Nox. "Care to go for a ride, Emil? I'd love to pick your brain further."

It's tempting to ride a phoenix, but I'm not flying away with some stranger. "I'm going to stick with my people."

"Suit yourself. Safe journeys, everyone." Wyatt strokes Nox's neck and the phoenix spreads his magnificent wings. They shoot across the blue sky like a shadowy star.

I watch the Halo Knight take off, envying his closeness with a beautiful phoenix.

Out of all of my lives, I wish one had been more like his.

TWENTY-NINE
IMPERSONATE

NESS

Since being locked in the panic room two days ago, I've been forced to memorize new lines in advance of my interviews where I'll be posing as Carolina and Eva. Roslyn gives me her latest script and I can't believe the big news that's being dropped here: Brighton revealed last night online that he has powers. It's not clear from these sides which ones, but I care more about the fact that Emil is seen alive and well too. If I can get back downstairs, I can report that news to their mother. I can barely focus, so relieved that Emil is okay, and honestly, a little grateful that his brother is packing powers to help keep him alive since I can't trust Emil to take care of himself.

I'm on my bed, almost done memorizing the pages, when the slow knock I've grown up with catches my attention. The

Senator has returned and he doesn't look like himself. His thick glasses don't hide the deep shadows underneath his reddened eyes. He's lost noticeable weight in his cheeks and the public will be sure to scrutinize what that means for him.

"You look like hell."

"Campaigning to be the leader of the free world isn't without its sacrifices," the Senator says. I expect some comment about how he tried to do away with me to further his goals, but he doesn't seem to have that snideness in him at the moment.

"Sounds like you've got some more competition out there."

"The Infinity Kings? Another threat we'll neutralize."

I'm sure Brighton came up with that name. I hope there's truth behind it.

"I trust you're prepared for your interviews," the Senator says.

"Just about got the new lies memorized."

"If you don't sell those lies as truth we will kill those women right in front of you."

"Then you'll lose your leverage against me."

The Senator smirks. "You can't possibly believe that we're relying solely on their lives to get you to cooperate."

I don't know if he's playing mind games with me, but the threats while I do his dirty work are really pissing me off. "I said I got this! Unless you're here to run lines with me, back off."

Jax appears in the doorway with his hand raised as if he's going to have to telekinetically restrain me. I stay seated on my bed.

The Senator doesn't seem the least bit intimidated. "I am here to let you know that we've secured the Silver Star Slayer for the interview with a set of pre-approved questions. He's a tremendous supporter of mine and giving him this spotlight will increase a platform that has been very generous toward our cause."

The Silver Star Slayer is a deranged vlogger. He's always red in the face as he explodes with conspiracy theories such as an airplane that went missing because it was swallowed up by a prime constellation. The first video I watched of his in full was about the Blackout. He claimed that the brawl between the Spell Walkers was the result of Aurora Lucero discovering an affair between her husband, Lestor, and Finola Simone-Chambers. He had shared all these pictures of Lestor and Finola close during battle to support his theory of how much they can't live without each other.

"You should do him a favor and send him to a psychiatrist instead," I say.

"That wouldn't serve me," the Senator says.

It wouldn't. The Silver Star Slayer will always be outspoken against anything a gleamcrafter does. A celestial on a plane was once praised for teleporting into the pilot's cabin to save the captain, who was having a seizure, and the Silver Star Slayer posted a whole video about how vulnerable all passengers are on a plane when a celestial can take over as quick as a snap. He absolutely hates the Spell Walkers, always blaming them for the destruction to public property when they're fighting for their lives or saving others.

"Be ready in thirty," the Senator says.

"I know Luna was busy during the Cloaked Phantom," I say before he can leave. "What are you going to do with me when it's time to swap me out with my replacement?"

The Senator stops at the door. "That will depend on your performances moving forward, Eduardo. We can either write you back into the show, or we can write you out for good."

The attic has been redone for the interview. The walls and windows have been blanketed to avoid anyone recognizing this space from the many photos available of the manor online. I know from the scripts that when speaking as Eva and Carolina that I won't be disclosing where we're supposed to be, and the Silver Star Slayer will be signing one hell of an NDA. Not that it seems necessary with the way he's fawning over the Senator in the hallway.

"Time to suit up," Roslyn says after she's finished setting up the camera and the ring light.

I morph into Eva—my brown skin lightening, hair growing longer with a patch where Eva has been pulling too much, beauty marks appearing on my cheeks, eyelashes extending—and I shrink a little into the chair.

"Don't worry about the black eye," Roslyn says as I'm in the middle of building in all her bruises. She holds up a tablet where she's video-chatting with Dione, who's downstairs in the panic room with Eva and Carolina. Roslyn compares my features with Eva, who looks terrified beside her four-armed former best friend. "Lose a little more hair."

"I got it right," I say. I look more groomed than Eva since I'm not supposed to appear as if I've been locked away for a week.

"The dramatics will benefit us. If you'd like, I'm sure Dione will rip out more hair to make it true."

I do as she asks, reminding myself that her time will come.

"Stick to the script," she says before calling, "We're ready!"

I keep my hands folded in my lap. I'm not familiar enough with Eva's composure when she's relaxed, having only spent intimate time with her when she was stressed and crying, but I'm hoping that I can sell this to the Senator's team and signal Iris that something is off about her girlfriend.

The Senator escorts the Silver Star Slayer inside, a white man in his early thirties with a navy tie over his hideous lime-green shirt that looks like it might glow in the dark. He has auburn hair and brown eyes that already hate the celestial he sees sitting before him. He approaches me cautiously, as if he suspects Eva's healing power is somehow violent.

"Russell, this is Eva," the Senator introduces.

I get up to shake his hand, hiding my amusement when he steps back. The Senator assures Russell that he's safe and reminds him that Jax is right outside should anything happen. It's so pathetic watching Russell put on a brave face to impress the Senator when I remember how many years I was guilty of that same crime.

I want to believe that people can stop falling for obvious lies, but the truth is that some of them aren't even being fooled.

"Hello," Russell greets awkwardly as he settles in across from me.

The first time I met celestials as a kid I was tense like this too, swearing that someone might melt my insides with a single stare or control my mind to commit crimes. I truly believed that people with powers were all dangerous and that the laws so many worked hard to put in place were to protect people like me. It took too long to figure out that this wasn't ever about security and always about dominating.

"Thanks for taking the time," I say, programmed from my days with the media.

Russell nods and signals for Roslyn to begin filming. I'm sure he's eager to move on to Carolina, who can't hurt him. He turns to the camera with his chest proud, body language as big of a liar as he is. "Today's interviews are being filmed from a discreet location to protect the whereabouts of my guests. First up as you'll see here is Eva Nafisi, who was brought to our attention last month when she was featured in Brighton Rey's series about the Spell Walkers. But lately she has had a change of heart. What inspired this, Eva?"

"The Spell Walkers are crumbling," I say, and it's one of the honest things that will come out of my mouth—Eva's mouth— in a web of lies. "There have been struggles for leadership, and secrets kept from one another, even a really big one from my girlfriend. Some trust can't be healed." I take the pause that Roslyn wrote in for me even though any Intro to Acting class will often encourage you to ignore the descriptions, but the only way I'm going to survive is to play by all their rules. "The Spell Walkers are my family. They took me in when I was running for my life, but I'm tired of being a target."

"Who's targeting you?"

"Gang leaders and alchemists have always wanted to make good use of my healing power. But I was recently taken hostage by the Blood Casters. A former best friend of mine, Dione, hurt me and forced me to use my power to save horrible people." I take a deep breath, knowing the lies that come next. "Then I was saved by enforcers. They weren't able to detain Dione, but they arrested some acolytes and have kept me somewhere safe for the past three days."

There's nothing about this statement that will draw any immediate attention. Nothing too specific about the incident and no details shared about the acolytes' identities or the prisons they would've been sent to if these were real accounts. I'm counting on Iris and the Spell Walkers to know better and dig deeper than everyone else who will accept this as fact.

"Have you reached out to anyone?" Russell asks.

I shake my head. "I tried reaching out to Iris, but she'd already vacated the hospital. It might be for the best until this all blows over. I love Iris, but I'm starting to question if we fit as well as this T-shirt her mother bought her. She leads people into battle with her powerhouse strength, and I'm this pacifist who heals them all after. I think I need to find my own way."

"What will you do?"

"I plan on donating some blood to a medical center I can't name. If I can help create some breakthroughs to heal patients with my blood, I'll be a hero in a way that's more me."

"It's certainly better than healing terrorists," Russell says with the most aggression in his voice of this entire interview. That line wasn't scripted. I choke on a response and ultimately say nothing. He grins. "Thank you for your time, Eva."

"Cut," Roslyn says. "Wonderful job, you two. Russell, we'll need a few moments to escort Ms. Nafisi out of here and bring in Mrs. Rey, but I believe the senator is wanting to show you his personal office."

Russell's trying so hard to hold back his smile and play it cool. No matter how much I hate it, the Senator is a hero to many. The Russells of the world are so ready to vote him into office. It makes me sick.

Once they walk out, I glow in gray light and become myself again. "That comment wasn't preapproved."

"Not to you," Roslyn says. "I asked Russell to sneak that one in. Who doesn't love a little improv?"

If she were my friend or anyone I was even one-thousandth interested in getting to know, I would share that improv was my least favorite part about acting, no matter how useful it's been to adapt to all situations as a specter with infinite faces. My instinct to not say anything when Russell challenged me seems to have played right into Roslyn's hopes. They'll now be able to broadcast Eva's guilty expression as she didn't negate the Spell Walkers being terrorists.

"Get dressed," Roslyn says.

Gray light washes over me again. Dark hair with gray streaks, kind eyes, arms that lovingly hugged Eva, hands that were once used to nurture the best person I've ever met. One look in the camera and I'm so perfectly Carolina Rey that even she would confuse me for her reflection.

I hate the words they're going to make me say.

A few minutes later, the Senator and Russell return. The Silver Star Slayer definitely has on his big boy pants this time as he mistakes me for a powerless mother. He doesn't look me in the eye

253

as he shakes my hand and I'm tempted to snap his wrist. Instead I soften my demeanor and express gratitude even though all I can think about is how he'll get what's coming to him one day. There's no way that Brighton won't use his new powers against the Silver Star Slayer; I wouldn't mind watching that video.

The cameras begin rolling.

"My next guest doesn't have any powers herself, but her children do. Last night your sons uploaded a video threatening those who get in their way," Russell says. No one showed me the livestream, but I doubt there were threats. "Brighton has abused his platform to spread misinformation about the Spell Walkers, claiming they're good. It's always been clear to me that he's very troubled, but I'll admit to being surprised about Emil. What darkness possessed him to become a specter?"

"It's complicated," I say, which is true in ways that the Senator and his team don't even understand. "What you have to understand is that my boys have been through a lot this past year after losing their father."

If Emil and Brighton watch this, I wonder if they'll assume their mother is leaving out the obvious details to protect them. I have no idea if the Senator has been clued in to the resurrection revelations, but I would hate for Luna to weaponize that against Emil.

"Grief doesn't give someone authority over others," Russell says. "Do you not see the value in trusting our government?"

I know the response I'm supposed to say, but I pause. The Senator can't be trusted with this country. I'm ready to rat him out, to transform back into myself because I don't give a damn if they have to kill Russell to protect my secret. It's not as if he's a source of good in this world. Roslyn holds up the tablet and Dione is choking Carolina. Russell only lives to see another day because I want Carolina to be able to.

"The government deserves our trust," I lie.

I stay in character the rest of the interview, echoing the lie that Carolina was also rescued by the government, sharing the story about Emil to illustrate what a kind soul he was before he chose the specter life, going on about seeking attention in a private center for heart complications, and the charges Carolina may face if she doesn't cooperate with the authorities.

"One last question," Russell says. "If you could send a message to your sons right now, what would you tell them?"

"Don't be so high and mighty, and don't get yourselves killed using powers you shouldn't have. You're all I have left."

Then, on command, I get myself to cry. Actors always make it look so easy, but I learned that's not the case for everyone. They cry because they're tapping into their own personal wells of pain, and my trigger is thinking about how much my life has gotten worse without my mother.

The camera is switched off and Russell shows no sympathy for me. He immediately returns to the Senator's side. "Thank you so much for trusting me with these interviews, sir."

"Oh, please. I'm grateful to have incredible supporters such as yourself," the Senator says.

"I'm having friends over the evening of the debate. We can't wait to watch you destroy Sunstar." There is so much hate in Russell's heart that I'm sure he's actively cheering for Sunstar's literal demise like so many others. "Please let me know if I can be of service to you again."

"Absolutely, my friend."

"And feel better!"

Roslyn escorts Russell out.

I drop my morph, and the Senator sits across from me.

"Does it make you proud how you're cheating to win?" I ask.

"I am fighting fire with fire, Eduardo. Celestials have always had the advantage over us, and I will do whatever it takes to level the playing field in this country. The work you have done so far has been incredible, son. People are arming themselves with wands for protection, and a dozen celestials have been killed since your videos have been posted. The American people understand that I'm the solution to this great threat our nation is facing," the Senator says as if he's trying to convince me of all this once again.

It's not a surprise that celestials have been killed, but the confirmation hurts. I have no access to even seeing their faces, which might be a blessing so I can't be so haunted by them that I transform into them in the middle of the night.

Gray light washes over me and I morph into the man sitting across from me. "This is the face of the nation's greatest threat. No matter what you tell yourself."

The Senator grins. "That face is very presidential. No matter what you tell yourself."

THIRTY
THE NEW EMBER SANCTUARY

EMIL

I grew up thinking Storm King State Park wasn't real because its name feels fresh out of a fantasy novel, but it's legit. Months ago Dad talked about taking us all there when he got better. He had so many plans for us, all of them involving Ma too, and she's not with us either. During this hour-long car ride with Brighton and Prudencia, I've brought up how maybe Wyatt and Nox can track down Ma the same way they found Tala. It's just enough hope to hold on to.

We drive past countless trees, freshly grazed by autumn with their orange, red, and yellow leaves. The deeper we get through the park the more we see massive boulders along the side of the road with different phoenixes painted onto them. The bright paintings are so bold they could probably be seen from the sky.

Prudencia follows the path as I finally answer the seventh of Wesley's calls and immediately apologize a thousand times and update him on everything.

"So you're on the way to their super-cool phoenix palace?" Wesley asks.

The Halo Sanctuaries I've seen images of over the years are gorgeous: a Gothic mansion in New Orleans that worships obsidians like Nox; a town house a quick drive from the Grand Canyon where gray suns have been known to dive; a hilltop castle in Paris that tends to crowned elders so they're comfortable in their immediate old age. I wonder what the New Ember Sanctuary looks like; I'm keeping myself in suspense since this may be the only time I'm ever personally welcomed inside of one.

"We should be pulling up soon, I think," I tell Wesley as we drive through a clearing and a brown phoenix with emerald-colored wings and a scorched belly lands inside the nest of a tree. These evergreen blazers are true champions of nature, best known for swallowing any flames during forest fires as if it's nothing but scorching hot food. If I weren't on the phone I'd record this sighting. "I don't know how long we'll be here, but—"

"You have some nerve," Iris says, surprising us all as her voice comes over the speaker. "Not only did you run away from safety at a time when your powers aren't dependable and Brighton is new to his, you left Wesley, Ruth, and Esther vulnerable by letting them think you were home. What if they'd been discovered and needed your help while I was out looking for Eva and Carolina?!"

I must be so damn red in the face because I'm burning up. "I'm sorry, it all happened so quickly. This Halo Knight's phoenix might be able to track down Ma and Eva; then we can all team up—"

"No! Teams are built on trust and communication, and you didn't honor either of those when you all stole Wesley's car without telling anyone."

"You're so right, Iris, we didn't mean—"

Brighton turns around from the front seat and snatches the phone. "You're one to talk! Don't come down on us like we got Wesley's family killed, when Atlas might be alive if you'd been honest with Maribelle about everything!"

We hear nothing but Iris breathing for a few moments. "I hope Maribelle's hospitality will be as generous as ours. You've chosen your side. Don't contact us."

The line goes dead.

"Bright, why'd you have to swing at her like that?"

"She was acting all high and mighty, like we're the bad guys!"

"Iris is grieving too," Prudencia reminds him. "Maybe not as hard as Maribelle, but I'm sure she's already blaming herself. You're better than that, Brighton."

It's hard getting Brighton to stay quiet, but if he's actually trying to make something work with Prudencia, he needs to get better at not lashing out at our friends and allies. I'm tempted to call Iris back, but I'm going to give her some space.

We drive around a mountain and there's a drawbridge stretching toward a home fitting for Halo Knights—a two-story stone castle with turreted-observation towers that are reaching for the sky. If Iris doesn't ever want to see us again at the cottage, hopefully we can all cram into a closet here or even the garden shed that overlooks the Hudson River. Wyatt, Tala, and Maribelle are waiting outside the Sanctuary's front doors while Nox and Roxana bob for fish in the nearby stream.

"I'm not driving across that old-looking bridge," Prudencia says as she parks the car off to the side.

We walk across with the river flowing beneath us. Roxana eyes us for a moment before swallowing another fish whole. All Halo Knights are vegans, but they don't push that on the phoenixes in their care. While phoenixes are generous spirits to their companions, it's the Halo Knight creed that they serve phoenixes, not the other way around.

"You made it," Wyatt says. He checks his watch. "Good time too."

"How'd you get here so fast?" Brighton asks Maribelle. He looks around. "Did you drive Atlas's car?"

"I parked the car back at the loft last night after messaging you. I hitched a ride with Tala."

"But she hit you!" Brighton says.

"Not as hard as she hit you," Maribelle says.

Brighton's black eye has darkened significantly in the past hour. Though nothing is more beat than his ego since he couldn't overpower someone without any powers of her own. He looks as if he wants to challenge Tala to another round. She looks like she would welcome that.

Wyatt grabs the brass door knocker that's shaped like an egg. "Before inviting you inside we must remind you that we are all guests on these sacred grounds."

"Considerable exceptions are made for you specters." Tala

stares us down, lingering longer on Brighton. "Any harm that befalls the phoenixes will be paid for with your final breath."

Wyatt scratches his head. "Uh, just be careful with the phoenixes, please."

He pushes open the door and I don't feel worthy of being within these walls or under this majestic sky. A rainbow of phoenixes are flying across the courtyard. The closest I've come to a sight like this is back at the museum where we had the model phoenixes hanging from the Sunroom's ceiling. A sky swimmer dives into a lake, splashing a woman who is chasing after a little sun swallower.

"Quite the sight, yeah?" Wyatt asks.

"Yeah. Legit music to my ears too." I wish I could understand all these squawks and chirps and get in on all of the conversations. "I'd listen to this any day instead of people cursing each other out on street corners."

"We may not be able to understand them, but I'm positive the phoenixes are swearing up storms at each other too."

The unity between phoenixes and people seems utopian, especially given everything going down in the city. I'm not likely to find a sun swallower's ankles chained or beak sealed shut here like back at the Apollo Arena where that poor phoenix was forced to battle that golden-strand hydra. Watching that sun swallower fly away is a good reminder that I haven't completely done harm in my time as a Spell Walker. But the lives I've saved don't outnumber the ones I've lost.

"So what's the deal with this place?" I ask Wyatt to distract myself. "Does the New Ember Sanctuary have a specialty?"

261

"It's in the name, no? The Haloes tend to phoenixes upon their resurrections. Each breed has their own need, especially according to their True Age of how many lifetimes they've lived."

Another evergreen blazer, this one the size of a hen, flies directly onto the raptor glove of a man who is looking my way. No, he's staring me down. I'm uncomfortable so I turn away only to find pretty much every other human outside my party watching us closely with rage in their eyes.

"These people hate us," I say.

Wyatt lets out a low whistle. "They're certainly not fans of specters with phoenix blood, but our commander Crest made a call and ordered for their cooperation as we explore our work. Granted access to the castle is one thing. Acceptance is another."

"We should bounce then," I say.

"Bounce?" Wyatt asks.

"Leave," I clarify.

"Oh, no. These trainers are harmless. They've all seen the videos of your powers and will know better than to try and scrap with you, Infinity Son."

If only the Halo Knights knew how much respect I have for phoenixes, if they knew my true story about how I became a specter, I doubt they would see me as a threatening weapon. "Feel free to tell them I'm harmless. Luna Marnette stabbed me with an infinity-ender blade and my powers haven't been working right since then."

"Good gods, she stabbed you?"

I'm surprised that surprises him. He might have scars on his neck, but I have them across my body during my short time in this war. "I was trying to protect Gravesend."

Wyatt's blue eyes follow Brighton as he tries petting the sky swimmer in the lake and gets splashed in return. "And Tala tells me Gravesend's essence is now coursing through Brighton among that of a hydra and ghosts. Between that mouthful and Maribelle's soap opera family drama it seems I've arrived at an exciting time to help."

"I swear you're going to turn on us any second and attack," I say.

"It would probably be to my advantage to keep that fear alive, but I'm disastrous with any weapon. I pierced my own mum's shoulder with an arrow."

"Yeah, but how long ago was that? When you began training?"

Wyatt blushes. "That happened this summer." His little snicker that follows reminds me of people who find something funny at funerals and are struggling to keep it together. "Anyway, Tala's flair for combat suits her role as a field Halo, but I work more closely with the phoenixes themselves."

"Then you should be more pissed off at me and everything I represent," I say.

We've almost caught up with the others at the opposite gate when he rests his hand on my shoulder and stops me. "I've traveled the world meeting with countless organizers that specialize in alchemy, caging, slaughtering, and hunting to get them to cease all harm for their own personal benefits. I've met specters who either don't value creature lives or believe they're more equipped to do good with powers that don't belong to them. You're the first specter to say you want to end this too. Your first life may have started this mess, but you're not stoking that flame, Emil."

It's almost as if I can't feel every other Halo Knight's eyes on me knowing I have one who believes in me.

"That said, to pay for Keon's crimes against phoenixkind, you have to clean up all droppings from the grounds." He cracks a smile.

I almost smile back as we rejoin the group, but things feel so tense between Brighton and Tala that I'm scared another fight is about to break out. Even if Tala throws the first punch, we're the ones who will be blamed for bringing chaos to the Sanctuary. I doubt Wyatt will be able to vouch for us then. I stand at Brighton's side, ready to hold him back if he gets bold.

"Anyone care for a tour of the castle?" Wyatt asks. "It's been years since I've last been here, but it's truly marvelous and—"

"This isn't a field trip," Tala interrupts. "While your parents may be living their best lives in London I can't say the same for mine. If you can't help these specters figure out this potion, then send them packing so we can fully focus on the Blood Casters."

"Absolutely," Wyatt says. Tala walks away without another word and Maribelle is ready to follow. "I'd give her a moment, Maribelle. Personally, I'd give her an hour because I've learned the hard way what happens when you try to be helpful." Wyatt mimics getting punched in the face.

"I'll take my chances," Maribelle says as she jogs across the courtyard to catch up with Tala.

"Wouldn't you all stick together? I thought you were all team-mates," Wyatt says.

"Think again," I say.

"Friends?"

I let out a little laugh.

"Duly noted."

Wyatt takes us into the castle. The great hall isn't as big as I expected it to be, but its greatness is legit. I step inside a circle of bronze statues, admiring all these well-crafted phoenixes, and I back away when I notice a Halo Knight kneeling before one in prayer. Colorful banners hang from the high ceiling and whoever sewed the patterns did so lovingly; the gray sun with its golden feathers in particular is so beautiful I want to make it my phone background. Brighton confuses the sky swimmer at first for the century phoenix since they're both blue but once I correct him he takes a selfie under the right banner. Not even being able to tell apart Gravesend's breed from phoenixes known for flying underwater is the thousandth reason Brighton shouldn't have her powers, but I'm staying shut because I don't want to ruin this experience.

We pass a circular room with all sorts of weapons on the walls—staffs, crossbows, daggers—and two blindfolded women are having a swordfight. I'm so nervous as metal clangs against metal, but no matter how fast they are every sweep and jab of the sword never cuts into either Halo Knight. Wyatt explains that these extreme training methods are one of many reasons he has avoided taking on a more active combat role like Tala. Brighton swears he could endure all of this, but also doesn't think it's necessary to be well versed with weapons since he's such a powerhouse. There's a frightening truth there.

265

While crossing the bridge to the next tower, the second courtyard comes into view. There's a young Halo Knight sitting on top of a blaze tempest, the phoenix with a body the size of a small hound. The blaze tempest has massive wings that carry them through the air and I'm so nervous the child is going to fall off, but they're being supervised by an older Halo on their own phoenix.

Wyatt points to a corner where a sun swallower is breathing fire onto a large suit of armor that's sparkling. "You see that there? My great-great-great-grandmother fashioned the very first armor for phoenixes."

"She created Herculean Feathers?"

Years ago, I was in a flea market and stumbled onto a Polaroid of a phoenix with armor that perfectly fit its head and body. I thought this was some kind of servitude until I researched it at home and discovered the Halo Knights used these armors made of diamond and sun-dust to give phoenixes an extra layer of protection in battle.

"Incredible, yeah? I certainly didn't live up to my family's legacy when I failed to construct Herculean Feathers for Nox at age fourteen, but it was more practice than anything since Nox isn't a war phoenix."

Brighton watches in awe as the sun swallower's deep orange flames keep everyone at bay. "This is incredible. How do we get our hands on some pet phoenixes?"

He's the smartest, most clueless person I know.

"Phoenixes aren't pets," I say.

"Certainly not," Wyatt says. "Just last week I freed a domesticated crowned elder from a woman in Tampa who was calling herself the Phoenix Queen. A phoenix's home is their choice."

I would give anything to tap out of this war as a soldier and instead become a guardian who saves phoenixes from being caged, eaten, worn, and, most critically, slaughtered for their powers.

"I didn't mean pet-pet," Brighton says. "But having some phoenixes can give us the upper hand. Especially for Emil, since his powers are down—"

"Bright, chill."

I'm trying really hard to bury my rage. It's bad enough that we're specters with the blood of creatures that are literally worshipped here in this castle, but now he's suggesting that I make up for my damaged, stolen powers by using a perfectly fine phoenix who doesn't need to fly into my battles.

"I'd love to borrow Emil for a bit," Wyatt says. "Could I interest you two in some lunch?"

"Yes, please," Prudencia says.

"I got to catch up on my DMs anyway," Brighton says as he glares at Wyatt.

He takes us all past the kitchen that smells of baked bread, soup, and potatoes. Prudencia takes Brighton's hand, settling him down, but he still looks over his shoulder as they walk into a dining area with three long tables that remind me of our high school cafeteria.

I take a deep breath.

"Pardon me if that was inappropriate," Wyatt says.

"What? Stopping me from dropkicking Brighton?"

"Precisely. Saving phoenixes is my heart's work but preventing brothers from dropkicking each other is of utmost importance too." Wyatt's dimpled smile catches me off guard. Anytime I experience even the quickest jolt of joy I feel guilty because the war is raging. Wyatt's work is significant, but he doesn't seem to have the weight of the world trying to straight-up flatten him. "You really wear your stress, you know that? I know somewhere that might help you."

I'm missing the sounds of the waves back at the cottage and wouldn't mind another nature moment to try and center my anxiety. Wyatt asks a passing Halo Knight for directions to some room, I don't catch the name, and he can't even hide his own enthusiasm. I bet he's terrible at keeping surprise parties a secret. He jogs up the stone steps of the south-facing tower. My recovering wounds make the climb a little harder for me without any of the adrenaline that's pushed me forward so far, but when I get to the top it was worth every single ache.

The room is one massive nest with three baby phoenixes who immediately stare at us. The sun swallower has patchy orange and crimson feathers and their wide black eyes lose interest in us as two evergreen blazers charge. The world's most popular firebird coughs out the tiniest of flames, which sends the young brown-and-green phoenixes tripping over themselves as they flee. The sun swallower's chest proudly puffs out.

"This is a nursery of sorts," Wyatt says.

"Can I hide out here forever?"

"Be my guest. I wouldn't mind having some of my ashes spread here."

Maybe to a Halo Knight that's not a grim sentiment, but I'm

less concerned about what will happen with my ashes and more hung up on what's in store for my next life if I can't break out of this infinity cycle.

Wyatt carefully scoops up the sun swallower. "Want to hold her?"

"I shouldn't."

"Come on. She doesn't bite. Though she might burn off your eyebrows if she's feeling gassy."

I tense up as the memory of Luna stabbing Gravesend replays in my head. Her last cry. Her dark blue blood spilling down my chest before Luna drained the rest over the cauldron. "The last phoenix I held was killed."

"But you weren't her killer. You were her protector."

I think about the look in Gravesend's eyes as all life vanished. "I failed."

"You think we don't fail?" Wyatt rubs the neck of the phoenix pressed against his chest. "Sun swallowers like this little lady are treated as a delicacy in many top-tier restaurants. A plate can cost upward of a thousand pounds. The treatment in those kitchens is cruel. The phoenixes are locked in cages, killed and carved and cooked and served. Unfortunately for sun swallowers, they're reborn from their ashes a full day later, cursed to die over and over to be someone's dinner." There are tears in his eyes and he kisses the phoenix's head. "I've lost more fights than I've won setting them free from those conditions."

I don't know what's worse, Gravesend losing all of her future lives after her first death, or all these caged phoenixes betrayed time and time again.

I step closer to Wyatt, and my hand hovers over the sun swallower. She flinches, suspicious of me, only settling down once I
brush her smooth feathers. I'm scared I might drop her, so I sit on
the floor and the evergreen blazers climb my ankles and race into
my lap. The sun swallower burrows her beak into me, and I sense
some comfort from her, the same way I could detect Gravesend's
thirst for war.

"They've taken to you," Wyatt says, drying his eyes.

These phoenixes crawling all over me remind me of the
BuzzFeed interview where Wesley was playing with puppies.
Brighton probably watched it ten times. Man, he's probably sliding into BuzzFeed's DMs right now trying to set something up
for himself. I don't need that kind of attention.

"I wish I had my camera," Wyatt says.

"All good."

This is one of those moments I swear I'll remember in my
next life.

An evergreen blazer pecks at my stomach, and I'm lucky
they're still young because their beaks grow sharp enough to
pierce through trees as adults.

"I can sometimes sense what a phoenix is feeling," I say.

"Yeah?"

"The first time it happened was when I was close to Gravesend's egg. Her song was this beautiful chaos that told me how
lethal she would be." There's a part of me that doesn't want to talk
about these powers that I shouldn't have so Wyatt won't see me as
a specter. But this is why I'm here. I've got to share these insights
so we can stop this. "Then I felt her warning me of danger after

she hatched. That's when she was stolen from me and . . ."

Wyatt sits beside me. "It's odd that Luna wanted a century phoenix. If killed, wouldn't she want to be reborn sooner than one hundred years?"

"I was told by . . ." I remember the conversation with Ness in the supplies closet where he laid out everything for me. The sun swallower cuddles up against my chest and maybe she can feel my emotions too. "I was told by an insider that Luna has been very calculating. Maybe the regenerative essence of the golden-strand hydra has some effect on the century phoenix's rebirthing?"

"I'm sure many alchemists who had hoped to accomplish a similar elixir of their own would've overlooked century phoenixes since resurrection may ultimately feel like death if they return a lifetime later to find their loved ones gone and the world changed. She's certainly a genius if this is the case. Evil genius, but a genius nonetheless."

If only we had someone as brilliant on our side to solve this power-binding potion.

"You recall nothing from Bautista's or Keon's lives," Wyatt states.

"Nope. Luna believes she fractured my ability to remember past lives when she stabbed Bautista with an infinity-ender blade. I'm only alive because she didn't deliver an instantly fatal blow during that lifetime."

"But then that would mean that Bautista knew he was Keon. Perhaps there's a chance we mend that ability for you or even . . ." There's so much life in Wyatt's eyes as his thoughts have carried him away, like he's flying away on Nox to his next destination.

271

"What if . . . But no . . . except not impossible all things considered . . . work our way back and then . . ." Wyatt stops talking to himself as he stands. "Emil, take care of these little nuggets. I have matters to discuss with Tala." He has one foot out of the door when he stops. "It's clear I mean nuggets as the little precious babies of gold they are and not to be eaten, yes? Wonderful, wonderful."

Wyatt leaves, this time for good.

The sun swallower and evergreen blazers continue crawling all over me, and even though I'm not fully convinced I deserve it, I take Wyatt's words to heart that I'm not the same as the killers I'm trying to stop. Playing with the phoenixes is a small joy I give myself, and I'm going to keep my eyes open for more.

THIRTY-ONE
PAPER BIRD

MARIBELLE

This may be a paradise for some, but watching Tala scrub Roxana's belly with a sponge makes me miss a city of people trying to kill me.

"So Wyatt seems to have gotten on your nerves," I say.

"He's very irritating."

"You two seem like tolerant exes."

"We've never dated because I'm not his reflection." Tala throws the sponge back into a bucket and sits next to me on the bench. "Also because I'm a lesbian. Wyatt is an exceptional Halo Knight who will do great things, I've thought this since meeting him two years ago. But sometimes it's hard being around him. It's as if . . . it's as if he's walking sunshine in a colorless world. I know that death is part of the cycle, but my loss is still fresh and I can't imagine a future where I'm giving out fun Sanctuary tours or flirting with someone upon meeting them."

I relate to so much of what she's saying. I'm further along on this journey of grieving parents, but I still have great distances to travel too.

"Atlas is the reason I wasn't angry all the time."

"No one would've described me as quick to anger before my parents died."

"It's like you've lost yourself."

"All the good parts of my soul," Tala says as she pulls out a piece of paper from her pocket and begins folding. "In some ways, the old Tala has burned out and I'm still getting used to the new Tala who has been reborn in her place." She focuses on what appears to be origami. I can make out the wings right before she presents it. "Paper bird."

"Is origami your thing?"

I didn't expect that from someone who engineers weapons.

"We weren't wealthy, so my parents always encouraged crafts to build something great out of something ordinary. My mother taught me how to make the paper birds for my tenth birthday. We used them as party favors and decorations. . . ." Tala's eyes search the sky as if she's waiting for her reincarnated parents to fly toward her, carrying her old soul.

The English accent breaks the silence. "There you are. Tala, we must discuss something that is absolutely skybreaking."

Tala composes herself. I see so much of myself in her with how quickly she can return to the world when her mind is elsewhere.

"What is it?" she asks.

"It's unofficial-but-potentially-official Halo Knight business."

"I'm even less interested in your secrets than I was your tour," I say.

"Then you won't mind that I snag this one for a moment," Wyatt says with a beaming smile, as if he won a match I wasn't fighting.

"Sunshine," Tala mutters as she walks after him.

She turns, throwing her paper bird, and it glides perfectly through the air and lands in my palm.

THIRTY-TWO
TRACK

BRIGHTON

I don't like being treated like I'm not valuable. I have millions of followers. I'm pretty damn brilliant. I have put hours and hours into building my online platform. So why am I being cut out of important conversations? Hopefully Emil is giving Wyatt a history lesson that the Spell Walkers drove me away when they pulled nonsense like this and I have no problem turning my back on the Halo Knights too.

I'm not doing a great job masking my annoyance for Prudencia. This mistreatment is going to sour my mood and threaten my chances at a real relationship with her. If this were a livestream I could hide my emotions, I'm a pro at turning on the confident Brighton for my Brightsiders. But Pru sees right through me.

We're in the dining hall and I finish my soup in silence, doing my best to ignore this Halo Knight staring me down as if I personally slit his phoenix's neck.

"Don't mind him," Prudencia says.

He's trying to catch a fire-bolt to his face.

We abandon our empty bowls and catch some air. I want to dash around from room to room, kicking down castle doors until I find Emil, but Prudencia wants to do some birdwatching, so we make our way down to the courtyard. I can't really identify any of these phoenixes, but I take deep breaths because I'm getting worked up again over how Emil and Wyatt took it personally when I hinted at wanting one. Emil is lying if he's saying he doesn't want a phoenix companion, and he's a true fool if he doesn't see the advantages of having one by his side to protect him in case I'm not around.

This war isn't ending anytime soon. Even once we manage to wipe out Luna and all her Blood Casters in New York there are still others spread out across the country wreaking their own havoc. They'll track us down. Not to mention all the alchemists who have sworn allegiance to Luna. If Emil's powers haven't bounced back by then and I've got to take down all of these foes I won't be around to babysit him.

A blue phoenix descends from the air and lands a few feet away from us. I'm pretty sure this is a century phoenix given how much it looks like a slightly older Gravesend. Longer tailfeathers, fuzzier chest, bigger bronze beak. Prudencia kneels before the phoenix like she's going to bow and offers her palm. The century ignores her and takes an interest in me.

"Not me, buddy. Go to her."

The phoenix cocks its head like I've told some riddle. Then I realize I'm the riddle. Gravesend's blood must've called out to this phoenix but I'm very clearly not a firebird. The century comes closer, inspecting me. Perhaps there's some extension of power to be gained here, or a bond I can build so this phoenix will align itself with me. I'm not sure how the Halo Knights go about claiming phoenixes, but this could be my way in, especially if I'm not able to fly for whatever reason.

I cautiously reach out my hand. "You bite me and I'll rain down fire on you."

Prudencia lets out a little laugh. "I could do without the threat, but it's refreshing to see the boy who grew back his arm concerned about losing his hand."

The century phoenix squawks and flaps its wings. It jumps on me before I can get to my feet to dash away and pecks my chest. I grab its body, squeezing, and the phoenix's beak hammers into my cheek before it suddenly flies backward—no, before Prudencia sends it flying. We've caught the attention of a couple Halo Knights who are laughing. I have blood dripping down my face and they think this is a joke.

"Did they sic that phoenix on me?" I ask. I'm ready to ask them myself with a fire-bolt when Prudencia grabs my hand.

"Let's find you a bathroom to wash that off."

I'm tired of all this walking around, especially when people are ignoring us when we ask for directions. I think the only way to get some respect is if we're wearing some store-bought phoenix Halloween costumes and demand them to serve us. Someone should teach these Halo Knights a lesson that it's okay to care

278

about human beings too—especially ones that are bleeding.

"Bright! Pru!"

We turn and Emil is coming down a set of stairs from one of the towers. Dad used to love saying when we had a pep in our steps and Emil certainly has one in his. I don't know where Wyatt is, but maybe he and Emil hooked up. Any other day I would be proud of him, but not right now. He notices the blood.

"What happened?"

"Some bastard phoenix."

"What did you do?"

"You for real? Do you think I maimed some phoenix?"

"I don't know what you've been up to."

"Likewise. What did Wyatt want?"

"He wanted to talk about my past lives, so he took me up to this tower with young phoenixes and—"

I force out a laugh that shuts him. "I'm happy that you're playing with phoenixes while I'm getting attacked by one. Did you at least bring up using Nox to track down Ma?"

Emil's flushed cheeks say everything.

"Wow, Emil."

"I didn't get a chance. Wyatt had some sort of breakthrough and he ran off to find Tala."

I'm boiling because I'm tired of Ma's kidnapping feeling like something that can keep being overlooked. "Whatever. I'm going to go for a run and wash up. Have fun telling Prudencia about the phoenixes."

I dash down the halls, and I'm a little dizzy from the blood loss. Wesley wouldn't have advised me running in bursts of swift-speed in this condition but I had to get out of there before I could lay into Emil. I find a bathroom and immediately get a wet towel against my cut until there's no more blood. I scrub my cheek clean and I'm left with a nasty scratch. It's frustrating and ridiculous that I'm not self-healing yet, especially since phoenixes and hydras both have that ability, but it wasn't instant for Emil, so I got to hang tight.

I'm not in a rush so I walk back, catching up on my messages. I've got a text from Nina, who I haven't heard much from since we broke up. She left a voice message after Dad died, but that's about it. Even with everything that's thrusted my family into the public eye this past month, this is the first time I'm hearing from her. Her little brother apparently wants an autograph. That kid snitched on us when Nina and I were planning on having sex. Normally I wouldn't do him any favors but it works out since I'm glad I got to have my first time with Prudencia. I tell Nina I'll send something when I get the chance. I really got to get my merch shop open.

"Brighton, Brighton, Brighton," Wyatt calls out to me. "You know, my mum is from Brighton. She took the train into London and met my dad. Great name you have."

I was supposed to be Miguel, but Dad wanted to honor his best friend and named me after him. Not that I'm telling Wyatt any of this.

He stares at my scratch. "Are you well?"

I cut right to the chase. "You said your phoenix loves tracking. Help us find our mother and the Blood Casters will be there too. Kill two birds with one stone."

Wyatt cringes. "Surely you understand that expression is distasteful around these parts."

"Please educate me on phoenix-friendly expressions after my mother is no longer locked away with major heart issues in a severely stressful situation."

He looks embarrassed. "Sorry, mate. Nox is indeed a brilliant tracker. Do you have any of your mum's personal belongings?"

"Not on me, but back at home. Can't you use my blood?"

Wyatt shakes his head. "'Fraid not. The Reaper's Blood will throw the whole hunt out of whack. It needs to be pure, and we sadly can't use Emil's blood either since . . ."

"Since he's not her biological son." This is the one curse the Reaper's Blood has cast on me, but it's still valuable. I may not be able to use my blood to find Ma, but I will use the powers the blood has given me to be her Infinity Savior. "Then what do we do?"

"I tell you what. We can send for some of your mum's clothes back at your house and see if Nox can pick up a trail. But for now we should gather your lot and meet with Tala and Maribelle in the library because I may have discovered a skybreaking way to channel your phoenix abilities."

"What? Don't keep me in suspense, especially not after you ran off with my brother like I'm insignificant—"

"I believe you can travel back in time."

THIRTY-THREE
REVERSING THE CYCLE

EMIL

The castle's library is intimate, but I'd happily kick up my feet on the gray chaise for hours, or as Wyatt would put it, spread my ashes here.

There are prints of different phoenixes above some knee-high bookcases, signaling the books that center on that particular breed. I stop in front of the century phoenix, grieving Gravesend, who won't ever grow up to spread her wings as massively and proudly as this illustrated one. Tala opens the balcony doors and air blows in. There are a couple chairs outside, but there's hardly any space to stretch with Nox and Roxana resting on the floor.

Everyone is gathered around a wooden table already, but I'm lagging behind as I admire all these colorful spines of books with general information about caring for phoenixes. I could spend the rest of my life here reading up on phoenixkind, armed with the knowledge to try and save them. That's not why we've been brought in here, so I grab a seat before Brighton can come down on me again for experiencing a second of leisure. There's a chandelier with beak-shaped bulbs and the light is casting over seven volumes of *The Firebird Compendium*. Wyatt is flipping through the pages of an eighth volume.

"Share your theory," Tala says as she sits on the back of Maribelle's chair.

"I'm finding the page I need for a smoother presentation," Wyatt says. "I'd hate to disrupt the flow once we get these wings flapping because—aha!" He murmurs the text to himself while nodding along. "Marvelous. Emil, sweet Emil, when discussing the range of your powers it got me thinking. A phoenix's most beautiful talent is rebirth, and we didn't know specters to be privileged with that ability until we met you."

I hadn't directly considered resurrection as a privilege. There are so many people who have died ahead of their times—Dad, Atlas—and yet I'm the one whose soul has been brought back twice already. For all we know, I'm the first and only specter who experiences this. Will this work for Maribelle since she's also part-celestial? Will it work for Brighton since his grand set of powers are technically incomplete? What about my enemies like Orton? Has he already been reborn as an infant and will grow up with the memories of our feud?

For the infinitieth time, I want out of this cycle.

"So what's the deal?" I ask.

Brighton leans forward. "Wyatt thinks we can go back in—"

"Buh, buh, buh, buh!" Wyatt shakes his finger. "You didn't take kindly to my 'low-budget science-fiction-movie rip-off' but that doesn't mean you can rob me of my dramatics." He shifts his attention back to me. "I was wondering perhaps if we could repair your memories and almost overlooked how phoenixes don't always return with their previous life's memories. That doesn't mean they're lost forever. It simply requires more of a journey."

"A journey back through time," Brighton says. "He thinks we can go back in time."

Wyatt's jaw drops. "You bastard."

Brighton smirks.

I'm not making the connection. "I'm sorry. What? How are we time-traveling?"

"Don't frame it too literally. Unlike your brother's accusation, this won't run the narrative of standard time-travel movies that come with a bunch of rules about not bumping into your past self or even so much as moving a single rock without changing the course of history." Wyatt sits on the table beside me with the book in his lap. "You see, phoenixes need history. When they resurrect they are carrying their past lives with them through time, but they can move backward if they desire—it's known as retrocycling. It's a necessary function for phoenixes whose memories have been fractured, such as yours, to return through their past lives and gather the wisdom they need to avoid repeating mistakes. If phoenixes can retrocycle, I don't see why you can't travel through your own bloodlines."

I always thought the memories of my past lives were lost in

time. I've read up a little on phoenixes retrocycling, but that's not something I thought I could pull off. After the Halo Knights were killed at the museum and Kirk was giving up Gravesend to turn me into some science experiment, he was speculating if I could slip into my previous lives. Luna didn't answer his question. I'm not sure if she even knows herself if this is possible for phoenix specters.

"You think I can work my way back through Bautista's life?"

"Perhaps. Then you can see for yourself what Bautista and Sera were planning with their power-binding potion."

Assuming any of this is legit, my life grows more and more surreal. There's a chance I can transport myself to the past and become one with Bautista? I really can't believe this. I turn and Brighton seems to believe it just fine. Envy is written all over his face.

"What about me?" Brighton asks. "And Maribelle. You said this would affect all of us, but we don't have past lives like Emil."

"Of course you doubt reincarnation," Tala says before Wyatt can speak. "And you continue to know nothing about the blood of the creature within you."

"A phoenix has two bloodlines," Wyatt gently says. "The first tracing back to their family. The second flowing infinitely from their personal life cycle. If my theory holds any weight, there will be opportunities for Brighton and Maribelle to retrocycle too through their familial bloodlines."

Maribelle's face lights up for the first time in ages, but a shadow seems to come over her as quickly. "I . . . I can't see Mama and Papa. Only Bautista and Sera."

"You can see Aurora and Lestor," Brighton says. "But I'm guessing they would have to be around Bautista and Sera. Shouldn't be too hard since they were all original Spell Walkers." A smile is creeping up on him. "I can see Dad with my power."

Much like Maribelle, I'm taken aback. I was on the edge of a thought of which moments in the past I'd love to reexperience with Dad, when I remember that even though he's my father we're not linked by blood. If this war ever settles and I get the time I need to process every ounce of trauma, I'd like to imagine myself finding peace over being secretly adopted sooner rather than later. But the goalpost seems to move further and further away any time the world reminds me that I was living a lie for eighteen years.

I bet I've got that same envious expression that Brighton had moments ago.

Then it hits me.

"Can Brighton only go back through the bloodline of someone if they're dead?" I ask.

"I believe so," Wyatt says. "The idea is you're connecting to other lives to aid the one you have."

I turn to Brighton. "So you could try to retrocycle to Ma. That'll tell us whether or not—"

"She's alive or dead," Brighton says, talking over me as if it's his idea.

I hope to everything that Brighton can't experience Ma's history.

"I'm so confused," Prudencia says. I'm realizing she's the only celestial in a room with Halo Knights and phoenix specters talking about past lives. "How do Halo Knights even know about a phoenix's process of retrocycling? I take it a phoenix didn't come back from their trip from the past and tell you about their vacation."

Wyatt shakes the book in the air. "My moment has come!" He opens to the page he bookmarked earlier. "Storytime, gentle-people."

Two centuries ago, when the Halo Knights were forming to combat injustices against phoenixes, insights were passed from one to the next to create a codex on how best to serve the firebirds. In those early days, there were many accounts of phoenixes inexplicably hibernating within their own fires. For some, hibernation lasted a day while others stretched for weeks. Each time the Haloes believed the phoenixes were preparing for their deaths, but the phoenixes in all cases were coming back smarter and stronger. A historian, Elodie Badeaux, traveled the world to explore this phenomenon.

I almost lose focus daydreaming about the life Elodie got to live and wishing it were my own, but I know good and well that I would've never been able to crack this code. Thankfully she was at the top of her game, interviewing all the Haloes about the specific differences in the phoenixes before and after hibernation. In one case, a sky swimmer in its sixth life seemed to have forgotten how to swim; then when she woke up after three days, she sped toward the ocean and gleefully dove in and chased dolphins. Elsewhere, a song-rook, best known for their ability to regenerate body parts, was victim to a hunter's bird trap and lost his foot, and as the phoenix surrounded himself in his violet flames, his

Halo companion said his farewells. Hours later the song-rook woke up from hibernation and immediately regrew his foot, to the grieving Halo's relief.

". . . these examples and more suggested that the phoenixes were tapping into their past lives to strengthen their present ones," Wyatt says as he closes the book. "This is a power that always exists in them. It's as instinctive as learning how to fly and as primal as breathing. Should a phoenix sense their muscle memory is off, they can simply go back in the past to remember it. Fascinating, yeah?"

"I witnessed this firsthand with Roxana," Tala says. "I was seven, and a boy in my training circle called her damaged because Roxana wasn't casting any thunderstorms after her most recent resurrection. I punched him in the nose."

"Of course you did," Brighton says.

"Care for a reenactment?" Tala asks.

Who would blame her at this point? Between Brighton shouting at Iris, who can literally rip his arms off—and happily rip them off again if they regrew—and now running his mouth to Tala, who's pissed at him for having phoenix blood, he can't keep his attitude together.

Tala turns away from him. "One evening, Roxana set her nest on fire and went to sleep. She didn't wake up the next morning, and I cried every night that followed, swearing I'd cared for her wrong. It was the most painful month of my life. And then she woke up. The sky thundered, and I danced in her downpour." This is the first time I'm seeing Tala beam as she watches Roxana. There's so much love there. I'm sure that month Tala believed her to be dead must've been unimaginable suffering.

"Similar situation with Nox," Wyatt says. "Two lives ago he was tracking a wounded phoenix in a forest and his senses couldn't have been more off. To this day I would put down ten pounds that he was only guessing. Then Nox stopped and began hibernating. I was familiar with retrocycling, but to see it in action was astonishing. I could've done without fending for myself in a forest for three nights, but Nox woke up and it took mere minutes to find the common ivory in a cave."

Wyatt is very proud of Nox too. His smile can light up the sun.

"How does this work for humans?" I ask. "Do we try and retrocycle in our sleep or something?"

"Here's where the guesswork begins. Tragically for you all there is no flame to light your path. Perhaps it happens in your sleep or you meditate or set yourself on fire or dance naked under the sun. I personally fancy the naked dancing experiment," Wyatt says as he looks me in the eye.

I'm burning up. I'm definitely rocking a vibe from Wyatt as I avoid his gaze. I don't know if he's super flirtatious with everyone or if he's going for it with me, but Wyatt is certainly more direct than any of my encounters with Ness. I'll never know what the deal was with Ness, but I always feel ridiculous even entertaining that someone as beautiful and brave as him would've been interested in someone like me. I'm probably imagining everything with Wyatt too.

"This doesn't serve me," Maribelle says.

"It might," Tala says. "You don't have control of your sensing power and that can make you a more lethal opponent to the Blood Casters. But only if you go straight to the source of your power."

Maribelle considers her words, but I wonder if that's going to be enough for her.

"Let's get started," Brighton says.

"Slow your racehorse," Wyatt says.

"No, my mother's life is on the line here."

"Absolutely, absolutely. I need some prep time to do some more research and decide on our best approach. I promise to share my findings by the morning at the absolute latest."

"What time should we come back?" I ask. I'm not sure where we'd even go since Iris doesn't want us back at the cottage. Maybe we'll sleep in the car.

"You're welcome to stay here. Two more guestrooms remain. I'll bunk here in the library. Tala, you mind escorting them?"

"Yes," Tala says.

"Thank you."

"You misunderstand. Yes, I do mind. I will work with them as long as this makes sense for phoenixkind, but I'm not putting mints on pillows or changing sheets," Tala says. She goes out to the balcony and lies down beside Roxana.

Wyatt leads the way himself, muttering about how much he's loving how good we're all getting on. There are two beds in each guestroom, and as much as I'd love to give Brighton and Prudencia some privacy, Maribelle makes it pretty clear she's not welcoming me in her room when she closes the door behind her. Hanging out in a library all night sounds chill, but this simple room with a black-and-white portrait of a flying phoenix and a view of the first courtyard will do.

"Until tomorrow," Wyatt says, tipping an invisible hat. "Perhaps later this evening if the mood strikes."

I stupidly turn away from the window and Wyatt is straight staring at me with lust in his eyes. He winks before leaving us.

Brighton laughs. "Oh, bro. That Halo Knight is hard for the Infinity Son."

"I don't think it's because he's the Infinity Son," Prudencia says. "Sorry, Emil, I'm not calling you that. Friend pass. But I do think Wyatt is interested."

"You should've taken him up earlier and ridden his phoenix," Brighton says with suggestive eyebrows.

Prudencia smacks him in the chest.

"Bright, bigger matters at hand."

"I'm looking out for you! You've never even kissed a guy and there's a Halo Knight with your favorite accent making a move on you."

On paper Wyatt is someone I should explore something with, I get that, but just because a phoenix-loving, handsome English guy might be into me doesn't mean that Ness is kicked out of my head and heart. Ness gained my trust, time and time again, and that's saying a lot considering he had multiple chances to kill me. He paid the ultimate price trying to save my life. The world grieved him after the Blackout, but I'm one of the few people who knows that he was still alive and now he's dead for real because he wanted to save me. I got to honor Ness by making sure his father doesn't become president. And to do that, I have to disempower the Blood Casters who are only supporting Senator Iron's case that gleamcrafters are dangerous.

I can't undo their wrongs, but I can try to make things right.

I have to go back to my last life to do good in this one.

THIRTY-FOUR
PAWN TO QUEEN

NESS

I'm in my bedroom dreaming up ways to beat the Senator.

The first step is incapacitating Zenon, wherever he's stationed in the manor, so he can't sound some alarm if I manage to get past Jax and morph into someone else to escape. The polling numbers I last saw were favoring the Senator, and I'm sure he's only gained more support since the propaganda videos, but if I can go live on national TV wearing the Senator's face, I'll own up to every single crime of his.

No more White House. Straight to jail.

There's a gentle knock on my door and Luna slowly enters in a crimson cloak that contrasts her sickly white skin. It's the first time I'm seeing her in the seven or eight days since she broke into the manor and built some arrangement with the Senator. She's also alone without even June at her side.

I could take her right now.

Luna picks up an unlit candle from my bookcase and smells it. "Eucalyptus. One of nature's many deceptions. It invites you in with its smell but its oils are a welcomed touch to any poison."

"You lied to me," I say, cutting to the point.

"When?"

Her question is genuine. She has trusted me with her life, with her pursuit for immortality, and who knows how many times she's lied to me.

"About the Senator," I say.

"You not asking the right questions isn't my fault."

"Would you have told the truth?"

"It's best to hold one's cards to one's chest until it's necessary. You were already more than willing to work for me—to work against your father." Luna sits beside me on my bed, bringing me back to the days when she first took me in and cared for me. "Besides, your betrayal proves why I was wise to keep secrets from you. There are many Blood Casters spread across the country, but the few I keep at my side are the ones I trust the most. The things I've asked of you could land me in prison, make me a target, but I asked them of you because it was important, because I believed in you."

There's a softness to her voice, like a mother trying to get her child to understand something very important without yelling.

The day of the Blackout, after June saved me and brought me to one of Luna's hideaway homes, Luna surprised me with lulling words of second chances. I didn't see it back then, but she was manipulating me into talking about my struggles with the Senator. She set herself up as the trusted ally who would keep me safe if I worked for her. Even though it meant risking my life to become a specter. It wasn't an easy decision, and the Cloaked Phantom was rapidly approaching. But it felt like a sign when Luna obtained a shifter wounded by a hunter, and Luna told me the poor creature could live on in spirit if I fused its blood with mine. I agreed and drank the potion thinking my new life would be better, thinking I could trust this woman who nursed me back to life with tonics when my body was dangerously morphing against my will.

Never in my life did I feel more special than when Luna taught me to shift. I was so dazzled by her praise that I couldn't see how she can transform without any gray lights.

I get up from the bed and sit at my desk. "Hopefully your next Blood Caster cooperates. Yeah, Dione told me what you were up to the night of the constellation; I'm not the only big mouth."

Luna turns to the doorway. "I'll be sure to have a word with her," she says, and then her green eyes land on me again. "It's unclear how much time I have left in this world, but I know that time isn't best spent nurturing new specters. I was using the Cloaked Phantom to fulfill a favor. Your father and I could only dream of creating a replacement for you since I've never met a single person—celestial or specter—who could transform into another as faithfully as you have. Recruiting another could be manageable for jobs with low stakes, but not changing the world as we're asking of you."

I would rather be fired from this job instead of staying on as their top employee. "Now that I've dressed up as Eva and Carolina for the Senator, I take it you're going to have me pose as the Spell Walkers next?"

"It was an idea, but then the Spell Walkers will piece together that you're alive and potentially find proof and methods to discredit your father's campaign. The same precautions are in place from when you would go undercover for me—never impersonate someone who will have a credible alibi. Eva and Carolina won't as long as they stay within our reach." Luna coughs, violently, and I fight back these old instincts to help her. "But when the time is right, you may get to wear your lover's face for us."

A chill shoots up my spine. "I don't know what you're talking about."

"I strung together the most groundbreaking alchemical formula since Keon Máximo discovered how to give humans the power of creatures. Do not mistake me for a fool who can't see young love." Luna might get that haughty smile knocked off her face if she isn't careful. "It must've been painful when you carved into him like he was nothing but roasted meat. How much harm do you think would befall him if everyone knew the truth about who he is? About who he was?"

It's my understanding that a lot of people grieved Bautista de León. There were so many memorials for him across the country, even fans across the world were impacted by his death too. But there were many that celebrated this news. And then there's every living soul who hates specters with their entire being who would take to the streets if they could pin all their anger on Emil. They wouldn't even care that Emil doesn't have a single memory from those lives, or that he's his own person who would never do what Keon Máximo did. He could become the most hunted person alive.

I've hurt Emil enough for one lifetime. I can't let others know about all of his.

"Why hasn't the Senator used this yet to villainize Emil?"

Luna grins. "As I told you, I only reveal my secrets when they benefit me. I have given Iron a blueprint to success that stands strong without him knowing that resurrection is possible."

"Why do you still care about keeping secrets? You're dying. Set the world on fire."

"You spent the better part of this year under my care, and you still think I'm nothing but a match. There has been a lot of death, I would never deny that, but I have always been in pursuit of resurrection and immortality—of life in all forms. Out of the hundreds of alchemists across the globe, I'd wager only dozens are worth anyone's time, and for the most part, we have failed humanity. No one has figured out how to cure the common cold, cancers, deadly infections, blood illnesses such as mine." There's color in her cheeks, but she still looks the weakest I've ever seen her. "Some have bought time, but never all of it," she adds with a sadness.

Her illness, haimashadow, is simply described as a sickness that blocks life. There's no known cure, though Luna was always hoping the Reaper's Blood could regenerate her arteries and make them good as new.

"If you care so much about the world, Luna, maybe you should've spent more time trying to protect those in it."

"I don't have to care for those who won't mourn me."

"It wouldn't hurt you to be more selfless," I say. She could've learned a lot from Emil if she weren't more interested in torturing him.

"There is nothing wrong with being selfish. You're allowed to have an agenda born out of your own need—fame, love, security, power, revenge. For some, it's all those and more."

It seems really greedy, but I've wanted all of these things too. There's been a lot of privilege in being a politician's son with my own bodyguard and living in a manor with a panic room. Not to mention all the financial security we've had. I dreamed of trading convention stages for the ones on Broadway and theaters across the country. Red carpets, press junkets, popping into drama schools to share my wisdom. I was looking forward to getting older and discovering the power of my own choices, but instead I'm wondering how I can get my revenge on the Senator and Luna, who stole my free will with manipulation and threats. And there's love, which maybe starts with running into a building to save someone when you're finally free to become yourself.

"I see it in your eyes that you don't disagree," Luna says.

Even though I swear I'm masking my emotions, she still sees through me.

"What's your point?" I ask.

"That it became clear to me ages ago that I wouldn't achieve dominion over life and death in an average life span. It takes alchemists decades to master their craft, and even supreme ones such as Keon and myself were advanced thanks to the works left behind by those before us. Loss has put me on my journey, but don't you think it would be a great sadness to rebuild the world and not live in it? That doesn't seem fair at all."

"And it doesn't serve you," I mock.

She's stone-faced. "It does not. What I want most in this world is my dear sister, Raine, to be more than ashes in an urn. I have gone through incredible, unnatural lengths to bring her back to life, and despite my many breakthroughs and discoveries, I needed more time to solve the puzzle of true resurrection, which the Reaper's Blood would've afforded me."

She'll die before I apologize.

"For the longest time, I carried many regrets. There were opportunities to claim powers of my own, especially when I was young enough that it wouldn't pose the great risks to me that we've seen with those who are older, but the dawn of specters was still new. Their powers may be extraordinary, but above all, specters are still mortal; even my miracle June won't live on forever. Thankfully, I didn't make any rash decisions, since there's nothing to suggest that phoenix blood on its own would've brought me back as I am, and we've seen that to be true with Keon and his scions. The creation of immortality always meant playing the long game, and I've done just that, from working alongside Keon to nurturing my marriage to empowering all of you Blood Casters."

"I didn't know you were married." Before she can say anything, I add, "I get it. It wasn't my business."

Luna's smile is interrupted by another cough, blood painting her palm. She wipes it on her crimson cloak, not bothering with a handkerchief. "Once Keon was killed by the Halo Knights and

299

didn't resurrect, I believed him dead and sought out other ways to get closer to death. There were quintuplets in Colombia, all brothers haunted by their deathlike powers."

I prop my elbow on my desk, finding myself pulled into this story that feels like a fairy tale. The eldest brother, Fabian, could hear and understand ghosts, but was so tormented by their pleas that he took his own life. Mattias's howls grew to be so piercing that an entire town's combusted brains traced back to him. Santiago secluded himself to avoid his visions of imminent deaths. Álvaro could smell someone's bones and blood and predict how much time they had left. And the youngest was Davian, whose touch was so deadly that his mother died from childbirth.

"Santiago was the last living brother when I arrived in Colombia, and while I would've loved to work with Fabian and his direct line to ghosts, I arrived at Santiago's house with promises of helping control his power so he could return to the world," Luna says proudly, and as someone who agreed to shifting powers for the same dream, I'm not surprised that he embraced her. "I gained his trust, and he welcomed me into his home and heart. I was given everything after our marriage—the family's estate, their darkest secrets, even a child with great potential who is no more. I don't consider myself superstitious, but even I would say that family was cursed."

I'm wrapping my head around how she was a wife and mother and I never knew any of this. I can morph into her and capture the exact shade of green in her eyes and the cracks in her lips and the wrinkles in her neck and the dark red tongue from her daily tonics. But that's all surface. I can't ever imitate the shadowy heart inside her.

"Did Santiago take his own life like his brother?"

"No, I gave myself the honor of killing him. I took great joy in watching his eyes glow as he foresaw the death I planned for him, and how powerless he was to stop it."

I can't even pretend this is shocking. This is the same woman who murdered her parents when she was young. It all tracks. "Sounds like he didn't serve you."

"He gave me a child, and through that, I learned how to nurture those with powers. The Blood Casters were born years later."

"Thanks for the history lesson. It's great to know you've always been this horrible."

Luna lets out a little laugh. "You once believed me to be the lesser evil—that your father was an even more dangerous criminal. You wondered about your next assignment. I'll have you know that you'll be impersonating Nicolette Sunstar in the upcoming debate. The plan is quite diabolical, designed by yours truly. But I am simply buying time until I can make my next move, and when I can, I'm hoping that these personal confessions of my past will have regained your trust. I don't have any family left, though I consider you mine."

I don't want to show my anger, but there's no face I can hide behind. "You would have more family if you didn't kill everyone off."

She inhales a deep breath as she rises from the bed and makes her way to the door. "You don't—"

"Shut up! You think you're some manipulation mastermind and bragging about using others, as if the Senator isn't using you right back."

I expect her to call for Stanton to punish me for lashing out like this, then I remember that he's not in the picture and she's in my house and she doesn't hold full power over me anymore. Luna grins, like she's proud that I've stood up to her.

"It's true that no matter how calculating one can be in a round of chess, the queen can still be overtaken by an unsuspecting force. But the game continues as long as the king stands, and a pawn may cross to the other side of the board, stronger than before. What I'm asking of you, darling Ness, is if you are on my side when I return to power or an enemy to be conquered?"

THIRTY-FIVE
MORNING NOX

EMIL

The only thing better than falling asleep to phoenix song is waking up to it.

I've been so haunted by the sound of Gravesend's final cries, it straight rings through my bones, but this morning I'm gifted new sounds as phoenixes call out to each other before taking to the sky. A phoenix's cycle is life and death, but the past twenty-four hours have been the first time ever I'm getting to see so many of them live. Mad love to Brighton and Prudencia for giving me the bed by the window so I can experience all these sights. Sunlight creeps onto me as a common ivory flies past, so close that I could've brushed its silvery tailfeather.

I wish every day could start like this. But today we may prove

303

Wyatt's theory nonsense, and then the Halo Knights will kick us out of the Sanctuary.

I'm going to make the most of this while I can. I sneak out while Bright and Pru are still sleeping, her arms wrapped around him. I greet a Halo Knight good morning, but she continues extinguishing the lit sconces without a word to me. I'm trying not to take it personally. Part of me wants to tell them all that I didn't actually choose this life for myself, but maybe I'm better off this way, instead of them knowing I used to be their number one enemy, the guy whose work has caused great devastation to all creatures, including the phoenixes the Haloes care for.

I keep my eyes low until I get to the courtyard. I hang out under the shade of an apple tree because the sun is really going for it up on these mountains. Watching these phoenixes in the sky makes me wish I could've shared this experience with Ma and Dad. For our tenth birthday, I got a blue kite shaped like a phoenix, and Brighton took pictures of me flying it around on his new camera. I badly wish I could retrocycle to that day—the four of us stretched out on the picnic blanket Abuelita sewed for us, eating arroz con gandules and tostones with garlic and playing Uno in the park until we couldn't stand the bugs anymore.

Wind picks up behind me, and there's a quiet thud. I turn, expecting to find a fallen apple, but there's an obsidian phoenix staring at me with pitch-black eyes. His cabbage breath blows my way and I'm frozen in place until Wyatt dismounts Nox. Then I'm stuck for other reasons. Wyatt's muscular thighs are tight against his shorts. His gray mesh crop top reveals abs that are paler than his toned arms; I guess his abs don't get as much sun as the rest of his body. He's sweating all over, and the white headband holding back his brown hair seems to have soaked up some of it.

"Snuck up on you," Wyatt says.

"Yeah. Nox is quiet."

"Crucial for a tracker."

"Were you tracking me?"

Wyatt sits on the grass. "Nox and I always begin our days with a flight. The sun can be bloody blistering, but he's a cranky bird if he doesn't have it his way. I spotted you walking toward this here tree when returning, but I'd be more than pleased to personally seek you out next time."

The way he can hold a gaze makes me so nervous.

"So is the heat why you're wearing that?"

"You noticed, yeah?" Wyatt's closed-lip smile is a turn-on even during questionable times, I can't lie. "Here's the business, love. Our signature cactus-leather jackets with phoenix feathers are beautiful, true works of art, I'd never deny that. But it's absurd to wear them when the sun is high. The mesh tops are winners— they're stylish, they're flexible, they're breezy. I'm thinking about getting some matching shorts so the lads can breathe."

He looks down at his crotch proudly.

"I don't see anything," I say.

Wyatt's jaw drops and he holds his hand to his heart. "Ah, sweet Emil has died and an arsehole rises from the ashes. Interesting, interesting. Perhaps I should strip down so you can see for yourself."

I definitely walked right into that one. "Nah, you're good."

"You sure? I love being naked, and I wouldn't mind seeing

305

you wear my clothes. I bet you'd look bangin' in all of this your-self."

A mesh crop top is pretty high up on the list of clothes no one will catch me wearing. I'm not trying to make my bones and scars more visible. But Wyatt's flirting takes me back to that art supplies room with Ness. I remember the smell of paint and paper, how hot I got when he said he believed my body would be as solid as my face, how safe I felt when his hands were roaming around me to clean my wounds, and how close I was to asking him to open his eyes so he could see me. And now he never will.

"Are you okay?" Wyatt asks.

"What? Yeah, yeah."

"You seemed to be in a pretty sad trance. I'm sorry if I over-stepped."

"No, you're fine." I don't want to get into it right now. I'm associated with enough death as it is. "I'm just taking in the Sanc-tuary while I can. I'm sure we'll have to bounce once we fail at retrocycling." He doesn't deny it. The pressure to get it right so I can stay here longer has only grown. "It would no doubt be my favorite power if it worked for my own lifetime. I'd use it to see my parents together again, even one more time."

Brighton's got it good if his powers can carry him back to Dad's life. He spent last night talking about how great it would be to see our parents when they first met and even experience all their highs and lows. He was very clear that he would avoid any moment that looked even slightly intimate because he doesn't want to be scarred for life. Prudencia must've nudged him while my back was turned or something because he seemed to come to his senses and remember that I can't witness anything from Ma and Dad.

"No one knows for sure whether you can go back through your present life," Wyatt says. "But I agree it seems unlikely, since the purpose of that ability seems to be to hop back to a previous life."

"Brighton swears that something being unlikely doesn't make it impossible."

"That's the smartest thing to come out of his mouth. Well, his mouth through your mouth. That all sounds terribly awkward."

"Yeah, go back in time and undo the hell out of that one, please," I say with a laugh. "Actually, if you could go back in time, is there a particular moment you have in mind?"

"Ah. Love this question."

Wyatt mutters different ideas, but he clearly won't commit to any of them. I personally want to know more about his favorite book, which he wants to go back and witness himself finishing for the first time. "It feels like cheating, but I'm most keen on moments with Nox. I'm not even saying that because he's right here," he adds with a smile. Nox eats an apple off the tree, paying us no mind. "One possibility: I was struck for days after we first flew together. It was honestly better than sex, and let there be no doubts that I've had loads of great sex."

It's definitely not a plot twist that Wyatt has been busy. I wonder if he's hinting at something with a committed partner or casual encounters. Maybe a combo of the two. He's what, also eighteen? Nineteen? Twenty? He's definitely living up his life more than I am. I can only imagine what my situation would look like if I had even a tenth of his confidence.

"That sounds like a great choice," I say, skating past his sex comment.

"But if I had to choose one moment, I'd go back to when Nox finally chose me."

"What do you mean?"

"What, do you think Halo Knights call dibs on a phoenix and fly off merrily? We have to prove ourselves worthy. We reckon Nox was in his nineties when his former companion died. That bastard was apparently abusive, and if he were alive today, I would hold his face to the fire for all the aggression he took out on Nox."

In moments I go from wondering about Wyatt's sex life to remembering that he's a Halo Knight who may have killed before.

"Nox had trust issues and wasn't bonding with anyone else. He seemed especially irritated with me at age eight. I was very annoying, believe it or not. I'd begun training to become a Halo Knight around that time, employing all my nurturing lessons to show Nox that I was safe. But Nox was hard to woo. Over the years Nox seemed to regard me more favorably, but still wouldn't commit to me by the time I was thirteen. I was the only one among my trainees who didn't have a companion. They treated me like I wasn't worth the dirt between a phoenix's talons."

Five years is a long time to wait. "There wasn't another phoenix that caught your eye?"

"Absolutely. There was a queen slayer who'd recently resurrected, and I thought it would be lovely to care for one like my dad, but whether or not Nox was on the grounds with us or away on some adventure, I knew Nox was the right one for me.

Our friendship was flickering; I simply had to tend to the fire. Then Nox returned after being gone for months. He was skeletal. Dying." Wyatt gets up, as if magnetized back to his companion, and he kisses Nox between his eyes. "It's an odd thing to grieve a phoenix you know will resurrect, but obsidians need roughly three years before respawning. Nox let me hold him as he died, and I protected his ashes in an iron crate. When Nox came back to life I was a blubbering mess, I'd missed him so much. He flew onto my shoulder and nibbled my ear, and we were each other's."

"What do you think made Nox ultimately choose you?" I ask.

"I think he understood that not only would I never hurt him, that I would show him the love he deserves. Frankly, I would've waited the rest of my life for him." He turns to Nox. "Don't go getting any ideas, my beauty. Seven years was plenty."

This is a beautiful memory Wyatt has shared, one definitely worth retrocycling to. I'm determined to create a world where Wyatt, and all these other Halo Knights, never have to fear someone killing their phoenix companions to steal their powers. That problem began with Keon and will be resolved by me if it's the last thing I do in this life.

THIRTY-SIX
INFINITY SENSES

EMIL

We're gearing up in the Sanctuary's meditation room. It's a simple space with racked candles, incense, a banner of a sun swallower, and a vaulted ceiling with windows wide enough for phoenixes to enter, since they're welcome here as much as anyone else. Or should I say, *more* than anyone else. It's hard for us to feel welcome when a man wraps up his prayers early because he doesn't want to be here with us. Tala hands us mats that she borrowed from one of the housekeeping families, and we roll them out on the floor. She intentionally gives Brighton the smallest one, intended for a child.

I sit in a triangle with Brighton and Maribelle while Prudencia leans against the wall.

Wyatt opens his logbook. "I spent the greater part of yesterday exploring different potential methods for a specter to retrocycle. Humans don't hibernate in the traditional sense, but we do sleep, and perhaps more importantly, we dream. I imagine retrocycling will feel much like a dreamer with intense lucidity, but the success rate for that is not in our favor."

"Based on what? Data from ordinary people?" Brighton asks. "We're above their level."

"Be my guest and prove how powerful you are by mastering a muscle that doesn't naturally exist within any human being."

I can practically feel how badly Brighton wants to do just that.

Maribelle is fidgety, like she's forgotten how to stay still. "We don't need to know what won't work. We need to know what will."

"You lot are no friends to suspense. Fine. I believe it is in our best interest if you set yourselves entirely on fire," Wyatt says, showing us a page in his logbook of three stick figures with flames around them. "I take it there will be no concerns since you're used to the fire already."

"Yeah, but not our entire bodies." I've gotten stronger since getting my powers, but throwing fire still isn't easy. The weight of it all is so tiring.

"Your own fire doesn't hurt you, yes?"

Brighton and Maribelle say no, but I say yes.

"Not usually," I say, remembering how the charged-up fire-orb I threw at the force field in the cemetery knocked the air out of me. "But it's been more painful to use my powers since Luna stabbed me with the infinity-ender."

311

"I'm sensitive to that, love; I don't want to put you through pain—"

"Then don't," Prudencia says. "I know you want to protect phoenixkind, but I'm speaking up for my friend. The last time Emil even so much as conjured a fire-orb he didn't have it in him to throw it. He put himself through that to save our lives."

Wyatt looks like he wants to counter, maybe mutter something to himself, but he nods instead. "Understood. Brighton, you're welcome to experiment too, but perhaps our focus should be on getting Maribelle to retrocycle since she will have access to Bautista's life as well."

"Fine by me," Maribelle says.

"I want to try," I say.

"You don't have to," Prudencia says.

"Yeah, bro, don't put yourself through that," Brighton says.

"This is one of the rare times I can make the most of these powers without actually fighting," I say. I wasn't up to full strength during our Crowned Dreamer battle because of all the pain Ness had inflicted on me, but the constellation helped my powers. I can use them, I just have to be the strongest I've ever been at withstanding the pain. "I swear I'll tap out if the fire becomes too much."

Brighton and Prudencia seem wary while Wyatt is glowing with gratitude for my efforts. I know he's not trying to throw me in danger, but either way, this is worth the risk. It's how I can make good on Keon's crimes.

I straight wish that doing the right thing was enough to overcome fear.

Wyatt walks us through everything else. Tala will coach us on measuring our breaths plus focusing and together they will try to guide us on our journeys back. We know this all might be pointless, but we're asked to believe in this fully, otherwise we may not be able to connect to our pasts and our bloodlines. I have no reason to think this isn't possible. I might be my roadblock if I can't tough it out.

Before we begin, Brighton twists around. "Pru, film this."

"This is a sacred space, and most importantly, you're calling forth a sacred power," Tala says with an edge. "The Halo Knights will determine whether or not a specter's ability to retrocycle will become public knowledge."

"Yeah, Bright, we're trying to make becoming a specter less exciting," I say.

"I know, but—" He stops himself. "You're both right. I'm sorry."

Brighton apologizing is stranger than watching him grow three heads and everyone seems to agree. Prudencia is the only one smirking. Thank the stars she's getting through to him.

Tala seems suspicious, but for once she doesn't have to fight back. She leads us through some deep breaths for what feels like an hour but in reality is probably only ten minutes. Even though I got some good sleep this whole thing is only making me more tired. "Focus on the lives you haven't lived, think about what you need from them, what you hope to gain from going back," she says. "Remember that phoenixes weren't taught to use this power. It was pure instinct. Follow yours."

"When you're ready," Wyatt says. "Ignite."

THIRTY-SEVEN
THE SCENT OF BLUE

MARIBELLE

I begin with Sera.

I will forever be a Lucero and wear that name like a badge of honor, but in blood I'm a Córdova and a de León. This biological connection with Sera will bring me closer to her, to helping me better understand her psychic powers, which have passed down to me. But I'm resisting. Mama and Papa actually taught me how to use my powers. I was seven when I stood on the balcony of the house we were staying in and I told my parents I was going to jump and fly like them. They told me I wasn't ready but I jumped anyway and before I could crash through the dining table Mama caught me. Her hands are the ones I want to feel around me now.

I can't resist Sera. I don't know how much she loved me, whether or not she wanted me, or if I would've been safe with her, but I have to accept her if I'm going to reach her. I can't keep acting as if she doesn't matter because she doesn't have any bearing on my life today, or because I feel guilty I'm not honoring my real parents. Sera being my mother doesn't mean Mama wasn't.

In the darkness, I struggle forward as if there's an actual road I'm traveling, one paved with guilt and grief. The more I think about Sera raising me, the more my senses feel out of control. It's like I'm separating from myself, like I'm being reborn as the daughter I would've been if Sera hadn't been killed. I believe I can smell the color blue—ocean waves crashing into each other, baths with Atlas where he would get carried away with shampooing my hair for his own amusement, clear skies I can now fly within. I listen to pain—when I was a girl trying to glide from one tree to the next and smacked through the river's surface, the way my heartbeat was so loud in my head when I held Atlas's corpse.

This is unlike any sensation I've ever experienced, so I must be getting somewhere. I trust my instinct and grow my senses. I feel lost and found inside a space that's warm and cool and everything and nothing. There are whispers invading my head and heart and clarity strikes me like lightning. As suddenly and oddly sure as I am that my own birth felt like being woken up by starlight, I know the person I'm hearing is Sera Córdova even though her voice is completely foreign to me. I have no idea what she's saying, it's as if she's expecting me to read her lips that I can't see, but something about this space bridging our bloodlines allows me to understand the emotions behind her words—there's love, there's panic, there's sorrow, there's defeat. Then finally relief.

I think I'm somewhere near the very edge of her death.

THIRTY-EIGHT
THE SOUND OF SKIN

EMIL

I got to get to Bautista.

I visualize the gray and gold flames, trying to center myself, but it's hard when I hear the fire already roaring around Brighton and Maribelle. The fear of disappointing Wyatt creeps up on me, but I got to push that thought out and keep my eye on the prize. I concentrate, heating up, and I bite down on my bottom lip to keep from screaming and ruining Brighton's and Maribelle's progress.

No, I got to stop. I cut out everyone else. I'm the only one in the room.

I train myself to believe that I could overheat like a supernova right now and no one else would die.

I'm trying to—no, I have to run with this faithfully. No doubts.

I'm going to walk through Bautista's life. I'm going to somehow find the right moment I need to learn the true names of the ingredients for the power-binding potions. I think about them all, memorized from all the time we've spent researching: burnt-berry, Shade Sea water, cumulus powder, feather-rock, ghost husk, crimson root, dry-tear, and grim-ash. Once I'm Bautista again, once I'm in his flesh and bones like I'm possessing him, I'm going to get all my answers. I'm going to bring his knowledge back with me, knowledge I would've been born with if Luna hadn't killed me. No, him. No again.

I'm going to know everything I should know if Luna hadn't killed us.

Someone whispers in my ear, but I can't understand the words, even though my gut tells me it's not some foreign language. It's strange, but I almost feel like I can smell the words. They're rank like some of the times at Nova when I didn't brush my teeth because we were too busy strategizing how to stay alive or I was too depressed to care.

Man, this doesn't make sense, but I swear I can hear gold. It's heavy, but I wouldn't compare it to an actual block of gold. The weight is like my gray and gold flames. But these flames aren't mine. They're Bautista's and I can practically hear his skin, the way it must've panicked when those gold flames were first set alight, all those nerves hushing once it was clear that he can't be harmed.

I'm feeling closer and closer, moving into his life—our life.

Bautista will be Emil, Bautista has become Emil, and Emil was Bautista.

We are one; we're not even we.

Fire rages around me and my tongue is thick with blood. I'm tasting death. No, wrong again. I'm tasting life, I'm tasting the infinity cycle. There are explosions of pain throughout my body and I want to be comforted by my parents, but I don't know the souls who parented Bautista. I'm slipping without this knowledge, like I should know those people as clearly as I know Carolina and Leonardo Rey. The fire and explosions grow tenfold, and staying in this space is as difficult as flying with weighted wings.

I'm falling, falling, falling back into my own life, and even though I trust that I'm safely sitting in the Sanctuary, the dizzying sensation and inferno within me feels like I'm an earthbound meteor.

And I no longer believe I can't hurt those around me.

THIRTY-NINE
THE WEIGHT OF NOTHING

BRIGHTON

I better not find Ma.

If I succeed at seeing her past, that means it's too late. If so, it's absolutely game over for Luna, every Blood Caster, every acolyte, every friend of a friend to the gang. It won't be enough to disempower our enemies and have them locked up like Emil wants. If my mother is dead, I will send them all to their graves.

Anger is demolishing my focus while also making my silver and sapphire flames grow.

My instincts are practically shouting at me to convince myself that Ma is dead so I can test this retrocycling theory. It reminds me of childhood when Emil believed we could jinx our fortunes by talking about them too much, especially in regards to becoming celestials; one could argue that he was right on that one.

I'm leaning into thoughts of Ma's fatality, searching for her throughout time. I'm not sure when I'm trying to go back to. It could be any time I guess. I decide on my birth. It could be good for me to understand that day for what it actually was. The day that I was born alone while Emil was reborn somewhere nearby. It also means I get to see Dad as he welcomes me into the world. I remember how Ma looks from all the pictures in our albums. Dark hair pulled back in a bun, no makeup, both me and Emil cradled in her arms as she smiled at Dad.

I'm waiting for some sign that this is working. A tingle, some dizziness. I stack more and more details about Ma to see if it will trigger something: Carolina Rey, only child; she took dancing classes as a kid but quit when her nerves got the best of her; she went to Comic Con while she was pregnant to get an autograph from her childhood crush; she never understood how her mother knew when she was sneaking up on her until Abuelita told Ma about the visions on her seventh birthday; she was devastated when her father died before he could walk her down the aisle like they always dreamed; she was never able to narrow down her favorite day because she said she was blessed with many.

Nothing.

On the one hand, there's so much relief that Ma is alive and I can save her. On the other hand, if she's alive, what conditions is she being put through?

Before I go racing out of here, I have to be sure that I actually have the power in me—that I can trust this proof that she's alive. The flames are roaring around, drowning out Wyatt and Tala as they discuss something. Sweat is dripping down on me. I'm so hot I want to stand under Roxana's rainstorm until I'm shaking cold. First things first: prove how extraordinary I am by retrocycling to Dad.

I once again try to return to the day I was born, except this time from Dad's perspective. The memories come just as easy to fill out his history: Dad never missing episodes of Monday-night wrestling even though it's staged, because he loved any sport with celestial competitors; the way he loved organizing our hardware cupboard, putting all loose screws and tools in labeled envelopes; how he used to talk so much as a kid that Grandpa would add a dollar to his allowance for every hour he didn't utter a single word; his habit of falling asleep in front of the TV; how fondly he spoke of his friend Brighton, who apparently saved Dad from a lot of beatings on his block.

Nothing.

I open my eyes to check if anything has changed, but I see only Maribelle and Emil sitting in towers of fire as Wyatt, Tala, and Prudencia look on, concerned. I'm immediately right there with them. I swipe the sweat out of my eyes so I can see clearly. Emil and Maribelle have nosebleeds mixing in with the gallons of sweat cascading down their foreheads. Strangely, their teeth are chattering so hard they might crack if we don't gag them with a shirt or something. In both of my attempts to retrocycle, it never felt as extreme as this looks.

They've pulled it off. They're going back to Bautista's and Sera's lives.

321

"Brighton!" Prudencia grabs my hand. "Are you okay? How are you feeling?"

"Nothing happened," I say.

"So Carolina is alive. That's a really good start. There's hope for her."

Prudencia is watching Emil, and I think we're both questioning if there's hope for him.

"This doesn't look normal," I say. The heat radiating off Emil and Maribelle is intense. "Should we wake them up?"

Wyatt walks circles around them. "Many tried waking up their phoenixes, but when most creatures and animals are hibernating, they only wake up when it's their time."

"My brother isn't a phoenix! If we can't wake him up, let's get a fire extinguisher or buckets of water!"

I'm going to shake Emil awake. I surround my hand in silver and sapphire flames, hoping it'll hurt less as I touch Emil's fire, but if worse comes to worst and I lose a hand, I can grow a new one. I reach for him when Maribelle gasps, her dark yellow flames vanishing.

Maribelle frantically looks around the room. "I heard her."

"Who? What happened?" Tala asks.

"Sera." Maribelle fights back tears in her eyes. "I think she was dying."

Tala takes this in. "Maybe her death was the closest doorway into her life."

Wyatt nods along. "Brilliant. The point of the cycle isn't to begin at the beginning, but to connect your beginning to her end." Wyatt's eyes widen as he bounces. "Oh, my holy blazes, we bloody did it!"

I want to punch this guy. "You're celebrating this while my brother—"

Emil screams as his gold and gray flames dissipate. His eyes are wide like he's seen something horrific; I wonder if I looked anything like that when Dad spat his blood on me before slumping over dead. Emil is shaking uncontrollably until Wyatt wraps his arms around him. Emil cries as he presses a hand to his sides, hiding his face in Wyatt's shoulder.

"You're safe," Wyatt says. He places a hand on Emil's forehead. "You're burning up."

"He was sitting in fire, genius," I say. "Bro, what happened? Did you see Bautista?"

He doesn't say anything.

This is unearthing so many awful, powerless feelings from over the years. I don't know what I did wrong, but I'm really confused over how Emil figured it out before me. No offense to him, but come on. Not only am I stronger as the Infinity Savior with Reaper's Blood, but learning has always been more instinctive to me. Emil couldn't even assemble his tiny dresser—that came with instructions!—without my help.

"That was a whole other world," Maribelle says. The last time I saw her gaze this distant was hours after Atlas died. "I felt like I was everywhere and nowhere. The more I accepted Sera as my mother, the more my senses were overloaded with things that don't make sense. I smelled the color blue as memories of my life came into focus."

Emil perks up, more blood smeared across his face. "I stopped rejecting my connection to Bautista. Stopped pretending that I didn't used to be him. Then I swore I heard the gold fire on Bautista's skin even though he was nowhere in sight."

"Perhaps it's a synesthesia of sorts," Wyatt says, ignoring Emil's blood on his shirt. "Senses may be bleeding into each other as you traverse into other lives."

Is this why retrocycling didn't click with me? I used logic: think about the past, go to the past. How could I have known that heightened senses were going to lead the way? Emil and Maribelle need to enlighten me on the details that prompted everything.

"Bright, did you see Ma and Dad?"

"No, but we should all try again. Let's go."

"No way," Emil says. "I got to chill for a sec."

"It's more draining than you can imagine," Maribelle says to me. "I'm starving and exhausted."

Tala helps Maribelle to her feet. "Let's get you something to eat."

"I need a nap," Emil says. "Or a sleep. And some ice for my wounds."

"I'll prepare a salve for you," Wyatt says. "We can revisit this when you're all feeling up to it."

Prudencia must be able to sense that I'm about to fight back because she rests her hand on my shoulder. I can't believe I'm watching Emil, Wyatt, Maribelle, and Tala leave like there isn't more work to be done here.

"This is a gigantic breakthrough and they're all going to grab a bite and nap away," I say.

Sometimes I feel like I'm the only one truly committed to making this world a better place.

"Brighton . . ."

"I know. I'm sorry."

I have to bite my tongue. I'm relieved she can't read my mind because I would only support her argument. Nosebleeds and shivers and feeling hot is child's play compared to my blood poisoning and arm literally burning off. But if I spoke that truth right now I would be insensitive to Emil's and Maribelle's exhaustion and empty stomachs.

Prudencia hugs me. "I'm on your side. All I'm saying is we don't know what they've been through."

"I should find out. I'm going to try again now that I know more."

Prudencia looks me in the eyes. "There's no world where you weren't."

"So you'll stay with me?"

"I'm here."

"Will you record me?"

"This is still a sacred space I want to respect," she says. "But I won't fling your camera to the skies if you only use the footage for research."

"Good compromise," I say and kiss her. There's one thing that could stop me from trying to retrocycle right now.

"What are you doing differently this time?"

This is the hardest thing I'll ever have to do. "Maribelle found herself on the edge of Sera's death. I think I have to go back to Dad's. I have the unfortunate advantage of having been there."

Tears are forming in Prudencia's eyes. "Brighton, you don't have to do that to yourself."

"If it means saving Ma, I do."

No one can contest that.

I prop my phone against the wall and ready the camera. I don't repeat all of Tala's breathing exercises, I trust I can get myself in the right headspace. I close my eyes, ignite my fire, and I paint the picture of my most traumatic day ever.

Dad and I were in the living room. There was standard city noise outside the window, nothing special. Dad was wearing the green bathrobe I got him as a welcome-home gift after some time spent in the hospital; his temperature frequently dictated whether it was on or off. He sat on the couch with his favorite book, *The Last Great Earthling*, telling me how, during his most recent reread in the hospital, he couldn't stand the narrator, and how there was no chemistry between the couple. I've tried reading the book before, and I thought Dad was wrong on both counts, but it was fun watching him getting angry over a story he has cherished for so many years.

That's when his death began.

The sickness turned on him so suddenly that he ripped the book's cover, tearing the man standing on earth in half. I'm waiting for my heightened, nonsensical senses to take over, such as the glossy cover screaming in pain or feeling Dad's lungs squeezing as if I was cutting off his air with my bare hands, but nothing comes. I'm fighting back all the tears and waiting for a nosebleed, but nothing. When the heat of my own fire becomes too much, I call it quits.

"Cut the camera."

FORTY
POWER COUPLE

BRIGHTON

"I have an idea."

I'm getting some air in the courtyard with Prudencia. She's been watching this family of white phoenixes for the past few minutes even though they're just being birds. I don't expect much from pigeons, but phoenixes should always be doing something cooler than trailing each other.

"Is this about retrocycling again?" she asks.

"Sort of. For whatever reason I can't access that power, but if Ma is alive, then we need to figure that out sooner. Let's drive back into the city so I can pick up something of hers from home. Then Wyatt can track her."

"Good point. Let's do it."

"Thank the stars, I was nervous you'd find some reason to say no."

"I was considering waiting to make the trip with Emil, but I know you would just hijack someone's phoenix and go yourself."

"You know me well."

We return inside the castle, waking up Emil to tell him our plan. He's so drained that I'm not sure he fully registers that we even spoke to him before he falls back to sleep. We leave the grounds, crossing the bridge back to the car. Prudencia is beautiful as she concentrates on the road and gets us out of the woods. On the road she blasts some music, tapping the wheel as she sings along. I pull out my phone to film her.

"Don't post that anywhere!"

"Why not? You'll get so many new followers."

"That's exactly why. I'm still trying to lie low."

"But wouldn't being the Infinity Queen to my Infinity King be fun?"

"I prefer being the Infinity Independent Woman."

"That doesn't have a ring to it."

"You would say that, Infinity Boy."

"I prefer Infinity Man."

"You would say that too," she says, smiling.

For how powerless I've been feeling, Prudencia has been lighting me up the entire drive back into the city. I'm sure she's being extra flirty and fun to distract me from everything that's been going wrong and I really appreciate it. Partners shouldn't only be there to witness your troubles. They should also help you get your mind off of them. I've got to make sure I'm doing the same for her moving forward.

There's something big that's been on my mind since the Cloaked Phantom, when everything changed between us. But I can't wait around for some special constellations to give me permission to be bold.

"Can I ask you something?"

"That's always been such a strange question. Are people really answering no and carrying about their day?"

"So your answer is yes."

"Correct."

"Do you love me?"

Prudencia is quiet until we stop at a red traffic light. "Maybe I should've asked what your question was about before answering. I wasn't prepared for that one."

"Sorry. It occurred to me that I said it to you and then we had sex, but didn't get to talk about any of that because of my powers."

"Saved by the powers."

"You don't have to answer. Never mind."

Prudencia keeps driving and we're getting closer to home. "I obviously love you, Brighton, and I'm clearly attracted to you. But I need some time to figure out if I'm in love with you. I'm an eighteen-year-old orphan who's been on the run with my best friends for weeks and my head has been a little foggy."

"Do you regret coming into my room that night?"

"Not at all. Don't make me regret it."

That's a great start and it won't end after everything we've been through.

Pulling up around the corner of my block makes me feel like the Brighton who used to live here is some past life of mine. It's easy to remember the Spell Walkers fighting Stanton on this street the day Emil got his powers, but those childhood memories of playing around with the neighborhood kids feel so distant. I always knew I was going to grow out of those friendships and do better things, but to me that meant moving to Los Angeles and starting film school. Not becoming a local hero who's too busy to respond to DMs from friends I used to play tag with.

"I don't have my key," I say as we start going up the stairs of my building.

"I really try not to use my you-know-what for personal reasons, but I'll let it slide today."

"You should let it slide every day."

"Before I had to use my you-know-what to stop Orton from torching you and Emil, I went almost two years not using it," Prudencia says as we reach the fourth floor and stop in front of my door. "But now Infinity Independent Woman has to strengthen up."

She makes sure the coast is clear before telekinetically unlocking the door. I take down the eviction notice on my way inside.

The apartment is still messy. I was last here with Maribelle the night of the Crowned Dreamer. She posted about Atlas's death on Instagram and then I pitched her my idea to steal the Reaper's Blood; she was immediately on board.

"You know Maribelle was the last girl in my room? Pretty epic, right?"

Prudencia fakes the biggest gasp and clutches my wrist. "Aw, how was she? Was she amazing? I'm so happy for you!"

"No, don't be happy, be jealous."

"Did she make you feel like an Infinity Man?"

"You know I've always been excited to bring you home as more than a friend and you're being a bully," I say, turning away from her. Then I spin back against my control to find myself face-to-face with her and her glowing eyes. "That was hot."

She's about to kiss me when my bedroom door opens.

I'm expecting—hoping—it'll be Ma because who else would possibly be in here. A stranger walks out of my room. He's pale with shaggy brown hair, a torn white shirt, and eyes that look tired as if he was sleeping in my bed. This better not be some looter or superfan.

"Who are you?"

He answers with burning eyes and throws a white fire-orb at us.

We duck, and the fire-orb sails over our heads and explodes against the wall. I dash-tackle the specter into my bedroom.

"Why are you here?"

He head-butts me off of him and gets back to his feet. I dash again, this time shooting straight through him as if he isn't there and crashing into my desk. He phased . . . one of the ghost powers that I don't have. Then I realize the last specter I fought with white fire was Orton. He's casting another fire-orb when my TV flies straight into him.

"He has knock-off Reaper's Blood," I say, remembering how Luna said she only experimented with the mixing of essences on some but saved the ultimate pure blood version for herself

I'm about to attack when the stranger vanishes from under the TV. I keep looking around, expecting him to pop up from behind me. This is my first real fight since getting my powers and I'm more than ready to make an example of this specter so the rest of the world will learn what happens when you cross me.

"Maybe he left," Prudencia says, looking out the window.

We go into the living room.

"I'm guessing Luna sent him in case we came home."

"He's probably on his way back to Luna."

I hear clicking coming from the kitchen. I gesture for Prudencia to be quiet as we creep up to find the specter standing over the oven with a fire-orb. My eyes widen as I grab Prudencia and dash through the living room right as there's a thunderous explosion and storm of fire blasting out of the kitchen. Dark smoke fills the apartment immediately as the fire alarm goes off. Another explosion rockets from the apartment beneath us, and another, and another—the specter is taking us down with this entire building.

"Are you okay?" Prudencia asks.

I'm in shock as I turn to find the fire spreading toward us as if this home isn't sacred to my family. Even if we had the money to start over after Dad died we never wanted to leave because this is where he and Ma raised us. But now all our furniture and pictures are being swallowed up by flames.

I should've been faster to kill that specter.

"Brighton!" Prudencia shakes me. "We have to go." She grabs my hand, leading me toward the fire escape.

"Wait. My neighbors . . . I've got to make sure they all get out."

She looks torn, but nods. "Where do we start?"

"You open every door and I'll run into every apartment. But you get out of here as soon as you're done."

The sprinklers have been activated already and the wet floor is shaking beneath us. It might cave in if we're not fast enough. Prudencia telekinetically slams open every apartment's front door before moving to the next level, working her way down. Residents are already filling the halls and I'm trying hard not to slip as I dash in, shouting for everyone to evacuate. My lungs are sucking in this bad air, but I have to keep moving. So many lives are at stake. By the time I've reached the second floor, Prudencia is losing time as she helps an elderly woman down the stairs. I bang on the few doors that haven't been opened yet, relieved when the residents come out.

"You've been on the news," one man says.

"You need to leave," I say, dashing to the ground level to find every apartment cleared right as Prudencia vacates with the woman.

I breathe in fresh air, holding Prudencia's hand as we cross the street to join the rest of my neighbors. We're all watching flames eat up our building—our home. I stare at the huge hole in the wall where my kitchen used to be, and tear up.

"It's all gone," I say weakly.

"We saved a lot of people," Prudencia says. "That's what matters most."

"Yeah, but . . . we didn't get to grab anything of Ma's."

I feel powerless to save her all over again.

FORTY-ONE
DAYROSE

EMIL

There's a knock at my window.

I shared the bread from my dinner with this common ivory and she's probably back for more. I turn over from my bed, up from my third nap since almost retrocycling, and Wyatt is somehow hovering outside even though he isn't a gleamcrafter. I realize what's what. I squint, just able to make out Nox, who is blending into the shadows tonight. I struggle opening the window, pain shooting up from my reignited infinity-ender wounds, but I manage. Wyatt hops inside and Nox zooms away.

"Is my door broken?" I ask.

"Sweet Emil, I kindly request that you welcome more flair into your life."

"Sure thing, I'll schedule that in after I go back in time."

"Fantastic." Wyatt digs inside his satchel and withdraws a mason jar containing a thick liquid I can only describe as red mud. "Here, good sir, is your Dayrose salve."

I unscrew the top.

"Wait, don't!"

But it's too late. This Dayrose salve, whatever this is, doesn't smell like any rose. I gag so hard, screwing the top back on immediately. The stench reminds me of this time that I cooked some veggie pasta for the family, but some of it got left in the pot while we were away for a few days, and it molded so bad that Brighton threw up on the kitchen floor upon smelling it. Wyatt lowers his headband to cover his mouth and nose before passing me an extra so I can do the same.

"Possibly the worst smell in the world," Wyatt says. "I'd rather be around Nox when he's having stomach issues and I promise that's no garden stroll."

My eyes are watering. "What the hell is Dayrose?"

"It's a flower that smells quite lovely on its own, but you mix anything with a couple corpse flowers and you get that assault on your senses. The salve was created to heal phoenixes whose regenerative powers are on the slower side, such as the queen slayers. As much as those phoenixes viciously conquered dragons, they often returned from battle wounded."

As tragic as the extinction of dragons is, I'm pretty relieved I don't have to go up against any dragon specters.

"I must've missed every detail about Dayrose in all my studies."

"That's because it's a trade secret. Halo Knight exclusive." Wyatt sits on the windowsill, lifting his headband to breathe in some fresh air. "Though if we're being honest, I believe there's a future path where you become a Halo Knight. Certainly controversial since you're a specter, but that won't always be the case."

Back when starting up community college was supposed to be the next phase of my life, I was excited to dive deeper into researching phoenixes. I believed working with Kirk at the museum was going to pair well with all my academic lessons. I thought there was a chance I could even take over the exhibit one day.

I never dared to dream about becoming a Halo Knight.

This would be an amazing opportunity for me. It's not as if I can ever return to my normal life with people knowing me as Fire-Wing and Infinity Son. I could probably even be safe here and learn how to better protect phoenixkind. But there's no way they would actually welcome me as one of their own.

"It's a cute thought, but we both know that's never going down."

"What's wrong with that? There are two ways to become a Halo Knight. The first is being born into it, a wonderful life hack I was privileged with. Or you can make significant contributions to phoenixkind. I'm not on the council, but between your gorgeous face and, oh, you know, retrocycling to find a potion that will banish the essences of fallen phoenixes from specters, you're a shoo-in."

Thankfully this headband around my face is hiding my blushed cheeks after Wyatt's gorgeous comment. "The only problem is that my past life causing this is pretty unforgivable, right? Making me a Halo Knight now would be like giving someone a promotion for fixing their own massive screw-up. One that cost lives."

"Well, our numbers are down, so we can't be picky," Wyatt says and I can tell that he's smiling behind his headband. "Truly, Emil, you have the heart for this. If you can create this potion and get rid of your powers, you are well on the way to joining us. I would mentor the holy blazes out of you."

He's staring at me so damn lustfully that I need some air.

I hold up the Dayrose salve. "Should we go outside? I don't want to stink up the room."

"Wise man."

Every step getting to the courtyard hurts. I spot Nox resting in the moonlight, a favorite pastime of his apparently. This idea of me becoming a Halo Knight is the first time I've been excited in a minute. I'd get to work more closely with phoenixes, but I wonder if I'll get to bond with one or if they'll all sense the dead gray sun's essence that has been in my blood for three lifetimes.

We pass the front gate of the castle because Wyatt says the phoenixes don't respond well to the Dayrose salve's stench either. I'm truly not looking forward to smelling like this for stars know how long. We sit close to the drawbridge, the sounds of the river flowing calming me. I suck in one last deep breath of fresh air before reopening the mason jar. The smell is so intense I cough and cough against the headband.

"Do you have any spray inside that handy satchel of yours?"

"Afraid not. We're going to have to soldier through this one." Wyatt steps closer to me. "Will you do me the great privilege of helping you apply it?"

The flashback returns of Ness helping me in the art supplies room—of Ness touching me.

"I got it," I say.

"Be generous to yourself."

I scoop out enough salve to cake my fingers. I almost lift my shirt, but Wyatt's blue eyes are on me and I don't want him to see my bare body. I turn my back and lift my shirt, applying the salve across all my scars. I spread the most over my stomach since the wound from Luna's stabbing has been pulsing with pain. In seconds, something icy activates within the salve.

"Please tell me I don't have to keep this on all night," I say as I turn back around to Wyatt.

He doesn't answer. He's staring at me like I'm some work of art, which is ridiculous. "Believe it or not, love, but as forward as I have been with you I have been holding back some. I'm desperate to tell you how beautiful you are under the moon like some sappy poet, but I'm taking the hint that you're not interested in me. Does my breath smell like that salve? Or is there someone else?"

Not once have Wyatt and I even talked about who we're into, but I know that Halo Knight culture as a whole has always been really accepting of queer people. I wasn't counting on him to be so forward about this. Definitely not tonight.

"Are those the only two options for why I'm not falling for your charms?"

"You think I'm charming, then."

"No. I mean sure, yeah. You're cool people and your accent has scored you tons of points in my book."

"But?"

"There is someone. There *was* someone. We weren't dating or anything and I'm not sure what he thought about me, but I was attracted to this guy Ness."

Wyatt picks up a rock and hurls it down to the river. "Damn, that's a great name. I was hoping for a Chad or Bobby. I can conquer all the Chads and Bobbys."

I realize I have no idea why Ness picked that name. "His real name is Eduardo. He chose the name Ness after he became a Blood Caster."

"Way to bury the lede!"

"Believe it or not, that's not the lede. Ness was Senator Iron's son. The one who supposedly died in the Blackout."

Wyatt's blue eyes widen with shock. "Wow. Well, I see why you're resisting my charms. I can't compete against a bad boy who came back from the dead."

"He wasn't a bad guy. Ness faked his death because his father was a terrible influence on him."

"Joining your country's most lethal gang makes him good?" Wyatt asks, a surprising edge in his voice.

This isn't news to me, I've been a direct target of theirs for weeks. "The Blood Casters saved his life and offered him shifter blood to hide from his father. His choices sucked."

"I would die before I willingly take in the blood of any creature."

I don't want to throw Ness under the bus, but me too. Though it's not right for me to judge him when I still don't even know his full story. "Ness was good. He was forced to kill Luna's enemies, but he isn't proud of that. It traumatized him so badly that he would wake up in the form of his victims. And when he had the opportunity to run away, he came back to save me. I didn't see him die, but I'm pretty damn sure it cost him his life."

I'm shaking and it's not because of the salve.

Wyatt closes the space between us with open arms. "May I?"

I let him hug me. I've already cried into his arms once today; I don't have more tears in me. Thinking about Ness makes me feel both dead inside and guilty for being alive.

"Maybe he got away," Wyatt says. "He's certainly faked his death before. He could be anyone in this world."

I would love to live in that fantasy. I wouldn't blame Ness if he managed to escape the enforcers and decided it was too risky to try to find me again. If only I knew he were alive, I could find so much happiness in that thought alone, even if it meant we couldn't be together. I would spend the rest of my life picturing Ness as different people, questioning if the person who is staring at me for a second too long or smiling as they pass me on the street is Ness in disguise. I just want him alive and I want him with someone where he can be himself, even if it's only in private. I'd hate for that face to be hidden from the world forever.

But there's this gut feeling that something has gone terribly wrong with Ness.

The sound of the car pulling up catches my attention and we break our hug. Prudencia parks again at the other side of the drawbridge. They get out of the car and Brighton looks really beat up with his ripped shirt and bandaged forehead. He helps Prudencia, who's limping toward us. I run toward them, the salve already working its magic and reducing my pain.

"What the hell is that smell?" Brighton asks, taking a step back and coughing.

"I love you, Emil, but you smell like death," Prudencia says as she presses an ice pack against her black eye and covers her nose.

"And you two look like it. What happened?"

"We were ambushed by some specter," Prudencia says.

"With reaper powers. Ghost phasing included," Brighton says. "But we still had him beat."

I hug them both at the same time. "I'm so glad you're okay."

Brighton gags. "Seriously, did a phoenix piss on you? What is that smell?"

"A healing salve," Wyatt says. "Phoenix urine smells more like—"

"Did you get Ma's clothes?" I ask, interrupting Wyatt.

Brighton and Prudencia exchange the kind of glance that can't possibly mean anything good. Was the apartment raided? Everything tossed since we haven't been around to pay rent?

"Tell him," Prudencia says.

Brighton lets out a deep sigh. "Today wasn't exactly a win for Team Infinity."

FORTY-TWO
PREDECESSOR

EMIL

My home is gone forever.

Everything that belonged to us, to Ma, to Dad has been destroyed. Every day in this war it feels like we're getting closer and closer to being erased from history. Like someone will succeed in killing us sooner or later and the world will move on. Then I'll be reborn, maybe Brighton too, and there will be no remnants of the Reys of Light for us to connect to—no pictures, no art, no personal tokens.

Brighton and Prudencia are drained so they head to bed, but between all my rest today and this news, I'm wired. It's chilly out, even as the salve's effect begins wearing off, so Wyatt and I sit close, with our shoulders pressed together; we've both gotten used to the stench by now.

I'm about to break down when Wyatt asks me about what my home life has been like over the years. It's painful sharing memories of simpler times, but this is how I make sure my family's history isn't reduced to ashes. I go in on what it was like being the thought-to-be-younger-brother-by-seven-minutes to someone who has always been so naturally brilliant, and how lucky I was to have parents who loved me so much that I never even suspected that I was adopted. But everything started going downhill once Dad got sick. We were all so spent, Brighton was always snapping at us and others at the hospital, and things only got worse when Dad died. Now Ma is lost, and Brighton was awful to her, and we have no way of finding her.

Now that I've gotten started, it's like I can't shut up. Before I know it, I'm walking Wyatt through everything that's happened since getting my powers—joining the Spell Walkers, saving the sun swallower from the arena the night we took Ness hostage, Ness's faux betrayal that led to him cutting me with an infinity-ender, discovering Prudencia is a celestial, and the battle on the last night of the Crowned Dreamer where Gravesend died in my arms.

For how quick Wyatt can be with his responses, he's an incredible listener. I can tell he's fading, though, so I lie about how I'm ready to go to bed so he can actually get some sleep. He deserves some rest after all his research on retrocycling plus preparing the Dayrose salve for me. I take a quick shower, then head back to the room, and I'm up for another couple hours, listening to Prudencia snoring and some phoenix song, before I finally fall asleep.

I'm woken up way too early because of Brighton playing news

reports on his phone without any headphones in. Different outlets are covering the story of Brighton's battle with the specter, and I brace myself for what remains of our home. The building is burnt black and there are fire-escape ladders lying curbside, not doing anyone good down there. I find our windows on the fourth floor, the one to the living room shattered from when Ness was disguising himself as Atlas, and the ones to the bedrooms warped like every other tenant's. Shelters have been taking people in, and even though Brighton and Prudencia helped save the day, this all happened because the Blood Casters were hoping we'd make the mistake of going home. We've displaced all our neighbors for no reason.

I bounce from the room, going straight to the library, where Wyatt is already up and out on the balcony. He's wearing nothing but the same shorts as yesterday, a thick book resting on his abs as his feet are kicked up on a sleeping Nox's back. The sunlight hits his brown hair in a way that makes it glow like a halo. I can't tell if he's squinting because it's so bright out or because he's focused on the page, but it's a good look on an already-great-looking guy.

"Hey," I say, stepping outside. The sun instantly warms the back of my neck.

"You're up far earlier than I'd expected," Wyatt says. He closes the book and sets it on his lap, baring his chest. I manage to maintain eye contact, but I can feel my gaze working hard to drift to his pecs like magnetism. "Had I known you were up I would've invited you on our morning flight."

"Another time," I say. I'd love to take him up on that. It's something to get used to in case I ever get to become a Halo Knight.

"You've caught me at an interesting time, love. I'm reading up on your predecessor's history. Your first attempt at retrocycling was astounding, though I believe it will go more swimmingly if you focus on returning to the day of his death. Maribelle sensed she was close to Sera's, and since the two died on the same day, perhaps that will be your way in too."

"That works for me."

"Shall we have a little Bautista Book Club?"

There's only a few pages about Bautista in *The Halo Blacklist*, but Wyatt thinks it's all worth studying up on. There isn't a ton that I don't already know about Bautista from Brighton obsessing about him over the years and his profile at the museum, but refreshing my memory won't hurt.

Bautista de León was twenty years old when he was making headlines for challenging Blood Casters in New York. The gang had been robbing banks, intimidating judges and politicians, and killing alchemists who were attempting to create potions to neutralize their powers. Their streak had gone unchecked until Bautista started tracking their patterns, a skill that I definitely don't have. He was holding his own in fights, but as the Blood Casters began grooming other young people—later called acolytes—to do their dirty work, Bautista knew he needed a team. He formed the Spell Walkers to combat all oppositions to peace. It took a while before they won over the public, but they became a valuable force with their track record of saving lives and incapacitating Blood Casters long enough for the authorities to lock them up in the Bounds. Four years later, Bautista was killed inside a weapons factory, and while many mourned him, the writer of this text claimed that if Bautista ever surfaced again with a phoenix's illegal powers, the Haloes would make sure his next death was as permanent as Keon Máximo's.

"Not the happiest of endings," I say.

"Haloes have some fiery hearts," Wyatt says.

"Hopefully none of them find out their history books are wrong about Keon."

Since the Dayrose salve didn't restore me to full health, I decide to keep busy digging up more information about Bautista until I have the strength to try retrocycling again. I borrow Brighton's laptop, and he gets me started with a dozen tabs to review while he spends time in the training room with Prudencia. I feel some kind of way about him getting more and more comfortable with powers I'm dead set on binding, but we got to make sure we're strong enough to get close to the Blood Casters if we want to have any chance of disempowering them.

The first tab is a YouTube video of Bautista being interviewed remotely by an anchorwoman on CNN explaining his intentions with the Spell Walkers. I've seen broadcasts of him throughout the years, and even though this video is a repeat, it's the first time I'm seeing life in him since discovering our link. His head is buzzed and he's not rocking any facial hair. He's comfortable in front of the camera, and his charisma really sells him as the hero millions once celebrated.

Last fall it was announced that a movie about Bautista's life was in the works, and fans—Brighton included—were very vocal about which actors they believed could actually match his charm. But the studio canceled the project after the Blackout to distance themselves from the Spell Walkers. Brighton was pissed that the movie wasn't happening, but I wouldn't be surprised if he's been sliding into the DMs of producers trying to sell the rights to our story.

There's an article with links to Bautista's public killstreaks. I hold my breath while clicking into a grainy video of Bautista battling a hydra specter with two heads and four arms. The specter charges Bautista with an infinity-ender dagger, but Bautista is faster, shoulder rolling toward an ax that's laid out on the street. He scoops it up, sets it ablaze with golden flames, and swings it so quickly that I see one head decapitated before I close the video; I trust the second head came clean off too.

I groan into my hands.

"What's the matter?" Wyatt asks.

"I come from killers, and I'm an idiot if I think I'm going to get out of this war without following in their footsteps."

"It's inevitable in our line of work, no?"

I tell him all about how the Spell Walkers have argued this point too, and even though they're also interested in avoiding fatalities, I have no clue if they've killed before and what the circumstances were. Maribelle burnt Anklin Prince alive, and she's gunning for June's blood. And then there's Brighton, who, ever since we first got pulled into the orbit of the Spell Walkers, has told me that killing to save the world is different.

"I don't believe heroes should have body counts."

"Then I'm not a hero in your books," Wyatt says.

That catches me off guard. "Really? But you don't even battle."

"Again, it's in our line of work. Three years ago, I was visiting the States to investigate a farm in Colorado that was stealing phoenix eggs for breeding. It happened to be the night of the Future Watcher, that lovely little prime constellation that aids celestials with all forms of foresight. My mum and dad had seen it years before, so they stayed in to prep while Nox and I flew atop the Chalk Cliffs to stargaze. Unfortunately, a psychic had sold us out to an alchemist and specter aspirant on the hunt for a phoenix, and we were ambushed."

Wyatt looks even more horrified than when he was telling me about the history of cruelty Nox suffered from his former companion.

"You don't have to talk about this. I'm not judging you," I say.

"No, no. It's important. It was a firsthand experience dealing with one's violent desperation to become a specter. Paired beautifully with another great American problem—being held at wandpoint. The alchemist trapped Nox in an electric net that shocked him the more he resisted. I had one opportunity to snatch the wand and I took it. I cast spells, and while I didn't intend to kill them, kill them I did." Wyatt stares out the open window, fixed on the sky. "It was self-defense, but that's a lot to take on at seventeen. It took about a year of therapy before I accepted that I'm not like those predators. My hope for you, sweet Emil, is that you're kind to yourself if you ever have to kill for those you love. I can't imagine you'll feel alive if you have the opportunity to save them and don't take it."

After a sleep troubled with haunting nightmares of Bautista's heroics, I settle into the meditation room shortly after dawn, more determined than ever to make sure my life doesn't echo his. Brighton isn't trying this time, only observing with Prudencia, and he's managing a pretty neutral attitude about it, I got to say. Maribelle is eager to give retrocycling another go. She sits cross-legged in front of me as Wyatt and Tala remind us that the goal is to find Sera and Bautista on their last day alive.

"Understood," Maribelle says.

"How are you feeling?" I ask her.

Maribelle glares as if I have some nerve to say anything to her.

I could offer her a lifetime of apologies, and it wouldn't matter as long as Atlas is dead. Instead of bothering her anymore, I close my eyes and take deep breaths to mentally prepare for this next attempt to the past.

"Trust in your instincts again," Tala says in a hushed voice. "Remember the history, breathe it, and fly back to it."

I hear Maribelle's flames burst to life, and I ignite too. I haven't used the Dayrose salve since two nights ago, but thankfully my power is significantly less painful than before. I'm able to build Bautista's life, beginning with his voice, which I know better now from those broadcasts, and I search and search for a way into his last day. I feel stuck, like my legs are buried in sand, and I think about how desperately I want to figure out those ingredients so I don't have to be trapped in this war.

Everything becomes blurry as muffled voices surface. A

younger Bautista flickers against a darkness, screaming as he finds his hand on fire, telling someone that he doesn't want to be a weapon. I've been asked before if I ever experienced any flashbacks to lives I didn't live, and now I can say I have. For several moments I forget my own face and name and history. I'm brought back as Emil Donato Rey with this memory of Bautista begging not to fight, and I can feel his hopelessness like fingers in my throat, suffocating me. We share this pain across lifetimes. Bautista wanted an escape too, and I urge him to help me even though he's dead, even though I'm the new us, but it's like asking yourself to solve a problem you can't possibly know the answer to. Then Bautista, much older than the flashback, slightly older than the videos, flickers in the darkness again, mouthing words I've never heard him say—words like *dry-tear* and *crimson root*. The ingredients. I keep reaching for his voice like it's something physical I can grab and squeeze. The other ingredients keep coming to me, like how my hands always know what words I want to type into a text, a total connection between body and brain.

Then I'm standing on darkness. I feel like I should be falling forever.

Bautista appears before me. His hair isn't buzzed, it's brown and messy and probably overdue for a haircut. His shadow of a beard has grown out in patches. His brown eyes look like he's in need of sleep. Sweat bullets down his face. He's wearing a raggedy gray sleeveless shirt tucked into his black jeans, and dang he's got some muscular arms. It's no surprise that everyone saw a superhero in him. I suddenly feel determination and hope increasing within me, and getting this far is huge, but there's something off about these feelings, like a shirt that fits but I've spent the day not realizing is backward. I think I'm reading Bautista's emotions. I'm standing right in front of him, though he can't seem to see me, not even as the darkness shrinks around us, replaced with color and light that paints the wide room we're in.

There are metallic yellow beams above us and dried blood staining the white floor that's harsh on my eyes. There's a poster with safety precautions by the window. Then lined all along the walls are a range of weapons that are mostly only used by the military, like semiautomatic sniper wands and gem-grenade launchers. This is definitely the Incendiary Factory in the South Bronx, where Bautista was killed and a few blocks from where I was born. I already hate this place so much that I want to go back to my time, but then I turn and find a man in a chair holding something that might be more powerful than any weapon in this room—a vial with a thick liquid that reminds me of wet clay. Oh man, I pray to every damn star that that's the power-binding potion.

"This has to work," the man in the chair pleads. He isn't shouting, but his voice rings loud in my head. He has a black eye and while his jaw hangs open I notice he's missing half of his teeth. I'm guessing he's a few years older than me, but I wouldn't be surprised if he's actually my age and just aged poorly because of whatever he's been through.

It'd be great if sharing a space with Bautista could hook me up with everything he knows, or at least let me read his mind in the moment, but I'll take the emotions.

"Just like the other potions, this version of the Starstifler is a trial too," Bautista says, casting a glance at the blue journal lying open on the deactivated conveyor belt.

I've never heard of the Starstifler before, but the name tracks with its purpose. If all powers originate from celestial bodies such as stars, then this name is appropriate for when you bind them. I walk over to the journal. The pages are still a crisp white, not yellowed like in my time, with an index card lying on top. I try picking up the card, but my hand phases right through it, over and over. I'm only here as an observer; I can't touch anything. I lean over the index card and it's about the Starstifler, written in penmanship I recognize as Sera's from half of the pages in the journal.

Attempt #7—the Starstifler
bone tears (tears from a lamenting phoenix)
ghost husk (eggshell of a reborn phoenix)
feather-rock (shedding from a blood-plumed basilisk)
crimson root (root of a Dayrose flower)
~~riot pod (breath spawn shell)~~
water from the Shade Sea (saliva from a hibernating
    shadow-star hydra)
burnt-berry (crushed torch grains)
cumulus powder (a sprinkling of soil from high mountain
    that isn't frequented because it's infested by hydras)
~~crooked star (peculiar soil)~~
grim-ash (soot from a crowned elder)

I don't know how much time I have before I'm kicked out of this life, so I'm committing all this to memory as quickly as I can. Tears from a lamenting phoenix, heartbreaking but simple enough. Ghost husk are literal eggshells from a phoenix that's resurrected. Blood-plumed basilisk shedding, blood-plumed basilisk shedding, blood-plumed basilisk shedding. I've got Dayrose down thanks to Wyatt. I would've never cracked the code that water from the Shade Sea was saliva from a hibernating shadow-star hydra, and that's the point, but man, who knows how many times I can retrocycle, so I'm dead set on getting everything right now. Crushed torch grains, which I know are common. And the Halo Knights can hopefully hook us up with soot from a crowned elder.

I'm running through everything over and over—lamenting phoenix tears, phoenix eggshell, blood-plumed basilisk shedding, Dayrose, hibernating shadow-star hydra saliva, crushed torch grains, crowned elder soot—when Bautista steps closer to the man, pulling me with him even as I resist, as if we're tethered together.

This is such a trip, I wish Brighton were here to tag-team this with me. He'd be losing his mind about how Bautista smells like armpits and street cologne.

The Spell Walker founder stands before the man as he trembles to unscrew the vial, tucking it between his legs, and then holding out his forearm. Bautista grabs his wrist. "Take a deep breath, Price. I'm going to count down from three."

Price squirms. "As if you ever actually count down from—"

Bautista drives the dagger through Price's hand, and Price's yell echoes so loudly that I cover my ears. Blood spills into the vial, staining Price's pants too, and once Bautista seems satisfied with how much blood has gone in he puts the cork back on and gives it a shake like a bartender mixing a cocktail. "You'll heal any second now" is all he says. I would've apologized.

"Doesn't mean it hurts any less," Price says as the wound in his hand closes, leaving the faintest scar on his palm. "This is the power I'll miss the most. Got me through some rough times in the Bounds."

"And unless you want to go back there, you'll drink up," Bautista says, handing the potion back to Price.

"But it's so disgusting. Can't your woman make it tastier?"

"While I'm passing the feedback back to Sera, let's hope your phoenix fire doesn't burn you alive like the Blood Caster you replaced. Tell me, how is that pile of ashes doing?"

"All right, all right!"

Bautista's attitude is not what I expected after watching him appear so respectful and heroic in his TV interviews. I never thought he'd be so taunting. I'm definitely not. It really goes to show how the only things we share are these powers and a history as the first specter.

Price stares at the potion. I can't imagine it's going to go smoothly down his throat. He drinks up, and when he begins gagging, Bautista slaps his hand against Price's mouth and nose until he swallows. Price begins shaking, violently, and he sinks out of his chair. Bautista holds the back of his head as Price screams, "It's burning me!"

"It'll pass," Bautista says.

I sense Bautista is lying. He's sure Price is about to die. He's actually sympathetic for this Blood Caster.

Price's eyes go dark as an eclipse and Bautista steps back in self-preservation. Price lets out another yell that hurts my ears, like he's shouting directly into them. White flames swallow his body whole, and it reminds me of Orton burning to death all over again. Bautista feels hopeless until the flames vanish and Price takes a deep breath.

"You okay?" Bautista asks.

Price sits up. He holds out his hand, as if he's trying to cast fire, but nothing happens. Multiple attempts and nothing. "My powers are gone," Price says.

"Stars," Bautista says.

Hope shoots through both of us so powerfully that I can't tell mine apart from his.

"My Caster days are over!" Price says with a high laugh.

"Everyone's Caster days are over," Bautista says as he gets up and grabs the journal, running out of the room and dragging me along like a shadow.

FORTY-THREE
MOTHER

MARIBELLE

There's a chill in the darkness that feels like the wintry winds the day Mama and Papa were killed, and then Sera Córdova manifests out of nowhere. She's stunning. She has my brown skin—I have her brown skin—and while my hair is usually braided behind my head, she wears hers fanned out and it trails to the middle of her back. She's in a white blouse with a beautiful blue ring and silver bracelets. As the darkness shrinks around me, I can smell flowers and herbs, and hear a cauldron bubbling and a baby crying.

Sera picks me up out of a crib—baby Maribelle. I must be a couple months old. She's softly singing me a song about a girl who makes a crown out of branches from her garden, and I'm so upset that I've never heard this before that rage builds in me so quickly that I might burn down this room that appears to be an alchemist's lab. But serenity and an urge to comfort wash over me, even though those don't jive with how I think I should be feeling. It's as if I'm somehow tapped into Sera's and baby Maribelle's feelings too. The baby settles against Sera's breasts, like a mother's song and touch is all she needed.

"You want to help your mother, my sunflower?" Sera asks. I've never heard that nickname before, but I can feel how lovingly she uses it as much as I can see it in her warm brown eyes. She points at the steel cauldron and herb-loaded mortars on the polished counter. "I am making a potion for your tía Aurora to help her feel better. She's been ill lately ever since losing a loved one. I can't bring back her loss, or make her instantly happy, but I can make her body kinder to her during this sad time."

"Aurora isn't my aunt," I say aloud, but Sera doesn't hear me.

I want Sera to speak more about Mama's loss and sadness. Is this around the time that her own mother passed?

The door bangs open, and I instinctively hold up my fists to fight, but I'm settled down by Sera's cool composure. A man I quickly recognize as Bautista appears, looking pretty grimy, as if he's been fixing up a car. I always remember him as the leader of the Spell Walkers, and I would salute him if he could see me, but wrapping my head around him being my father is a whole other matter. If I couldn't clearly read the excitement in his face, I feel some triumph in his heart. I must be able to feel him as well because we're all a family, and as Wyatt said, that's one of the two lifelines phoenixes have. Juggling four sets of emotions at once is dizzying.

He steps fully inside, and Emil walks in after him. We see each other, and thank the stars I'm not feeling whatever he's got going on inside. He's muttering something to himself, eyes closed in concentration.

"It worked!" Bautista says.

Tears are brought to Sera's eyes as glee and pride soar within. "The Starstifler worked?"

He puts down the journal on the counter. "You did it, my beautiful vision!"

Sera and Bautista kiss, love exploding so fiercely that I imagine my own family with Atlas as if he were still alive. This was going to be us in the future. Heroes and parents.

Bautista kisses the baby on her forehead. "You hear that, Maribelle? Your parents are making a better world for you."

"I pray to the stars the potion isn't used against our kind," Sera says. "We have to be selective about who we introduce it to. Maybe only the other Walkers so it stays in the family. I wouldn't even trust the government right now. They could use it on Maribelle whenever she comes into her powers."

"If she does," Bautista says. "My blood may have ruined that for her."

"I know she will."

"You're the seer. I'm sure she'll take after her powerful mother."

"She would be lucky to have your fire, my sunray."

"Once these streets are mine, I'm putting my fire out. Full-time dad," Bautista says with a smile as he kisses baby Maribelle's forehead again.

What would my life have looked like if they weren't killed?

Would the Blackout have ever happened with Sera around to predict the catastrophe clearly instead of my nagging gut feeling that I couldn't make sense of? Would we have all transformed the world for the better by now so we could've had our own home after the streets were cleansed of violent specters?

Sera's eyes glow like one full moon bouncing between her left and right eye. We're being warned of a danger so intense that we feel it in our bones, picking at our skin; this is what my power should feel like. Even though I can't see what she's seeing, I have history to define the moment she's dreading. Terror squeezes at her throat and she can't speak their fates. One moment she was imagining a hopeful future, the next she was seeing that none of it would ever happen. Death may move quickly, but there's solace in knowing she can prepare.

If only I could've braced myself for Atlas.

"Sera, what did you see?" Bautista has never been more frightened either.

"Our end," Sera whispers. "But only mine and yours. There's still hope for Maribelle. My mother can never know she's my daughter. She'll hunt her down and use her powers like she used me."

Bautista is trying to stay strong, whereas Emil is crying like this is his own family. In a way, it is.

"What do we do?" Bautista asks as his own tears break through. "It was hard enough hiding your pregnancy this year."

"I have a plan," Sera says. She's sobbing, her lips quivering as she plants a long kiss on baby Maribelle's cheek. "I'm sorry I won't be around, my sunflower."

This is the apology I heard during my first attempt at retro-cycling.

"How much time do we have?" Bautista asks.

Sera almost doesn't want to answer, but time isn't on their side. "Minutes. My mother and her forces will be breaking in as we speak."

Rage takes over Bautista as his eyes burn like an eclipse and gray flames burst around his fist. "She isn't coming anywhere near our daughter. Not unless Luna wants to die with us."

Even though I can't feel Emil's shock, I know we're the only two people in the room feeling it.

Luna is Sera's mother—and my grandmother.

FORTY-FOUR
HISTORY

BRIGHTON

Emil and Maribelle are glowing like rays of sun. They're sweating within their gold and gray and dark yellow flames and while words occasionally slip out, I have no idea what's actually happening. All I know is they must have successfully retrocycled.

I can't believe this. Emil is meeting my hero, his past life, while Maribelle is with her biological mother. How does it work? Have they become them? Do they have any control? No one thought they would, but we didn't know any of this was possible before we came along. The rules for a phoenix don't have to be the same rules for specters with phoenix powers.

Thirty minutes in, Prudencia asks, "What if they're stuck?"

"It hasn't even been an hour," Tala says. "Phoenixes don't go in and out."

Wyatt nods. "The only gray sun on record for retrocycling returned from hibernation after two days."

"I'm not sitting here for two days," I say.

"Then let's hope Emil and Maribelle can find their way back sooner," Wyatt says.

"By trusting their instincts?"

"It's gotten them this far."

But how far is that? Truly. They're limited by what they could do, even someone as special as Maribelle, a celestial-specter hybrid. I'm the Infinity Savior, and the reason I must not be able to retrocycle is because I don't have all the powers my Reaper's Blood has promised me. Even if the ghost powers don't have much to do with my phoenix ones, everything is packaged together within me and is sure to affect each other, just like how Maribelle couldn't fully fly until she activated her fire too.

I might be left out now, but once I have all my powers, I'll make their retrocycling and everything else they can do look like child's play.

Count on it.

An hour passes, then another, and I spend the next three replying to my YouTube comments and answering a few questions on Instagram, but by the eighth hour of waiting around, I'm beginning to wonder if my brother and Maribelle will find their way back to our time.

FORTY-FIVE
SERA CÓRDOVA

MARIBELLE

I'm the granddaughter of the woman who has taken everything from me.

This is some cursed darkness I've been born into. I've always loved being a celestial, but I've never wanted these powers less than I do right now. I crave family drama more along the lines of my mother not speaking to my grandmother because she doesn't approve of my father or arguments over how best to raise me. Instead there have been hidden pregnancies, secret parents, and a villainous grandmother like some awful fairy tale.

I share blood with the most feared gang leader who is behind the deaths of Mama, Papa, Sera, Bautista, and Atlas. I want to rage-cry, but Luna's made sure there's no one to hold me anymore.

Emil tries approaching me, but I hold out my hand. I don't want his comfort.

"Are Konrad and Finola back?" Sera asks.

"I don't think so," Bautista says. "Iris's appointment with the savant should be happening now. Do you think they're okay?"

"I didn't see them getting harmed in my vision," Sera says.

"What did you see? How does it happen?"

"What does it matter how it happens?! We're dying, Bautista. The best thing we can do right now is make sure our daughter and our friends don't die with us!" Sera is shaking as she switches off the cauldron's fire. "I didn't even get to finish the potion for Aurora, and I'll never get to see Maribelle speak or watch her walk. It's happening too soon, far too soon. I hate these visions that only show me pain and death but never life."

The baby is crying, but Bautista tries shushing Sera to calm her down instead. He holds her face to his chest and rubs her back. Neither of them are particularly settled by this.

What Sera says about the visions only showing pain and death syncs up with how my psychic sense has only ever warned me of danger. I don't know where this power comes from. An ancestor of Luna's? My grandfather? Whoever that is. As much as Sera believes she wants to see my future as if I have some beautiful life, she would only see how the world has gotten worse and taken me down with it.

"We have to bring Maribelle to Aurora," Sera says.

"No, come on. I'm getting you out of here. We'll prove your vision wrong," Bautista says.

"This warning is written in the stars, and even we're not

powerful enough to change the fates. Grab the journal. There's still time to set up the Walkers for success against the Blood Casters."

As Sera leaves the room and rushes down the hallway, I'm dragged with her, like she's the earth and I'm a moon pulled into her orbit. Bautista catches up, clutching the journal. Emil is side by side with me.

"Are you okay?" Emil asks.

I'm surprised I can hear him. I ignore him like I can't.

Sera and Bautista are rushing through the hall, dreading their deaths, but not saying anything to each other. Had Mama and Papa known they were about to die, they would've used every last minute to express their love for one another. But I was grown when Mama and Papa died. Here I'm a baby who needs my biological parents to pass me on so I can become who I am.

I can't believe I'm going to get to see Mama and Papa.

Sera stops in her tracks, then shoves Bautista to the side as she steps back, a stream of acid sailing past where they stood. We all turn and a man in a gray jumpsuit and venom-green eyes gives Sera and Bautista a creepy-ass wave with his scaled hand. Bautista wastes no time blasting golden fire his way, but the basilisk specter moves as smoothly as Stanton has.

"Take her and go!" Bautista says.

He tosses the journal to Sera before launching another attack, unaware if he'll ever see her again. Sera drops the journal, and as she scoops it up and runs away, an index card is left behind. Emil pointlessly shouts her name as he pointlessly tries to pick it up.

"Those are the ingredients!" Emil says.

"Memorize them!" I shout as Sera pulls me with her down the hall.

This is the moment in history that explains why two more decades of specters were allowed to grow, causing more strife between those with powers and those without. A warrior's carelessness sparked by a mother's determination to protect her daughter. All the deaths, from Mama and Papa to Finola to Konrad to Atlas—would they still be alive if this power-binding potion had made its way into the world? Would Luna have given up the fight if her efforts were so easily countered?

It's like I've been thinking all along—I'm touched by Death.

I just didn't realize it's been this way since the beginning.

Sera has nearly reached the end of the hallway when I see my parents pop out of one of the rooms, wands at the ready. I'm stunned and it's like I've forgotten how to breathe as I marvel at them. I never thought it would be possible to see my parents again, let alone at a time where they're a couple years older than I am. Mama is so beautiful; I wish I resembled her more. Her dark hair isn't long like I've known it, but cut to her shoulders with a golden wreath wrapped around her head that brings out the green flecks in her brown eyes. Papa is as handsome as all the photos made him out to be, and it's not surprising to me that he was the player in the group. His thick eyebrows are one day away from a unibrow, and I almost want to laugh given how serious Papa got about waxing later in his life. They're both wearing dated power-proof vests, our Spell Walker insignia sprayed on in silver graffiti.

"Blood Casters have broken in," Sera says.

"Look out the window; we're surrounded by acolytes," Mama says.

This surprises Sera, her fear building. "I don't have a lot of time, but Bautista and I need you both to take care of Maribelle."

"We're staying and fighting," Papa says.

"No, you have to go! I had a vision, and I need my daughter out of here!"

Mama holds Papa's wrist, which I've always seen her do to get him to listen. "We'll fly Maribelle somewhere safe. Anywhere in particular we should meet you?"

Sera is rocking baby Maribelle back and forth while brushing the full head of hair I was born with. She tearfully looks up at Mama and Papa and even though I can't sense their emotions I trust they know what's coming as clear as a vision. "This is my and Bautista's last fight. I've seen our corpses in the very near future, and the only way you can help us is by taking care of our daughter."

Papa is shaking his head. "Sera, you're not going anywhere. Maybe you're reading the vision wrong. Don't play into it."

Mama is crying, and whenever she cried in life, it was always hard for me to watch. This time I won't turn away. "I know it's hard, Lestor, but her visions have never been wrong. The last time we didn't trust her power, it only broke our hearts even more. . . ." She places one hand on her stomach and rubs Papa's arm, soothing him as he fights back his own tears.

I'm confused until I realize that Mama must've had a miscarriage—a loss that Sera would've foreseen. I don't know how painful that must've been for them, and if they ever planned on telling me, but I want to hug Mama and Papa so much.

The desperation and devastation is building within Sera. "I wish more than anything to have seen our girls grow up together. . . . I'm heartbroken I won't even get to see my little sunflower blossom. But you two can. I need you to raise Maribelle as your own. Do not let anyone, especially the Blood Casters, know that she's mine. I can't have my mother using her the way she's used me my entire life."

Mama nods immediately, so ready to welcome me as her daughter, and Papa is still in shock. "We'll love her as we already have," she says. "It will never feel like a charade, but what do we do if her powers take after Bautista? There is no fire in our bloodlines."

"Then bind them," Sera says as she hands Papa the journal. "Bautista tested my potion on Price, and it worked. When she's older and safe, you decide what she knows or doesn't. But her life is more important to me than the truth. Understood?"

"Yes," Mama says.

"Lestor?"

"You and Bautista saved our lives. We'll do anything for you," Papa says.

Sera stares into her daughter's eyes. "Be strong and be loved, Maribelle Córdova de León. Your father and I have constellations of love for you." She kisses baby Maribelle's forehead and squeezes her against her chest before passing her over to Mama.

There's something about this handoff that makes me feel like I'm watching myself being born.

"Be well," Sera whispers to everyone.

Papa opens the window and he's the first to fly out. Mama makes sure the blanket is secured around the baby before pausing to give Sera one last look. Then Mama smoothly flies outside, and Sera and I watch them soaring into the distance.

This is the first time my family took to the skies together. And the last time my birth mother ever saw me.

FORTY-SIX
BAUTISTA DE LEÓN

EMIL

In every great time-travel story, the person returning to the past brings spoilers with them.

Even though I know Luna is ultimately the one who kills Bautista, I'm still not sure how this battle is going to play out between the original Spell Walker and this basilisk Blood Caster. I so badly wish I could take over so Bautista can catch up with Sera and Maribelle and say his goodbyes, but I'm powerless in this space.

Green acid flies toward Bautista and he shoulder rolls into a room with shelves of colorful gem-grenades. He's calculating something as he ducks behind one of the dozen barrels in here. I almost hide with him, but the Blood Caster can't see me when he comes in.

"Who was that precious baby?" he asks.

Back at Gleam Care, when Stanton attacked, he was able to track us quickly. I don't know if this Blood Caster has the same abilities, but he's moving fast in the direction of Bautista. I can sense that Bautista is nervous. I don't know if it's because he's in a room of explosives or because an adversary might figure out that Maribelle is his daughter.

The Blood Caster stops in his tracks, sniffing the air, and Bautista hops from behind the barrel and jumps into this unbelievable swing kick that connects with his jaw; it's hard to picture myself doing that, and I can actually fly, unlike Bautista. They trade blows, missing each other every time until the Blood Caster is building acid in his mouth and Bautista chops him in the throat and takes him down with an ankle sweep.

Bautista runs to the doorway. "I'm not going down alone," he says as he throws a golden fire-orb into the wall of gem-grenades. He charges down the same hall where Sera and Maribelle ran off, so focused that he doesn't see the index card with the potion ingredients on the floor. In moments, the loudest explosion I've ever heard echoes through my ears as fire and electricity blow apart the room. An alarm rings through the halls. Bautista continues running away like he's a track star escaping an apocalypse, never once looking back at the electrifying, fiery chaos raging behind him.

Once he's in the clear, he stops to catch his breath. He doesn't feel any remorse for killing the Blood Caster, or destroying the property. I could've never protected my life as quickly as he protected his. But if I had to take care of Brighton? Maybe. I hope I never have to find out. I repeat the ingredients over and over to make sure I no longer have to be a soldier.

The former Blood Caster, Price, comes running down the hall. "What's happening? Are we under attack?"

"No, I thought blowing up the place could be festive," Bautista says.

"You enjoy being a dick; I'm going to get out of here—" Price stops talking as a spear with green flames pierces him from behind and he drops dead as quick as a blink.

We turn to find a crew of reinforcements—two Blood Casters and a group of acolytes, guessing from the look of them. The man who threw the spear with phoenix fire has a black ponytail and huge muscles. He might not have his spear anymore, but he could probably crush someone with his burnt hands. There's a woman with three eyes, one of them shut, and four arms with fingers that won't stop twitching; hydra-blooded for sure. These must be some of the earliest Blood Casters, if not the first. The acolytes are dressed in gray turtlenecks and black pants, much different from the jumpsuits they wear today.

Bautista holds up two fiery fists and tries to assert as much confidence as possible; they don't know yet that they'll be successful in killing him.

"I killed your pet snake," he says. "Who's next?"

"Perhaps me," a woman's voice calls, and the acolytes part so Luna can make her way to the front. She must be in her late forties, early fifties here, with her dark hair beginning to gray. She moves and breathes easily. If Luna is as dangerous as she is in my time, I can only imagine what action she saw in her full health.

She smiles at Price on the floor. "The traitor is dead. Marvelous."

"All he wanted was a better life," Bautista says.

"Don't we all?" Luna muses. "Where's Sera?"

"Long gone," Bautista lies.

"She won't get very far."

"Neither will you," Bautista says.

He thrusts his fists forward repeatedly like he's in front of a punching bag; it's a technique I'd be smart to try out as long as I have these powers. Seven fire-orbs fly toward Luna and the phoenix Caster defends Luna with a shield of green fire. The hydra Caster runs along the wall, and as Bautista focuses on trying to burn her, he leaves himself vulnerable to fire-darts to the chest and is blasted backward.

I scream as the fire burns me too. I don't go flying like Bautista, but I still clutch my chest wishing I could do something more than stand here and take it. I didn't know I would experience Bautista's pain like this. . . .

The Blood Casters pin him down.

Luna unsheathes the infinity-ender dagger from her belt. "Shame that Sera isn't around to see this. Though perhaps she already has. . . ." She hovers over him and presses her hand against her heart. "I promise you, my dear Bautista, that if you dare appear in another life to oppose me, I will kill you over and over until you learn your lesson. Be forewarned that I plan on being around for a very long time."

I try to break my hold on my past life so I don't have to feel this pain, but Luna is swift and stabs him in the stomach. Bautista and I scream, echoing over each other. His blood rises around the dagger and flows down his sides. His healing power tries to activate, but the same pain from when Ness and Luna stabbed me ignites, over and over, and it's unbearable. Bautista fights for air, and I feel dizzy, struggling to breathe myself. He knows he's going to die, but I'm freaking out that maybe I might die too. We have no clue if the phoenixes who've retrocycled were impacted by the deaths in their bloodlines, and I wish I'd learned more about how many of those hibernating phoenixes actually woke up, and if any of them fell over dead because they didn't return to their own life in time.

"BAUTISTA!"

Sera runs over with present-day Maribelle at her side. She slides to her knees, so bold that she doesn't pay any mind to the Blood Casters crowding Bautista. She shoves away Luna, who laughs. Maribelle suddenly starts holding her stomach and screams; can she feel his pain too, even if she transported to Sera? I can't focus as Sera slowly pulls out the infinity-ender from Bautista's stomach. Everything is too agonizing to notice a difference. It's so odd to feel all his pain and not see my own blood running down me.

"We won," Sera says with tears flooding down her flushed cheeks. "We won. Not them! I will see you in the beyond, my sunray."

His body is shutting down, but when Sera kisses him, there's so much love that blasts through me. Love that I've never known because I've never taken this leap. Bautista wants to stay here, he wants to keep living, and I do too, but darkness conceals everyone, and it's just us, dying together.

Then, right on the edge of death, gold and gray flames drop

around me and I'm screaming in my own body.

I'm alive, I'm back.

I'm drenched in sweat and I haven't felt this dizzy since when I used my powers for the first time. Brighton, Prudencia, and Wyatt are all at my side, and they want to know if I'm okay, if I saw Bautista or became him, if I discovered the ingredients. But it's too much too soon.

My body is still aching, and I lift my shirt—not giving a single damn who sees—to make sure that there isn't a hole in my stomach from where Bautista was stabbed. The only scars are my own. How Luna killed Bautista is what she intended to do to me the last night of the Crowned Dreamer.

I rock back and forth, haunted by how I felt Bautista's death. I watch Maribelle in her dark yellow flames, hoping she can return to her own body before she has to feel every ounce of pain as her biological mother is killed too.

FORTY-SEVEN
HONOR

MARIBELLE

Sera is still alive, but all her light has left her.

Bautista's pain may have left me, but Sera's heart is so shattered it's as if I'm reliving Atlas's death all over again. Except she doesn't have my rage. For all her talk about how she and Bautista won—a code to let him know they succeeded in getting baby Maribelle to safety, maybe even figuring out that power-binding potion—her brave face has fallen.

Luna rests her hand on Sera's shoulder, and Sera doesn't bother shaking her off. "You were worthy by my side. We were going to create a world where you wouldn't need to worry about losing your loved ones as I have. No more visions of danger and death because everyone would be safe, untouchable. Instead you both betrayed me and tried to undo all my work. Tell me, my one and only. What do you think of this world of death as you hold his corpse?"

Sera looks her mother in the eyes. "It's unfortunate I won't be around to watch you die." She turns to Bautista and kisses his lips for what she feels will be the last time. "I've seen the end already. Get on with it."

"Very well," Luna says. There's remorse alive within her, but her need for survival is sharper.

Luna grabs the infinity-ender dagger, pulls Sera's head back by her hair, and slices her throat. Sera ungracefully crashes against Bautista's shoulder, blood pooling under her. By the time the pain begins, darkness takes over and it's only me and Sera dying in it until my familiar dark yellow flames vanish and I'm back in my own life.

I suck in the sharpest breath and almost punch Tala as she tries pressing a cold towel against my forehead.

"I'm back, I'm back," I whisper.

"You're okay," Emil says, still sitting where we first started.

Retrocycling has the potential to be beautiful. But this was a nightmare.

"I'm going to kill Luna," I say.

"What happened?" Tala asks.

"Can someone fill us in already?" Brighton asks. "Curious minds."

I'm half expecting to feel Sera's emotions, but I only feel mine since I'm no longer by her side. There's one takeaway I keep rolling around in my head. "How did we not know that Luna was Sera's mother?"

"Wait—what?!" Brighton asks.

Everyone is as surprised as I was, and this is the problem. Sera being an alchemist herself wasn't enough of a clue, but it's certainly an important piece of the puzzle now. Why didn't Mama and Papa tell me? Sera said it wasn't necessary for me to know that I was her daughter, but why couldn't they have trusted me with the knowledge that Sera's mother was Luna? Maybe to them it didn't matter, but it's yet another family secret, and this better be the last one I hear from anyone or so help me.

"How did we not know?!" I shout.

"I'm remembering something," Emil says. "When Luna had me hostage, she mentioned something about a traitor enthralling Bautista. She didn't say anything else about them, but Sera fits the bill."

"Why didn't you mention that sooner?"

"It didn't seem important with everything else we had going on," he softly says.

The number of ways I've been screwed over by this sad excuse of a chosen one is astounding. "I plan on honoring Sera by undoing all of Luna's work. You better have memorized those potion ingredients because I'm not reliving that again!"

Emil nods vigorously. He grabs the journal and begins marking the true names of the ingredients. I hear him talking about crushed torch grains before I tune him out.

All the pain I've been through this year feels cruel. It's as if the gods hidden in the constellations hate me, as if they're punishing me for defying nature with my existence as a hybrid celestial-specter. Grieving my parents and Atlas has been hard enough, but living in Sera's heart as she loses the love of her life and the father of her child? Of me? I have to repay blood with blood, and all roads lead back to Luna.

Tala takes the journal from Emil and reads. "I'm not in love with exploiting a phoenix's pain to use their tears, but it's certainly better than all potions that call for their eyes and talons. There's an underground market in the city where I've done business before. They should carry some of these rarer ingredients."

"We're going to get a bloody Nobel Prize out of this, yeah?" Wyatt asks. "Well, posthumously awarded to Sera and Bautista." Everyone is staring at him. "Messing around, of course. Long live our phoenixes, heh."

"Maribelle, ride with me?" Tala helps me up. "Everyone else stay put."

"We can help," Brighton says.

"You can help by keeping your famous face away from the public," Tala says.

He turns to me as if he wants my support, but I'm following Tala's lead here. "We need discretion."

"Fine. But this fight is all of ours," Brighton says.

"Absolutely. As long as it's understood that Luna is mine."

It's my duty to kill my last living family member.

FORTY-EIGHT
OBLIVION NIGHT

EMIL

It's wild how much time I lost while traveling to the past.

I already didn't get enough sleep last night, but now I'm so drained. Brighton brings me two salad bowls with tofu, quinoa, and chickpeas, and I could easily throw back another. I've already given Wyatt my official report on everything that went down while retrocycling, and while he's busy updating his commander, Brighton is still picking away at every last detail. I swear he won't chill until he can grow out a beard like Bautista.

"He had more edge than I expected," I say.

"Of course. No one ever saved the world by being casual about it," Brighton says. That feels like a slight against me. He picks up his phone. "Are we sure we can't do any content about retrocycling? Now that we have the potion ingredients, we can make sure that if anyone even thinks about trying something then the Infinity Kings will stop them."

Prudencia rests her hand on Brighton's shoulder. "It's not in our best interest to brag about retrocycling. We need to surprise the Blood Casters with the Starstifler so they won't be prepared."

"Good point," he says.

"We're also going to be drinking the potion ourselves," I remind him.

Brighton looks like he's fighting back a massive eyeroll. "You do understand that immediately drinking the potion won't solve any problems, right? It's our responsibility to use our powers to protect as many people as possible before the election. Otherwise all this country will see is more havoc because heroes aren't stepping up to save them."

"I know that—"

"Then buckle up, bro. If Sunstar wins, she'll still need a few months to set up the Luminary Union, so we'll continue defending the country until then. But if Iron takes the White House, we'll be in this for the long haul until we can set this world right."

There's a part of me that thinks Brighton wouldn't mind Senator Iron winning the election so he can keep playing hero. I don't want this, I've never wanted this, and I'm so damn nervous that Brighton is going to keep pushing back the goalposts on when we give up the powers. And the truth is that I doubt he ever will give them up, though I don't understand why. He could easily make a living out of being Brighton Rey, the dude who was once infinite. He could chill back and engage with his millions of followers and publish some tell-all memoir about what it was like being on the inside of this war. But I know my brother too well. No spotlight will shine bright enough unless he's the Infinity Savior.

I tell Brighton and Prudencia I need air and then bounce.

I head straight to the library without a second thought. I enter cautiously in case Wyatt is still busy with his virtual meeting, but it's quiet and completely empty. I'm nervous he might be sleeping, wherever he's set up his bed in here. I step quietly and find Wyatt lounging in his usual spot on the balcony, dressed in the leather Halo Knight jacket with black feathered sleeves I haven't seen him in since we met three days ago. Nox is eating away at some of the foliage wrapped around the stone railings as a sun swallower blazes across the dark sky.

"Man, your view is way better than mine," I say.

Wyatt turns with a dimpled smile. "My view is rather fantastic," he says while looking me up and down. "But yours is six feet of gorgeousness too."

"Walked right into that one," I say.

"Glad you did. Are you here for a celebratory toast? You did something absolutely skybreaking, love. I'm proud of you."

I'm frozen, staring at the stars. There's been a lot of hate from strangers, calls to do more from Brighton, unappreciation of my efforts from Maribelle, and sympathy from Prudencia, but no one's been proud of me. Even I haven't been. "All I did was go on the journey. You're the one who figured out the road."

Wyatt leans forward solely so he can pat himself on the back. "Crest was pleased to hear the news. It's been difficult for him, adjusting as commander, since he wasn't exactly next in line by a long shot, but when all those Haloes were killed he had to rise to the challenge. Doesn't matter that he's only thirty-three. The Bronze Wings are now his responsibility."

"Bronze Wings?"

"Yeah, it's the biggest division of Haloes. The Council of Phoenixlight restructured a decade ago to better manage the thousand or so active Halo Knights around the world. The Bronze Wings are those who have been Haloes for under twenty-five years, then it's Silver Wings for fifty years, and Gold Wings for seventy-five years and beyond. While many of the Gold Wings are councilmembers who pass down their knowledge to us, Crest is going to have the great pleasure of letting them know that one of our group's youngest—and most handsome—worked out how to get specters to retrocycle."

"I hope they appreciate how brilliant you are."

"They'll either commission a statue in my honor or bury me alive for training humans to better use phoenix powers. Frankly, I'm not sure I can survive a sculptor's failed attempts to capture my magnificence, so I'll opt for the elders burying me with a flashlight and a long book."

"I'll go up against these elders instead of Blood Casters any day."

"They're mostly good people. I'm curious what they'll think of you."

"I hope there's some forgiveness. Brighton's got me pretty worked up over how much longer he thinks we'll have to be the Infinity Kings. I want to make the world a better place, just like he does—not only because it's what I owe, but because it's the right thing for anyone to do. That better world just looks differ-ent for me. It looks less like a Spell Walker's and more like yours."

"It's not a life without its heartache, but the wins of a Halo Knight are absolutely wonderful."

I lean against the stone railing with my arms folded across my chest. "It must be really beautiful the day someone gets to become a Gold Wing. To know that you have spent your life doing the right thing."

"Doing the right thing means taking care of yourself too. My mum has always gone on about how self-care isn't valued nearly enough, especially in our culture, with how much of ourselves we give to the phoenixes. We have more to offer when we take care of ourselves. I'm not sure how much time you spend doing that."

I think about how Wyatt has talked about having great sex and how that's something I've always been interested in with some-one I'm dating. I really hoped back in high school that something could've gone down with Nicholas, who trusted me with the secret that he was a celestial, but that didn't work out. Then how hyped I was giving that guy Charlie a tour at the museum before he revealed himself to be someone who didn't give a shooting star about the lives of phoenixes. And of course Ness, who is so damn special that it feels insulting to even think of him so immediately after thinking of someone I was never going to get along with. But I always hold back, keeping my truths from myself, from others.

"I don't want to be a Spell Walker or the Infinity Son or anything high-profile. I want to be a discreet Halo Knight and figure out the most effective way to protect phoenixes."

"I think you would be a divine Halo. Now I know you can fly, but are you afraid of heights?"

"Not really," I say. "Though I'm not super experienced like Maribelle. I've only flown great distances a couple times."

Wyatt gets up from his chair and rubs Nox's neck. "No matter. Your power will be gone soon enough—despite what your brother might think—and if you're going to be a Halo Knight, you should be familiar with what it's like to ride a phoenix."

I shake my head because this is so absurd. "Nope, sorry, I don't deserve—"

"Why not? We may carry our pasts with us in every life, but we don't have to be defined by them. Please show yourself a thousandth of the care you show others."

For over a month I've been working hard to be the hero that everyone needs me to be and rarely fueling myself with happiness. That moment alone with the young phoenixes in the tower made me stronger, did something amazing for my soul.

"What if Nox throws me off midflight?"

"Then you'll be thankful we haven't clipped your wings yet. Come on, I want you to see the world that's waiting for you on the other side of infinity."

Wyatt scratches around Nox's beak and hops onto his back. I can't believe this is happening, not even as Wyatt hoists me up with him. There's no saddle, which I know is out of respect for the phoenixes, and I feel like I'm sitting on a stiff mattress that's covered with a smooth, feathery comforter. I run my fingers through Nox's thick black feathers, sensing that he doesn't mind me. It makes me feel better that he doesn't distrust me after everything he's been through during his lives. I'm able to relax more on top of him, as much as one can when riding a phoenix that's bigger than a horse for the first time.

"Hold on," Wyatt says over his shoulder.

"Around you?"

"Feel free to hug Nox's arse if that's preferable."

I inch closer to Wyatt, wrapping my arms around his stomach and locking my fingers together. I lean into his back and can smell so many adventures on his jacket—fresh pine, wet grass, maybe even a couple flowers thrown in there; I wonder if one is Dayrose. He tells me to hold on tight, and I don't think it's necessary until Nox kicks off into the air. Then I hang on like I'm trying to merge into one being.

Flying on Nox is such an odd, freeing sensation, different from doing it by myself. I don't have to try; I can kick back as we sail across the Sanctuary's fields and put New Ember behind us. Wyatt confidently steers Nox over the roadway that we originally arrived on by car, but now we're seeing the tops of trees, and a dozen evergreen blazers chase after us.

"Hold on like your lives depend on it!" Wyatt shouts over the roaring winds.

Nox screeches as he jerks and shoots toward the moon, and I'm so nervous that I'm going to fall off and drag Wyatt down into the forest with me, but the obsidian adjusts, and we're higher than I've ever been before. I take in the mountains below us, thinking they could make for a challenging hike even with my strong New Yorker legs that are primed for long walks, but I only ever want to be up in the air from here on out.

The moon and stars are still so damn out of reach, and I want Nox to take us even closer. It's like Nox can sense my feelings and does the exact opposite. We dip like the world's most intense roller coaster toward the glistening river. My fingers dig into Wyatt's abs when it seems like we're about to go underwater, and I have no idea if obsidians do well there like sky swimmers. Nox smoothly transitions into a glide, his belly skimming across the surface of the river and his massive wings splashing water back at us. Wyatt is laughing as I shiver against him, the crisp air even colder now that I'm drenched. A surge of joy rockets through me, and my cheeks hurt from smiling.

"Skybreaking, yeah?"

"Skybreaking," I echo into his ear.

I wonder if he can sense the smile in my voice the way I do with his.

We're back in the air, but we move like a gentle wave, up, down, up, down.

Wyatt spins and faces me, patting my knees with so much enthusiasm. I hold on to his legs though I can't lie, it's not strictly for balance.

"How you getting on with all of this?" Wyatt asks as he shakes some water out of his hair.

"Best night in a minute." I fight back some serious shivers because I don't want this to end, but my chattering teeth betray me. "And a little cold."

Wyatt takes off his jacket and holds it up. I try to turn him down because I'm me and I can never accept help without feeling weird about it, but he's thankfully him and works a little harder to help anyway. I slide into the first feathered sleeve, and I feel this rush of power, power that has nothing to do with stolen phoenix fire. It's like I can change the world on good heart alone. The Halo Knight jacket has some weight to it, and I want one of my own.

"Thanks for coming along," Wyatt says.

"You're kidding, right? Thanks for these incredible views," I say as I turn back to where the New Ember Sanctuary feels far off, like a star. "I don't just mean the mountains and river. Your perspective too. It's been a huge struggle reckoning with my history, and every day I feel like I'm moving deeper and deeper into a dark space. I straight-up haven't wanted to live a few times, and I want to feel more grateful for this life that I shouldn't have."

"Of course you should have your life," he says.

I look to the sky, so full of stars—you can't catch a sight like this in the city. I imagine that each star belongs to those who have fallen in my life and beyond—Dad, Ma, Ness, Atlas, Gravesend, Bautista, Sera, the other Spell Walkers, every celestial who was murdered because of fear and hate, and every creature who was hunted for power.

"I didn't grow up believing in souls reincarnating like you did, Wyatt. And since learning that I have past lives, I've been surrounded by death." I hold out my hands, bracing myself for sharp pain as I conjure a fire-orb, but I'm okay because of the Dayrose salve. "You've given me hope that I can do incredible things with these powers. That I can make sure the gray sun whose blood is in mine didn't die in vain."

"You have a bright future ahead of you, love."

"I'm going to make sure of that. I died with Bautista—I once died *as* him. I never want to feel that death again, but I do want what he had in his life. Even in the middle of all the chaos, Bautista still found time for a love that was so epic he sacrificed himself for it." I think about when Ness returned for me back at Nova, how invincible I felt. And how much I wish I had made that clear to him right then and there. "It's so hard to be open to happiness when people are missing and dying, but I'm never going to get anywhere in life if I'm waiting for everything to be perfect. If all goes according to plan, this might be my last life, and I got to start somewhere—and with someone."

The fire-orb is making his eyes glow until I crush it between my palms because I don't want to burn him. I can still make out his lips in the darkness, and he's paying attention to mine too. The wind whistles as Nox continues to take us over mountains and rivers, though I'm only focused on Wyatt.

My heart is hammering as he reaches for my hair and pulls me to him, our faces so close that I suck in my breath. His dimpled smile is the key that unlocks me, that frees me like riding a phoenix on a beautiful night. I kiss him, our lips pressed together, and I'm running so hot I might explode.

I didn't expect any of this when I walked into the library tonight—flying on Nox, kissing Wyatt, welcoming happiness. It would be so easy to be miserable and alone during a war even though I want more, but this is the first of hopefully many winning moments while I'm still fighting the bigger battle. And the life Wyatt is offering me as a Halo Knight is one I hope to live.

His hand slides under the jacket, and I tense as he grabs my side, almost breaking the kiss. I'm not used to this. I'm not opposed either. I run my hands down his pecs, fighting away all these ugly thoughts that someone like Wyatt only wants me because I happen to be gay and around. Then I remember how Ness asked me to only be with someone who thinks I'm beautiful because of who I am. I think that was true for Ness, and I think it's true for Wyatt too.

I lean away from the kiss though our foreheads remain pressed together and we're still holding on to each other. His smile gets another quick kiss out of me.

"You get better and better, love."

"So do you, Skybreaker."

When I manage to look away from his blue eyes, I notice that we're back at the Sanctuary. I could have stayed out all night like this, but that's not fair to Nox. Wyatt dismounts first, and he holds my hand as I hop off. Completely unnecessary and fully welcomed. I don't let go of him as I turn to pet Nox, thanking him for this incredible ride.

We enter the library, and I realize I'm not ready to go back to my room.

"I really liked holding you tonight," I say with my eyes to the floor because letting those words escape was vulnerable enough. "Can I stay here?"

"My door's been open since the day we arrived," Wyatt says.

He leads me to the farthest corner of the library where a sleeping bag is hidden behind a waist-high bookcase with tomes organized by color, like a rainbow of literature. All the colors vanish as he switches off the light. We're both wet, so we strip down to our underwear, and I change into one of Wyatt's dry shirts; he got me in his clothes like he wanted. We share the one pillow with our lips a breath apart and hold each other as phoenix song plays outside like nature's greatest playlist. Except I'm too wired to think about sleeping.

Today, I went back in time so I can save lives, and tonight, I changed mine.

FORTY-NINE
FOREVERMORE

MARIBELLE

It's late when Roxana gets us to Saffron Square in Brooklyn. Tala sends her away since she'll be vulnerable in the market.

We go down into the abandoned train station where seven years ago construction was halted after wild basilisks kept swallowing workers whole and chewing the steel tracks between their fangs. I remember Mama saying how much she didn't envy the celestials contracted with killing the basilisks, and how outraged the Save the Serpent activists were.

I had no idea there was a whole underground market operating here. It's always a strange feeling when visitors know your city better than you do, but Tala has done business here before.

There's graffiti all over the walls: a celestial telekinetically strangling a basilisk with the train tracks; green blood dripping from a slit palm and forming a girl and her serpentine shadow; a subway entrance shaped like a snake's mouth with *SHED* spelled in fangs; and the biggest piece is of a basilisk with windows trailing down three flights of steps like a train that's delivering us straight to the market.

"Welcome to the Shed," Tala says as she puts on her mask, its beak still broken from our fight, and she passes shoppers with her shoulders high.

Glowing lanterns hang above the twenty or so booths, though it's mercifully still dark enough that people don't seem to be recognizing me. It's close to one in the morning and there are easily a hundred people down here. How many are here to save the world and how many want to keep ruining it? I've smelled worse in my life, but the way someone has gone heavy on incense to cover the worst of humans is still horrible.

On the flight over, we reviewed which four ingredients we need, and Tala has already begun haggling with vendors. I admire a candleholder that's shaped like a crystal skull as Tala trades one of her tranquilizers for saliva from a hibernating shadow-star hydra.

We need the shedding of a blood-plumed basilisk, and we can't think of anyone better to ask than the man who has contacts that make his eyes look like slits and tattooed arms that are supposed to make him look scaly; it's not impossible that he's a specter, but personally, I think he's overcompensating. On the shelves behind him are snake eyes, some as large as apples, in glass jars; jewelry made of fangs; and hideous snakeskin shoes that thankfully went out of fashion years ago. Tala points to what looks like a belt made of rubies on the third shelf. She trades the last gem-grenades in her bag for the dead skin.

Surrounded by all these herbs and chemicals and essences, I'm impressed with how good alchemists are at understanding the properties of ingredients to create effective potions. Anyone can brew if told what to throw inside a cauldron, but discovering everything yourself is a true skill. It must've been awful growing up with Luna as a mother, but if it meant that Sera learned the craft at a much faster rate, then I'll make sure her childhood effort wasn't in vain by using this shadow-star hydra saliva and blood-plumed basilisk shedding and everything else against Luna and her army.

We ask around for the soil that Sera named cumulus powder. One woman thinks we'd have an easier time finding fresh strawberries growing in a December snowfall. But a man who has seen better days directs us to a woman named Gemma toward the end of the line.

The booth has lanterns hidden behind the purple curtains, making it glow like a sunset. The vendor looks to be about Mama's age, and she's wearing a black veiled dress as if she's returned from a fancy funeral.

"Are you Gemma?" Tala asks.

She nods as she counts her cash. "What do you need?"

"Soil from a high mountain. Maybe from Aconcagua or Everest."

Gemma looks at us for the first time and grins. "What do a Halo Knight and a wanted Spell Walker need with soil of that nature? Putting together a potion?"

"That's none of your concern," I say.

"No, but I can't help but be nosy when people come looking for rare items. That soil is often used for purging creature toxins, though it's hard to get your hands on some without those blasted hydras biting them off," Gemma says. "It'll cost more than cash."

Tala reaches into her bag. "I created bladed stars that explode in lightning."

Gemma laughs. "Young lady, I applaud your innovation, but that doesn't interest me. What else do you have?" She looks between us, but the only item of potential interest I'm carrying is the oblivion dagger. And I'm not trading a surefire way to kill June for the chance to make a potion to disempower her. Gemma's eyes land on Tala again. "I'll take your jacket."

"No," Tala says. "Take my crossbow instead."

"Once again, your weapons do not excite me. I'm well protected already." Gemma's eyes suddenly burn like an eclipse. My psychic sense triggers as two extra arms punch out of Gemma's sides, reach behind her, and pull out two wands from underneath a blanket. "Now, a Halo Knight's jacket is a collector's item that several clients of mine would take an interest in."

"This jacket was given to me by my parents, who were murdered weeks ago."

"Condolences," Gemma says with enough honesty that I don't set her on fire. "But that's my price. I want to live and manage my business and maintain my reputation as having the best high wares, young lady."

Tala tightens her jacket close as if it's freezing down here, when actually the sorrow in her amber eyes tells me she's about to part with it. She strokes the black feathered sleeves, and I hope it's of some consolation to Tala that Roxana is still alive to produce enough feathers to start again. Tala takes off the jacket, her wings and talons and beak tattoos exposed. Before she hands it over, she asks, "Where's the soil?"

Gemma stares as her hydra-grown arms unlock a chest and pull out a pouch that's patterned with blue and white stripes.

"How do we know this is legit?" Tala asks.

"You not knowing the product isn't my fault," Gemma says as she swiftly snatches the jacket and hands over the pouch. "But if it turns out to be nothing but park dirt, you can find me down here dressed like one of you until I have a buyer."

Tala storms off, and I chase after her.

"I'm good with snapping off her arms if you want to steal back your jacket," I say.

Tala stops in front of a booth selling ointments that claim to prevent phoenixpox. "There's no honor in that, but there is some in the sacrifice I made. It's better to lose something sentimental if it means saving phoenixes everywhere."

Her devotion to phoenixkind makes me feel selfish for not even offering the oblivion dagger. But she made her choice, and I quietly made mine.

"Excuse me," a short man says, trying to get to the booth. He has a dark, thick beard peppered with gray, and he's wearing a tracksuit. He does a double take, and it's clear he recognizes me. Then he looks especially petrified when he sees Tala's mask. He immediately runs away, snaking his way through the crowd.

There's something familiar about him. Was he one of the Brew dealers I confronted during the night of the Cloaked Phantom?

Or one of those pharmacy alchemists I'd hoped might have some affiliation with Luna?

Then I know. I never met this man, but back when the Spell Walkers researched Emil's life before bringing him onto the team, we learned that his boss at the Museum of Natural Creatures wrote a nonfiction book about some journey with phoenixes. What I remember most was this black-and-white author photo of him wearing a white turtleneck and a raptor glove. I couldn't help but laugh at how serious he was trying to look while he rested his chin on his gloved fist, and even Atlas couldn't hold back his smile at how funny I found it.

"That man is Kirk Bennett. The museum curator who would've hired your parents to protect Gravesend, and then traded her egg away for Emil."

Tala breaks into a sprint, shoving shoppers out of the way, and I follow in the path she's cleared. Kirk runs past the stairway and through a dark tunnel where there are no lanterns in sight to light his way. I cast fire, but Tala is still several feet ahead of me, tracking Kirk by his pounding footsteps. She dives forward and tackles him, his face splashing in a deep puddle; he's lucky if it's only dirty water.

My fire-orb illuminates his face. "We haven't had the pleasure, Kirk."

"Please let me go," he says. "I didn't do anything!"

"Innocent people don't run away like you did. What are you doing here?"

"I'm running an errand," Kirk says.

"For what?"

He's biting his tongue until I inch the fire-orb closer. "For whom—Luna."

I tap Tala's shoulder and ask her to ease up on him, but she's too furious. "What are you getting for her? Where is she?"

The Starstifler can wait if we get a location on Luna now.

"I don't know where she is! I'm picking up some oils and herbs used to strengthen phoenixes, and an ointment for shifters. She's planning on sending someone over to grab them in the next few days."

I'm not going to camp out in his home. That can turn into a trap quickly.

"Do you know who I am?" Tala says.

"A Halo Knight," Kirk says.

She rolls him onto his back and removes her mask. "My parents were murdered in your precious museum over a job you didn't honor." He tries to apologize, but Tala's fist connects with his chin too fast and hard. "Your word means nothing." She drives her knee straight into his stomach. "You profited off phoenixkind and couldn't bother protecting the precious first life of one who had centuries of lives ahead of her."

Kirk begs for her to stop as she raises her fist. "Please! I'll do anything! You want Luna? We can set up a trap for whoever comes for her order. They'll know more than I do!"

Tala finally gets off of him. "You have ten seconds to get out of here."

"Thank you, thank you!" Kirk is gasping for breath as he runs down the tunnel.

"Do you believe him?" I ask.

"My parents once believed him. I won't make their mistake."

Tala chooses an ordinary arrow and loads it into her crossbow. She aims with nothing but the sound of Kirk's running to signal where he is. She takes a deep breath as tears slide down her blushed cheeks. He's one of many people responsible for the death of her parents. Tala shoots the arrow through the darkness, and the fleeing footsteps stop and his anguished cries echo through the tunnel.

"He deserves to be a stranger to breath forevermore," Tala says. "But I'll settle for having him locked up for his crimes against phoenixes and my family."

FIFTY
THE SILVER STAR SLAYER

BRIGHTON

One look at the news proves that I'm not this country's problem child.

Allegations against celestials have been increasing lately. Sometimes it feels like there's a new one every day. But the three that have dropped this morning are rough: the invisible high school coach spying on students while they're changing in the locker rooms; the boss with fire in his eyes as he corners his assistant for refusing dates with him; and the mother who blinded the children who bullied her son at school.

"I don't know how Sunstar is going to counter Iron during Monday's debate," I say to Prudencia as she finishes her breakfast. "I got to get back out there, try to help."

"We blew up a building the last time we tried to help," Prudencia says.

"Technically, the other specter blew it up."

"I'm sure we can trust Iron to make that distinction."

"I want to give Sunstar something to fire back with."

"Brighton, no matter how much good we do, Iron's people find ways to twist it." Prudencia takes my hand. "I know you're feeling powerless even though we know you're not. But it's not safe right now. You couldn't even go home without getting attacked. We're lucky no one died that night."

I'm relieved none of my neighbors got killed. I am. But this is one of those moments where I'm grateful Prudencia is telekinetic and not telepathic because she would be disgusted to read my mind and see that I wouldn't mourn some losses for the greater good.

It's hard to be the Infinity Savior when I can't save people.

"Okay," I say, which feels like a weak promise I might break at any moment.

"Maribelle and Tala should be back with the potion ingredients soon, and then we can disempower the Blood Casters for good. That'll paint Sunstar and her proposal for the Luminary Union in a better light. Sit tight with me for a little bit longer?"

She kisses me behind my ear, then twice down my cheek, and then finally my lips. We fall back onto the bed, and she sits on top of me, closing and locking the door with her telekinesis, which has definitely become a turn-on for me. My phone keeps vibrating, but I ignore it as my hands reach underneath her shirt and as

401

her hands unbuckle my jeans. Even though we had the room to ourselves last night, we didn't have sex because we weren't sure when Emil was going to pop back in, but tonight I'm assuming he's with Wyatt again or curled up with some phoenixes outside, I don't care. I'm about to kick off my pants when Prudencia grabs my phone.

"You have so many notifications," Prudencia says.

"Day in the life," I say, sitting up to kiss her, but she stops me.

"Brighton, this looks serious."

I should've melted the damn phone when I had the chance. I take it from her and see everyone's tagging me across all platforms. Everything is linking me to some new rant from the Silver Star Slayer. I can't wait to see which conspiracy theory about me has everyone so riled up that it's cut into time better spent having sex with Prudencia. The video title pisses me off: *True Allies of New York.*

I press play, and Prudencia and I are shocked to see the Silver Star Slayer sitting beside Eva. Prudencia immediately wants to check in with Iris, but we watch first. So Eva is being detained by enforcers. Does this mean Ma is too? I'm so tempted to skip ahead. Eva doesn't share any of the big secrets revealed among the Spell Walkers, but she's clearly beaten down by the weight of everything. Donating her blood sounds worthwhile, though I'm sure the government will be more interested in using it to heal their enforcers and military instead of actually researching it for everyday citizens. The interview ends and transitions straight to the next.

Ma is alive. She's actually alive, like I've been saying this entire time! A rush shoots through me like when I drank the Reaper's Blood, but just like when the elixir started turning on me, I crash really hard. Why is she with the Silver Star Slayer? She explains that she's being detained too, though I hate that she's cooperating with him.

The Silver Star Slayer finishes his rant about how the government is on our side; then he glares at Ma. "One last question. If you could send a message to your sons right now, what would you tell them?"

Ma looks so exhausted as she takes a deep breath. "Don't be so high and mighty, and don't get yourselves killed using powers you shouldn't have. You're all I have left."

There goes those words again. High and mighty. Even after our last argument, this is what she decides to put out there. She may as well have just directly said how much I've disappointed her by drinking the Reaper's Blood.

As for the Silver Star Slayer, he's on my damn list of people who have horrible, burning hot things coming their way.

"This is great news," Prudencia says.

"It's a great start, but we have no idea where Ma and Eva are."

"I'll call Iris. Maybe she'll have some ideas on where to begin the search."

I fix myself up as I head for the door. "I'll find Emil."

I open the door and dash down the hall, bursting with so much power and life because our mother is alive. This is my most personal opportunity to show the world why I'm called the Infinity Savior—and why you don't mess with my family.

FIFTY-ONE
SUNRISE

EMIL

I've had some chill mornings here at the Sanctuary, but this one is the best. Wyatt's arms are wrapped around me, his body pressed against mine inside this sleeping bag. Sunlight and phoenix song are slowly filling the library. I'd definitely want some of my ashes dropped here.

I'm telling Wyatt more about my family, using the last ten percent of my phone's battery to show him some memories from my camera's album. There's a photo of Ma hugging me and Brighton on the day we graduated, and Bright is holding a framed picture of all of us plus Dad.

"Brighton wanted to create one of those infinity series where you take a picture with the last one you took. The next one would've been after we graduated from college. Then landing jobs we love. Meeting people we love." I'm pretty sure I'm not in love with Wyatt, though it's possible my head is just going up against my heart right now, but I know for a damn fact that I'm straight blushing because talking about love with someone whose arms are wrapped around you feels big. "The ultimate plan was to have some huge family picture with my and Brighton's partners and kids."

"That's bloody sweet. You can still do this," Wyatt says.

"It feels like we would be jinxing ourselves by doing it without Ma. Like every time we take a picture we're guaranteeing someone photographed won't be around next time."

"Rubbish, love. Keep finding time for your life as if you don't have a lot of it left, but don't forget that you're fighting for your future too. Make sure you're setting yourself up for greatness—becoming a Halo Knight, infinity pictures with your families, bonding with a phoenix. Perhaps including your phoenix in your family pictures and your phoenix's family and the families of your phoenix's family and the—"

I flip around and shut up a smiling Wyatt with a kiss. He slides his fingers through the collar of the shirt I borrowed from him last night, trailing my collarbone. Our bodies are reacting in some super-solid ways, especially since we didn't have sex last night because I didn't feel up to it. I think I've got some work to do on myself before I'm ready to take off all my clothes in front of another person, especially someone who's put so much work into his own body. Nothing wrong with making out though; I can tell I'm really getting the hang of it by the way Wyatt moans into my mouth.

The library door slams open so suddenly that I gasp. Memories trigger of the enforcers busting into Nova, and I'm scared that they've found us again. I try crawling out of the sleeping bag, but it's tough as Wyatt tries doing the same, and then Brighton rounds the corner and his eyes widen; I think I would've preferred enforcers.

"Whoa!" Brighton turns around. "Sorry."

"Bright, go!"

"Bro, no! Get dressed. There's something you need to see."

"Fine, wait out on the balcony!"

Brighton listens, and I find my way out of the sleeping bag. I put on my pants, damp from the river, and tell Wyatt to stay put. I meet Brighton on the balcony, one hundred percent unable to look at him.

"Now I know why you never came back to the room," Brighton says.

"We didn't do anything," I say.

"There's no need to lie—"

"I know, which is why I'm not."

"We'll circle back to this later. More important matters anyway. Ma's alive."

All embarrassment forgotten, I turn to Brighton with tears already forming in my eyes. "For real?"

Brighton hands me his phone with a video loaded. I'm nervous that it's going to be something horrible, like when Stanton beat up Brighton on camera, but it's an interview that starts off with that Silver Star Slayer creep and Eva. I watch the whole thing with the heat of the rising sun on my neck, and I'm so relieved

Ma and Eva are alive, but there's something off about this.

"Ma would've called us," I say.

"They're not letting her."

"But she has rights."

"These are people who treat us like terrorists. The only way enforcers are giving Ma a call is if they believe it'll lead them to us." Brighton is so pissed that he looks like he might hurl some fire-bolts into the sky. "This has got to be some political move to stir up more trouble before the election."

"Why wouldn't they use an actual news network?"

"Probably because using the Silver Star Slayer is a middle finger to me."

Too many mind games. "What's our move?"

"I'll grab Prudencia, and we can all figure it out together. I'll be back in minutes, so you don't have time for whatever it was you and your boyfriend were or weren't doing," Brighton says, and dashes away.

"He's not my boyfriend," I say to no one.

But I'm not against it.

A couple hours in the library and we haven't come up with any leads.

Prudencia managed to get Iris on the phone right as she was on her way out with Wesley to hit the streets, even though there's no guarantee Eva and Ma are even still in the city. Brighton has posted response videos online, running his mouth about the

Silver Star Slayer and how Iron is messing with our heads and possibly harming our mother. Strong words, but he's not pulling any punches. Wyatt watched the interview once and confirmed our gut feelings that there's nothing in that setting that we can use to determine where it was even filmed.

"I'm this close to knocking down Iron's door and demanding to know where Ma is," Brighton says.

"Don't see how that will help with your image," Wyatt says.

"I don't care!" Brighton shouts.

The door opens, and Maribelle and Tala enter.

"This is the loudest library," Maribelle says. "Do I want to know?"

"Big updates since you've been out," Brighton says, and then fills them both in on everything that we know.

"It's all happening," Tala says, setting down a bag on the round table. "When it rains, it pours. We have the ingredients."

I open the bag, laying out all the ingredients and admiring them like pieces to my new favorite puzzle. This is how we'll create the Starstifler, a potion that has been hidden in time for decades, and we'll change the fate of specters everywhere. I'll bind my powers, I'll work to become a Halo Knight, I'll fight this war in a way that's more me. For the first time since those gold and gray flames appeared, I actually believe there's life beyond them.

Brighton stares at the ingredients too, but I don't think he's seeing what I'm seeing.

"It's going to take three days to brew," I say.

Prudencia packs up everything. "We better get started."

"Enjoy that. I'm going to sleep," Maribelle says.

"Same," Tala says.

"Only wake me if we've tracked down literally anyone we're looking for," Maribelle adds.

I let them go, and Wyatt leads us to the on-site lab where he had prepared the Dayrose salve for me. The room is small, occupied by a Halo Knight who is using a poster on different alchemic elements to teach a child about brewing. We give them as much space as possible, setting up near two silver cauldrons. I run back for the journal and return just as Brighton and Prudencia finish rinsing the cauldrons. Wyatt goes into a cabinet and hands me a jar of crushed torch grains, a couple Dayrose roots, a vial of phoenix tears, and packets of a crowned elder's soot.

"I'll fetch the eggshell from one of the nests," Wyatt says.

"Make sure it's from a reborn phoenix, not a first-timer," I say.

"On it, Hot Wings." He winks as he leaves.

Brighton snickers. "England and Hot Wings here may have been on each other last night."

I ignore him, crushing the blood-plumed basilisk's dead skin as instructed in the journal. We slowly find a flow through our first potion, triple-checking every step to make sure we're making good use of our limited ingredients. Prudencia sprinkles the soot and torch grains into the steaming cauldron, and telekinetically stirs while Brighton boils some phoenix tears with the ground-up basilisk skin.

"The end of specters is really beginning," I say.

I'm a mix of pride and anxiety all weekend as we work on the Starstifler. There's a schedule we're supposed to stick to so that nothing goes wrong, but of course Brighton would rather train and enhance his "signature moves" instead of wake up in the middle of the night to check on the potion that will one day bind his powers. I don't say it out loud, but I'd rather lose more sleep to see this through myself than risk Brighton sabotaging it.

By Monday, everything seems to be going smoothly, though spirits are still down since we haven't gotten any concrete updates about Ma or Eva.

"Hosting a debate watch party in an hour," Brighton says.

"Watching Sunstar demolish Iron will be a nice break," Prudencia says.

"We should take a shot every time Iron lies."

"We would die."

"You might. Emil and I are the Infinity Kings."

Brighton smiles and tries to get a fist bump out of me but I shake my head.

Prudencia and I sprinkle shavings from the phoenix eggshell into the potion and meet up with Brighton and Wyatt in the library. We gather around Brighton's laptop, ready for Sunstar to show this country why she deserves to be the next president.

FIFTY-TWO
ECLIPSING

NESS

Ask me anything about Nicolette Sunstar.

She was born in bright lights at the zenith of the Dazzling Compass constellation. She has a birthmark shaped like an hourglass above her left knee. She received her middle name, Penelope, from the aunt who first got her interested in justice. She loves traveling to cold climates, especially Alaska when the aurora borealis paints the sky. She's the daughter to a marriage counselor and bookshop owner. She has always filled her home with the greenest of plants, which she nurtures without using her power. She met her husband during karaoke night in college and Ash Hyperion was drunkenly singing a love song. She begins her day making breakfast with their daughter, Proxima, usually blueberry pancakes, and preparing her for school.

She deserves to be the president of the United States.

For the past week, I've been reviewing all the materials given to me about her.

I've read the three-hundred-and-eighty-four-page paperback about her life, *Our Country, Our Universe*, twice. I've been glued to an internet-less tablet and watching over thirty hours of interviews and speeches. I've been given the debates too, which I've rewatched ten times because of how Sunstar embarrasses the Senator on national TV as she recounts all his failures.

But she's going to lose this election because I'm going to lie to the country while looking like a carbon copy of her.

I'm in a limousine with the Senator, Bishop, and Roslyn in the back and Jax and Zenon up front. Dione is tailing us in a town car with Luna and June. Since leaving New York and arriving in Boston for the debate, I've been hoping that some natural catastrophe would swallow all of us into the pit of the earth so some of the country's absolute worst can die already, but unfortunately it's a lovely night.

We arrive at the host site of the debate, Doherty University. Even though the college has historically favored celestial rights, that might die tonight after I hit them with Sunstar's new celestial supremacy stance. Attendees are filling the campus grounds as we drive to the rear of the building.

"Showtime," the Senator says. "Get rid of your face, Eduardo."

I glow gray and morph into a white bodyguard with pitch-black hair. I'm given shades so the media will have a harder time identifying me if any of them bother to investigate. This twenty feet between the car and the building is the first time I've been outside since being held at the manor. It's impossible to enjoy the fresh air without feeling like I'm suffocating under the Senator's control.

The young greeter escorts us to a green room, rambling to the Senator the entire time about what a big fan she is and how she'll be applying for internships if he gets into office. The Senator claims he's honored, but I know he can't wait to be rid of her. Unlike Sunstar, who spends her time getting to know everyone in the community, the Senator mostly aligns himself with those in power; a young woman directing us to a room hardly fits that bill in his eyes.

"I'll come and grab you in fifteen minutes," she says.

"Much appreciated," the Senator says, shaking her hand with both of his. The moment the door closes behind her, he turns to Zenon. "Status?"

Zenon's eyes glow. "The person running surveillance in the camera room has no eyes on us."

The Senator's forced smile drops. "Fantastic. Roslyn, notify Luna. Zenon, locate Sunstar. Time is limited to execute the swap."

Bishop looks pleased, as if all this corruption is some surprise party he's been planning for ages.

Zenon continues vision-hopping. The Senator must be paying a fortune for this former soldier who survived in battle and led his squad to numerous victories because of his abilities to orient himself from the perspective of others in situations like this. "Sunstar is in a room with her family and Senator Lu, though the

413

senator appears to be on her way out . . . and she's gone. Security is blocking the room number, but Lu has now passed the library. I would estimate twenty paces."

"That will do," the Senator says.

"Incoming," Roslyn says while looking at her phone.

June and Dione appear out of nowhere. Jax looks as if he'd be ready to hurl her across the room if it weren't for Roslyn's warning.

The Senator stands tall, beaming with pride. "You all know your roles. Eduardo, you play yours wrong and Sunstar's entire family will be killed. If I can't be president, she won't either."

His ego will be the death of millions.

"Understood," I say.

"I'm watching every move you make," Zenon says.

"I said I understand."

June is given instructions on how to find Sunstar before she holds on to me and Dione, and we disappear. As we all fade in and out of rooms, it feels like my body is coming apart every time, just like when June rescued me during the Blackout and then transported me to Luna. This trip is thankfully shorter, but still nauseating as all hell.

We appear inside Sunstar's green room. They're all holding hands as Sunstar leads them in prayer. Dione grows a third arm and grabs three wands from her belt and aims them at Sunstar, Ash, and Proxima. The family break into laughter at the end of their prayer, and then are stunned to find three uninvited guests in here with them.

"If anyone calls for security, you're all dead," Dione says.

Sunstar pushes her trembling twelve-year-old daughter behind her, and Proxima's lips are quivering as she peeks around at us. She's staring at us like we're monsters, and she's right. I'm just grateful she doesn't see my actual face in this moment.

Ash's eyes glow silver like coins and there are wrinkles in the air. I'm suddenly exhausted, and my rapid heartbeat has slowed down. This is his power to manipulate consciousness at work, and I welcome it. Dione's arms have fallen to her sides, and I might pass out any moment. Then my morph will drop, my identity will be revealed, and they can take me into custody so we can expose the Senator as the fraud and terrorist he is.

June fades away and reappears behind Ash. I try to shout, but I don't have the energy as Ash continues to induce me into sleep. June steps inside the congresswoman's husband, possessing him instantly. The wrinkles in the air even out as June forces Ash to yank his daughter to his side.

Inside Ash's body, June opens his mouth and there are no words. Only the sounds of howling winds that chill me to the bone.

"He's possessed," I say. This reminds me of when Emil tried warning the Halo Knights at the museum that June had possessed one of their own, and Luna smacked him. "Don't do anything stupid."

Sunstar looks as if she wants to fill this room with burning light, but she stands still. Sudden movements don't end well for celestials.

I still feel drowsy, but it passes shortly, like in the morning when you manage to finally get yourself out of bed.

"Please don't hurt my family," Sunstar says.

"We won't if you cooperate," I say, even though I don't fully believe that's true.

"You'll be coming with me," Dione says.

"I'm supposed to be onstage in minutes. The authorities will know I'm missing."

"No, they won't," Dione says, gesturing to me with all three arms.

I remove the shades as gray light washes over me. My skin smooths and darkens. My hair grows to my shoulders. My nails turn white. My black bodyguard outfit is replaced with the same dark green suit Sunstar wore for her campaign visit in North Carolina.

The real Sunstar looks at me in horror.

"Problem solved," Dione says. "We can't impersonate all of you, so your husband and daughter's survival depends on their performances during the debate. We have people in the audience tasked with watching them. If they don't appear supportive or even so much as speak to anyone else, they will be killed on the spot."

Sunstar nods. "Proxy, baby, do everything they say, okay?"

Proxima is shaking, even after June steps backward outside of Ash. Ash hugs Proxima, scaring her at first, but assuring her that it's him. Dione and June grab Sunstar, who is staring at her family, unsure if she'll ever see them again.

I don't know if she will either.

"We have eyes on you in here too," Dione says. "Do the right thing and support your wife."

They all fade away, and for the first time since being held captive, I'm left alone in the outside world with good people. But I can't let them know I'm on their side, no matter how scared they are. Zenon is watching us this very moment, and if I even so much as apologize for all the harm I'm about to cause their family, they may not live to see it.

I'll go onstage and debate the Senator with all the scripted lies I've memorized.

I plan on sneaking out one great truth while on national TV.

FIFTY-THREE
THE DEBATE

NESS

"Welcome to the third and final debate."

Tonight's moderator is Hugh Cooper, a news personality who has been very critical of the Senator in the past and will hopefully challenge him tonight when I can't—when Sunstar would. He explains that none of the questions for the segments have been shared with the candidates in advance. He requests silence from the audience throughout the evening so everyone present and watching from home can focus.

"Please welcome the Democratic nominee, Congresswoman Sunstar, and the Republican nominee, Senator Iron."

I cross the stage, meeting the Senator in the middle for a handshake. He's exuding so much confidence in his presidential suit, knowing this debate is in the bag. I'm tempted to drop this costume now and expose him, but when I turn to the crowd and find Ash holding Proxima close, I continue to cooperate instead for their well-being.

The Senator and I take our places behind our podiums. There's a notepad with three pens. Sunstar is a diligent notetaker, a behavior I'll be expected to keep up. Darkness falls over the audience and there's only a time clock that's visible. It's a small mercy so I don't have to watch Proxima quivering anymore.

"I'd like to start off this evening talking about the economy," Hugh Cooper says. "In the last debate you both shared your views on the decline of available jobs, and I want to ask what you will do to ensure growth so those living in this country will thrive in it. Senator Iron, you'll go first in this segment. You have two minutes."

"Thank you, Hugh, and thank you to Doherty University for graciously hosting us," the Senator says, masking his disdain for this pro-celestial campus with a smile.

He immediately talks about the great honor he's had working alongside the laborers in New York and traveling to meet others across the country, expressing their heartbreak at spending hundreds of thousands of dollars on education only to find themselves shut out of dream jobs by celestials who can do the job in the snap of a finger. He cites one of our propaganda videos about a construction worker who can no longer support his family after being replaced by a celestial with advanced telekinesis.

"Power shouldn't come before passion," the Senator says.

"Thank you, Senator. I'd like to ask the same question of Congresswoman Sunstar. How will you improve the economy?"

Sunstar's plans to increase minimum wage and create higher taxes for the wealthy is a country I'd love to live in, but instead I work the lines written for me. How celestials should continue to invade markets outside of their interest and collect payments originally allotted for manual laborers. The Senator is quick to counter, right on cue, about how many Americans are in debt and without homes because of unavailable jobs.

The gloves stay off from that point forward.

On the topic of wand violence, the Senator defends everyone's right to bear arms since he considers celestials to be walking weapons. For health care, the Senator deflects how many celestials aren't insured because of their powers and instead advises for broader guidelines that would allow better coverage for properties damaged by gleam, and he completely doesn't mention how that would suit his donors and raise taxes on everyone else. He dismisses the idea that underground camps have made their way into our country, designed to hold pregnant celestials hostage throughout their pregnancies to prevent the children being born under the skies and reaching the full potential of their powers.

I'm not some bystander in the audience. I'm one of the two liars on this stage.

I've been tasked with portraying Sunstar as someone who is cracking under the pressure of her campaign, especially in light of the Silver Star Slayer's videos, and I argue back with an aggression that Sunstar hasn't once demonstrated in any of her debates. When asked, I don't condemn specters as a whole, stating that there are good, well-intentioned people who seek out power to further their lives, and I applaud the risks they take, especially those who are older, given how blood alchemy isn't always kind to their bodies. I want to warn everyone, no matter their intentions, that becoming a specter isn't worth it, but I'm too busy not offering sympathies as requested by the Senator to those who have lost their children because of gleam cross fires.

I can't imagine that the celestials currently holding seats in government aren't cringing during this entire debate. Maybe some of them will even be suspicious, having worked with Sunstar and shared her views for how she would shape the country. But between the Senator presenting himself as a grounded candidate who will be remembered as strong and me fighting back—sure to get Sunstar labeled as unhinged—it's impossible to believe anyone will expect anything except the Senator taking the White House next month.

Hugh Cooper regains control. "We're wrapping up shortly, so I'd like to shift and ask you, Congresswoman, about your recent announcement of your plan to abolish the Enforcer Program and put an organization you're calling the Luminary Union in its place. What would you say to Americans who are nervous about relying on powered guardians?"

I don't know all of Sunstar's intentions on this since only one video of her talking about it has been shared with me, but I suspect she simply wants to stop seeing people in her community killed by enforcers who use wands charged by celestial blood. I can't push this message, and may the stars have mercy on me.

"The Luminary Union is designed to protect the public, but

namely the extraordinary celestials who are the backbone and heart of this country. It is time that we become the authorities and leaders."

"So you're giving even more jobs to celestials," the Senator says. "And leaving our citizens disadvantaged against those with power. This vision for the future is bleak and will only lead to more Blackouts. I promise no one wants to receive the call that I did telling them that their child was blown up because of a power brawl between Spell Walkers, whom you not only won't condemn, but would bring into the fold of your new division. Can you really look me in the eye and tell me in front of the American people that the terrorist group that killed my son should become our new law enforcement?"

The anger on Sunstar's face is the realest it's been all night.

I try arguing that the faults of some cannot fall on an entire community, but the Senator is louder and more forceful.

"I didn't think so! I didn't think so! Americans refuse to build the bricks of your celestial supremacist country." The Senator comes out from behind the podium, creating an intimacy with the audience hidden in the darkness. "A Sunstar presidency is preventable, but we should be concerned that she's gotten this far. We have a record number of celestials in seats of power, and you've heard the rumors of qualified opponents who wanted to serve you but were too intimidated to run against celestials. Between stories of Sunstar using her husband's hypnosis to control minds of politicians and voters, we have to protect ourselves now!"

I want to argue that mind control isn't even a real power, and that Ash would never use it that way if it were, but it would be pointless even if I were allowed.

To my horror, they're applauding him.

The Senator points at me. "You deserve to be locked up in the Bounds."

The applause grows louder and Hugh Cooper is having a difficult time getting the audience to settle down. I'm terrified that I coexist in a country with these people.

"Thank you," Hugh Cooper says as everyone finally quiets down. "I'd like to open the floor for closing statements. Congresswoman Sunstar, you may go first."

I stare directly into the camera. I'm supposed to push some more Celestials First ideals, and I've figured out how to do it my way. "Celestials are fireflies who have been suppressed for so long, suffocating in jars that have become our homes. We demand to be freed from our jars, but we need your help to unscrew the lids. Thank you."

This might sound like nonsense to the majority of this country.

I only need one person to understand.

FIFTY-FOUR
BREAKING

EMIL

Sunstar is talking about fireflies.

I pop my head up from Wyatt's shoulder and drag Brighton's laptop closer to me, rewatching the closing remarks. This entire debate has been wild with how Sunstar has hit absolute one-eighties with her stances, but what if something has gone terribly wrong? And maybe even a little bit right?

"I think that's Ness," I say, staring at my frozen still of Sunstar.

"Ness-Ness?" Wyatt asks.

"What are you talking about?" Brighton asks.

My heart is absolutely pounding against my chest, even though I've barely moved. "Look, for the past two hours we've been confused about why Sunstar seems so off and is saying so many dangerous things. What if that isn't her?"

"That's a big leap, especially since we think he's dead," Brighton says.

"But we don't have proof that he is," Prudencia says.

"Ness calls me 'firefly.' Iron must be using him, and this must've been some code for me to know what's what. Think about it, the last time I saw Ness he was being carried away by enforcers. Someone would've definitely told Iron about that, right? Maybe Iron is using Ness's powers to win this election."

Everyone looks uneasy, like I'm reaching for this to be true. I don't know, maybe I am. I never got any closure with Ness. I barely even got a beginning.

I replay Sunstar's final remarks again.

"She's—he's—talking about fireflies suffocating in jars that feel like home. Maybe that's code for Iron's house and he's being held hostage there."

"Bro, you're giving off major conspiracy-theorist vibes. If everything you're saying is true, wouldn't it be really risky for Iron to put Ness on a national stage?"

"Yeah, for sure, but maybe Iron has something on Ness to keep him in check."

Maybe some promise for freedom? Things were so bad at home that Ness chose a literal gang over staying there. Or maybe he's being blackmailed for everything he's done as a Blood Caster. Above all, Ness has wanted his life back, and he's not going to have much of one behind bars if his identity and crimes are exposed.

Prudencia's eyes widen. "Iron could have Carolina and Eva as hostages too."

"But they're with—" Brighton shuts up.

"The government," Prudencia says.

"If that was even them in the videos," I say.

Brighton opens another tab on his laptop, and we rewatch the Silver Star Slayer's interviews. I can't speak for Eva, but everything about Ma's appearance still seems so legit. Ness is also an incredible shifter who could pull off passing as them as much as he has Sunstar tonight.

"That's definitely Ma," Brighton says. "She's even talking about us being 'high and mighty' like in my last argument with her."

"But if everyone is housed together, Ness would know," Prudencia counters. "We don't know Eva well enough, but I don't think she would've quit the team. No matter how upset she was at Iris for lying."

"Then what really went down with this saved-by-enforcers narrative?" I ask. "The Blood Casters wouldn't be working with Iron, right?"

What could possibly possess them to do that?

Nothing is clear, but there are enough stars that don't connect into a constellation that I got to see what's going down. "I think we should go investigate," I say.

Brighton laughs and claps. "You have been grounding me since I got my powers, and now you're talking about storming into the home of a gleamphobic presidential candidate to save your other boyfriend?"

"I don't have a boyfriend!"

Wyatt has been quiet while we've been trying to work this

out, but I feel the weight of his silence now as if I said something wrong. He's not my boyfriend and same goes for Ness. But whatever drama comes out of this, now is definitely one of many reasons why I'm not trying to mess around with romance in the middle of a war.

"Bright, if you're not game, fine. I'll fly back into the city myself if I have to."

"No, I'm good to go. Just wanted to be clear whose idea this was in case we're thrown into the Bounds."

"This is a bad idea," Prudencia says. "If we're wrong, this will only prove everything Iron has been saying about gleamcrafters behaving as if we're above the law because we have powers."

"If we're right, we save our mother, Eva, Ness, and Sunstar," Brighton says.

Prudencia nods, but still looks uncomfortable. She's right to feel so and I'm right there with her. Everyone we're hoping to rescue might already be dead.

Wyatt lets out a deep breath. "You lot are truly operating under the gigantic assumption that the man who might become president may have kidnapped your loved ones and staged a public debate with his shape-shifting son."

"Yup," I say.

"This country is awful."

"Yup," I say again.

"I'll take to the skies with you, love," Wyatt says.

"Thank you," I say, hoping he doesn't feel obligated, but we can definitely use the backup because stars know how much security the senator must have.

We get ready quickly, having no idea if Iron is returning from Boston tonight or heading off to somewhere else. It's going to take us over an hour to drive back into the city, and if Iron flies back by helicopter, we're screwed. Nox unfortunately can't carry all of us, so Prudencia gets the car ready while Brighton updates Maribelle to see if she's game to come with us. What really sucks as I run back to mix more phoenix tears into the Starstifler potion is that we're a few hours away from being done with it. We could've brought this with us to try it out on any Blood Casters.

But we can't afford to wait. Not when Ness just risked his life to send me that message.

I ride backseat in the car so I can strategize with Brighton and Prudencia, and Wyatt, Tala, and Maribelle fly ahead on the phoenixes. I haven't felt this much hope in a minute, and I'm going to be a disgrace to Bautista's legacy if my actions get us all captured—or worse—right as we were about to make history of our own.

We all reunite a couple blocks from Iron's house. The phoenixes are hiding out by the river, staying within whistling distance. Brighton tried to reach Iris and Wesley multiple times in the car, but they never answered, not even when we used Prudencia's phone, so he left a message and that's that. It's going to be the six of us—four powered, two armed with weapons—against however many Blood Casters and security guards are watching over the estate. Once inside, we'll break into two groups of three—the

Reys of Light plus Wyatt, and then Maribelle, Prudencia, and Tala—so power is evenly distributed.

"No killing," I remind everyone.

"No promises," Maribelle says as she leads the way.

The house's surroundings are hidden behind hedges. I peek through the front gate and notice a security guard with dark gray hair walking past a fountain; not going that way. Brighton dashes up the block, and we all keep to the shadows as we run after him. He returns with the good news that the south entrance doesn't have any visible guard, so we rush there. Prudencia telekinetically pushes open the gate, slowing down when it creaks, and we all slide through before the doors close. The lights are off in the backyard, and I'm so nervous we're going to set off sensors like I know some rich people have.

I freeze, as the same security guard from before rounds the corner. His eyes glow as he begins raising his hands, but Prudencia locks his arms at his side and clasps his jaw shut all in one move; all that time she spent practicing her power back at the cottage is already paying off. The guard struggles to break free, and Brighton dashes over and knocks him out with three punches.

"MVP so far," Maribelle says, patting Prudencia's shoulder.

Brighton removes the guard's handcuffs from his belt and binds his arms behind his back in case he wakes up. We drag him behind a bush too, hoping this buys us even an extra minute if someone else is here.

Prudencia telekinetically opens the door and no alarm goes off. We're all immediately in some sort of telepathic agreement to no longer speak as we step inside. We're in a sunroom with blossoming plants and white wicker benches. I'm so nervous about this hardwood floor giving us away if someone else is here. Tala leads Maribelle and Prudencia through a dining room and away from us, and Prudencia and Brighton exchange a concerned look; I'm going to make sure they get back to each other.

I slowly make my way up the steps, and when one begins creaking I pull off my foot. We all skip it and find ourselves on the second floor with portraits outside an office. Brighton peeks inside and comes right back out. If this is one of those houses that has secret hideaways triggered by twisting some old high school trophy on a dusty shelf, we're not going to have much luck tonight. The master bedroom and two bedrooms are empty, leaving one more room down the hall.

I open the door and find what has got to be Ness's room. The green curtains are drawn, and he's got this really interesting wall with black diamonds. He's definitely alive, judging from the way this place has been lived in, with its empty glasses, potato chip wrappers, clothes thrown around. I always thought when someone I liked brought me home that they would actually be bringing me home—not dropping clues during a national debate for me to break in and rescue them. And not with my brother and some other guy who I'm catching feelings for at my side.

"He's alive," I whisper.

"And not in here," Brighton says.

I can't help myself as I go over to his bed. If Ness and I were normal, we could hang out here, play games, talk about books, keep getting to know each other. Maybe even throw back some kisses and fall asleep holding each other like I've gotten to do with Wyatt at the Sanctuary.

There's a paperback about Sunstar on his pillow. I can't believe we figured all of this out, all thanks to him giving me that one clue during the debate.

A phone rings from within our group, and Brighton quickly silences it with the guiltiest look on his face. "It's Wesley calling," he whispers.

Wyatt rolls his eyes. "Did you seriously not consider putting your phone on silent before breaking into a politician's home? Quite frankly, I'd advise that for any future break-in of yours."

"Shut up."

"Is it too late for me to join the other team?" Wyatt asks.

"Bright, we'll call Wesley back, but for now—"

There are footsteps, and for a second I dare to dream that it might be Ness, but when we all turn to the door, we see a bodyguard with glowing eyes and electricity crackling around his fists.

FIFTY-FIVE
THE VOID

BRIGHTON

The bodyguard wastes no time hurling lightning at us.

I dash-tackle Emil and Wyatt out of harm's way, and the desk behind us explodes. Celestials using their powers so aggressively for a candidate who hates them are among the dumbest people I know. From the floor, I throw a fire-bolt at the bodyguard and lay him out in the doorway.

I help up Emil while the bodyguard groans. "No point sneaking around anymore, so I'm going to run around the house. You two stay close."

"Be careful," Emil says.

I dash out of the room, feeling the bodyguard's nose crunch under my foot, and I pay no mind to his anguished cries as I go up the next flight of steps and toward the attic. The door is locked—this could be where Ma is being held. I blow it open with a fire-bolt. No one is in here. It's a massive attic that I would've loved for a bedroom if I'd been wealthy enough to grow up in a house like this, but the space only has a camera on a tripod, chairs, and a desk. Maybe for the Silver Star Slayer interviews?

I go to the desk, hoping to find some proof of Emil's big theory in case we can't find our people. There's definitely been campaign work happening up here, with some Iron-Bishop pamphlets, tax statements, and rally receipts. I open a binder and find transcripts of a couple anti-gleam videos that were released recently. Right as I'm about to close it, I notice some of the pages have edits in red.

These aren't transcripts. They're actual scripts.

Iron's team must have Ness putting out propaganda too.

For the first time in my life, I'm truly terrified of Iron. If this is all true, then we're up against someone more dangerous than Luna and the Blood Casters.

I hold the binder close, turning to find that security guard with dark hair I triple-decked outside. "That wasn't personal. Neither is this."

I charge a fire-bolt, but the guard is faster. Heavy winds blast from his palms and extinguish my flames as easily as breathing on birthday candles. I try dashing forward, but it's like trying to run through a tornado, and I'm thrown off balance. His winds carry me to the attic's ceiling, and I lose hold of the binder. The guard extends one palm to keep me pinned with his winds, and with his other hand he gestures like he's squeezing something. I don't understand what's happening at first until I'm suddenly wheezing over and over—he's dragging the oxygen out of me.

This can't be the end.

There's no way in hell this is how I'm going out. If I'm ever going to die in battle, it's going to be epic and at the hands of a worthier opponent. Not some Dark Side Atlas literally sucking the life out of me. Except I can't break out of this hold. I can't believe some nobody is going to kill the Infinity Savior.

I can't breathe, and even as my temperature drops hard and fast, practically sub-zero, I can't help thinking that I'm going out just like Dad, fighting for air. I'm dizzy and feel weightless as I fall from the ceiling. The lack of oxygen must be getting to me because the world loses all color, and shifting lights and shadows transform everything like some old-school photo negatives. This must be it for me. I'm about to slam against the floor when instead I sink through it, falling back into Ness's room, where Emil casts fire against that celestial from earlier, and the flames are blinding me. The sounds of winds follow me as I fall through the floor again, even though that Dark Nobody is still up in the attic and I'm somehow crashing through the kitchen. No, I'm not crashing—I'm phasing through this house—and I go through one more fall before slamming down on a tiled floor and suck in the biggest breath.

My ghost powers saved my life before I could die.

I have all three sets of powers the Reaper's Blood promised, which makes me more than the Infinity Savior, I'm the—

"Brighton!"

Ma.

I turn, and there's a massive black box inside a yellow

434

gleam-shield. This is one of those lofty panic rooms. I can't see Ma through the door's window, but she keeps yelling that she's inside. I hear Eva too. They're actually alive. The Senator is going to burn for this. For now, I have to rescue them.

"I'm going to get you out!"

"There's a button on the wall!" Eva shouts.

I find the keypad with the emergency button and the gleam-shield switches off.

Upstairs, there's an explosion, followed by people shouting and glass shattering. I hope my side is winning so I have more time to free Ma and Eva. The door won't pull open. These panic rooms were built to keep out celestials, but what about specters with ghost powers?

There's no one in my life who can be my phasing instructor the way I have Emil for my phoenix powers and Wesley for swift-speed. I'm all I have—and all I am is more than everyone else. If anyone can go inside a room designed to keep people out, it's me.

I focus on the panic and determination that must've awakened my power, and I think about making myself weightless again until the world loses color again and the sound of howling winds rages inside my head. I'm nervous that I might fall through the earth as I take my first step forward, but that's not the worst of it. It's difficult and freezing like walking through a cold, furious ocean and I'm suffocating like I'm drowning in it.

Once I'm inside, the lights and shadows readjust, and I try to catch my breath but my crying mother pulls me into the tightest hug. I'm not complaining.

"I'm sorry for everything, Ma."

435

"Me too, my shining star, me too."

She takes a good look at me, and I hate how underfed she looks.

"Who else is here?" Eva asks. She has bruises around her body.

These monsters who harmed them will meet their ends. Even if I have to possess them all one by one and walk them off skyscrapers.

"We've got enough backup," I say. There's no time to break down why Iris and Wesley aren't with us. "This power is new, so hopefully I can make it work with all of us."

I grab their hands, and Ma squeezes like she never wants to let me go again. We step toward the door and begin phasing through. It's even harder, like I'm a tiny boat with two anchors thrown overboard, and I'm ready to quit when we break through to the other side. I'm the only one gasping for air, and Ma and Eva don't seem affected in the slightest.

We go up the stairs and Ma is shaking the entire time.

It's absolute chaos up here.

Maribelle is fighting a guard on the steps, and she balances herself on the handrail as she kicks him so hard that he tumbles down. Tala and Wyatt are in a dizzying fight with a woman who keeps teleporting in and out, and she always lands a hit on one of them. Emil is rounding the corners of various big furniture pieces as he shoots fire-darts and dodges more lightning attacks from the same celestial as before. And Prudencia is battling the silver-haired bodyguard with a grandfather clock suspended in the air between them; his winds are beginning to overwhelm her and she might get crushed.

436

"Start moving for the door," I say.

"No, don't leave us," Ma says, holding on to me.

I phase my hand out of hers and rush over to Prudencia. The bodyguard is getting the edge over her until I dash into him so hard that he flies through the windows of the sunroom; he should've stayed down when we handcuffed him outside. Prudencia telekinetically slams the grandfather clock down, and the chimes are so distracting that Maribelle surprises the teleporter with a fire-arrow and knocks her out too.

"Pru, get my mom outside!"

I don't even wait for her reaction before dashing toward Emil, skidding to a halt as the bodyguard attacks. I grab Emil and hope to every star that my power doesn't fail me now. The lightning phases through us, exploding in white-hot sparks against the fireplace. While Emil is shocked, I hurl a fire-bolt straight into the celestial's chest and he lands in the ruins of the grandfather clock.

"I saved Ma and Eva; let's go!"

We yell for everyone to follow us out of the house. We run past a statue and get to the front gate, which Prudencia has pushed open with her power. The Haloes whistle for their phoenixes and Emil runs straight into Ma's arms. There are sirens in the distance, so I give Emil and Ma three whole seconds before we have to keep it moving. It's such a rush as we make it back to the car and peel away, Emil and I sitting with our mother's arms wrapped around us and crying together.

We did it. The Reys of Light, the Infinity Kings—mostly me—saved our family.

FIFTY-SIX
CHANGING THE NARRATIVE

NESS

I hide my smile as we walk through the wrecked manor.

This home that has belonged to our family for generations has been turned upside down. The bodyguards tasked with watching the grounds have been beat and bloodied, and Jax and Zenon are scolding them in the destroyed sunroom. Roslyn is outside speaking with authorities and reporters, keeping them away from the manor while Luna, Dione, and June hide out in the attic just in case.

The Senator is looking pale, like he's seen a ghost. His fists have been clenched since getting the news that his captives have been freed by the Infinity Kings, Maribelle, Prudencia, and a couple Halo Knights. Carolina and Eva are going to expose everything.

I wish I could've been here to greet Emil. But reuniting him with his mother is my big win tonight. It's given me some of my soul back.

Bishop steps over the cracked TV and rests a hand on the Senator's shoulder. "They'll all be locked away in no time, Edward."

"I know."

The Senator storms into the sunroom and we follow him, my face disguised as the same white bodyguard from when we arrived at the university. The Senator is known for being charming, but even he's not bothering to hide his absolute disdain at all the four guards who failed him tonight. "I entrusted you all with my home. I have stood by you even though my supporters have warned me of the ways celestials may betray me." He doesn't bother acknowledging Jax's and Zenon's undying loyalty.

"I'm sorry, sir," says one of the guards with silver hair.

"Your apologies won't save my reputation. Spinning this story in my favor will. Politics is steered by narratives. It will certainly make sense to the American people that after I dominated my celestial opponent in tonight's debate, Spell Walkers would attempt an assassination. My support skyrocketed after losing my wife and son, though the outpour when they hear this news will be monumental. The voters will see that I'm doing something right if these vigilantes were willing to have me killed instead of see me rise to power." The Senator walks in a circle around the guards. "Death is political, even the senseless ones."

He snaps his fingers.

Jax's eyes glow and he telekinetically breaks the necks of all four guards.

They all drop dead, and I turn away before their faces can haunt me. I try to reason with myself that anyone working for the Senator can't be good, and that Carolina's and Eva's lives are worth more than theirs. But I know all too well that people with good hearts get caught up in wrong situations. Sometimes even grow up in them.

"Burn their bodies," the Senator says. "We'll pin that on those Infinity Kings."

I'm sure Brighton has already burned people alive for unfollowing him on Instagram, but Emil isn't a murderer. I can't even picture him killing in self-defense.

"Drop the face," the Senator says to me.

The gray light washes over me to my great relief; holding all these morphs tonight, especially Sunstar's, has been weighing on me.

"It's no coincidence that this break-in, Eduardo, comes on the heels of the first time we let you out in public."

"I did what you asked of me," I say.

"Not completely. You went off script at the end."

"Going on about butterflies," Bishop says.

"Fireflies," the Senator corrects as he gets in my face. "Was that some sort of code for your allies?"

I shrug. "Or maybe the Spell Walkers have been waiting for the moment to attack since you filmed me impersonating their healer and Emil and Brighton's mother. Did you really think you were going to get away with that? Do you really think no one is going to notice that Sunstar was behaving differently and is now missing?"

"I believe all of this. This is a country full of easily fooled people," the Senator says.

I wish his voters could hear the way he talks about them.

"Edward," Luna calls from the top of the stairs. "I'd like a word."

"I'm in the middle of something," he says.

"You're interrogating your son over something you already know the answer to," Luna says. "Your time is better spent punishing him for his crime and testing his loyalty. Once and for all."

This is it.

Luna is finally going to tell the Senator about Emil's past lives.

In saving his mother's life, I just ruined his.

FIFTY-SEVEN
GHOSTLY

BRIGHTON

The Halo Knights haven't been welcoming since we returned to the Sanctuary.

They've been following the news and know about us breaking into Iron's home. They see that chief enforcers are expanding their hunt for us. I get that our spotlight has only grown brighter and brighter since I became the Infinity Savior. I don't want anyone storming these sacred grounds either, especially since Ma deserves some peace after everything she's been through. If there's danger, we'll handle it.

Wyatt and Tala agree to take first watch for any sign of trouble.

The kitchens are closed, so I risk pissing everyone off some more by sneaking in. Ma and Eva need a substantial meal after living off soda, soup, and crackers for two weeks. I cook an entire pot of bow-tie pasta and broccoli with lemon while checking in on social media. I have a flood of comments from celestials trying to cancel me and calling me a traitor to the cause for using my powers to not only seem above the law, but to attack a man of the law's home. The Silver Star Slayer is calling us dangerous instead of heroic, as if he understands the physical and psychological abuse my mother suffered. There's no telling what I'll do to him if I find out he knew. Celestial politicians are condemning our behavior too without knowing the full story. People turn on their allies too quickly these days.

Everyone will know the truth soon.

I bring the meal to the dining hall. Eva is talking to Maribelle as we await the arrival of Iris and Wesley's family, who we reached on the drive back. Emil returns with Ma just in time from standing guard outside the bathroom as she showered. She wanted privacy and protection and Emil gave her both. Prudencia is working on the Starstifler potion, which will be done sometime in the middle of the night.

Eva is half-asleep on the table and too sick to finish eating as Ma tells us all about how Ness was tricked into getting personal stories from them for the Silver Star Slayer's interviews. Then she confirms our suspicions about Luna and the Blood Casters working with Iron. It's despicable the lengths Iron's team has gone through to rig this election. I wonder how many of his supporters will even care that his bodyguards had no problems assaulting two women, one of whom is a pacifist who wouldn't fight back even if she had an offensive power.

"EVA!"

We all turn.

Iris is running so fast through the dining hall it's as if she thinks she's swift-speeded like Wesley, who's coming up behind her with Ruth, Esther, and Tala. Eva nearly trips over herself in her sleepy daze, and Iris picks her up into the tightest hug. I expect them to say how much they love each other or something, but they're both quiet and just breathing together.

This is the closest thing to a family reunion the Spell Walkers can have, but I only see one thing at this large gathering—our army is growing.

Everyone is packed into the Sanctuary's lab. This reminds me when we first gathered with the Spell Walkers in Nova's brewing chamber except we're not guests this time—we're in charge. It's almost two in the morning when we finish updating the Spell Walkers and Co. on everything we've been up to since first arriving here.

"Wow. Time travel," Wesley says. "It doesn't seem fair that we hosted you in our secret home too, only to miss out on all the cool time traveling."

"They also stole your car," Iris says, her arm wrapped around Eva's shoulder.

"Rules don't apply to time travelers."

"False," Emil says as he puts what little muscle he has into stirring the Starstifler, which is thickening like paste. How on earth is anyone supposed to drink that? It's going to be exhausting for him when he has to retrocycle again to figure out where he went wrong.

Ma fights back a yawn, refusing to rest because she misses us so much.

Maribelle is on my laptop with one earphone in. "Iron will be making a speech shortly."

"Aw, he's going to apologize for all the kidnapping and lies," Wesley says.

"I'm grateful to everyone for saving Eva and Carolina," Iris says. "I would've loved for it to have been less destructive, but we're at where we're at. What's your strategy to offset this?"

"Going to use my channels—the ones you hate so much," I say. I can't help but be a little petty now that the tables have turned. Maribelle smirks too. "My platform has grown, so we have Ma and Eva tell their true stories."

"But you don't have proof," Iris says.

"His supporters don't care about proof."

Iris scoffs. "They don't care when it suits their narrative, but they will challenge everything else. I'm genuinely shocked you didn't stream the whole rescue mission for your followers."

Prudencia grabs my hand. "It says a lot about Brighton that he didn't. Our plan wasn't perfect, but we did our best not even knowing if there was anyone to save."

I turn to Prudencia, noticing that Ma is smiling at her too. She's always known there's been something between us, and I'm happy she'll be around to watch us grow.

"That doesn't mean we won't take accountability for our actions," Prudencia says. "Brighton's idea for an interview is great, and we can let everyone know about the Starstifler."

"I thought we weren't mentioning that," I say.

"You and Emil are viewed as unnecessary threats since you're specters. You're not supposed to have powers in the first place, and if we can prove to everyone that you'll be binding them, it could go a long way in building back some goodwill," Prudencia says.

I want to let go of her hand, but I stay still.

"Oh, good," Ma says. "Send those powers back. The ghost ones are so unnatural."

Wesley's eyes widen. "You have spooky ghost powers too? We need to start a group chat."

"I phased tonight," I say.

"Superstar," Wesley says.

"But those powers are evil," Ma says.

I don't have my usual blood-and-bones instinct, but I can tell a classic gang-up is beginning. "Powers don't have some bright or dark side by nature. I saved everyone tonight with phoenix fire *and* dashing *and* phasing. All I've ever wanted to do was help and make a difference. I'm continuing the work that started with my series."

"What if you lose yourself?" Emil asks. "June doesn't speak."

"I'm chatting away, bro. And I don't appreciate being put in the same category as an assassin when I'm a savior."

"We just want to save your life too," Prudencia gently says. "Orton had all of your same powers and he went up in flames."

"We don't have any statistics on hybrid specters beyond that. This Reaper's Blood was designed with pure essences to be

446

stronger than others," I say.

"It was designed for Luna," Emil says. "You have her parents' ghosts in you. There might be some repercussions."

I'm not going to tell them about how unnerving and difficult the power is when active; they'll only use it against me. Slinging fire-bolts and running swiftly can be depleting, but those abilities don't cut off my air like when I'm in that ghost zone. Besides, there's still so much for me to explore. June doesn't seem to feel any physical pain and it wouldn't be the worst thing in the world to not have that slowing me down in combat.

"I'm still me," I say. "Just upgraded."

"Time-out on this," Maribelle says. "Iron is talking any minute now."

I gather with Emil, Prudencia, Ma, and Maribelle around my laptop while Wesley and Iris find it on their phones.

Let's see how Iron tries to spin his crimes.

FIFTY-EIGHT
THE SPEECH

NESS

I'm awaiting my punishment in the panic room.

The gleam-shield is humming. It's ridiculous that Jax turned it on when locking me in here as if I can shift into some insect and escape through the tiny vents. No one is using their gleam to get through this barrier. That's the point.

It's been almost an hour since Luna and the Senator started speaking, and they must be planning something awful for me. What could be worse than posing as Sunstar and tanking her chances at the election? For me, it would be anything that hurts Emil. I'm sure it would be great if they could get some footage of me posing as Emil and physically assaulting the camera. I'll die before I do that.

I'm bracing myself for that reality.

I snap up from the couch at the sound of the many footsteps coming down the stairs. Through the door's window I see the Senator and Bishop leading the charge, followed by Jax and Zenon, and then Luna with Dione and June at her side.

The Senator's appearance isn't as manicured as usual. He's abandoned his glasses and jacket, loosened his tie, undone his top button, and rolled up his sleeves like he's been doing some manual labor for once in his life. He turns off the gleam-shield and opens the door. "Eventful evening. I've seen tremendous, threatening powers in my life, but nothing as terrifying as resurrection."

"The dead should stay dead," Bishop says, looking at me.

"You've never known true loss, then," Luna says.

The Senator holds up his hand to silence them. "Resurrection is the greatest danger to our world, and the American people must understand what's at stake with Election Day approaching. There are numerous reporters outside our gates wanting a word about the invasion in our home, and you will have the great honor of delivering this news, Eduardo."

"But they think I'm dead," I say.

"That's why you'll be delivering the speech as me," he says as he withdraws a folded sheet of paper from his pocket.

I step out of the panic room and take it. "This is a horrible idea. The general public doesn't even know resurrection is possible. You're better off keeping this quiet."

The Senator steps into the panic room. "Stop putting your hormones before your country, Eduardo. It's embarrassing for me as a father and a politician. I will not allow us to become more vulnerable to those who already outpower us. Do you want our soldiers going into war against enemies who can come back to life on the battlefield? This country needs to take a stand now against those who will allow this imbalance to come to pass. This includes the Spell Walkers, the Blood Casters, and every last alchemist who can build this army against us."

He nods at his team, and it all happens so suddenly.

Bishop shoves Luna into the panic room, and she falls flat on the floor. He slams the door closed. Zenon quickly turns on the gleam-shield as June races for Luna, and when she collides into it, she's blasted across the room and phases through the wall. Dione runs at the Senator while growing an extra set of arms, only for Jax to telekinetically snap her legs, bones puncturing as she falls. I'm tempted to run, but Dione's screams are enough of a warning.

Zenon's eyes glow. "June is returning."

"From where?" Jax asks.

The top half of June's body ascends from the floor, and she grabs Dione before they both sink away like the concrete is quicksand.

"They're teleporting," Zenon says. "I'll stay alert."

"We caught the big fish already," Bishop says.

The Senator pushes me up the stairs with everyone following as Luna screams my name as if I can, or would, help her. "That alliance is over," he says. "I'm giving you one last chance to maintain ours."

"Screw that. Go give your own speech."

"If your friends were bold enough to break into my home, I wouldn't put it past them to attempt an assassination."

I don't even have to ask him if he's willing to let me die in his place. He already tried to have me killed for his future.

"The press is waiting," the Senator says. "Read every single word as I have written it."

"Or what?"

"You haven't come this far to die now, have you?"

He makes it impossible to think of him as my father when he threatens me like this.

Gray light.

I transform into the Senator once again, mirroring his loosened tie and rolled sleeves. He studies me. Does he know his face as well as he thinks he does? I know it really well from all the times he was up in mine yelling at me to be better, to give him space to work when I wanted him to spend time with me. There were some evenings during my Blood Caster days when I was on edge whenever I saw someone who bore the slightest resemblance to him. His face has haunted me, and I'm wearing it now to lie for him like I have my entire life.

"That power is remarkable," the Senator says. "Don't disappoint me."

"Not sure that's possible," I say as I leave, followed by Bishop.

I pass Grandpa's statue, wishing he'd been a better human being instead of the gleamphobic piece of shit who raised another one. Flashing cameras greet us at the gate. The last time the media swarmed to the manor like this was after the Blackout when the Senator was grieving me. They're back for another lie.

Roslyn silences all the reporters and photographers.

I open the speech, a full page handwritten by the Senator.

Interesting how he can find the time to write up these lies in minutes but can only spare a sentence for my birthday cards, if that. There's so much suspense in the air as everyone waits for me to speak.

I'm silent as I quickly read through the speech.

It opens with grief for the bodyguards who were killed by Emil and Brighton.

Lie.

How the Spell Walkers want to assassinate him.

Lie.

How resurrection in humans is real with phoenix blood.

Fact.

How he is responsible for the capture of Luna Marnette.

Fact omitting the greater truth.

How all vigilante groups are uniting to become invincible.

Lie.

How Emil Rey is the latest incarnation of Keon Máximo and Bautista de León.

Fact.

How the Senator is the true hero this country needs.

Lie.

I look up at everyone with genuine tears in my eyes, knowing what has to happen next. The Senator must be stopped. It's frightening how quickly he's adapted to tonight's events. He wrote all of this before he even detained Luna. In the time we've been back, he plotted a whole betrayal to try and save face.

This might be the last time I'm let out of my cage.

I rip up the script with a pounding heart. "You're all being lied to! The Blackout was orchestrated by—"

A spell bangs through the air.

There are screams in the crowd, but I can't see where anyone is going. I'm on the floor with blood spilling out of my stomach and gray light washing over me to show the world my true face.

One last time.

FIFTY-NINE
FURY

EMIL

Senator Iron has been shot on live TV.

I'm horrified while standing beside my mother, and her hand squeezes mine. No matter how much we don't mess with this guy, especially after everything he put Ma through, this isn't how justice is supposed to go down. Brighton and Prudencia are staring at the screen in shock as pandemonium erupts outside Iron's front gate—the one we escaped through hours ago. Even blood-thirsty Maribelle looks away.

"Not good," Wesley says as Ruth steps away from the video streaming on his phone.

The cameraperson still has eyes on Iron on the ground as others run away. First I think someone is flashing a light on him, but I know that gray glow. My eyes immediately water. I might throw up.

"NESS!"

The real Iron hobbles past the gate, and he has a black eye. Did Ness fight back? Iron is breaking down in tears as he calls for help and presses down on Ness's wound.

"HE'S A LIAR!"

The news teams are hovering all over them as if it's more important to cover this groundbreaking story of Ness being alive all along and impersonating his father instead of getting him medical attention. Someone tried to kill him and these vultures can't even give him some damn dignity.

This was probably Iron's doing. He's punishing Ness for helping me.

Punished.

I step back, and Prudencia stops me from accidentally knocking over the cauldron with the Starstifler.

I'm blazing hot thinking about how much Ness deserved a better father, someone who loves him so much that he couldn't possibly be a suspect in his attack. Gold and gray flames burst around me as if I can protect Ness. I might burn down the Sanctuary's lab. Everyone's telling me to breathe, but I can't control myself.

Brighton braves my fire and wraps his arms around me, shouting as he drags me toward the wall with swift-speed. Before we collide, we phase right through, out into the courtyard.

"Go for it!" Brighton yells as he crouches in pain.

It takes me a sec to figure out what he's telling me to do.

I give in to my fury and shout at the night sky, hurling fire-orb after fire-orb toward the stars until it looks like a gold and gray meteor storm shooting over the river. I've disturbed some sleeping phoenixes, even scared some into flight. I exhaust myself and collapse to my knees, and Brighton wraps his arms around me and tells me to breathe over and over long enough that I finally listen to him. I cry against my brother's chest, hating this life that forces me to grieve Ness again.

SIXTY
UNMASKED

NESS

First there's darkness, then the smell of salt water, then extraordinary pain.

For a beat, I wonder if someone has stolen an organ before remembering what happened outside the manor. I've been hit by a lot of spells during my time as a Blood Caster. Most have blasted me across the room, or at worst, stunned me. This one tore through me. I thought I was going to bleed out.

I try touching my wound, but my arms are bound.

I open my eyes, and the light hurts even though it's not that bright. I'm strapped into a stretcher. Someone is taking me to Gleam Care. I turn my neck to find the Senator watching me. He has a black eye and a cut lip. There are life jackets above his head. I'm not on my way to receive medical attention. I'm back on the same boat where we first reunited.

The destination is obvious.

"You tried to make a fool out of me," the Senator says. "Thankfully Jax has impeccable aim."

"He didn't kill me," I say, my throat raw.

"You weren't useful to me dead. This time. The country already saw me grieve you. What they needed this time was to watch me condemn you—my son who came back from the dead. It's a sign of my strength and commitment to protecting everyone from celestials and specters. I've been playing the long game thanks to my friend here. . . ." The Senator spins my stretcher and Luna is handcuffed in the corner with her eyes closed. "Then of course I beat her before she could try and cheat me out of my victory."

"You talk too much," Luna says with a bored sigh.

"Enjoy the conversation while you can. You'll miss it when you're in solitary confinement."

I've never seen Luna look this defeated before. Does she really not have something up her sleeve? Is June going to pop in any second now and vanish with her leader? Maybe Luna will show me some final mercy and have June carry me away too because I'm all out of moves now. It's up to Emil and the Spell Walkers to cast a light on the Senator's crimes. Outsmart him.

"Do you remember when you were little and you were rooting for me to become President Iron so you could live in the White House? You should be proud of yourself. It required some nudging and threats, but you did this!"

"It's not over. You can still lose, especially without my power to lie for you."

The Senator laughs. "You think I don't have this election in the bag? In the eyes of this country, I defeated that supremacist Sunstar in the debate, I have apprehended the alchemist responsible for many of our terrors, and I sentenced my son to a life behind bars for their protection. And if that isn't enough, all isn't lost."

The impossible happens.

His eyes burn like an eclipse and the black eye and cut lip glow in gray lights and fade away as if they were never there. And that's because they never were. I blink multiple times, not wanting to believe this is true. Then I piece it all together. The Senator and Luna both left together on the night of the Cloaked Phantom. Then he came back sick. . . .

"How? That alchemy doesn't work well for people your age."

"Perhaps in the hands of some untrained alchemists, but I worked with the best alive. Luna warned me that it could have dangerous results, though once I saw how valuable your power was I knew I would still need it on my side after you inevitably betrayed me. Who better to do all this dirty work than the only person I ultimately trust?"

This man is absolutely diabolical.

He worked me to the bone, but he'll have a long career ahead of him if he can do everything himself. What better way to paint himself as a saint than by making monsters of his opponents?

"I should've poisoned you," Luna says.

"I thought you were, after drinking that disgusting creature's blood. Eduardo, you should've seen that hideous shifter. It was as if a coyote had wings made of fish scales."

No one knows a shifter's true state since they all take on different forms, but most are wise enough to blend in with other animals and creatures. The wounded shifter I got my powers from looked like a small red elephant with jackrabbit legs and a lion's tail. I cried watching it die, whereas the Senator was repulsed by the one that's made him powerful.

I stare at Luna. "This will go down in history as one of your worst crimes."

"Of which there are many," the Senator adds. "But don't discredit yourself, son. You made this happen too." He again glows gray and shrinks a couple feet, and his hair grows long and black with some silver in front. His pale skin becomes slightly darker than mine and breasts grow from his chest. His face's tight skin becomes relaxed, natural, and beautiful with brown eyes and high cheekbones. "I'm proud of you," he says with my mother's voice.

This is cursing her memory.

"STOP IT!"

I use all my strength to try and pop these straps.

The Senator takes on Mom's laugh. Then a bump grows on her nose that can only be found on the Senator's and her round jaw squares like his too. He's bathed in gray light. "I'm still ironing out the tricks, but I'll get there."

The deck door opens. "Docking, Edward," Bishop calls down.

"End of the line," the Senator says. "I can hardly wait to get started in the office and I'm looking forward to the many terms I will serve. It brings me peace knowing that if I'm ever voted out I can simply morph into the next president and continue the great work I've started to protect this country from people abusing their powers." The Senator releases a deep, proud sigh. "Think of me in the White House from your cells. If you survive long enough."

The Senator has fooled the world without these powers. Now that he has them, he'll destroy it as the President.

SIXTY-ONE
VILLAINIZED

BRIGHTON

I'm keeping up the good fight for Emil's privacy.

Ma wants to let him cry in her arms, Wyatt wants to hold him, and Prudencia just wants to keep him company, but he asked to be alone, and it's staying that way. We brought some chairs out into the hallway though so we can be with him at a moment's notice if he changes his mind.

Everyone is exhausted. Before going to sleep in Maribelle's room, Eva generously healed my burn marks from Emil's fire. There's a shortage of available rooms, so Wesley and Ruth joined her, and Maribelle doesn't care that Iris is there too. I wish Ma would go take Emil's bed in our room, but she's being stubborn and resting in her chair.

"He must've really cared for him," Wyatt whispers.

I honestly didn't understand Ness's whole thing. He didn't seem like a Brightsider himself, to be fair. But he did a lot for my brother. "They bonded," I say.

"He cared about Emil too," Ma says with her eyes closed. "He said Emil made him feel warm."

Wyatt stares at the floor.

Whenever Emil is ready to talk, I'll be here for him. I expect he's going to end whatever this Wyatt situation is immediately. I know my brother, he's got to be feeling really guilty right now for getting romantically involved with Wyatt while Ness was alive and still thinking of him. Even bonding with our mother.

I'm on my phone typing up the format for the interviews I'll film tomorrow morning when I switch back to BuzzFeed's coverage of Ness's discovery to find an update. Prudencia inches closer when I press play on the video. It's of Senator Iron standing on a dock and addressing reporters.

"Thank you for your patience on this impossible evening," Iron says as he tightens his jacket. "There were so many nights after the Blackout where I would wake up and forget that Eduardo was dead. I never in a million years suspected he was alive and being corrupted by the Blood Casters, and later by the Spell Walkers. He was manipulated into putting power above all—country, family, justice. To punish me after a successful debate against Congresswoman Sunstar, he tried to destroy the campaign he once fully believed in with the powers of a shifter." He brushes his black eye, wincing. "I'll admit, if this weren't such a public affair I would get my son into a rehabilitation program to rescue him from this darkness, but my loyalties can't only be for

463

my family. They must also lie with the American people. My son is not above justice and has been sent to the Bounds alongside the terrorist Luna Marnette, who poisoned Eduardo with her powers. I have failed the memory of my late wife, but I hope this heartbreaking gesture proves my commitment to making this country safe from gleamcraft supremacy."

Iron doesn't answer any more questions as he steps into a black car and drives away.

Prudencia and I immediately charge into the library and Emil's head pops up from the table in a panic.

"He's alive, he's alive," we both say.

"What?" Emil wipes his eyes.

Ma and Wyatt follow us in and we replay Iron's speech.

Emil bursts into more tears. "He's being sent to the Bounds? This isn't a win."

"It can be," I say. Everyone's looking at me like I'm insane. "It wouldn't be our first break-in tonight. We're already tracking one-for-one in success rates."

"This isn't some politician's home in the suburbs," Prudencia says. "This is a federal prison on an island."

"And maybe our last chance to save Ness," Emil says. "He's never going to get a fair trial."

No one protests.

"This country is going to villainize everything we do," I say. "But we know we're the real heroes. Let's go save the day."

SIXTY-TWO
STRATEGY

MARIBELLE

"Am I really the only one who's going to keep calling out these bad ideas?" Iris asks.

"Yes," I say.

We've all been rounded up outside my guest room, where Esther is sleeping and being watched by one of Ruth's clones. The weight of breaking into the Bounds is heavy enough on everyone's shoulders, and I'm not sure they have the fumes this late at night.

"I can phase us in and out," Brighton says.

"It's still breaking the law," Iris says.

"You've never cared about saving people unless you benefit," Brighton says. "This is just like when the Blood Casters kept me hostage, when Stanton was kicking my ass and humiliating me and you didn't want to rescue me."

"That wasn't only Iris," Wesley says. "I agreed with her then and I agree with her now. We're seen as the face for the celestials in this country. It's not going to be a good look if we kick down the doors of the Bounds to rescue someone everyone thinks is a terrorist."

"But we know he's not," Emil says. "Ness could pull back the curtains on everything his father has done."

"The truth doesn't matter!" Iris shouts. "It's supposed to, but it doesn't! I know that's a harsh reality but it's one we live in."

"Then what do you suggest we do?" I ask.

"Luna being locked up goes a long way, but Iron continues to blame us for the Blackout and has been using Ness to lie on a grander scale for weeks. We need to turn our focus to finding out what happened to Sunstar and hope to save her so she can rebuild this country for our families."

Wesley, Ruth, and Eva seem to be in agreement. Saving Sunstar is important. But Iris doesn't have the full story on my family.

"Justice hasn't been served. When I retrocycled, I discovered that Luna is my grandmother. Though, hey, maybe you've been sitting on that secret too," I say.

Iris's face is frozen in surprise, her eyes glazed and lips parted. She might be a liar, but she's not an actress.

"That criminal turned us into orphans, Iris. Tala lost her parents too. We need to make sure that Luna being locked up isn't another trick from Iron to make himself look good."

"And if it isn't?" Iris asks.

"Then we end Luna once and for all."

466

Iris puts her hands in the pockets of her father's corduroy jacket, which has always been so big on her. "I'm sorry," she says sheepishly. "I won't pretend to understand the nightmare of being related to that monster who has ruined our lives. We're here to help you through that because even though you piss me off like no one else, you're still family to me, to all of us. Take the higher road, Maribelle. Killing Luna won't bring you peace."

I not only witnessed Luna murder my birth mother, but I felt that blade across Sera's neck. The Blackout took Mama and Papa away from me. Then, when Atlas brought me some light, he was killed too. It's as if my heart has turned to stone, and the only way to break through is by making sure the source of my greatest pains has met her end.

I turn away from Iris. "We should get moving. Who's in?"

"Team Infinity," Brighton says, standing between Emil and Prudencia.

Tala already has her crossbow ready from standing guard outside. We might have to fight over who gets to kill Luna.

"I'll be enjoying a book and a bubble bath if we don't get arrested," Wyatt says.

"I can't leave Esther," Ruth says with her hand to her heart. She's always been a sweetheart who feels guilty when she shouldn't. "I'm sorry. Carolina, you're welcome to spend the evening with us. I'll do better to protect you if there's more trouble."

Carolina offers a warm, tired smile. "Thank you."

"I'll be here too," Wesley says. "Maribelle, I hate to play this card, but . . . Atlas's parents are still jailed for going above the law with their powers. He wouldn't want you locked up too."

I'm not going to have Atlas's memory used against me, and I won't get caught.

"I won't be useful to you," Eva says. "I'm going to stay."

Iris grabs her hand. "Me too. I didn't lose you to run away again so soon." She addresses Emil and Brighton. "I can't stop any of you, but I will also guard your mother with my life if enforcers find us."

"Thank you," Emil says.

"Let's go," Brighton says.

Tala leads us to a closet with training gear, not allowing anyone to wear official Halo Knight armor. I still have my power-proof vest, but Emil, Brighton, and Prudencia put on gray ones. Wyatt is nervous when Tala fills a bag with gem-grenades because bringing weapons into a prison with powerful criminals is a bad idea, but so is breaking into one. Emil and Brighton take a few moments with Carolina, promising they'll look after each other.

Everyone sees us off, which is an infuriating gesture from those with powers refusing to help. Roxana carries me and Tala over the mountains as Wyatt and Emil are close behind on Nox. Prudencia and Brighton tail us with the car.

I feel powerful under these stars, but they won't give me strength where we're going. The underground cells in the Bounds will weaken me, but I only need to be strong enough to throw fire-arrows into Luna—one for every person she took from me.

SIXTY-THREE
CELL

NESS

I'm blindfolded as guards carry me through the island and into the Bounds. I only hear the screech of the cerulean phoenix that circles the towers, the harsh winds, and Bishop instructing the guards to process Luna for solitary confinement and me for a cell with minimal supervision. Between this and the fact that they haven't cuffed me in any neutralizing gauntlets, I guess I'm not the threat they've made me out to be.

I'll die here knowing the truth—and knowing that they know it too.

I can tell we're inside when the winds stop, replaced by the sound of gates clanging. Throughout the halls it smells like sweat, burnt flesh, and rank vomit.

I stop keeping track of where we're going after the third flight of stairs. Doing so only tricks me into thinking there's a chance for escape. If I couldn't break free from my childhood home, I have no chance inside this labyrinth. There's power in resigning to your fate.

Inmates are cheering and roaring as I'm pushed through the halls. They see someone young, but they have no idea what power I have. I could probably use that to my advantage for a day or two.

A cell door is opened, and I'm unstrapped from the stretcher. By the time I remove my blindfold, the door is locked. I groan as I sit up. There's a bed, a toilet, and a bloody handprint on the wall. I have a dozen neighbors down this hall and Bishop is watching me from outside the bars like I'm some caged animal.

"Did you ever think you'd be back here under these conditions?" Bishop asks.

"I don't need small talk. This is punishment enough."

"You're on my turf, Eduardo, and I'm doing you a courtesy so you're not surprised when your door suddenly opens within the next hour." The stupidest thought that Bishop might try to help me passes through my mind. "These cells sometimes get overcrowded, and when that happens my guards unlock cells for survival of the fittest. I unfortunately can't be on the premises when this happens, but I'm looking forward to hearing about the results of a new game to make it extra exciting—Hunt the Shifter."

This is why I was blindfolded.

This is why my power wasn't neutralized.

This is why they're not bothering to put me in a custom cell.

I'm about to be in for the final fight of my life.

SIXTY-FOUR
REBEL

EMIL

I'm standing on the dock, staring at the Bounds across the river.

Between breaking into Iron's home and getting ready to storm into a prison, I feel like Bautista's rebel spirit too. I can't only look at the good though; I got to wonder if I'm growing corrupt like Keon too. I have no idea what pushed Keon to create specters beyond the usual theories of him wanting power, but maybe his heart was steering him toward unlawful acts too.

Brighton and Prudencia finally arrived minutes ago, and they're currently deciding which is the best rental boat to "borrow" to get them across and back as if we're going for some new record on most crimes in a single night. If only Brighton could fly and Prudencia could trust her power to carry herself across the river. Meanwhile, Maribelle and Tala are strategizing on how to defeat the sky swimmer that's known to guard the prison. Nox and Roxana are standing in the river, bobbing for fish.

Then there's Wyatt, who comes up beside me. "This evening has become a touch too exciting, hasn't it?"

"I'm sorry. I bet you're wishing you didn't stop Tala from having us all blown up."

"You're foolish to think I regret meeting you, love. If I may be so direct—"

"You always are."

"—I'm hoping our time getting to know each other isn't at an end. I understand things are a tad complicated and I'll give you the space you need. But I really love when you hold me as we fly through the skies and when I get to hold you back at night. I'd hate to lose that so soon."

It's not fair that he's hitting me with this right now, not when I'm a river away from Ness, but I can't act like I'm not moved by it. He's beautiful, confident about himself though bordering on conceited, devoted to phoenixkind, and keeps dreaming up a better world for me as a Halo Knight. I'm really into everything he's talking about too—my arms wrapped around him as we fly around on Nox, how we don't have to talk over the winds to feel connected, and how much easier it's been to sleep because I'm with him.

I just can't give him anything in return until I figure myself out.

"Hey!" Brighton calls, sitting inside a four-seater jet boat with Prudencia. "We're ready!"

We all gather around and review our plan once we get inside the Bounds. Split up into pairs of two—Brighton and Prudencia,

Maribelle and Tala, me and Wyatt—to cover more ground. There's one phoenix specter on each team, and hopefully our fire will be enough to melt whatever cell Ness is in. We're not expecting our phones to work underground, so if we hear chaos, we're supposed to blow on whistles the Halo Knights have used when training phoenixes and run toward the danger to make sure none of us get captured during this mission.

"Special request to alert me if you see Stanton," Tala says. "I'm going to cut that snake's head off for killing my mother."

"Very dark," Wyatt says.

"And duly noted," Brighton says.

"How much time are we giving ourselves in there?" Prudencia asks.

"Until we find Ness," I say.

"That's not going to fly," Maribelle says. "One hour."

"There's four towers to search."

"Bro, I'm going to dash around, but we'll have to call it quits at some point," Brighton says.

"Then I'll stay."

"Then you're forcing everyone else to stay too because I'm the door getting us in and out and you know I'm not leaving you behind."

Brighton is staring at me, and I know he's one hundred percent serious.

I can sacrifice myself all I want, but I can't force everyone to do the same.

I agree to the terms, not knowing how I'll be able to live with myself if I can't save the person who keeps risking death for me.

SIXTY-FIVE
STRIKE

MARIBELLE

Lightning flashes and rain pounds the river as Roxana flies Tala and me toward the Bounds. Prudencia is telekinetically piloting the speedboat away from the phoenix's storm as Emil and Wyatt blend into the night on Nox. Everything is smooth sailing, as Papa used to say, until a phoenix pops out from the river's surface and shoots into the sky with water spraying from its large wings.

"Please don't attack us," Tala says, hoping this won't have to get violent between the phoenixes.

The sky swimmer flies toward us at furious speed. Its wings begin burning in cerulean flames and the phoenix flaps the fire toward us with the force of a gale. Tala sharply steers us away from the attack, and I hold on to Roxana's strong yellow feathers for balance. The sky swimmer dives toward the speedboat, about to collide until Nox swoops up out of nowhere with a breath of bronze flames that scares the sky swimmer back underwater.

I try searching for shadows in the river, but it's too dark out. The sky swimmer emerges behind us and speeds toward us. "Tala, attack it now or—"

The collision of phoenixes is so powerful we're both thrown off Roxana's back. My dark yellow flames carry me back up, but Tala smacks straight into the river. Wyatt dives off Nox to search for her. The sky swimmer is scratching away at Roxana with its talons, and the light howler is screaming like never before.

I hurl fire-arrows up at the sky swimmer, striking it in the back. The phoenix spins and pursues me. I fly away in terror, looking over my shoulder to see the sky swimmer catching up. My power isn't strong enough to take the phoenix down, so I brake in the air just long enough for the sky swimmer to fly over me, and I make my way back to Roxana as quickly as possible.

I drop onto Roxana's back as she wails, not knowing how to soothe her, but knowing I need her.

Halo Knights have vowed not to harm other phoenixes, even if it means putting their own lives at risk.

I'm not a Halo Knight.

I scream the command that Tala used when we first met: "STRIKE!"

Roxana opens her mouth and massive bolts of lightning strike the sky swimmer out of the air, again and again, and before it crashes into the river, it explodes in a massive blue fireball. Ashes cloud the air and feathers float on the water.

My muscles are throbbing from Roxana's lightning as I steer her toward the island, landing moments before everyone else. Tala jumps off Nox, her teeth chattering, as she observes the slashes across Roxana's belly.

"I had to kill that phoenix," I say.

"Thank you for saving mine," Tala says as she guides Roxana toward the shore, getting her to lie down so the gentle waves can cool her wound.

"How long until that phoenix resurrects?" Brighton asks.

"Sky swimmers need an hour, maybe two," Wyatt says.

"Depends on how old it is," Emil adds.

"Then we better keep it moving," Brighton says, moving across the beach.

Tala kisses Roxana between the eyes. "I'm coming back for you."

I admire her strength as she runs toward the Bounds, her crossbow at the ready.

Maybe we'll both fire arrows into Luna at the same time.

SIXTY-SIX
THE BOUNDS

BRIGHTON

Showtime.

We make our way up to the Bounds, sticking to the shadows the entire time. Maribelle is able to sense danger beyond a tree, grabbing Emil's arm before he can fall down a trap where a blood orange basilisk is curled around a spike, its tail rattling. Prudencia telekinetically covers the hole with a nearby boulder, leaving enough space for air and moonlight but not enough to burst up and kill us.

There are four towers, and we stand outside the closest.

I prepare them for phasing, assuring them they won't feel anything.

They're lucky that way.

I turn on ghost mode, straining for air and freezing as I peek through the thick stone wall. The hallway is filtered stark white and shadowy like an X-ray because of my power. I get everyone through as quickly as I can, beginning with Emil, Maribelle, and Prudencia so they can defend me if guards appear in the meantime. I get Tala through right as it feels like some blood vessels might pop behind my eyes, and as I grab Wyatt, I'm certain I'm going to pass out and we'll both be frozen inside this wall forever.

Emil grabs my wrist, pulling me into the prison. "You good?"

My breaths are shallow. "Just a lot of people," I say as color fills the world again. "Got us through."

Prudencia rubs my back, and her touch grounds me in my body. "You all go ahead. Time is limited."

Maribelle and Tala take off down one hallway, dark yellow phoenix fire lighting their path.

"Play this smart, Bright," Emil says, holding out his fist.

"Stay alive, bro," I say, fist-bumping and whistling with him.

I don't think either of us ever thought this childhood handshake would follow us into a prison.

"I'll protect him," Prudencia says as she hugs Emil. "Get going."

Emil and Wyatt run the opposite way, and Emil looks over his shoulder before they round the corner, as if this might be the last time we see each other. He's forgetting that we're the Infinity Kings—we're going to go on and on and on.

"This is a literal nightmare," Prudencia says. She keeps looking back and forth down the two hallways as if someone is going to emerge from the shadows. "It's even darker than they make it look in documentaries."

I hold her hand, trying to stay strong. We go down a curvy staircase and reach a level that smells like backed-up toilets and body odor. We cover our noses with the headbands and cautiously go down a hall toward a buzzing sound. Behind a wall there's an electric fence surrounding the cell of a sleeping inmate. Prudencia leads me away.

"What's the rush? That could be Ness for all we know."

"We don't have time to interview every inmate who might be Ness in disguise," Prudencia says.

"You tell that to Emil when we leave without Ness."

"Ness has no reason to hide anymore. Everyone knows he's alive. Where would they have put him? Solitary confinement? A custom cell?"

"His power isn't dangerous enough for that," I say.

Those custom cells are more for the likes of powerful people like me. If I had to design a cell to lock up someone with Reaper's Blood, I'd start with shackles to prevent any dashing at unsuspecting guards, put them inside a tank of water so any phoenix fire will be short-lived, and entrap the specter in a gleam-shield to prevent them from phasing through any wall, ceiling, or floor. I bet I'd still find a way out.

We continue on, finding more traditional cells with inmates who start shouting when they see us. Prudencia and I stay in the very center away from reaching hands; if anyone touches her, I'll shove a fire-bolt down their throat. I scan everyone's face, but no Ness.

"I bet some of these prisoners would have great stories for Celestials of New York."

"I'm going to unfollow you in real life," Prudencia says.

"Hey, I'm just saying—"

The ceiling bulbs flash red and metal grinds as all the cell doors slide open.

The inmates have been freed.

SIXTY-SEVEN
MANHUNT

NESS

My heart is beating as fast as the flashing red lights. The other inmates cautiously step outside their cells as the doors open. I don't know what powers they possess, only that they're probably not as lethal if they're in these standard cells. That doesn't mean they're not dangerous.

Unless everyone else has been falsely imprisoned too.

There's static coming from the speakers in the corner. "Attention! Before you start blowing off some steam and beating the lights out of each other, you got to know something," says a low voice I've never heard before. "Those of you who weren't incarcerated until after late January will remember that a senator's son was one of six-hundred-something people killed during the city's Blackout. Except he wasn't. Eduardo Iron lives and breathes in

481

this prison. He became a specter for the Blood Casters and will be standing trial for acts of burglary, trespassing, selling hallucinatory drugs, aggravated assault, identity theft, and terrorism."

In other words, I'm here for life, if they let me live.

I'm fighting back tears on how corrupt this place is.

"Eduardo has the power to shift," the voice continues. "He can look like anyone—a stranger, your cellmate, even yourself. If you're looking for an extra challenge while blowing off some steam, whoever hunts down the shifter before dawn will be rewarded with thirty minutes on the roof this morning."

I don't doubt the lure of that grand prize. Breathing in the air before being banished back to this darkness could be as welcome as a hug from a loved one.

The red lights stop flashing as the speaker says, "Happy hunting."

There are shouts and cheers, even a roar, echoing through the halls.

A bald man with a three-headed hydra tattoo on his forearm is talking with someone while staring at me. There's one clear tell that I don't belong here: I'm not wearing one of the lime-green jumpsuits. I charge the opposite way, hearing them call after me.

I fight through the pain of my stinging wound, glowing gray midrun and giving myself the jumpsuit and a new face before blending into a crowd of celestials beating each other to death.

A lot of people mistaken as me in disguise will die tonight.

SIXTY-EIGHT
FIREFLY'S FLAMES

EMIL

"Hide-and-seek with the shape-shifter just got infinitely harder," Wyatt whispers as we hide in a stairway.

"And he doesn't even know that we're trying to find him," I say.

Just when I thought this place couldn't be more monstrous, the guards are siccing the other inmates on Ness as if this is some acceptable practice. More than ever I'm terrified to be here though I have zero regrets. Ness might think he's alone in this fight, but I'm going to back him up.

"Perhaps it's time we regroup." Wyatt tugs at his whistle.

"No, someone might think we should bounce."

"Not the worst idea."

"I'm not leaving without Ness," I say, staring Wyatt in the

eyes. I'm indebted to Ness for saving me over and over even though we were strangers who only met less than a month ago.

"Of course," Wyatt says, though it's clear he knows the dangers he's risking for a cause he doesn't believe in. "What do you propose we do to find him? Shout his name over and over?"

"No, but you're on the right track. We don't go looking for him. We make him come to us."

"How do we do that?"

I conjure two gold and gray fire-orbs, hoping to draw Ness to my flames.

SIXTY-NINE

SOLITARY CONFINEMENT

MARIBELLE

Ever since the announcement, Tala and I have failed to travel through the Bounds unnoticed.

My fire-arrow collides into the chest of a woman trying to touch me with her electric hands. Tala kicks off a wall and drives the butt of her crossbow into someone's forehead, laying him out. She fires an arrow into the shoulder of another inmate charging toward her, and he collapses in agony. I skip over a couple of the ten or twelve bodies piling up and we continue our hunt for Luna.

There have been over one hundred steps spiraling down from where we began, as if solitary confinement is in the center of the earth. There is every possibility in the world that we'll get caught by the guards and buried away in one of these cells too, but the memory of this alliance with Tala will make me feel less alone. Grief can be so isolating, and Tala and I have been united by revenge over the murders of our parents in ways that Iris and I were driven apart.

Luna may not have gotten her hands dirty, but the monsters she created are the reason we all lost our loved ones. We'll slay the monsters next.

We reach the lowest level. I light our way through what feels like a dark cave. There's a woman shouting and banging on a door, and it isn't until we get closer that I realize she's not locked up. Tala aims her crossbow, but I stop her from taking a shot through the darkness, like when she killed Kirk.

"This is your fault!" the woman shouts, crying. "You swore I would become a Blood Caster!"

"Luna," I say.

The young woman turns and white flames run up her arm. There's something familiar about her. Her hair looks choppy, but that's not it.

The stars be damned, she's the specter that Atlas and I were pursuing the very first night of the Crowned Dreamer. Atlas had gotten a tip that a specter attacked her own family, and we rushed to the scene, pursuing her for blocks before we brawled. She was powerful too, and I needed a gem-grenade to take her down. That was also the night we first met Brighton and Emil, days before Emil's powers manifested; some might even call our paths crossing destiny.

The same can be said for this woman who was arrested after Atlas and I flew away.

"Do you remember me?" I ask.

"You have fire now," she says.

"Turns out it was always in me," I say. "Is that Luna in there?"

She nods. "She gave me power and claimed she cared about me, but was nowhere to be seen when I was locked up."

"There is no part of me that cares," I say. "Luna is ours to end." The woman holds out her palms like she's about to unleash some fire. "Take a second to think. You're outnumbered, and your power has been dampened from your time here in the Bounds, away from the stars. I've only grown stronger and less patient. You choose what happens next."

The specter looks between us and the door, weighing her choices.

The white flames vanish, and so does she into the darkness.

Tala wastes no time running toward the cell, eager to make sure that Luna's breath remains a stranger forevermore. She drops a gem-grenade and blows down the door. We stand outside the tiny room where Luna is pressed against the wall.

My grandmother eyes us like the reapers we are.

SEVENTY
HUNT THE SHIFTER

NESS

I'm staying alive by posing as dead men.

One man was telekinetically shoved so hard into a wall that his neck snapped. I wore his puffy cheeks and shock white hair while limping past a trio hunting for me. I found another dead on the floor, strangled by his own stretched-out, supple arms, which coiled around his throat like a snake. I imagined his face not being so purple as I morphed into him to climb the stairs undetected. For the past ten minutes, I've been walking around as someone with thick eyebrows and a face shaped like a teardrop—before he was burnt unrecognizably by a wounded woman with electric hands.

No disguise is safe for too long in the Bounds. I either run the risk of bumping into someone who knows the person I'm impersonating or drawing suspicion for being unrecognizable. Maintaining someone's features I captured at a quick glance is growing more difficult as I keep face-swapping under the stresses of being literally hunted by unleashed convicts.

I find my way into a small room with sterile white floors and four octagonal cells with plexiglass walls. This is one of the rooms they use for holding when creating effective containment for new inmates. When Bishop gave me and the Senator a tour years ago there were security guards monitoring all of the celestials, using these special tablets that could manipulate the conditions if the celestial was acting out. There's no one for the guards to supervise at the moment, which makes me wonder if they've been freed too so they can join the hunt.

For once, I have some peace to catch my breath.

I glow gray.

It shouldn't feel like such a relief to be myself again, but not using my power is exactly that.

I pick up one of those tablets, scrolling through the features: temperature adjustments as high as one hundred and fifty degrees and as low as negative fifty, electrification between one hundred and three hundred volts, air decompression, and toxic gasses. I don't know a single gleamcrafter that could survive all of these.

The prison system has always been flawed, even during my ignorant days of fantasizing with the Senator about how I would punish the celestial who killed my mother. The procedures in the Bounds are so inhumane because the architects and guards simply don't see celestials and specters as humans. The Senator's supporters don't care, especially as Bishop keeps masking this disturbing reality as dominance and security.

If not Sunstar, maybe someone else will end this cruelty.

I'm not counting on it.

The door behind me bangs open, and I quickly morph back into the man with the teardrop face. Two women are too distracted fighting to notice me. I hang around long enough to see one breathe ice onto the other's swinging fists, freezing and shattering them with one slam into the wall. The woman's agonized scream follows me out back into the hall, and if I live long enough, her face will haunt my nightmares.

I run up the stairs, straight into more barbaric chaos.

I keep changing, gray light after gray light after gray light.

I round a corner and bump straight into someone with a firm back. I hope he doesn't think I'm trying to start a fight. Then he turns and my heart races.

Stanton.

His dark green veins are popping more than usual through his pale skin. This is the weakest I've ever seen him—underfed, bruised, scarred across his face and arms. He shoves me to the floor, staring down at me with his furious yellow eyes. He sees nothing but a red-haired white man with a scar on his neck and I hope it stays that way.

"Watch where you're going," Stanton says.

"I'm sorry," I say. A sign of weakness.

He's walking off, dismissing a pathetic soul who isn't worth his time when he sniffs the air. He stares at me menacingly as people fight behind him. "You can change your face, Ness, but you can't change your scent."

There's no point denying the facts. But making some up could help. "The Spell Walkers got me thrown in here," I lie. "Luna too. We got to find her; she can't defend herself. I think she's in solitary confinement."

"Your heart is racing," Stanton says.

"I have an entire prison hunting me. Didn't you hear?"

"Your heart is racing because you're a liar," Stanton says.

The ice-breathing celestial from the holding room appears and I point at Stanton and shout, "That's Eduardo Iron!" Her eyes immediately glow like snowflakes made of stars and her cold breath freezes Stanton's feet to the floor.

I get up and run, shoving people out of the way, knowing that won't hold Stanton for long. I keep an eye out for anything that could mask my scent, willing to douse myself in gasoline if it could throw Stanton off. I time my morphs in the seconds between brawls I pass, and even if I've caught more attention from other inmates, I trust I can fool them quickly in the way I can't this basilisk specter. That's only if I have the will to keep changing. I'm nearly out of breath and my wound is bleeding, and if my life is almost over, then I should die as me.

Fear drives me forward as I turn to find Stanton snapping the neck of someone in his way. He's pursuing me like a basilisk set free from a cage. I don't deserve the vicious end that he would give me. I look ahead and dark smoke is coming up from the balcony. I'm nervous running through it, thinking it might be some toxic power, but it gives me some great cover. I cough my way through, seeing a fire on the next level down.

The flames are gold and gray.

My heart races, so wild that I'm sure Stanton could detect me from the other side of the world. I only know one person whose fire are those colors.

Then there he is, alongside a Halo Knight as they drag mattresses out of cells and throw them into the burning pile.

Emil is stronger than he believes.

His beautiful face is the last one I expected to find inside the Bounds.

I make my way for the stairs, taking careful steps when I feel a foot on my back. I tumble down, banging my shoulder, my knees, my elbows, and my face slaps against the bottom step. I spit blood, surprised to be alive and wanting to be more than ever.

I use every last ounce of my strength to shout, "Firefly!"

SEVENTY-ONE
WINNER

EMIL

That stranger called me firefly.

Before his gray glow finishes, I'm running toward him. The beautiful brown of his skin returns, the once-shaved sides of his head have grown out since I last saw him, and he looks like he's been through hell with all these bruises and cuts and blood. I cradle his neck, and I suck in the biggest breath at being able to touch him again.

"You're alive, you're alive," I say, which is more important to me than I ever could've known.

"Firefly," Ness says. It's my favorite word.

Wyatt crouches, lifting Ness from under his arms. "Come on, champ, let's get you out of here."

I want to stay here and hold Ness, but Wyatt's right; we got to get out of here before he's recognized.

My chest tightens as someone steps out of the smoke— Stanton. I waste no time throwing fire-orbs, hoping to lay him out again just like back at Gleam Care. One catches him in the shoulder and he slams on his back. I grab my whistle, blowing on it over and over, praying to every damn star that my full squad will hear this over this chaos and come help us.

Wyatt lifts Ness onto his shoulder and runs past the burning mattress, but not fast enough. Stanton recovers and dodges every fire-dart I throw over my shoulder. His footsteps pound the floor and it's too late; he grabs me by the back of my neck and throws me against the wall. Stanton rips Ness off of Wyatt's shoulder and slams him onto the ground like a sledgehammer. There's fear in Wyatt's eyes, which Stanton seems to be drinking in before throwing him back toward the fire.

Stanton pounces on me and rages against my face with his fist.

"You thought you were free of me?"

Whenever I try to concentrate on setting my own fists on fire, he breaks my focus with another hit.

It's hard to keep my eyes open. . . .

I don't even feel the punches anymore. . . .

It's getting dark, even though my healing power tries to find the light. . . .

Someone tackles Stanton off me, but it's a blur.

First I think it's Ness being an idiot and saving me for the infinitieth time. He's still on the floor, struggling to breathe.

Same for Wyatt, who is groaning in pain.

The person isn't blurry anymore.

It's my brother, rescuing me like a hero who has fallen out of the sky.

SEVENTY-TWO
INFINITY REAPER

BRIGHTON

No one tries killing my brother.

My physical strength is no match for Stanton, but that doesn't stop me from punching him with flaming fists. His eyes burn like an eclipse as the green veins in his neck darken. I roll out of the way before he can spit his acid on me. Stanton lunges at me and I become intangible in time for him to phase through me and straight into the wall.

He tried assassinating me before I had these powers. Now I'm the ultimate success story he can't destroy. I've suffered so much abuse at the hands of Stanton: outside my apartment on the street, punched between the eyes at the cemetery, beat up while held captive, and then at the hospital when I was dying.

"You don't seem up for this rematch," I tell him before dashing behind him and punching his head. "Different fight now that I'm not tied to a chair, right?"

Stanton swings again, and I hit him with a fire-bolt.

I feel like a character in a video game facing off against the final boss, underwhelmed by how easy it is. This is one of the deadliest specters the city has ever seen and he can't even get a hit on me. But as I look around at Emil, Wyatt, and Ness, hurting on the floor, I'm reminded that Stanton is really strong. I'm just stronger.

"Brighton!" Prudencia appears, finally catching up after encouraging me to follow the whistling. "The guards are firing down on people with their wand-turrets. It's out of control. We— Behind you!"

Stanton grabs me and lifts me up. I try phasing away, but then I remember how June also couldn't use her ability whenever someone physically grabbed her. He races toward the balcony, hurling me over—I can't fly, I can't run on air, I can't fade around like a ghost. I'm flipping forward and glimpsing the four levels I'm about to fall down when I'm sucked up through the air, landing on my feet right beside Prudencia, whose eyes are still glowing.

"You're amazing," I say.

Prudencia telekinetically pins Stanton to the wall. "Go get everyone up!"

I rush to Emil. His face seems to be healing; Stanton won't be so lucky when I'm done with him. "Bro, we got to go."

"Ness," he breathes.

"You saved him, he's here," I say. I turn to Ness and spot three guards coming behind Prudencia. "Pru!"

497

They aim their wands and cast spells.

Prudencia spins, her hands up, and I dash-tackle her just before the spells can hit her.

The guards continue firing at us, but I hold on to her, and the spells phase through us until they've unloaded all the charges in their wands. That's the problem with those weapons—their power is limited. I blast them through the air with fire-bolts, proving how little control they could have over someone special like me.

Stanton runs toward me, and I do what has to be done.

I phase my hand through his chest, squeeze his heart, and rip it out.

His snake-slit eyes widen and I kick him over the balcony, watching his body fall into darkness. His heart drips red and green blood and I set it ablaze in sapphire and silver flames.

I smile over how I conquered a monster who tried to kill me, whose reign is over forever because I had the courage to end it once and for all. It feels incredible to not hold back my potential.

Saviors defend lives. Reapers take them.

SEVENTY-THREE
THE SMILE

EMIL

My brother's face is lit up by the sapphire and silver flames burning our enemy's heart. Brighton's smile may as well be a promise to his powers that he'll never bind them. He's not throwing out human vibes. It's like the phoenix, hydra, and ghost essences are fully converting him into someone—something else.

What color is my brother's blood?

"Bright, what did you do?"

"I killed Stanton."

"I know that! Why?"

"He had to die," Brighton says.

"He's already in prison, where he deserved to rot," Prudencia says.

Brighton throws the flaming heart over the balcony. "He will rot. His body will, at least."

"Bloody hell," Wyatt says as he looks over the railing. "I strongly believe that we should bounce up out of here, as Emil would put it."

He's right; I can't get into some argument with Brighton right now. I help Ness up and he's bleeding so much; I wish Eva had come along after all.

If we phased through the wall right now, we would find ourselves underground or even underwater, so we're climbing the steps with Brighton peeking out at every level to see when we're safe to escape. Prudencia keeps blowing the whistle to attract Maribelle and Tala, and I have an ear out for them, but nothing.

"I should search for them," Wyatt says.

"Please stay with us," I say. I can't start this all over again.

"But—"

"No, we'll wait for them at the top."

I don't know how much time we can offer with Ness bleeding out, but we'll do our best.

We go up the next level, and guards behind wand-turrets are rapidly firing spells down the path we need to go. Brighton's eyes burn as he steps out and everything shoots right through him. He's drawing all the attention on him long enough for Prudencia to telekinetically deflect the spells back into the turrets, damaging them all.

"I'm slowing you down," Ness breathes. "Just go."

Too many people are trying to play hero right now.

I ignore him and notice across the tower that inmates are

fighting guards who are blocking one of the entrances. One celestial casts funnels of water while another throws lightning, and they electrocute the guards right as one is setting up a gleamshield; individually these celestials might be subdued, but united they're a force. This revolt isn't surprising given how abusive these guards are known to be, literally forcing them to fight each other.

Every single Bound needs the full-blown investigation that Sunstar stands for—stood for?

Then more horror strikes—the inmates bust down the door and run back into the world. How many are innocent and how many are guilty?

Gas creeps out of the high ceiling vents, and I wrap my headband around Ness's face and cover my nose.

"We're leaving," Brighton says.

"I'm not leaving without Tala," Wyatt says.

"You think you're not," Brighton says. He grabs Wyatt's arm and drags him through the wall. He returns by himself. "Emil, you're both next."

I shiver as my brother touches me, horrified by how heartless he seems. I take a deep breath on the other side of the wall, so relieved to have escaped the Bounds. Wyatt cursing Brighton's name instantly reminds me that we're leaving people behind. Brighton and Prudencia phase out. Brighton runs for the boat and Prudencia does me the great favor of telekinetically carrying Ness, who looks like he's floating through the air.

"Wyatt, Wyatt, we got to go," I say, grabbing his wrist.

"Tala is still in there!"

"They might still escape, but I need your help now. I think

501

we have to fly Ness back to the Sanctuary fast or he might die."

"Gleam Care can sort him out."

"Everyone thinks he's a criminal, and being broken out of the Bounds isn't going to make him look innocent. Please, I know this is so selfish, but I can't let Ness bleed out on this island after everything."

Wyatt rests his hand on the wall as if he can feel his way through it before turning away and running toward our crew.

I hate that he's choosing me.

I catch up, watching as one inmate flies into the air toward freedom as others run into the river and begin swimming. Some gleamcrafters are making a move for the boat, and Brighton dashes ahead, attacking them with fire-bolts until they are laid out or back away.

I mount Nox as Prudencia telekinetically sits Ness between my legs, and I hold him exactly how I'm used to holding Wyatt. Ness groans, placing his hands over mine, and leans his head back on my shoulder. This is a moment of comfort I want to live in fully and appreciate, but as Nox begins our rapid ascent toward the stars, I look back at all the chaos caused by my selfishness—Roxana waiting for Tala, who may never come, abandoning Maribelle, and how many dangerous criminals have been unleashed on our city again so I can save one innocent.

This will be the crime I'm remembered for in this lifetime.

SEVENTY-FOUR
MARNETTES AND CÓRDOVAS

MARIBELLE

I want to begin Luna's end but I'm not sure where to start.

My family has spent years fighting her, and it's surreal to finally have her so vulnerable in front of me. This deserves more than instant arrows, no matter how much chaos is happening in these towers.

"This is certainly a disappointing final chapter to my journey," Luna says as she slowly sets herself down on the bed. There are blood smears around her lips and hand. "I have accomplished more in my life than most will in lifetimes, and yet I failed in my grandest ambitions. Time was not on my side, but dying now is more merciful than a slow death in this cell. I thank you both."

"You should've welcomed death after Brighton shot you," I say.

"Dying under the Cloaked Phantom would've been more poetic," Luna says. "I'll admit, I believed Brighton Rey would be the one to kill me with my own powers, to make this full circle. A Spell Walker and Halo Knight joining forces suffices too, if not a bit boring." She turns to Tala. "Who exactly are you?"

There is hate and heartbreak in Tala's eyes as she finally comes face-to-face with the woman who ordered the murder of her parents. "Tala Castillo, Bronze Wing."

"Beautiful name, but I meant more of why you're here with your pretty crossbow."

"You killed my parents."

Luna studies her face. "I'm afraid I'll need some more information. You Haloes haven't exactly stayed out of my affairs over the years."

"The museum," Tala says.

"Ah, yes. Recent. That was a slaughter, though some of them fought bravely. We can pretend your parents were among them." Luna turns to me. "The night of that gala was interesting. Upon losing your lover you cast fire and then burned my dear Anklin Prince alive. Neither Lestor nor Aurora Lucero possessed those abilities. Was this a latent power from generations ago?"

She truly has no idea of our personal relation. "I'm only coming to understand more about my family since that night."

"Family secrets?"

"Secrets kept to protect me from family—from you."

"Pardon?"

"I'm the biological daughter of Sera and Bautista. They hid

504

their pregnancy from you so that you couldn't use my power the way you used Sera for hers."

Luna rises from the bed, closing the space between us. I don't flinch. She's already hurt me in the only ways she possibly can. Her green eyes stare at me in confusion, and she cocks her head. "This would be an odd lie. You said you've only come to discover this weeks ago?"

"Word was passed on to me and I've been able to project myself through my bloodline and into the past to see Sera and Bautista. I saw how much they loved, how much they wanted to raise me. I felt her death as you slit her throat," I say, pulling out the oblivion dagger and pressing it against her neck. "My entire life has been thrown off course because of you."

Unlike when I was retrocycling, I can't feel Luna's emotions anymore, though it's clear she isn't scared to have her life threatened. "You successfully retrocycled."

"You know about that?"

"My parents—your great-grandparents—were professors. My mother studied phoenixes, my father hydras. A romance that developed over heated debates about the long-standing war between creatures. Growing up, my sister, Raine, and I were raised on stories of phoenixes and hydras. I brought a lot of this valuable information to Keon, but with the phoenix specters as a whole, retrocycling has seemed so beyond their capabilities when none of them could even resurrect as themselves. . . ." Luna steps away from the dagger, pacing the small span of her room. "But, my dear granddaughter, if you possess this power, then you may

505

be the key I've needed all along to unlock treasured secrets buried in the past."

"You're just trying to live."

"Now that you've given me a reason to. I've been dispirited this evening, since Edward Iron betrayed me before I could betray him, but now there is hope again. Your grandfather Santiago was one of five powerful brothers with deathlike powers. He could foresee imminent deaths, and when we married, he gave me all of the family's secrets. One in particular will be of great interest to you."

I've never done any digging into the Córdovas. I wasn't even obsessing over it too much until I got to see Sera and Bautista and feel their love for me. This grandfather of mine has the same visions as Sera except I don't see anything. I only sense threatening forces.

"Get on with it," Tala says, keeping an eye out the door.

"Patience, Halo Knight. You'll appreciate this tale too," Luna says, returning to her bed. "After my sister died, I demanded we cremate her. I was hoping to one day discover a way to resurrect Raine from her ashes like a phoenix. I began my journey seeking resurrection and have found myself on the path to immortality after the creation of specters. Around the time I met Santiago, I was learning more about ghosts . . . and he taught me how to bring them to life."

"A living ghost?"

"Don't be so surprised—my very first success story is the reason your parents and boyfriend are dead."

I'm trying to connect the stars. "June is a specter with ghost blood."

"She is. She was also dead. The practices I inherited from the Córdovas only function for deaths not long past, which was most unfortunate for Raine but has still given me hope. Though admittedly, I wouldn't bring back Raine if she functioned like June; alive, but not quite."

"What are you claiming you can do for us?" Tala asks.

"That with knowledge collected from a trip to the past and the ashes of your dearly departed, I can restore them as if they were never away from this world."

I drop the oblivion dagger and it clatters at my feet. "You can—"

"I can bring Atlas back to life."

SEVENTY-FIVE
SKYBREAKER AND SHAPE-SHIFTER

EMIL

The flight back to the Sanctuary is tense.

Nox isn't super built to carry three people, but he thankfully manages as Wyatt guides him through the skies. I'm tightly holding on to Ness, still completely blown away that he's alive, that he's someone I can wrap my arms around, that I can breathe him in. He's dizzy at these great heights, so I let him close his eyes, but I need him to keep talking because if he passes out I'm not sure he'll wake up. He keeps thanking me over and over, and when words feel like too much, he squeezes my hands with both of his to let me know that he's awake; I can feel the thank-you in his touch too.

I don't know where to begin with breaking down everything I've been through to Ness, especially with the handsome Halo

Knight flying us to safety, but I pray to all these damn stars that that's a problem I'll get to have if Eva heals him in time. Then there's Wyatt, who put my heart before his so we could save the life of a shape-shifter he doesn't know.

I'm indebted to them both, and I have no idea how to repay them.

The sun is rising as we fly over Storm King State Park and the castle finally comes into view. A cycle of phoenixes take flight to begin their day right as we're landing in the courtyard. This is normally when Wyatt and Nox would wake up and fly too, and instead, the obsidian phoenix goes under the apple tree and lies down.

"I'll go and disturb Eva's sleep," Wyatt says, muttering about how envious he is for sleep of his own as he jogs off.

"You still with me, Ness?"

His head is bobbing forward, his body getting limper by the minute. "I'm with you, firefly." An evergreen blazer the size of a bloated pigeon hops over to us. "Pretty green bird," he says drowsily.

I'm nervous I might have to start slapping him awake when Wyatt, Eva, and Iris come running through the courtyard, breaking up a fight between sun swallowers. I carefully rest Ness on the grass to prepare him.

Eva immediately investigates his injuries. She takes a deep breath, bracing herself. Her tired eyes glow like a rapid sunrise as colorful lights shine over Ness's bloody wound from the spell. Iris holds on to her girlfriend as Eva absorbs Ness's pain. Ness is breathing better by the time Eva heals the other battle scars across his body and face. The pinks, greens, oranges, and blues vanish as quick as a blink when Eva's work is done.

"You're okay," Iris says as she rests her chin on Eva's shoulder.

"Thank you so much," I say.

"Wow," Ness says, sitting up. He lifts his holey shirt and examines the smooth skin that's still slick with blood but no wound. "You're a true miracle worker."

"Happy to help," Eva says.

"Helping shouldn't hurt so much," Wyatt says as he walks toward Nox.

That definitely felt targeted at me.

"He filled us in," Iris says as she helps Eva to her feet. "I haven't heard anything from Maribelle obviously, but I'll wake up Wesley to see if she reached out to him."

"Okay. I'm so sorry that we had to leave, it was getting grim in there and—"

"It was an impossible mission with one victory," Iris says, though I think she's hiding behind some diplomatic nonsense when she can keep it real with me. She shakes Ness's hand. "Thank you for your work."

Ness shrugs that off. "Don't thank me. I did more damage than good."

"You did," Iris agrees. "But we're personally grateful for the good."

Eva hugs Ness, a celestial and a specter united by freedom from an unlikely captor. "I'm glad you're okay," she says.

"You too."

Iris takes Eva's hand. "We should let them catch up."

510

"Actually, would you mind taking Ness to the kitchen quickly? I got to check in on the potion." I turn to Ness. "You've got to be starving, right?"

Ness is reading my face like some scholar on expressions. "I should eat, yeah," he says even though he knows something's up.

They all walk off, and Ness looks over his shoulder a couple times, too concerned about me to really take in the castle or the phoenixes or his new lease on life. Once they're out of sight, I go straight to Wyatt, who is lying beside Nox on the grass with his eyes closed.

"Can we talk?" I ask.

"I'm sleeping," he says. "It's been a very, very long night."

"I know. You've done so much to save my people. I can't thank you enough."

"There are ways that you can try—" Wyatt shuts up, like he has some automatic flirtation function he forgot to turn off. "It was my pleasure to help."

"Except helping shouldn't hurt so much, right? Look, I know that you're respecting my headspace as I figure everything out for myself but I want to respect yours too. It was really big of you to risk your life to save Ness's knowing what he means to me."

Wyatt sits up, his blue eyes looking more like an ocean as he tears up. "That's precisely why I did it, Emil. For you. Ness's imprisonment was tragic, yes, but he wasn't some helpless, caged phoenix I've been trained to rescue. I've taken vows to serve phoenixkind and protect my fellow Haloes, and instead we abandoned Tala and Roxana. This hasn't been sitting right with me since our flight back."

511

I haven't seen this side of him before. He's so upset that he's crying, something I relate to.

"You told me to start being more selfish, and I'm sorry that's come at a cost to you."

"I hope it'll pay off for me in the long run. Ness is a good man who saved your family too, I would never deny that nor would I ever say anything bad about someone I don't know. I'm simply hoping that I see you on the other side of infinity." Wyatt looks tempted to kiss me, and part of me wishes he would so I know there's still something good between us, but instead he lies down with his back to me. I fight back my own temptations to cuddle up to him, wondering if I'll ever get the chance to do so again.

I return to the castle and head straight for the lab. Brighton and Prudencia should be back in the next ten to twenty minutes unless they had a pit stop so he could rip out someone else's heart. The journal is lying open beside the cauldron. I follow the last instructions, soaking the Dayrose root in phoenix tears and setting the potion to a high boil. This will be ready in minutes, and then I'll figure out when I might meet up with Wyatt on the other side of infinity.

There's a knock on the door, and at first I think he's a ghost because I'm still not used to Ness being alive, let alone here in the Sanctuary. He walks through the lab, paying no mind to anything but me, and straight into my arms. The last time we hugged was when I ran straight into his arms for coming back to help me at Nova, and before that was when we were parting ways, unsure if we'd ever see each other again.

"You shouldn't have rescued me," Ness says, holding me close.

"Got to live up to my nickname," I say.

"Popping up like a firefly in the night." He steps back to look me in the eyes. "It was a great surprise, don't get me wrong. But busting into the Bounds? I don't know that I could've pulled that off."

"You would've tried. I owed you the same respect."

Ness sits on a stool, grinning up at me. "I guess we're stuck in our very own infinity cycle, taking turns saving each other from doom. Hopefully we don't get separated again. I like the idea of us staying together. A lot."

"Me too."

There's so much unspoken between us that when I'm reading between the lines it's like I'm finding all the right words in caps lock.

I'm blushing and turn to the Starstifler as if there's more for me to do here besides make sure it doesn't blow up in its final minutes brewing. "How are you feeling?"

"Physically? All healed up, but exhausted. Emotionally? Relieved to be here and terrified that someone will drag me back to the manor or the Bounds at any moment. Psychologically? Destroyed over how a father could try to have his son killed and then greet his resurrection by using his powers for political gain."

"He tried to kill you?"

"The Blackout," Ness says, and explains everything to me about how Iron and Luna tag-teamed that terrorist attack to gain support and sympathy for the presidential campaign. "I've only ever been a pawn in their games. Someone to carry out missions and then sacrificed for the greater good."

I already wanted more for Ness when I thought his father was just abusing his powers, but to discover that Iron tried to blow up his son? There are no words.

"You're probably thinking it can't get worse, right? Luna turned the Senator into a specter with shifting powers of his own."

I don't give a shooting star what anyone says; this insanity feels like it's ripped out of some dystopian novel, and I'm scared I might be one of the heroes expected to save the world.

"Okay, that's absolutely wild, but we can stop him. This is the power-binding potion from Bautista's journal. You just mix a specter's blood into a vial of the Starstifler and their powers won't work anymore."

"Knowing our luck, it won't work."

"I've seen it work. I sort of went back in time."

"You did what?"

There's so much to catch him up on, all the way back to the Crowned Dreamer battle where Brighton stole the Reaper's Blood, but I focus on what brought us here to the New Ember Sanctuary—our temporary split from the Spell Walkers, discovering Maribelle and I could retrocycle, going through Bautista's and Sera's lives, learning about Luna being Maribelle's mother, and bringing back the ingredients to the Starstifler.

Ness is staring in awe. "I've just been grounded in my bedroom and impersonating a bunch of people."

"That's definitely a lot."

He begins pacing around the lab. "This makes sense. Luna was telling me about having a child, which was news to me and . . . I never thought it was Sera Córdova. Being the Senator's son ranks high in awfulness, but so does being Luna's granddaughter."

"No offense, but Maribelle pretty much only went to the Bounds to kill Luna."

"None taken. I hope she gives her the death she deserves." He stops pacing in front of the cauldron. "So this can disempower the Senator."

"And us," I say. I turn off the cauldron and the Starstifler smells like nature, which my city nose appreciates. "It's ready."

I let it cool down while reflecting on everything that had to happen to get to this point. My powers had to manifest, no matter how much pain they've put me through ever since, and now I'll be able to protect so many people by disempowering the Blood Casters, Iron, and any other specter. But no matter how much Prudencia and I tried cracking Sera's codes, we owe so much to Wyatt and his theories that got all the retrocycling in motion. Part of me feels like he should be here with me now as I'm using the steel baster to fill up the first vial of Starstifler that's existed in my lifetime.

"That doesn't look very drinkable," Ness says.

"That Blood Caster downed it." I fill up six vials and hand him one. "You can too. Enjoy your freedom."

Ness eyes the potion. "So I drop some of my blood into this and then my powers are gone?"

"Bound, but yeah."

"I'm looking forward to drinking this once I'm positive the Senator is no longer a threat," Ness says, setting the potion

515

down on the counter. "Once he realizes that I wasn't killed in the Bounds, he'll come looking for me again. This time he won't even have to be discreet about it since everyone knows I'm alive. The media can circulate my face while not knowing that he can change his."

I don't want to know what it's like to be hunted down by an entire country at that scale.

"But if you drink it now he can't ever force you to use your powers again."

"Then what, Emil? Do I become some honorary Spell Walker? Or am I going to get kicked to the curb because I might not be worth the trouble I attract?"

"Where I go, you go."

"But why? I barely know you, but you're also the only person alive who I trust. Why are we going through such great lengths for each other?"

I lift my shirt, only high enough to show him the scar in my side from where he stabbed me. "You did this to save me and I believe you. Trust goes two ways."

"But even that . . . killing you would've been more merciful. Instead I keep protecting your life and you keep protecting mine. Why are we doing this? Are we friends? Or are we more?"

"I think we're more than friends." My heart is hammering as he steps closer to me. "But I also thought you were dead and . . ." It really sucks that retrocycling doesn't let me change the past because I would like to avoid everything I have to say now. ". . . I started connecting with Wyatt. He's not my boyfriend, but we've been bonding since I got here and I'm even thinking about becoming a Halo Knight. It's not like the world is going to forget my face after I give up my powers, so I might as well keep doing some good." He takes a step back and I want to grab his hand, but that's not right. "I'm sorry."

"For what? You didn't do anything wrong."

"I feel like I did."

Ness shakes his head. "You thought I was dead, and even then, you've never owed me anything. But I am interested in how you feel now that you know I'm alive."

I've had so many regrets these past few weeks, so many things I wish I had done and said. "I want to get to know you better. Not just who you've become because of this war, but who you were before it and who you want to be when it's done."

"If it ever ends," Ness says.

"I'm going to make sure of it," I say, shaking a Starstifler. "I want to make sure you never have to hide your beautiful face ever again."

Ness smiles. "Beautiful, huh? You've come a long way from only being able to say my face is solid."

"I'm trying to have fewer regrets. Life's heavy enough."

"What do you want to know about me?"

There's so much, but I start simple. "How'd you choose your name?"

"It's the name of a star in the Cloaked Phantom. It's the dimmest star in that constellation, and that's what I liked about it. I've been growing up with a lot of eyes on me since my mom was killed, and my classmates thought my life was flashy because I was working all those political circuits. This power was finally going to give me some discretion to figure out who I wanted to become." He takes my hand in his. "Things took a turn with all the Blood Casting, but I can't get too upset since it led me to you too. Maybe one day when everything settles we'll get to morph into something together, firefly."

The way he calls me firefly and gently brushes my palm has me blazing inside. He's reading my face, like he knows how successfully he's seducing me with his touch. I'm not fighting it. I'm pushing away all my guilty thoughts about the Halo Knight I first kissed while flying on a phoenix because Ness is back from the dead and I want to stoke these flames for once in my life.

I put my hand on his heart, and it's beating as fast and hard as mine.

My lips practically fly to his, and I kiss the shape-shifter who has always found me beautiful because of who I am and has never wanted to change me. He's kissing me back, taking charge as he picks me up and sets me down beside the cauldron. My palms are on his cheeks as his tongue slowly slides across mine. I'm not ready to strip down to nothing yet but I take off my shirt and I don't ask him to keep his eyes closed this time. I'm hoping everything I've thought about him is right, that he's not about to be disappointed by what he finds underneath. He smiles even though I don't have a single ab in sight, like seeing more of me is enough to make him happy. He removes his own shirt and presses his bare chest against mine, and it's the first time I've ever been flesh to flesh with someone like this. Our bodies have been through so much before this point, and maybe, one day, our bodies are going to go through some really great things together.

However long I live in this lifetime, this moment is something I'll never forget.

SEVENTY-SIX
FAMILY

NESS

This is the safest I have felt in weeks.

Firefly's embrace is everything and I want our lips and bodies to stay locked.

I'm not stressing over the Halo Knight, especially since I don't know their business. I'm keeping my attention on Emil, who's haunted me so much that I've woken up in his form and I wonder how that will change if I get to hold him when I finally get to fall asleep after this hellish night of being shot and hunted in the Bounds.

There's shouting in the hallway and the first thing I hear is "Pru, just talk to me!"

Emil breaks our kiss. His tired hazel eyes widen. "Brighton and Prudencia are back," he says, putting on his shirt.

His brother is always getting in the way of things.

I get dressed too and follow him out of the lab.

"Hey!" Emil calls.

Prudencia stops. "Great. Emil, take over. I just spent an hour in the car with your brother while he tried to justify murder."

Probably best for Emil not to mention what he's been up to.

"You make it sound so ugly," Brighton says. "Stanton was beating the life out of Emil and tried to throw me over a balcony. It's self-defense."

"People don't usually smile when ripping out hearts, Bright," Emil says.

"I was happy that he was dead! That monster tortured me. I'm not throwing a party, but don't expect me to grieve someone who tried assassinating me."

I'm certainly not going to mourn Stanton either. He was an absolute terror and everyone should be able to sleep a little easier now that he's dead. But I'm certainly not jumping into these family affairs.

"I'm just nervous," Emil says. "Never in a million lifetimes would I kill someone."

"Well, Keon and Bautista beg to disagree," Brighton says, not caring when Emil tears up. "You might find yourself having to change your tune soon enough, because all those Bounds escapees are running loose, and we're going to have to round them up. . . ." He points to me. "Especially with your father blaming everything on us."

"He's already given a statement?" I ask.

Brighton pulls out his phone, swiping away his many

notifications to show me and Emil a news video.

There's footage of the Bounds captured by a drone, and black smoke is pouring out of one of the four towers; they haven't cited Emil as the source thankfully. The large yellow phoenix back on the island is now seen flying away with three silhouetted passengers as a storm follows them toward the city.

"Please tell me that's Maribelle and Tala and not some convicts," Emil says.

"Hopefully. Though I'm more concerned about the third person," Prudencia says.

I flush in anger. "Don't tell me Luna talked her way into survival."

The video cuts to the Senator outside the manor. He's still fooling the press with his fake black eye and cut lip. "Our country is under attack and neither our sitting president nor my opponent has condemned the actions of the Spell Walkers and the Halo Knights who broke into the New York City Bounds in the middle of the night. Let me be the first to say this terrorism won't be allowed when the country is under my supervision." He takes the most insincere pause. "I believe my son, Eduardo, coordinated these efforts in the event he was ever captured, and he succeeded in escaping along with many other dangerous criminals. Be wary of anyone speaking ill against me from this point forward—it may simply be Eduardo in disguise hoping to elect Congresswoman Sunstar into office so that those with power make totalitarians out of those without."

I almost throw Brighton's phone, but he snatches it out of my hand.

I try to take deep breaths. "This is what he wanted all along. Another crime to pin on those against him." There's no beating him. This fantasy to bind the Senator's power so I can reboot my life won't ever come true. If he's still shifting around this country, then so am I. I can't pursue any dreams, any relationships without fear of them being used against me. "Shit. Emil, there's something else. He knows about your past lives. I was supposed to expose you, and when I broke script, that's when I got shot. The Senator can make you public enemy number one by telling everyone you're immortal."

Emil looks frantic. "I'm not immortal! If I die, I'm dead."

"That's not how he's going to spin that."

"So everyone's going to blame me for what Keon caused—I don't have a single memory from that life! Now this is going to endanger so many phoenixes, and the Halo Knights can barely keep up with saving them now."

Brighton shakes his head. "I say this with the greatest offense, Ness, but your dad is a dick."

I ignore him, comforting his brother instead since he can't be bothered.

"What's to stop Iron from exposing Emil now?" Prudencia asks.

I shrug. "He might blackmail me into returning to him."

"No!" Emil says, clutching my wrist.

Then that English accent comes from behind me: "It's a worthy sacrifice," Wyatt says.

"You trying to kill me off?" I ask.

"No, not at all. This has nothing to do with the obvious and only to do with the threat against phoenixkind that is preventable."

Emil shakes his head. "I wouldn't believe Iron if he claimed he'd keep that secret buried away."

Brighton claps, bringing the attention back on himself. "The only way we can combat all these lies is with action. Those criminals breaking out of the Bounds is a miracle for us. We can put them all back in their place and prove we're the real heroes." He starts typing into his phone while walking away. "I'm going to see if there's been any criminal activity yet."

"Pardon me, but did Brighton rip out his own heart too?" Wyatt asks.

"You got to get him with the Starstifler fast," I tell Emil.

"It's done?" Wyatt asks.

Emil nods. "He doesn't want to bind his powers until after Sunstar is elected and creates her Luminary Union."

He's fooling himself if he thinks Sunstar still has a chance at this election. If she's even alive.

"Firefly, it took me years to really understand what a threat my father is. I'm going to need you to get there sooner with your brother."

"But . . ."

"There's no buts here—"

"He knows his brother," Wyatt cuts in.

"Want to bet?" I ask.

"Just chill," Emil tells us both. He turns to Prudencia. "What do you think?"

Prudencia's arms are crossed as she tries to keep her head high

524

after this long night. "I'm torn. The Stanton kill is scary, but Brighton has shown reason since having those powers. There were a lot of things we talked him out of doing."

"Good point," Emil says. "I'll talk to him. Maybe bring in Ma too."

There's a flash of hope on his face, short-lived because even he knows deep down this intervention won't work. But he's going to keep lying to himself until his brother flat out shows what he's capable of. Just because someone's family doesn't mean they won't hurt you.

This is going to be a hard lesson that I already know all too well.

SEVENTY-SEVEN
TRAITOR

BRIGHTON

My popularity is at stake, and with that, my power.

I've lost over one hundred thousand followers since we broke into Iron's house last night, and as more people are waking up to the news about the Bounds, I'm expecting a bigger drop. I'm being tagged in all these *INFINITY TRAITOR* memes from Brightsiders who think I've betrayed their trust and ruined the perception of gleamcrafters, as if there was all love before I hit the scene. I'm exhausted because unlike these keyboard warriors, I've been out in the world making a difference while they criticize every move I make. I almost snap at them, but that never goes well.

I have to earn back their support.

I'm in the library, really tempted to close my eyes for even ten minutes on this table but I'm sure I'll wake up to even more people dragging the Infinity Kings and Spell Walkers and Halo Knights since nuance doesn't seem to be taught anywhere. No one is ever going to make me feel guilty for breaking the law to rescue my kidnapped mother. End of story.

It would be comforting to know my supporters are backing me up, but I think they're being drowned out right now. It may be time to figure out how to make them feel more involved beyond reposting. I should grow a support network that's inclusive of everyone whether they have the gleam or not. We need people working cameras to protect our image and others fighting criminals to protect our streets. This movement can start off nationally, then go global.

United, my factions of Brightsiders—got to keep my personal branding—will re-create the world.

Emil knocks on the door. "Hey, Bright," he says softly.

I'm on edge, anticipating a confrontation. "No reports of criminal activity so far. If you want me to clear out so you and Wyatt can bunk up some more let me know. Or are you and Ness a thing now?"

Emil's gaze is like he's trying to calculate this himself. "Not a thing," he says, then looking around the library. "We'll see."

"All right, well, today we absolutely have to film Ma and Eva so they can tell their side of the story. Do you think Ness would do a video too?"

"You'd have to ask him," Emil says.

"He'd be stupid not to. An interview with a thought-to-be-dead presidential candidate's son who got powers and joined a

527

gang is not one people will ignore."

"You heard the senator; he's already got everyone thinking Ness is a liar," Emil says.

"Iron's story is the only one out there right now. That will change once we speak up."

"Look, I came to talk to you about something else."

"I'm not going to keep repeating myself on killing Stanton, bro. He's powerful and had to be stopped. It's not like I ripped out defenseless Luna's heart." Though I guess I killed her in my own way when I stole the Reaper's Blood. I hope Maribelle has thrown Luna off that phoenix by now. "There are bigger threats at hand."

"I'm scared you're going to become one, Bright. I'm begging you to really hear me on this. The Starstifler is ready and I think you should drink one."

He's never going to let this go. I'm finally showing everyone what a true hero looks like and they're so used to the sanitized versions in our generation that it scares them. This is why nothing has changed. "You had no problems with my powers when we were using them to break out Ness, but now that you've got what you want I'm a threat? You can't have it both ways. This city needs me now more than ever. If this is too much for you, drink your potion and go figure out if you're trying to screw Wyatt or Ness or yourself. I have real work to do."

Whenever I lash out at Emil like this he's usually tearing up or storming away, but he's just standing there frozen. It's like this life has finally made him numb.

I get up and pocket my phone. I'm not hanging around here while he feels bad for himself.

"Brighton?"

Before I finish turning Emil punches me so hard in the jaw that I bang straight into a bookcase; he's finally cracked. He pins me down. I try phasing out from under him, but I'm stuck because of his hold on me. He pulls out a small knife, one of the ones from the kitchen, and my brother slices my forearm. I shout as Emil yanks my bloody flesh.

"What are you doing?!"

"This is for everyone's own good!"

Emil runs for the door.

Everyone's own good? What the hell does that—

No. I won't let him.

I bite my tongue through the pain and dash toward Emil, grabbing him before he can even leave the library. He elbows my stomach and squeezes my new wound. It stings so much. I dash backward, dragging him with me, and I swing him on top of the table. I blast it in half with a fire-bolt and Emil caves in between the cracks.

"You're not taking this from me!"

I hit him with a flurry of punches, so betrayed by my brother. This is different than every other fight we've ever been in. He has no business trying to force this change on me.

I'm suddenly thrown off of Emil and straight into the wall, banging into an art print of some green phoenix. I look up from the floor and Prudencia and Wyatt are both shocked to see me laying into Emil like that, but not as much as I am to see Emil also standing beside them, holding on to the arm of our horrified mother.

The Emil who's sitting up glows gray. That bastard Ness was posing as my brother.

The real Emil stares like he doesn't know me.

SEVENTY-EIGHT
OVERPOWER

EMIL

Our brotherhood isn't enough to stop him.

By the look on Brighton's face, he didn't know the person he was beating up wasn't me. All of those punches were intended for me. I keep trying to ask Ness and Brighton what went down, but I piece it together when I see my brother's bleeding arm and Ness holding on to some flesh.

"Did you plan this?!" Brighton shouts.

"Emil had no idea," Ness says as he limps toward me. "I'm sorry, firefly, but I had to show you the truth."

I would've happily died never knowing this truth.

Brighton's eyes burn and fire snakes around his wrists. He hurls a fire-bolt while Ness's back is turned and Prudencia tele-kinetically sweeps it out through the balcony. I hurl a fire-orb at him so fast, but it phases through him. He stares at me, maybe even a little more surprised than I was to find him punching my face in.

"Go get a potion," I say to anyone, and Wyatt runs off.

"I'm not drinking it," Brighton says.

"Please, Bright."

"These powers are mine—I almost died for them!"

"You almost died because of them!"

"I'm not Dad; I'm a survivor!"

There's complete silence in the room except for Ma gasping. Phoenixes are screeching outside but somehow my beating heart feels louder. I can't even fight back the tears, thinking about how grateful I am that Dad isn't around to see Brighton being so absolutely horrible.

"Don't insult your father's memory like this!" Ma shouts. "If he were around, he would tell you that you're not supposed to be playing judge, jury, and executioner with these unnatural powers."

Brighton is red in the face. "None of you appreciate how extraordinary I am! The Spell Walkers treated Emil like he's some chosen one, when I'm the one who has defied death to become the most powerful gleamcrafter in the entire world. I will make the most change and protect everyone from anyone using their powers to terrorize. Overpowering the enemy is how wars are won, and that will sometimes mean deciding if someone lives or dies."

I remember my nightmare of Brighton terrorizing everyone with all his reaper powers. I tried to shake that off as nothing but a dream, but maybe that was my subconscious trying to brace me for this dark reality.

"Am I your enemy?" I ask.

"If you're not with me, you're against me."

"Then overpower me."

Brighton and I stare each other down, and in an instant, we draw fire.

My gold and gray fire-orbs blast apart his silver-and-sapphire fire-bolts, driving straight into my brother's chest.

This is not a fight I want to have, but it's one I got to win.

SEVENTY-NINE
SHINING BRIGHTER

BRIGHTON

I should've known it would come to this.

My chest burns from the fire-orbs, but I won't be the only one in pain. I throw fire-bolt after fire-bolt as I rise and they all explode in the air as Emil keeps countering with his own attacks. It takes so much agonizing soul-searching for Emil to justify fighting actual enemies, but now that it's me he has no problem being so aggressive. He can't dominate me like this, not with his one set of powers. I dash in a zigzag, dodging his fire-orbs, and I'm so close that I'm about to uppercut him with a flaming fist when Prudencia telekinetically shoves me back across the library.

"Stay out of this!" I shout.

"No! I've been with you both since the start and I'm seeing this through to the end," Prudencia says.

"You're supposed to be on my side."

She shakes her head. "You're supposed to convince me that your side is worth taking. I've never worried about Emil abusing his powers, but I can't say the same for you."

"So what, you preferred me when I was powerless?"

"You're the same person, Brighton. The powers only shone a light on how much of a dangerous egomaniac you are."

Something inside me is cracking, and instead of giving in to the heartache, I retaliate: "You don't deserve to be with someone great like me. Go run back to your pathetic ex."

Prudencia grins like I've told some joke. "You really think I'm so weak to be heartbroken by that. Your pride is wounded and always gets in your way of admitting when you're wrong. Get yourself under control now so you don't have to live a lonely life."

"I have millions of people who love me—"

"Your followers don't know the real you! Your fake persona is why I've never been able to trust myself to fall in love with you."

"I can't save the world with your love. Keep it."

Prudencia turns her back on me as Ma takes hold of her hand.

Wyatt returns to the library, and Ness takes the potion from him. He squeezes the blood from my flesh into the vial and begins shaking it. My arm still hasn't healed. Emil's phoenix powers are stronger than mine, even I have to admit it. Stronger fire, self-healing, flying, retrocycling.

That can change.

We've attracted the attention of Iris, Eva, Wesley, and Ruth. They're all staring at me like these divided lines aren't surprising. Since the jump I've been treated unfairly.

Emil takes the potion from Ness. "I know you want to do the right thing, Bright. We all love you and we can put this all behind us if you end this now."

I've been overpowered and wounded. I'm outnumbered and exhausted. I am ready to end this. I meet Emil in the middle of the library. I grab the Starstifler, appreciating how something so small can bind someone so powerful. I uncork the vial and it smells like a park after a rainstorm. I breathe it in as my heart races. I smile at him, and by the time he sees my eyes burning, I've already phased right through him and wrapped my arm around his neck. I shove the Starstifler between his lips, holding back his head to make him swallow. This may not work since it's not his blood, but I hope it can make him weaker and give me the upper hand in every fight moving forward.

The Starstifler flies out of my hand, smashing against the wall and staining it.

Prudencia tries wrenching me off of him and the others are charging me, but I phase through the floor with Emil and we land right into the courtyard. I keep his mouth covered, sealing his nostrils too so he'll be forced to swallow what little of the Starstifler he did drink. He begins burning my hands, but I shout through the pain and don't let go. He's got to be running out of air and he'll have to choose between taking a breath and swallowing the potion or passing out.

Gold and gray wings burst, blasting me backward. My entire body feels like it's on fire as Emil is knelt over, spitting out the potion. He holds up his hand, ready to defend himself if I attack.

"Why couldn't you just trust me, Emil? I supported you like a good brother!"

"I wasn't killing people!"

"You know I don't want to die!"

"If you go down this path, Brighton, you're not going to become some iconic Infinity Savior. This world will hate you and fear you so much that you'll never feel safe until you're standing alone in this world."

"If anyone comes for my life, I will send them to their graves."

We stare each other down, this threat and promise breaking up the Reys of Light, the Infinity Kings. No fist bump and whistle is going to save us this time.

The others are running across the courtyard and I'm smart enough to turn the other way, dashing out of the Sanctuary, across the bridge, through the trees, and keeping clear of the road in case they come chasing me. I can't outrun Wesley or the phoenixes, but this head start is everything I need to set myself up for success.

I'm going to prove everyone wrong.

I'm the weapon this war has been missing the entire time, and like a reaper's scythe, I will cut through those who stand in the way of a better world.

But I'm going to need an army.

I pull out my phone and study my reflection in my camera—dark circles under my reddened eyes, face flushed from the heat of Emil's wings, bruising from all the fights. I open Instagram and go live, letting everyone take in my appearance and the sounds of the river flowing alongside me as I begin my journey back to the city without a car or wings of my own.

"Hey, Brightsiders. I'm not sure where to start," I say as hundreds of thousands of people join the live. Some of the comments are already hateful while others are asking to hear me out. "There have been a lot of lies floating around out there and I wanted you all to hear the truth from me. I've had some better days, but I'm gutted right now. Everyone I love and trusted just betrayed me. I need some support, and I know I have to earn that with some honesty as epic as you all are." All my rage is building from everything that happened back at the Sanctuary. "This pains me, but these powers that almost killed me may not be enough to save me if I don't get some help. You all know that my brother, Emil, is powerful, but you don't understand how much. Just like phoenixes, Emil can resurrect. But this isn't his only life. In the past, he was one of my childhood heroes, Bautista de León, and before that, he was the first specter who started this all, Keon Máximo. I really thought Emil was going to do something good with this life, but he's proven me wrong—he's proven all of us wrong." There's no taking this back now and I wouldn't if I could. I'm redefining heroism. "I promise you all as the Infinity Savior I will do everything in my power to stop the Infinity Son. Even if that means becoming the Infinity Reaper to protect all of you . . ."

My brother's past lives will be the death of him.

ACKNOWLEDGMENTS

I write about death a lot and I struggle with life even more.

Writing has always been hard, but nothing has been more challenging than rewriting my first-ever sequel during a global pandemic and major mental health crises. Things have been dark, especially while in isolation, but I'm thankfully here, and you are too, and hopefully we can do our part in making this world a brighter, fairer place.

Huge thanks to my extraordinary editor, Andrew Eliopulos, for always deepening my stories and going on this journey through Infinity with me—and waiting nearly as long for me to turn in my edits so I can get it right. Jodi Reamer for being an incredible agent who understands that I'm a human and not a machine.

My HarperCollins family: Michael D'Angelo, Rosemary Brosnan, Mitchell Thorpe, Bria Ragin, Tyler Breitfeller, Jane Lee, Suzanne Murphy, Caitlin Garing, Kathy Faber, Liz Byer, Jacqueline Hornberger, Laura Harshberger, and Dan Janeck. And Erin Fitzsimmons and Kevin Tong for another gorgeous cover.

Thank you to Writers House and all my international publishers for getting my work out there.

My mom, Persi Rosa, who quotes lines of my books to her coworkers. And my brother, Andrew Silvera, who doesn't read any of them but champions me anyway.

My friends: Luis "12-20" Rivera and Jordin Rivera for never-ending calls of laughter and tears and love. Elliot "Chapter Two: Ness" Knight, who was physically with me when I began this book and mentally with me when I finished. Becky Albertalli, who listened to hours and hours of voice notes containing my highs and lows throughout the entire process. David Arnold and Jasmine Warga and Nicola Yoon and David Yoon for always cheering me on in every corner of life. Sabaa Tahir and Victoria Aveyard for being real fantasy queens I can always turn to. Angie Thomas for the greatest hype song to get me past the finish line. Arvin Ahmadi for Mexico—enough said. Dhonielle Clayton, Patrice Caldwell, and Mark Oshiro for a group chat of brightness and shade. And huge thanks to Marie Lu, who kindly gave me her blessing to open this book with the perfect quote from *The Rose Society*.

My Epic Reads tour sisters, Farah Naz Rishi and Abigail Hing Wen, for all the adventures at arcades and bookstores.

My therapist, who literally keeps me alive.

Booksellers and librarians, who give so much and don't get enough in return. Thank you for everything you've done, and I hope to everything that you're around forever.

Lastly, my readers who have followed me into my first series—I hope you love the rest of the Infinity Cycle.

TURN THE PAGE TO READ

"FIRST FACE,"

A LIMITED EDITION PREQUEL

SHORT STORY STARRING NESS.

FIRST
FACE
ADAM SILVERA

CHAPTER ONE
THE SENATOR'S SON
EDUARDO

Everyone thinks they know me.

To the public, I'm the young man who enthusiastically speaks out against gleamcraft violence after his mother was killed by a celestial. To my classmates, I'm someone they'll continue disrespecting unless my senator father clinches the presidential nomination. To the campaign staff, I'm a willing mouthpiece who will say anything to get into the White House—even lie. And to my father, I'm a loyal son who wants the best for our family.

I've gotten good at tricking all of them. I've had to.

I part my green curtains and see there's a light snow dusting the garden. Winter used to be my favorite season, but now I'm always grateful when the holidays become shadows behind me. Dad has never been the warm, cozy parent. Mom was always the one breaking out the Christmas tree the morning after Thanksgiving and singing songs as we decorated. She put a lot of care into her gifts too—two-player board games for us to play while Dad was busy, videos with personalized greetings from my favorite actors, mezzanine tickets to Broadway shows because I always preferred a bird's-eye view instead of being front row.

Now I get nothing but ties.

I choose a navy one today, thinking it will pair well with my peacoat. The D'Angelo High teachers gave us permission to dress down for this field trip to the Nightlocke Conservatory, but I don't get that privilege of freedom. Everything about my life is political—my social media, the movie tickets I buy, my old acting classes, and everything I wear. I could've spoken with the campaign manager about opting for a classy cardigan or thick sweater instead of my pressed white shirt, but I haven't liked Roslyn Fox since she was my father's secretary and she's even more insufferable now. The fewer conversations, the better.

Midterm exams are next week, and it's hard enough to stay on top of my studies when I'm pulled out of school at a moment's notice to hit the campaign trail with Dad, but now this trip to the Nightlocke Conservatory to learn about celestial histories is setting me back some more. I could fail all the tests I want if Dad gets elected president because every door in the world would open for me anyway. But that's not looking likely. He's falling behind in the primaries to his opponents Governor Horn and Senator Krause. Fingers crossed that Dad's influence and donations will continue to protect my grades regardless.

I go downstairs, hearing people in the dining room. I've gotten used to having unexpected company over the past couple months—it probably isn't fair to even call it unexpected at this point. Dad's official campaign office is on the Upper West Side, but he's been known to have some people over when his schedule is tight; when Mom talked about welcoming strangers into our home, I don't think this is what she meant.

Five people sit around Dad at the dining table: Roslyn is sitting the closest, as if that's going to make him want her as much as she wants him; a policy adviser who harbors a hate for celestials for reasons that no longer make much sense to me; the communications director, who uses my face all over social media to get out the word for those turning eighteen before the primaries; the pollster whose survey groups once said that Dad and I don't seem that close—ding, ding; and Barrett Bishop, who is the chief architect for the Bounds and a potential running mate.

If this country is lucky, an Iron-Bishop ticket won't happen.

"Morning, everyone," I say. They used to greet me like I was some prince, but it's become clear to them as well that they don't have to kiss my ass to be in good standing with Dad. The most basic levels of respect work just fine.

"Morning," Dad mutters while focusing on what looks to be the latest polling graph. He adjusts his glasses as if that's going to shift everything to his favor. He looks up at his team. "We're never going to win over voters at this rate."

"Not without a big win," Bishop says.

"Such as locking up the Spell Walkers in your prison," Dad says tensely. He looks as if he's about to bang his fist on the table. "Even with all our enforcers and scouts, how is it we haven't found them in our own city?"

"They're hiding behind their powers," Roslyn says.

A few weeks ago, Dad hosted a town hall where a man nearing death asked if the government has used jets to search for the

Spell Walkers in the skies because he was sure they were hiding in clouds. I was the only person in the building who could see the disdain for this conspiracy theorist in Dad's eyes as he responded respectfully.

"What about the Blood Casters?" I ask now. That gang of specters hunts, tortures, and kills people with powers given to them by their alchemist leader Luna Marnette. "Wouldn't locking them up and stopping their violence be a stronger signal?"

Dad is quiet for a beat. "They're off the radar too."

There's so much defeat in his voice. His dreams of taking the White House and claiming power over those born with their own are coming to an end. Even as a senator, he'll have a harder time restricting celestials if Congresswoman Sunstar's campaign gets her the Democratic nomination and goes on to secure the presidency. There are a lot of moments where a Sunstar win makes me really nervous. I'm working on figuring out if that's because Dad has taught me to be scared of her or because I don't want more emboldened celestials running around the world like gods who can kill mothers and then vanish off the face of the earth before they can stand trial.

It could be both.

"Don't concern yourself with the Blood Casters," Roslyn says to me. "We'll review some more Truth for the Youth talking points when you return from your trip."

"I'm studying later," I say.

Roslyn turns to my dad, knowing she has no authority over me.

"This country needs your service," Dad says.

It's not fair that I'm expected to serve this country when

4

I'm not the one running for office and I don't have any political ambitions. I'm more than a senator's son and I'm tired of my words getting people hurt—people killed. Like Rhys Stone, the fifteen-year-old celestial who could extend his limbs in unimaginable ways. He died with his stretched arms tied to opposite ends of a parking lot gate and tortured by people without powers and left for dead. His murderers were roused by one of my speeches and took their hate out an innocent boy who was walking home after meditating in the park with other celestials. Is this really serving my country?

"Sure," I lie.

I put on my peacoat and check myself out in the mirror. The coat is good—not the warmest but it's a stylish one to wear while dressing for the job my father wants. I almost put on a hat, but I don't want it flattening my curls. I would buzz-cut the sides of my hair if Dad weren't so concerned about it making me look too casual, similar to criticisms drawn toward Governor Horn's daughter. I hate how every decision I make in my own life is impacted by his choices. I stare into the mirror, knowing that logically this is my face, but still struggling to believe that, given how much I don't feel like my own person.

"I'm headed out," I say.

Dad gets up and meets me by the door. He rests his hand on my shoulder and looks me in the eye. "Keep making me proud, Eduardo."

These tiny moments of affection are how he's trapped me over the years. The pat on the back after I threatened to have Peter McCall drowned if he ever used his water power in front of me.

5

How Dad bandaged my hand after I beat down Harry Gardner. The praise after Rhys Stone was killed. I've attacked an entire community of people because I got some fatherly love from it. But every time I think about my mother, I know she wouldn't have raised me to be so hateful. I need to change and be someone she would've been proud to call her son.

It's hard when there's so much blood on my hands already.

Sometimes I think about how I would rather be dead than keep hiding my monstrosities behind this mask.

CHAPTER TWO
THE PASSENGER
EDUARDO

People must be wondering who's inside this town car with its tinted windows.

Back when Mom and I used to walk around the city, we would guess who were the passengers inside limousines and town cars. As a kid, I imagined people with phoenix wings and hydras talking into as many phones as they had heads. But I grew up fast after Mom died, and my guesses matured as much as I did. I assumed the passengers were politicians. One time I thought it was the president, but Dad said that he wouldn't be parked at a stoplight and he would be surrounded by a motorcade. In my dreamiest guesses, I kept wishing the passengers were actors, and I would get lost thinking about how amazing it must be to be someone everyone knows, someone who has to be hidden if they're ever going to get from one glamorous destination to the next. Theaters, sets, recording studies, premieres, conventions, all of it.

I'll never get to be famous for my own accomplishments.

The partition is up this morning, so I can't speak with my driver, Frederick, who I've known for years. He has two sons, who've come over a few times, but we don't ever really connect. It's clear they're not ever being themselves around me. When no one's watching, I catch them cracking crude jokes and shoving each other. But once I step into the picture, they're on their best behavior. I'd rather have friends who play rough and talk shit as long as they're being honest.

My bodyguard, Logan Hesse, is sitting across from me. He's my height, five ten, and I originally expected someone with a mightier presence to defend me. But muscle isn't as important when Logan can create domed shields that will protect us from any gleam attacks. It's a power that celestials such as Logan have helped regular people re-create, donating their blood to alchemists so they can create shields for vaults and panic rooms, but having him at my side has made me a lot safer. Not that anyone's tried to come at me like that.

I still think it's a special sort of trick to get celestials to work for the family of a man who creates laws that limit their rights, but Dad and many others pay them very well for their protections. It helps that Logan likes me enough.

"Did you watch wrestling last night?" I ask.

"There's no way I was missing that. I would've let you out of my sight to watch that main event," Logan says with a deep laugh. It's refreshing to have someone who will joke with me like this. "I shouted so loud when Hagen blasted Cosmo off the steel cage with that lightning bolt that I woke up my wife."

"I bet you needed your own bodyguard after that."

"It's no joke; she needs her eight of hours of sleep. I'll pay that price later, but the match was worth it."

I don't watch celestials wrestle. For one thing, it's all theatrics and not the kind I enjoy. But it's mainly because Dad has never wanted me to be entertained by celestials. I've known this since I was young. One day I was going to the park with my parents and I heard laughter above me. I looked up to find a boy in the air, higher than any building we were passing. He was laughing so hard and so loud that he was knelt over while pointing at another boy who was flying toward him, struggling, as if he was swimming through muddy waters.

I had pointed up to the sky and said, "I wish I could fly."

Dad was pissed. "If people were meant to fly, we would all be able to do it," he had said. "If you get too close to a flying celestial, they might carry you up to the clouds and laugh as they drop you out of the sky."

Mom was gentler, telling me that gleamcraft could be dangerous on one's body and mind. That powers create a sense of superiority. But the fear Dad planted in me was already taking root, making me reject celestials for so long.

It's frightening how one childhood moment can scar you for years.

Logan's phone rings and he answers. "Yes, sir?" He looks up at me. "But I would be leaving Eduardo vulnerable . . . Understood, sir."

"Who was that?"

"Jax. He said that I'm needed."

If Dad's head of security is calling Logan back, it must be

9

serious. "What's going on?"

"It's not my job to ask. Frederick should drive you home too."

I look out the window, just in time to see us rounding the corner to the conservatory. "I'm already here. I'll be fine."

By the nature of the job, Logan's expressions are all subtle, but I'm able to see the uncertainty in his eyes. His job depends on keeping me alive, but this isn't the first time I've been out in public without him at my side, and it won't be the last.

The car parks and Logan gets out, surveying the path from the curb to the conservatory's entrance. "Are you sure?"

"I'm not as big a target as Dad pretends I am. But if he becomes president, you'll be so attached to me that I might finally start watching wrestling."

I pat him on the back and walk toward the Nightlocke Conservatory, and even with the dozen footprints I've left behind in the snow, I feel his eyes on me the entire time.

CHAPTER THREE
THE CLASSMATE
EDUARDO

I always feel really important when someone holds a door open for me. It might be a sign of courtesy for most people, but for those associated with power, it's seen as respect.

I thank the greeter as I step into the Nightlocke Conservatory, staring up at the glass domed ceiling as I go through security. Snow caps the highest point, but the rest of the gray skies can be seen from inside. I'm sure the night sky must be majestic, but I see every single star as a weapon that makes celestials more dangerous. No, those are Dad's words in my head. The stars make celestials more powerful—that doesn't automatically make them dangerous.

The two people I'm most likely to call my friends wave me over. There's Luke Fey, whose congressman father couldn't get enough donations to keep him running as a presidential candidate and is prepared to endorse Dad, which makes things less awkward for me and Luke, who have known each other for almost five years. And there's Louise Kama, who is not shy about letting everyone know her father is the chief enforcer of New York City. I have some other associates, but Luke and Louise are the only two people in class who have my phone number and follow my private Instagram account, where I don't even post because I'm too paranoid someone might betray me one day.

"Look who finally made it," Louise says.

"Am I late?" I ask, checking the time on my dad's old watch.

Her red hair is tucked underneath a knitted cap and her bright green eyes always ignite something in me, and the way she had once stared at me for a second too long led to our first kiss. "I just don't want to be left alone with Luke."

"You know you can't get enough of me," Luke says. His blue eyes are pretty magnetizing too, though my favorite part about him has always been this champagne-bottle-shaped birthmark on his pale neck. He's a pretty good kisser too.

At one point or another, I could've seen myself dating Louise or Luke. We bonded so much over our hate of celestials, even the innocent ones. Unlike me, I don't see their anger losing steam. They'll give in sooner or later and finally start dating and probably stay together and pass down their teachings too. I'm not letting them take me down with them—though I pretend I'm still one of them.

"I don't give a hydra's tail about Noah Nightlocke," Luke says as we join our teacher Ms. Fitzsimmons and the rest of our class.

"Why'd you show up?" I ask.

"Change of scenery," he says.

"Uh-huh."

Ever since Luke joined some of my rallies years ago, he's always

12

been restless, sometimes coming onstage before I was done so he can explode with this charged energy against celestials. That attitude once made me feel safe around him.

Paper lanterns decorated with stars hang around the conservatory, such as the snake plants that are taller than all my classmates, a white bust of Noah Nightlocke, his portrait, glass cases with items of his from over the years, and the huge bronze telescope in the center of the room that already has people crowding around it for photos.

"Welcome, D'Angelo High!" says a man in a maroon vest. "I'm Deckard, and on behalf of everyone at the conservatory, we're so pleased you can join us this morning."

"Put a wand to my head if I'm ever a tour guide," Luke says. "Unless it's at the White House after your dad wins."

I want to be real with him about how my father clearly won't win, but I'm expected to show support all around.

"Noah Nightlocke was an extraordinary celestial who made even more extraordinary discoveries," Deckard says, gesturing to the portrait. Noah is painted with brown skin as light as my own, dark eyes, streaks of gray in his black hair, and a maroon half cape. "Mr. Nightlocke holds the record for spotting the most prime constellations that decorate our skies and empower celestialkind, such as the Scavenged Poet, the Loud Reader, and the rare Crowned Dreamer, which will resurface this September for the first time in sixty-seven years. Does anyone know the next prime constellation that will appear?"

Our classmate Aria's hand begins twitching, like she wants to answer, but she doesn't draw any attention to herself.

13

Poor Deckard keeps his phony smile plastered as he waits for someone to speak up. "Our next constellation will be the Cloaked Phantom in a couple weeks, and it is stunning—not to be missed. Our gift shop carries yearly calendars for all the prime constellations. The Cloaked Phantom has benefits for those with the power to morph their appearances, but it encourages everyone underneath its stars to take stock of their lives and pursue change for the better."

Luke doesn't bother fighting back his yawn.

Louise raises her hand but doesn't wait for Deckard to call on her. "All those constellations actually do is flood our streets with celestials, who use their powers to terrorize our people."

Deckard blushes. "While it's true that some crime happens—"

"A lot of crime happens," Louise says. "My father is the chief enforcer of this city, and I'm always worried about whether he's going to come home or not."

I want to stop her, but seeing as someone has already taken out their phone and started filming yet another of Louise's takedowns, I can't be caught defending a celestial without the media using it against my father's campaign. And then Dad taking that out on me.

"Enough," Ms. Fitzsimmons says.

"Fine," Louise says, having already gotten her fix.

I've done a lot of despicable things in my short life. I'm relieved that dating Louise or Luke isn't among them.

Deckard tries getting his bearings, but he's blushing more and more, absolutely red in the face over how he got owned by a seventeen-year-old whose father could have him arrested. It's

14

not as if celestials are always guilty of the crimes they're being charged for and brutalized over—one conversation with Bishop will reveal how proud he is of locking up innocent celestials in the Bounds before they can do any harm.

Then, just when it looks like the lesson about constellations will continue, the sky shatters.

Glass rains down on everyone, most of us too frozen to move, though some manage to run away screaming.

Two women fall toward me, one choking the other, and crash down on the floor.

Even before I see their power-proof vests with their group's sigil, I recognize their faces—it's Aurora Lucero and Finola Simone-Chambers.

Why the hell are the Spell Walkers fighting each other?

Their husbands, Lestor Lucero and Konrad Chambers, charge through the entrance and try to break up the fight. Aurora continues to strangle her squad mate until Finola breaks the hold, using her powerhouse strength to shove Aurora and the husbands off her.

I know I should run, but it's like all my instincts have been ruined by having a bodyguard. If Logan were here right now, his shield could prevent any shard of glass or celestial from harming me. But even as Aurora Lucero looks up at me, my feet are glued to the floor.

The Spell Walker lunges at me.

CHAPTER FOUR
THE TARGET
EDUARDO

I'm going to be the next Iron to die.

This is my first time meeting a Spell Walker, and the dark glare in Aurora Lucero's eyes tells me it will be the last. I try fighting her off, but it's no use. Luke and Louise are shouting for help as they hide behind a display. My heart is racing as Aurora's fingers dig into my shoulders.

My death will be as political as my life.

"Please, don't do this," I beg. "I'm sorry for everything. I can talk to my dad; I'll make sure he never comes for your people again! I'll get him to not run for office! Give me a chance, please!"

There's no bartering with this reaper, who has had enough of her life being threatened by my father. I might only be allowed to speak on stages with words that aren't even my own, but people in this Spell Walker's community have been hurt and killed because of me. I might not be able to fly like her, but my words have been powerful—more dangerous than most celestials.

Aurora slams me to the floor, my back lit in pain.

I don't want to die, but my father won't be able to use me anymore if I do.

Still, I feel like I'm plagued by every nightmare of violent deaths that I've had since Mom was killed. I try comforting myself that maybe I'll die fast like she did, but what I want more than anything is to live my own life, become my own man.

Meet myself.

But I won't get to do that. Not judging by the gem-grenade Aurora pulls out from her power-proof vest. She throws it toward one corner of the room, and Lestor Lucero jumps into flight and chases after it. Aurora throws another over Finola's head, and both Chambers attempt to catch that one; maybe together they can absorb the blast.

I'm sweating as I stare up at the snow that drops through the ceiling, right up until the moment when the conservatory explodes in red energy that swallows us whole.

CHAPTER FIVE
THE SURVIVOR
EDUARDO

I'm a dead man.

The blast obliterates everything—the metal of the telescope is screeching as it's split apart, the last of the glass shatters, the walls crumble down—but I shouldn't hear anything. I should be on fire, but I don't even feel hot. I'm a little cold actually. Dark smoke prevents me from seeing anything, when suddenly everything feels more chaotic—I smell burnt flesh, I feel blood soaking into my pants, I'm coughing and choking. I brace myself again for some sort of explosion and nothing happens. I crawl through the smoke, my hand landing on someone else's. I pick it up, immediately understanding that it's not attached to an arm. I gag, ready to vomit all over it.

Then, as the wintry winds push away the smoke, I see what's left of Aurora Lucero; cremation is probably the best route.

Everyone must be dead except me . . . and the girl who is holding my shoulder.

Immediately, she gives off the vibe of some ballerina's ghost in a horror story. But considering how she must have saved my life, she has to be some guardian celestial, like in all those cheesy made-for-TV movies.

The girl squeezes, and I feel like my entire body is fading away, like I'm nothing but wind.

Suddenly, we reappear on a pharmacy rooftop blanketed in snow. Then in the Union Square subway station. Then in the kitchen of some restaurant where a cook is boiling rice. Then in a storage locker where dust is collecting on someone's belongings. Then in a toy store with a child who drops his train when he sees us. Then in a park, where the birdsong would be welcome after all the destruction I just heard if I weren't so nauseous from all this transporting. Then outside of a bank. Then in the middle of traffic, my heart in my chest as we barely avoid getting flattened by a truck. Then in a staircase that smells like piss. Then inside some apartment with a lightwood dining table and a cauldron on top of it.

I don't reach the cauldron before vomiting all over the white rug.

I haven't felt this sick since stealing bottles from the liquor cabinet at Luke's and drinking with him in his bedroom.

Did he die at the conservatory? Louise too?

I turn, getting a clearer look at my savior. She's white, short, and looks bored. No, her expression is . . . blank. She must also be shocked by everything we experienced. I'm embarrassed vomiting in front of her, but the damage is done, especially to her rug. More likely her parents' rug since I'm guessing she's fifteen, sixteen.

"You okay?" I ask.

She doesn't say anything.

"Thank you for saving me."

Some celestials do right with their powers. My father knows this, not that he'll ever credit anyone outside those who are in his service. But I'm walking proof that when one celestial tried to kill me, another saved me.

Footsteps.

"I'm the one you should be thanking," an elderly woman says as she enters the dining room.

No matter how good a job Luna Marnette has done with hiding from the media, I still instantly recognize the leader of the Blood Casters from the few times they have managed to capture this supreme alchemist out and about. She's taller than I expected, and even though her frame seems frail, she holds herself up so confidently that I'm not sure I can take her in a fight.

I back up against a cabinet with fancy dishes, scared of Luna, as if she's one of the specters she's created. I turn to my savior again, wondering why a celestial is working for a gang of specters. Then again, anything is possible in a world where my father employs celestials even though he wants to ruin their lives.

I eye the door and make a run for it. The ghostly ballerina appears out of nowhere and punches me between the eyes. She kicks me so hard that I roll into a wall, gasping for breath. "What are you going to do, torture me?" I ask.

"Torture is certainly more interesting than execution," Luna says, stepping over my vomit and taking a seat at the table. "But I didn't save you to hurt you. I saved you to help me."

"Help you?"

"I have given you a blessing, Eduardo. Within the hour the world will believe you to be dead along with the Spell Walkers and however many innocent souls were in that conservatory with you."

My friends, my classmates, my father's enemies. They're all dead.

"So what," I say.

"I've studied your face during all your recent appearances. You used to have so much rage in you, but that's settled greatly. I see your doubts. You're not buying what your father is selling anymore, are you?" Luna grins as I stay quiet. "Still playing the loyal son. Quite a convincing role. You should be an actor." She doesn't wink, but I can see in her green eyes that she's toying around with me. "Your father's ambitions will continue to lock away your dreams."

"Cut the monologue and get to the point."

"How would you like to live your life away from your father?"

I don't say anything. I don't tell her that this is a dream of mine. But like everything else she's figured out about me, maybe she can read it on my face. I don't know what she's proposing, but if it's anything like getting me to start over at some witness protection capacity, it's more than I could've ever imagined about the day I get to turn my back on my father.

"This is in your future, but not immediately," Luna says. "You're no stranger to working for someone who's trying to change the world. But I require more action than standing on a stage and talking about your feelings. I need infiltration."

21

This doesn't make sense. "I'm not exactly going to have a great future if I get caught infiltrating lives."

"If all goes well, no one will know it's you. The Cloaked Phantom rises at the start of February. This constellation elevates the powers of those rare few with shifting abilities. A former specter of mine, Adrian Paige, was once trapped as a bird between the appearances of the Cloaked Phantom . . . frustrating several months, but a lesson well learned for the next shifter—for you."

She can't be seriously thinking about turning me into a specter—and I seriously can't be so desperate to hide from my life that I would become one.

CHAPTER SIX
THE LIAR
EDUARDO

I'm not a prisoner, but I'm not allowed to leave.

I've gathered from the view out the guest room's window that we're in downtown Brooklyn, a good thirty-minute walk from the bridge. I'm still nauseous from all the teleporting that girl—whose name I still don't know—did to get us here, but that's not why I've rejected a hot meal from Luna. I've grown up on so many horror stories of how alchemists can't be trusted, and I'm nervous Luna has poisoned the food and will refuse to give me an antidote if I turn down her offer to become a specter.

This room is pretty luxurious, like some of the fancy suites my family has stayed in over the years. Silk sheets over the queen-sized bed, brass bookcases fixed to the walls with photo journals lining the shelves, and a stunning painting of our country in the shape of stars, like some constellation of America.

I watch the news on the mounted TV, switching between channels as everyone covers the attack at the Nightlocke Conservatory. It seems as if a few people made it out, but I don't think that includes Luke and Louise. They were nowhere near the door as the gem-grenades exploded. As they are—were—I would never want them as long-term friends, but maybe they could've changed too. Grown out of how their parents also raised them. I'll never know because they were killed as quick as a snap.

There's so much rage, confusion, and grief over the Spell Walkers. I don't know if Aurora Lucero was actually coming there to kill me or if I was a happy accident. Though Dad has told me that only stupid people ignore coincidences. I've got to think that Aurora chose to hunt me down to send a message to my father and the other Spell Walkers disagreed. They all lost their lives trying to take mine.

What does it mean for the Spell Walkers that all the original members are now gone? Enforcers are expanding their search to track down the children, Maribelle Lucero and Iris Simone-Chambers, along with Atlas Haas and Wesley Young. This younger generation of Spell Walkers has been seen saving people here and there but not without damaging property or hurting innocent people along the way. If they're smart, they'll disband the group and never show their faces again.

It's strange seeing my name pop up on every channel like I was the only notable person in the Nightlocke Conservatory.

I go to Wolf News, the network that has always championed Dad the most. I'm shocked when instead of some report from an anchor, I see actual footage of Dad stepping out of the conservatory with a white mask around his mouth and nose. He's accompanied by firefighters and his bodyguards—Zenon Ramsey and head of security Jax Jann—and Logan is there too, looking absolutely miserable. He thinks he could've saved me because he thinks I'm dead. How am I supposed to let him live that soul-crushing lie? Hopefully Dad being the reason Logan got called back protects his job.

Dad approaches the crowd of reporters and removes his mask. I need to see something from him, something that proves I've been wrong about his lack of love for me. He clears his throat and tries looking strong at a time when no one could possibly expect that of him. "I've lost everyone. A celestial took Esmeralda from me and now Spell Walkers have killed Eduardo. My only son . . ." A tear slides down his cheek. "This is what happens when you speak out for justice, for security. Today it's my family, and tomorrow it's yours."

The reporters shout over each other to get their questions answered:

"Why did they come for your son?"

"What will you do about this?"

"Will you exit the presidential race?"

"Are you concerned for your safety?"

Dad turns his back on everyone, but the cameras follow him as he stares at the fallen conservatory, not a doubt in his mind that he's the last Iron standing. But I'm not sold on those tears he's squeezing out for the media; he does that whenever he's trying to appear more worked up for his audiences. I know the difference when his heartbreak is real and when it's performative. We were together at the manor when an enforcer came over to let us know Mom was killed by a celestial. Dad fell to his knees and couldn't breathe and refused media appearances for weeks because he couldn't function—that was true grief. Looking at him now confirms everything I've been thinking for years.

This is not the face of a man who will miss his son.

He was always happy to be my mother's husband, but being a father didn't seem to mean as much to him. To mean anything beyond having a legacy and a pawn.

He's a liar who didn't care about my life and doesn't care about my death.

I get up and search the loft until I find Luna in this grand living room with a silver chandelier and green velvet couches. I'm supposed to be terrified of her because of everything that my father taught me. But the way I see it, both of them want to use me; at least one of them plans to set me free afterward.

I'll do whatever it takes to finally become myself—whoever that is.

"I'm ready to change."

CHAPTER SEVEN
THE SPECTER
EDUARDO

Every night I go to sleep, I think about who I could be when I wake up, once I have my powers.

It'd be fun to take on the appearances of my favorite actors, but I don't want to play pretend with a famous person's life; I want my own. I've had some moments where I wish I could start my childhood over, maybe morph into a little boy who is adopted and fully loved by new parents and get the nurturing I've missed out on since Mom died. Other times I think about changing into a grown man who appears to have his shit together.

Once I have these powers, I can look like anyone. But I won't have to worry about choosing a permanent form and losing my face forever. Still, I'm ready to explore life as other people. We can listen to friends and strangers until the sun goes down, but we can never know someone's full story without going through the world in their bodies. I might be able to find myself after those journeys.

I don't have all my questions answered for what will be expected of me as a specter, but Luna has made it clear that I'll become a Blood Caster who takes down corrupt people. I'm done debating who's good and who's bad; I want to get these powers and do the job. If she ever puts me in a situation that I don't like, I'll shift into someone else and flee the country. Simple.

The latest primary polls have shown a big boost for my father, but I still don't think it will be enough to get the nomination. It's a small comfort that if he does, I can screw with him. Maybe morph into him and say a hundred outrageous things to reporters and tank his chances. But it's thoughts like this that only support everything he fears about gleamcrafters as a whole, and he'll take action against innocent celestials if I add fuel to the fire. The temptation to ruin his life is still really strong, truth be told.

The night of the Cloaked Phantom, Luna takes me to the rooftop of the building, the entrance blocked by the girl whose name I've learned is June. Everything else about her is as big a mystery as where the other Blood Casters have been these past two weeks, since June saved me at the Nightlocke Conservatory.

"It's beautiful," Luna says, staring at the constellation.

The stars are arranged like a theater mask I once got to wear during a play in sixth grade. I stare at the bright eyes in awe, wondering what they see as they look down at the world below. Can the Cloaked Phantom see how much I want to change?

"Why don't you give yourself power?" I ask.

"The constellations aren't as kind to people my age," Luna says. "Besides, I've designed a grander plan for myself—one you will be instrumental in achieving for me." She looks over her shoulder. "It's time, my miracle."

With her life-saving power, June walks through the door like it isn't even there.

I don't know what it's time for, but it's clear that soon I'll be different. I'll become one of the people I was raised to hate.

"I'm nervous," I admit.

"That's common. You may not love your life as is, but it is still one of comforts you're familiar with. The greatest changes hurt the most. What better time to shed your old self than under the stars of the icon of transformation." Luna wanders over to a steel cauldron resting on a generator and mixes the potion I'm about to drink.

If I'm going to leave my life behind, I want to make sure I'm starting fresh.

That begins with a new name.

My father originally wanted to name me Edward Jr., but my mother wanted me to have some roots with my Dominican side, so I became Eduardo. But I'm ripping out everything that connects me to my father; I won't even recognize him as such anymore. He's just Edward. No, that feels too personal. Moving forward, he's simply the Senator. And I'll use Mom's maiden name, Arroyo, as my new last name.

Who am I going to be?

I look up at the Cloaked Phantom like it's going to give me an answer.

"Do you know the names of the stars?" I ask Luna.

Luna turns from the cauldron and points. "Those two at the very top are Lerrel and Sillis. The brightest one above the left eye

29

is Shalev, and Mal is below the right. The dimmest is Ness—"

"Ness," I interrupt, feeling the name light me up like a firefly surrounded in pitch-black darkness. I like that this star is the dimmest in the entire constellation. I've spent too much of my life on the wrong stages and I wouldn't mind going unnoticed until I'm ready to present the best version of myself. "Call me Ness from now on."

"Very well, Ness."

I already feel like I'm shedding my father's influences.

As I'm wondering what I'll change next, there's an unnatural sound I've never heard in the city. It's like a dying roar. I turn to the source and find June standing by the cauldron with a tiny animal—the creature whose blood I'll need to have those powers. I don't know a ton about shifters, only that they're rare creatures who usually do a better job at blending in. This shifter looks like a baby red elephant with a lion's tail coiled around its jackrabbit legs. It must not be as heavy as it looks given how easily June is carrying it, but as she sets it down on the generator, the shifter lies down on its side and I see a patch of bloody flesh.

"What happened to it?" I ask.

"Hunters," Luna says.

"Yours?"

"The work was done for another alchemist. We intercepted the shifter."

I knew I was going to have a creature's blood fused into mine, but I didn't expect to meet it. It's like bonding with a chicken before it becomes your dinner.

"What are you going to do it?"

"Put the poor thing out of its misery and let it live through you," Luna says as she pushes back her ceremonial cape and unsheathes a knife from her belt. "You don't have to watch."

I stare into the shifter's eyes; they're as yellow as sunflower petals. Ness Arroyo will have strength, but I'm not strong enough to witness this. I turn my back and wish I could block out the shifter's wailing as Luna shows it mercy.

"It's dead," Luna says.

I still can't look. I stare at the constellation, reminding myself over and over that I'm going to find the most compassionate version of myself in the near future. That my streak of harm will be over soon enough. One creature's death tonight is better than the thousands of people who will die if Eduardo Iron were around to help his father becomes president.

Luna steps into view and hands me a potion.

I know there are no guarantees that I'll become a specter. So many people have been poisoned or even died trying. But I'm not going to back out after letting a shifter die so I can escape my life.

I unscrew the top and look to the stars as I drink the potion. It tastes like a fish-flavored tea and it runs smoothly down my throat. My body flashes in light as my heart rate slows down and my muscles relax, and it feels like my bones are rapidly growing and shrinking. I feel feverish and wish Mom were around to keep me company and feed me raw nuts and honey until I'm better. Luna doesn't seem concerned, but my gruesome death could have been her real plan all along—exploit my attempt at becoming a specter to embarrass the Senator's reputation. Then she tells me to breathe because she needs me alive, and I try. It's hard when I don't feel as if I have control over my own lungs anymore. I want to shout in pain at the Cloaked Phantom, but no sound comes out.

The greatest changes do hurt the most.

CHAPTER EIGHT
THE SHIFTER
NESS

I can be anyone I want. That's the hope.

Shifters are hard creatures to categorize because of their ever-changing forms, and we're still not sure if the one Luna killed could morph into other humans or animals and creatures. The latter isn't useful to Luna and I'm not trying to live my life as a bird either. None of that matters since I haven't had much luck turning into anyone since yesterday's Cloaked Phantom.

Sometimes specters show signs that the powers are taking and then nothing comes of it. But Luna is determined. She coaches me through quiet meditations that are so long that I miss the rowdiness of campaign stages. She shows me pictures of people—politicians, prisoners, alchemists—and tells me to shift into them, always a breath away from screaming at me in frustration before she collects herself.

"What are you going to do to me if this doesn't work?" I ask.

"I'm afraid we'll have to decide if you're still useful to me as

Eduardo Iron or arrange a death that will be more permanent," Luna says.

I study Luna's journals on everything she knows about specters with shifter blood, which is minimal since the success rate isn't as high as it is with other creatures, but it's a great crash course. Holding a form is difficult because you have to keep all the details of your guise along the edges of your mind or it'll all fall apart. There's also a warning to not repeat a single form too many times, as it can force you to disassociate and drive you to madness. There's all these notes about how taking the size of a person doesn't give you their strength, and how you can pose as someone small and surprise attack an enemy who isn't expecting you to be so strong. What's really key is that you can only transform into someone from what you can see. If you haven't seen the birthmark on someone's inner thigh, the gleam won't create that for you. These mistakes can get you killed.

"What happened to this shifter?" I ask, pointing at a sketch of one in the journal.

"Dead," Luna says.

"Do I want to know how?"

"Do you?"

There's enough pressure building as is.

I sit in front of the living room's standing mirror and get ready.

This is my ultimate second chance, the sort of comeback you usually only get if you're a phoenix. I want to live, but not if that means being banished back to my old life. I have to prove to Luna and myself that I can make the changes. I sit on the floor, concentrating on who I want to become; familiarity should help.

I start small—replace the scar on my knee with a scab, the molar that cracked and had to be replaced, the curly hair that got greasy before people stepped in. I feel movement through me, like waves slowly reaching the shore, and I keep fleshing out of my form: a couple feet shorter, my bones shrinking; muscles deflating as I lose tone; removing body hair as if I'm shaving it; and, finally, my face is five years younger.

I glow in gray light, and once it fades, I'm thirteen-year-old Eduardo Iron standing in the same sweatshirt and jeans I've been wearing the past few days.

"I did it," I say in my older voice, knowing I'll have to learn how to manipulate that.

"Indeed you did," Luna says with dreams in her eyes.

It's harder than the journal described to hold this form, and the gray light washes over me again and gives me back everything that I was.

Not everything.

Eduardo Iron is dead like the world believes.

Ness Arroyo lives on.

HAVE YOU
READ THEM ALL?